2010

Max and the Gatekeeper

Book III

The Descendant and

the Demon's Fork

James Todd

Cochrane

Special thanks to all my family and friends for their help and support. Thanks to all the kids who motivated me to keep writing. Thanks to East Elementary School, Cedar City, Utah for help with an excellent villain.

Copyright © 2010 James Todd Cochrane

Originally Published May 20, 2011

Second Publication June 1, 2011

Jacket cover by Susan K. Szepanski

Sketches by Beth Peluso

www.darkmoonpublishing.com

Library of Congress Control Number: 2011930781

ISBN 978-0-9797202-6-0

CONTENTS

1

Increasing a Collection

Janice, a short, round, middle-aged woman with blond hair, sat at her desk staring out the window at the rain falling in steady sheets on the darkened city. Her hazel eyes immediately locked onto the man resting against the lamppost. Even from the third floor of her office she recognized him as the same man who had been there every night for the past two weeks. He wore the same gray trench coat and dark felt hat. Though she couldn't see his eyes, she sensed he was watching her. She could feel it. The hairs on her arms and the back of her neck stood on end, at the fear of seeing him again. *Who is he? What does he want?*

She retreated to the water cooler, hoping a drink would help to calm her nerves and her suspicions. Navigating the empty cubicles decorated with tinsel and Christmas lights, her mind raced with possibilities for the stranger's being there. His lurking outside began a couple of weeks ago. Although he had never approached her or even entered the building, she somehow knew he was there for her. Her hand shook as she attempted to hold the paper cup steady under the tap.

"Are you okay, Janice?" Nathan, a fellow co-worker, asked, causing her to start, nearly spilling the water from the full cup.

"Ah, yes." She quickly composed herself.

"Are you sure? You look...petrified."

"It's just the rain," she offered as an excuse. "After most of the office left early for the Christmas Holiday, it just got kind of spooky in here."

"Well, it's supposed to turn to snow within the hour." Nathan stated. "We should have a white Christmas."

"Yes. Do you have big plans for Christmas?" she asked, relaxing slightly.

"Just staying at home with the wife and kids. How about you?"

"I'll be with family as well. Sometimes a quiet holiday is the best kind. Well, I have a report to finish before I head out. I better get it done before it gets too late. You have a Merry Christmas." Janice smiled and returned to her desk.

As she pulled her chair up to her desk, she spied the figure beneath the lamppost; still there. Grabbing the phone with one hand she pounded out a number with the other. "Hello, it's me," she spoke into the receiver. "He's here again."

"Who's there?" a voice responded through the earpiece.

"What do you mean, who? The same guy I've been telling you about. What do you think I should do?"

"Has he given you any indication he's after you?" the voice asked.

"Well, no. He hasn't actually done anything." She tapped her pen on her desk and glanced at the man again. "I'd still feel better if you'd come and pick me up."

"Are you sure you're not imagining things?"

"No. Have I ever been wrong before?" she asked as she noticed another straggling coworker get into the elevator located at the opposite end of her aisle.

"No. I'll be there in about twenty minutes."

"Okay. Thanks Mike. I'll see you soon." She put down the phone and peeked at the stranger to discover he had gone.

She stood up and leaned against the window for a better look. Pressing her face to the glass and blocking the light with her hands, she tried to spot the man. "Now where did you go?" she muttered to herself.

Janice didn't know what was worse, the fact the man had apparently left or that she could no longer see him. A strange uneasy impression crept down her spine like a slow moving glacier, chilling her skin. She worked her way around the office, checking other windows for a glimpse of the stranger.

Suddenly the power to the building died and all the lights went out. Janice froze, blinded by the sudden darkness. If not for the emergency exit lights and the streetlights shining in from outside the windows, the office would have been pitch black, still it took a moment for her eyes to adjust.

"Hello? Is anyone else in the office?" a man's voice called.

Janice released the air from her lungs in relief. "Bob, is that you?"

"Yes, I was just about to get in the elevator. But with the electricity out, I'll have to use the stairs, so I figured I'd see if anyone else was here before I started down."

Janice almost jogged towards the elevators. She slowed as Bob, a short elderly man with gray hair and a hitch in his step, appeared wearing a coat and carrying his briefcase.

"Janice, what's wrong?" he asked.

She pointed towards the windows, and at the office buildings beyond. "I just realized the power is only out in our building. Look." She indicated the still-glowing city lights around them.

"Oh, I wouldn't worry. This kind of thing happens all the time. Probably just a planned outage in the building in order to fix something." Bob smiled in the faint red light of an exit sign. "Come on. I'll wait for you."

Janice nodded, not completely convinced. "Just give me a minute to get my things." Her heart raced as she hurried back to her desk to collect her belongings. A little voice inside her head kept telling her that the stranger outside had something to do with the building's lack of power. She put on her coat and threw her bag over her shoulder before joining Bob at the stairway door.

Janice fought the urge to run while she waited every few steps for Bob to catch up. Her special gift, the one that told her when danger was near, screamed its familiar warning. She read her watch, which indicated that Mike should be only a few minutes away. At the bottom of the stairs, she held the door open for Bob and they strolled to the main entrance.

Before they reached the glass entryway, a yellow taxicab drove up in front of the building. Rainwater cascaded off the building and the taxi before splashing on the sidewalk and street, filling the building with echoing plops and drips.

"Right on time," Bob said as they arrived at the revolving door. "Do you need a ride?"

"No, Mike is on his way. I'll just wait against the building out of the rain." Janice managed a weak smile as she stepped into the revolving door. She exited the building and moved to the side as Bob made his way out of the opening.

"Have a Merry Christmas," Bob said as he covered his head with his briefcase and ventured out towards the taxi.

"Merry Christmas," Janice responded. As she watched Bob leave, what little sense of comfort she had felt in his presence fluttered away like air from a deflating balloon. *Hurry up Mike.*

Janice shivered as she huddled against the building to avoid the spraying water. The rain had dropped the temperature to a point where her breath created smoky puffs. She now wished she had worn slacks instead of the long dress that was letting in a chilly draft on her legs.

Just when she thought it couldn't get any colder, the stranger materialized out of the shadow of an awning across the street. It was as if she had entered an ice cave. Even the rain, acting as if it too had detected the change, had transformed into large, white snowflakes. Fear cemented Janice in place. She wanted to run, to scream, but somehow she couldn't make her muscles obey. Even her eyes remained focused on the dark figure.

"Janice. Janice," Mike's voice broke through the barrier of terror that had blocked all other thoughts except escape from her mind.

The relief Janice received from Mike's call rushed over her body, restoring life to her limbs. "Mike," Janice sighed, tears formed along her lower eyelids as she watched her husband hustle up the sidewalk towards her. She flung herself into his arms when he reached her side.

"Hey, hey," Mike's shocked voice whispered in her ear as he returned her embrace. "What's wrong?"

Janice sobbed into his shoulder; she felt ridiculous but couldn't stop the tears. "Can we just get out of..." Janice gasped as she lifted her head to see the stranger standing only a short distance behind Mike.

Mike spun on his heels in response to Janice's sharp intake of air and fearful eyes. Janice stood behind Mike, peering around his broad shoulders at the figure observing them from only a few feet away.

"Can I help you?" Mike asked.

Janice trembled behind Mike as large clouds of warm air floated from the dark where the stranger's face waited. "Yes," a calm, smooth voice answered.

The three of them remained rooted to the spot eyeing one another.

"Well? What do you want?" Mike asked sharply.

"I don't think you're going to like the answer to that question," the stranger responded, taking a step forward.

Mike and Janice inched a pace back, away from the figure's advance. "Whatever it is, I suggest you look elsewhere then!" Mike said.

"Oh, I wish I could. I really do. But your wife is very special to me." The man advanced another couple of steps.

"What do you want from me?" Janice screeched from behind Mike as they continued to retreat in reaction to the stranger's movements towards them.

"Why, I want your soul," he said, cocking his head to the side.

"What?" both Janice and Mike asked with surprise.

"Yes, I'm collecting them." The stranger put his foot down into a small puddle as he continued forward.

Mike started to laugh, "Well, you can't have *it*." He enunciated the last with extra fervor. "I think you need to get out of here."

"I won't be leaving until I get what I came for," the stalker's voice remained steady. Suddenly, a long forked tongue flicked out of the shadows of his face, stopping Mike and Janice in their tracks.

Janice's jaw dropped and Mike withdrew a small revolver from the inside of his coat. "Okay, we've had enough. I didn't want to resort to this, but either you get out of here or someone really will get hurt."

"I suggest you put that thing away and leave now before it's too late," the figure said taking another stride forward.

Mike raised the gun to the man's chest. "Stop right there! Janice, get out your phone and—"

Before Mike could finish his sentence, an unusual croak issued from the figure's mouth and the gun zoomed out of Mike's hand and disappeared into the darkness.

"You won't need that," the man hissed and took another deliberate step towards them.

Janice gasped and Mike wore an expression of utter astonishment.

"Janice, run!" Mike whispered out of the side of his mouth as he shoved her away.

"What?" Janice questioned with astonishment.

"Run," Mike yelled over his shoulder and pushed her back with his hand. Before Mike could relocate the stranger, the figure slammed into him. The force of the blow propelled him into Janice, driving them both onto the hard sidewalk.

Besides the sharp painful scratches on her hands and knees, Janice's clothing acted like a sponge absorbing the cold slushy water that covered the walkways. Mike dragged her out of the puddles and to her feet, away from the attacker. His sudden burst of energy forced Janice to run so she wouldn't fall behind. As they rushed down the street, Janice glanced back to see the stranger standing where he had assaulted them. The wet slushy surface splashed water everywhere with each footstep.

"Where's the car?" Janice asked through gulps of air. Her fear, mingled with the cold water she soaked up from the fall, caused her muscles to tremble.

"Back the other direction. We'll double back and get out of here," Mike said.

They turned right ducking into an alley between two buildings. Mike continued to jog at a pace that caused Janice to struggle to keep up. She worried she was going to trip over her own feet any second, and her lungs throbbed with exertion. She checked for the stranger again but couldn't see anyone.

"I think you can slow down," Janice said, tugging against Mike's pull.

Mike slowed to a brisk walk. His chest expanded and contracted as he attempted to calm his breathing. "I don't think we're out of this yet!"

"What do you mean?" Janice skipped to the side to avoid some trashcans.

"You saw what he did to my gun." Mike's head swiveled all around, scanning the area.

"You think he's like me?"

"I think he has special powers like you, but I don't think he's like *you*." Mike met her eyes.

She shivered at the look he gave her. "What are we going to do?"

"I know we've tried to keep your powers a secret, but if you have to use them to get away, do it!"

Janice had discovered her powers as a little girl when she launched a school bully into a brick wall as he attempted to beat up a friend of hers. She remembered how angry she was that the bully had pinned her friend to the ground and shoved grass up his nose. She lost several friends that day and many treated her like a freak after. Janice learned to control her emotions from then on.

She had told Mike her secret early on in their marriage, after she had stopped a car from hitting him in a crosswalk. The force of her ability had destroyed the front end of the car. Everyone at the scene thought it was a freak accident, but Mike had noticed the look on Janice's face. He didn't believe at first, instead insisting she perform little "tricks" knocking plastic cups off the counter. Her little demonstration convinced him.

"Do you think I'll have to..." Janice started when the stranger appeared at the end of the alley. He just stood there as if he expected them to join him.

"What do you want?" Mike yelled, his voice cracking.

The figure strolled into the alley. "Janice, of course."

"Well, you can't have her!" Mike said as he and Janice retreated a few paces backwards while keeping the stranger in view.

"Nevertheless, I will have her, or a part of her," the stranger said coolly continuing his approach.

"Janice, knock him flat," Mike spat in a hushed voice out of the corner of his mouth.

"You want me..." Janice started

"Yes! Do it now!" Mike said as the stranger continued his advance up the alley.

Janice closed her eyes and gritted her teeth. She concentrated so hard that the muscles in her face tensed up and her whole body started to shake. Suddenly all of the loose trash in the narrow alley around her started to vibrate along the ground. She clamped her hands together and her eyes snapped open, focusing on the dark figure heading up the alley.

"I can feel your magic," the stranger said as he drew within a few yards.

"What," Mike gasped and he placed a hand on Janice as if to stop something terrible from happening. "Janice! Janice! I was wrong! Please stop!" He grabbed her arm.

"You're too late. You can't control her," the stranger's voice sounded excited.

Janice screamed as her hands shot out towards the stranger. Mike jumped out of the way as a shock wave flew up the alley scattering debris like leaves in the wind. As the blast reached the stranger, he opened his mouth and inhaled Janice's burst of energy into his lungs. His chest expanded more than a normal human's torso could stretch. After the last of the force had stopped, the stranger turned towards Mike and exhaled the spell in a narrow stream of power that formed a ray of white, smoky light that shot through Mike's chest.

When the stranger had released the last of Janice's magic, Mike staggered backward before falling into a pile of trash and garbage cans.

Janice couldn't believe the scene that had unfolded before her eyes. The stranger had used her unique power against Mike. Her head pounded and her vision swam as she stumbled towards Mike. "Mike! Mike! No!" Her voice was shrill in her ears. She collapsed at his side.

Mike's eyes had rolled back in his head and his hands flailed wildly over the steam rising from the spot where Janice's spell had penetrated his chest.

"What did you do to him?" Janice cried, as she patted Mike's cheek in an effort to comfort and wake him at the same time.

"Me?" the stranger's voice, dripping with sarcasm, drifted over to them as he opened his long black coat. "Oh my, no. That was all your doing. You cast the spell. I can't control what you do."

Janice took her phone out of her pocket and started to dial, when, like Mike's gun, the phone flew out of her hand where it smashed into the wall. "What are you doing?" she screamed. "He's going to die!"

"Oh yes, I know," the man said calmly.

"What do you want with me?" Janice sobbed uncontrollably as she wiped snowflakes from Mike's pale face.

"I want your soul, Janice," the stranger said.

"My, my s-soul," Janice stammered as she turned her head towards the stranger. "I d-don't understand. W-why would you w-want me?"

"Oh, you are very special, Janice." The stranger stepped into the light and removed his hat. His flesh melted away to reveal a lizard-like head with razor-sharp hooked teeth. As soon as this terrifying vision revealed itself, it was gone and a man with wavy blond hair and a handsome face stood staring at her.

Janice screamed and stumbled backwards tripping over lose trash and garbage cans. "Why are you doing this?" she cried and another shockwave flashed towards the stranger, who deflected it as if swatting away an annoying fly.

Excitement pumped through Kacha's veins like fire as he gazed hungrily upon Janice. He could barely contain his joy at having his current victim in his grasp. "It's your magical abilities that make you special."

"Magic?" Janice gasped.

"Yes. You never realized your special powers were magic, did you? It is magic that has drawn me to you. That's the reason I need your soul. You see, magical souls are a lot stronger than normal souls."

"I d-don't understand." Janice cried harder than before.

"No, I don't suppose you do." Kacha smiled. He extended his hand and formed a claw-like hook. "*Ukradi dusho,*" he called. A ray of laser-like light shot out of his hand and up the alley. When the power reached Janice, she heaved as if to vomit. Out of the soft spot at the base of her neck, a small colorful light about the size of a marble escaped her body. Kacha drew his hand to his chest and the magic returned.

Janice's body remained in its convulsed state for several minutes before falling over sideways.

Kacha extracted a small jar from inside his coat and opened the lid to capture the soul that slowly floated towards him. After sealing the lid, he uttered a strange word and a thin pulsing light flowed over the jar. "That should keep you safe until I get you home," he said, watching the small round light drift as if suspended in the center of the jar.

After tucking the jar back inside his coat, he strolled over to Janice's body. "Another mysterious death for the police," he smiled. He then went to Mike. "You, on the other hand, would draw unwanted attention with that strange burn mark right through the center of your body."

Kacha held his hand over Mike's head. He cast another spell and Mike's body changed to ash. Kacha continued to watch as it dissolved into the puddles of water that covered the alley floor.

Kacha rubbed his arms and legs to help add some warmth to his aching body. He hated the cold. He checked the alley and surrounding buildings to make sure no one had seen what had happened and then made his way to the subway.

"Good evening, Mr. Field," the doorman said as he held the door open for Kacha.

"Evening, Steve," Kacha greeted as he walked into the lobby of his apartment building and thick warm air from the heated building relieved his freezing body.

"Out doing some last minute Christmas shopping?" Steve asked.

"Yes, I've just collected a very special present," Kacha said, and tipped his hat before heading towards the elevator.

"Good evening, sir," the elevator operator said as Kacha stepped into the lift.

"Evening," Kacha smiled as the man pushed the button for the top floor. "How's your wife?"

"She's fine, Mr. Field. Thank you for asking." The man watched the elevator control panel.

"When's she due?"

"In February," the man responded as they reached the top floor and the doors opened.

"Well, here's a little something for the happy event," Kacha said, dropping a hundred dollar bill in the man's hand. "Merry Christmas."

"Thank you, sir. And Merry Christmas to you, sir."

Kacha hummed "I'm Dreaming of a White Christmas" to himself as he strolled to his penthouse apartment. As he entered his lavishly decorated apartment, he turned up the thermostat and went to one of the back bedrooms. He switched on the light to reveal a sandstone floor with a hole in the center of the room. In the back corner sat a desk with an ornately designed hourglass with a handful of colorful lights dancing along its bottom. Next to the hourglass sat a large, open leather-bound book.

Kacha took the jar out of his coat and placed it beside the hourglass. He picked up the book and carried it to the living room where he plopped down in his black leather chair. "Where was I?" he muttered to himself as he flipped through the pages of the book. He stopped on a page with a crude-looking staff sketched on its surface, almost like a distorted cactus. "Oh, yes, the demon's fork!"

2

The Hunt

"Now, this is going to take all of your concentration," Yelka said in her melodic voice, looking straight into Max's eyes. "You first and then Cindy. Your ball, Max, is on the kitchen table."

Max, a wiry thirteen-year-old boy with wavy brown hair and green eyes, took a deep breath to relax. Ever since last summer when Max and his Grandfather had rescued Max's mother from Hudich and his minions, Yelka had continued to create lessons that stretched Max and Cindy's magical abilities. Her new obsession involved Max and Cindy transporting objects through the house without the item touching anything. She indicated when an exercise pushes you to your limits, that is when you grow.

Max wrinkled his nose at his short, elfin magic teacher and pictured the ball sitting on the kitchen table. Facing the open doorway from inside the science room on the second floor of his grandfather's house, he concentrated so hard on the ball that he could actually smell its rubber exterior. After another breath, he slowly extended one hand, "*pridi*." Max visualized lifting the ball off the table and moving it out of the kitchen. He carried it along the hall to the main foyer before gliding it up the stairs and turning it right down the hallway. He could see it in his mind's eye, floating through the hall and up the stairs before passing each room until it appeared in front of the open doorway.

A smile crossed Max's face as the ball zoomed from the hallway into his open hand.

"Very good, Max," Yelka sang and clapped her hands. "Now, it's Cindy's turn."

Max played catch with himself by tossing the ball a couple of feet into the air and snagging it again. He stepped out of the way and leaned against the wall. He continued to throw the ball as he watched Cindy get ready for her turn.

"Your ball, Cindy, is on the front room sofa," Yelka instructed.

Cindy nodded, her chin-length blond hair bobbing with the movement, and closed her bright blue eyes. After a short pause, she too held out her hand and appeared to be waiting for something. A few moments later, Cindy's ball hovered outside the doorway before flying into her hand.

"Well done, Cindy," Yelka beamed, a smile spreading across her golden-bronze face. "You both showed excellent control."

"Yelka, when can we learn a new spell?" Cindy asked, as she bounced her ball on the hardwood floor.

Max agreed.

"Hmm, since you both seem so eager to learn a new spell, I suspect you've already got one in mind," Yelka responded with her familiar singing tone.

"Yes, we have," Cindy piped up.

"After my encounter with Hudich last summer, I'd definitely like to know how to block evil spells," Max said.

"I think that's an excellent choice," Yelka replied in her sing-song voice. "It is a very useful spell and one that will push your current magical abilities to the limits."

"It can't be more difficult than the travel spell, can it?" Max stated and Cindy shrugged her shoulders.

"Oh, but it is. I think you both have come far enough that it's time to take an even larger step into the magical world," Yelka said. "With the blocking spell, speed and mental concentration are needed, because it actually involves two spells: one to help you anticipate your attacker's curse and the other to block."

"Two spells," Cindy inhaled as if understanding Yelka's meaning.

"How can we possibly anticipate what the enemy is going to hit us with?" Max wondered aloud.

"By reading their thoughts," Yelka answered.

"But don't they use different words for their spells than we do? How are we going to know what their spell is?" Cindy questioned. "Do we need to learn their language as well?"

"Max, wasn't Hudich able to block your spells on Kleen?" Yelka asked.

"Yes."

"So, he was reading Max's mind? That must have been one of the shortest reads of all time." Cindy elbowed Max in the ribs.

"Hey!" Max smiled as he continued to play with his rubber ball. After a short pause he added, "Does that mean Hudich knows our spells? Our language?"

"No, but Hudich knows how magic works and has mastered it," Yelka explained. "I'm going to show you something that might help you understand. *Come!*" Yelka said firmly and Max's ball flew out of his hand and into Yelka's.

Both Max and Cindy's mouths fell open as they stared at the ball, now cradled in Yelka's small, golden hand.

"How? What?" Max stammered.

"Wait, so, our spells have nothing to do with the actual words?" Cindy's eyes were wide with wonder.

"Yes and no," Yelka responded. "Verbalization is an important part of learning magic and helps the user visualize what they are doing, but the words are just that, words. We chose the words from a language that isn't well known. If the enemy hears words they understand, the whole process of blocking or deflecting spells becomes much easier for them. Only someone who truly comprehends magic can block spells completely. You need to be able to feel what it's telling you. I will give you both spells, but tonight I will only show you how to block because our time is short and I must soon return to Svet. You will have to practice together. Now, you don't want to let your enemy know what spell you are casting at them. That should help you with your speed before we move on to the second spell."

"Okay," Max and Cindy agreed.

"The spell to block is pronounced *oviraj*. The visualization is like placing an impregnable shield in front of you. You have already practiced a form of blocking spells with *pochasi* and *ugasni*. The spell to read magic is pronounced *beri misel*. The only visualization I can give you for this is to imagine you can hear another's thoughts or intents."

"Okay, give us a quick demo before you go so we have an example," Cindy said.

Yelka nodded. "Just once, though, because we are waiting on a call from Sky."

Max and Cindy exchanged a quick glance.

"Max you stand over there." Yelka pointed to a spot near the window as she took up a position about twenty feet away. "Whenever you're ready give me your best shot."

Max walked to the area Yelka had indicated and spun on his heel. He extended his hands and thought, *premakni*.

"*Oviraj*!"

Everything happened so quickly it astonished Max. His spell rebounded off Yelka and knocked him to the floor. "Wow," Max gasped as he tried to catch his breath.

"That was sick," Cindy laughed aloud. "You should have seen your face before you hit the floor. I thought you were going to have an accident."

"I thought you might try to trick me by *thinking* the spell," Yelka said as she helped Max to his feet. "I think that was a good demonstration of reading the magic, don't you?"

"Yes, definitely," Max said in a raspy voice, still struggling to get his wind back.

"I think that will leave you with plenty to work on," Yelka sang. "I expect results by our next lesson."

Cindy continued to chuckle as she watched Max rub his backside. "Do you want to practice the spell, now?" Cindy asked.

"I think I've had enough for the night," Max grimaced.

"Shall we go see what our moms are up to?"

"Sure," Max said as he headed for the door.

They meandered downstairs, into the smell of pine mingled with ginger, to find their mothers sitting in the dark, sipping eggnog and gazing at the twinkling lights on the Christmas tree in front of the window. The radio emitted soft Christmas music and the women chatted only periodically, clearly comfortable in each other's company.

"Max, Cindy, how was your lesson?" Max's mother, Rachel, asked as she spotted them entering the front room.

"It was good," Cindy responded, plopping down in an empty arm-chair. "Oh look, it's snowing!" she said, turning towards the window.

"I love snow," Max said as he went to the window and cupped his face against it. "By the look of it, it's been snowing for a while."

"For about an hour now," Cindy's mother, Mrs. Carlson, informed them, her blue eyes twinkling.

"Yep! It looks like we'll have a white Christmas," Max's mom stated as she took a drink of eggnog.

"Is there anymore?" Cindy asked.

"Eggnog? Yes, dear. It's in the fridge. And there are some gingerbread cookies on the counter," Mrs. Rigdon said, tucking a lock of dark hair behind her ear. "Help yourselves."

"Mmm, I thought I could smell cookies," Max said happily, stepping back from the window.

Cindy jumped to her feet and hurried towards the kitchen with Max right on her heels. When Max tried to pass her in the hall, she blocked his path, "No way, punk."

They ran, giggling, into the kitchen and just as they entered, Max cast his spell. "*Pochasi!*" Cindy went into an extreme state of slow motion. Max rushed ahead of her and grabbed the whole plate of cookies. Cindy's face slowly changed to an expression of "I'll get even."

"Boy, these cookies smell so good." Max floated the plate under his nose in a teasing manner. "I bet you wish you could have some." He snagged a cookie off the plate but before he could put it in his mouth, it flew out of his hand and into Cindy's.

"Thank you, loser!"

Suddenly, the floor started to vibrate and the humming of the force field rose above the Christmas music playing in the front room. Max and Cindy exchanged a knowing glance. Max snatched a couple of cookies from the plate and set it on the counter before they both raced to the third floor.

"Do you think Sky knows where he is?" Cindy asked as they climbed the spiral staircase.

"She hinted we should be able to catch him soon," Max responded.

Max stopped short as he and Cindy entered the third floor and watched as the huge and shaggy Ell—not Sky—exited the gateway. Cindy would never forget how he saved her life two summers ago in the world of the Zeenosees and knew that Ell would forever be their friend and ally.

What also added to their surprise was the presence of Olik, the very epitome of an alien. With his pale green skin, large black eyes, oversized head, and narrow mouth, he resembled everyone's idea of a green Martian. Instead of his usual silver jumpsuit, though, he wore a black one.

"Ell," Cindy smiled, anxiously waiting for Grandpa to kill the force field that separated them from the gateway.

"Hey, Olik. I thought it would be Sky, not you and Ell," Max said as the force field dissolved back into the five metallic stands arranged in a large circle around the gateway.

Cindy dashed to Ell and gave him a hug.

Max followed and put his hand on Ell's side, *Hello, Ell.*

Hello, Max. Are we ready to go?

We? both Max and Cindy thought.

Max turned to his grandfather who was adjusting the gateway control panel. "Where are we going?"

"Who said you were going anywhere?" Grandpa answered, not looking up from the control panel.

"Ell did," Cindy blurted as Yelka entered the third floor carrying several packs and an armload of coats.

"Well, since it is Christmas vacation and we can use all the help we can get, we decided to bring you and Ell on a little adventure," Grandpa said with a wink and ran his hand through his wavy gray hair. Even now, his resemblance to Mark Twain was remarkable.

"Sweet," Cindy said.

"The one condition is the three of you must stick together," Yelka said, handing out packs and coats.

Olik then gave each of them a long, silvery metallic staff with a button on the doorknob-like handle at one end and a small, cylindrical cup about an inch long and an inch wide on the other end. "These are for stunning. You activate it with the switch and then just touch your enemy with the other end. It will immobilize them for about twenty minutes. That should give us enough time to move him back to his world."

"And Sky? Why is she not here?" Max asked as he clicked his staff on and watched a small, blue flame dance around the edge of the cup.

"She's waiting for us. She said she will give us the details when we get there. Turn that thing off. We don't want any accidents," Grandpa ordered, donning his coat and slinging his pack over his shoulder. He then switched on the force field, followed by the gateway.

Everyone else put on their coats and watched the old-fashioned revolving mirror as it slowly began to rotate and pick up speed. After a few moments, a light appeared that engulfed the entire mirror to become the gateway.

"So we're still going to try and capture him alive?" Cindy asked.

"Yes," Olik said. "I've got another dimensional prison. Once we zap him, we will place him in it for transportation."

"Remember, this isn't a game." Grandpa walked into the light of the gateway with the others right behind him.

Max stepped down into two feet of snow. It was cold. Small white clouds of breath rose in puffs from the small group as they huddled next to an old, rundown barn nestled in the basin of a large valley. In the distance, lights from a city created an orange glow in the night sky. From over the hills, a strange buzzing seemed to rise and fall in volume.

"What do we do now?" Yelka pulled her ski cap down over her ears and shivered.

"We wait for Sky." Grandpa moved to the end of the barn, his steps crunching the snow beneath his shoes.

"Do you see anything?" Olik whispered as everyone tailed Grandpa.

"No, but she should be here." Grandpa turned to answer. When he looked around again he jumped backwards in surprise as Sky popped up right in front of him.

Sky, Max and Cindy's self-defense teacher, was a beautiful, medium-height woman from a different world. She had long blond hair, pale smooth skin, dark red lips, and sharp blue eyes. She wore dark, baggy clothing that usually held an array of weapons.

"Sorry about startling you." Sky waved everyone away from the corner of the barn. "We need to hurry. He's just made a kill and will be heading this way shortly."

Everyone exchanged worried looks.

"Do not fret. It is not a human he has attacked, but a deer. He's been very careful to avoid detection. He lives in the city but leaves it to feed and he has only been taking wild animals," Sky informed them.

"Where do you want us?" Grandpa asked.

"I think Cindy, Max, and Ell should wait in this old barn. That way, if anyone happens to be in the area, they won't see Ell. The rest of us can spread out along the edge of the valley in the direction of the city. He will bring his kill there to eat before he returns to the city. If we are quick and quiet, we should be able to stun him," Sky suggested.

"Wait." Olik thrust another staff towards Sky. "I almost forgot."

"Oh good, thanks," Sky's voice dripped with sarcasm and she gave Olik a strange look that suggested she really wasn't interested in making a live capture.

Grandpa ordered Max and Cindy, along with their enormous friend into the barn. "The walls of this thing are so deteriorated you should be able to see everything. Stay ready. We may need you to seal off his way of retreat."

Cindy put her hand on Ell's shoulder. *Come on, Ell.*

The three of them circled the barn until they found the entrance. There were no windows, making the darkness inside an excellent hiding place. They went deep into the shadows of the decrepit building and found some old straw piled next to a wall with plenty of holes through which they could observe the valley. Ell lay himself down on the straw and Max and Cindy sat, leaning against his warm flank as they eyed the others accompanying Sky towards the edge of the valley.

"How long do you think we will have to wait?" Cindy whispered.

"From the way Sky was talking, not very long," Max replied, his face glued to a large crack between two planks of the wall.

"What's making that buzzing?" Cindy asked after a few moments.

"I don't know, but it seems to be getting louder."

Suddenly, Ell's head jerked towards the entrance of the barn and he started to sniff with great huffs of air.

"What is it?" Cindy whispered fearfully as both she and Max put their hands on Ell's side.

He's coming.

How close? Max's pulse rose in nervous anticipation.

Not far. We should see him at any moment, Ell replied.

Max and Cindy pushed their faces up against some large holes in the side of the building to get the best possible view of the valley.

"Be careful," Cindy whispered, noticing the mists of water vapor as she exhaled. "Our breath is going outside."

Max positioned his head back from the crack as he too saw the white puff of air float through the cracks to the outside of the barn. "Good point." Max turned to agree with Cindy but her rigid posture told him their quarry had shown up.

Ell was on his feet in an instant and the hair on the back of his neck bristled like sharp spikes. Max had a second to wonder if the buzzing from earlier was growing louder or if Ell was growling.

On the side of the valley opposite the city lights, a hunched figure dragging something through the deep snow materialized out of the night. Every few feet the creature would stop and scan its surroundings. After appearing satisfied it was alone, it began its slow laborious heaving of the deer carcass.

"Something's wrong," Max whispered as the strange buzzing seemed closer now.

"What? The buzzing?" Cindy questioned.

"Well, yes, that too. But look, he's struggling with that dead deer. Haireens are extremely strong and fast. So, why is he acting like a complete wimp with that deer?"

Cindy took a moment to observe the Haireen's difficulty with its prey, and agreed that everything wasn't normal. "What do you suppose is the problem?"

"I'm not sure. It's taken him about ten minutes to pull that thing twenty yards." Max's brow furrowed.

"Ell, can you sense anything?" Cindy moved to Ell's side and placed her hand deep into his warm fur.

The volume of the noise continued to increase as the Haireen fought to get its victim to the other end of the valley. "Anything?" Max whispered.

"Ell says it's the cold that's affecting him."

Suddenly, the blaze of bright lights filtered through the deteriorating slates of the barn wall behind them as the buzzing changed into the distinct roar of snowmobile engines.

"Uh oh," Max said as he recognized what was happening.

Cindy raced to his side and found a hole to peer through.

The Haireen dropped the deer and headed towards the barn. Even now, his movements were slow and cumbersome as he trudged through the snow.

"What do we do?" Cindy asked as her head swiveled around the area. "There's nowhere to escape."

"Go invisible!" Max whispered. He rushed to Ell with Cindy right by him. "*Izginim se.*" Max placed a hand on Ell before they both vanished.

Cindy followed suit. "*Izginim se.*"

The rumbling of the snowmobiles' engines grew closer and their headlights danced through the cracks in the wall.

He's coming! Ell thought.

Max's heart pounded in his chest and his mouth became dry. He held on to the staff Olik had given him like a lifeline. "Get ready," Max's voice cracked.

"Should I call the others?" Cindy asked.

"There's no ti—"

Abruptly, a shadow fell across the doorway. For an instant, the lights of a snowmobile revealed the body of a man with a lizard-like head and rows of razor sharp teeth before he stepped into the darkness of the old barn.

Even with the thundering of the snowmobile engines, harsh, labored breathing floated through the dilapidated building.

The creature backed slowly into the barn, his head whipping back and forth as several snowmobiles zoomed by the barn and down into the valley. The creature crept back to the door and peered around the corner. He remained, still and silent, like a piece of petrified wood, all the while keeping his eyes on the speeding snow machines.

The sounds of the joy riders began traveling farther and farther from the barn. Finally, after the noise returned to the strange, distant buzzing, the Haireen moved. He appeared to be double-checking the area for anything that might have snuck in under the racket.

Suddenly, his head whipped around to the center of the barn. "I know you're there."

Max flipped the switch on his staff and the small blue flame flickered in the air giving off a pale light. Cindy's staff ignited next to him.

"Max! It is you, isn't it? I recognize your scent. The other must be...Cindy." There was a long slow sniff. "And you've brought some muscle." The creature faced them and snapped his jaws.

3

Discoveries

"What are your intentions?" The Haireen got into a crouched position as if coiling to strike.

"To take you back!" Max couldn't believe he had spoken. Cindy's gasp indicated he had surprised her too.

"Back where?" The creature groaned as if fighting some unknown pain.

"Where you came from," Max stated. "You won't be killing any more people!"

"Then let's get on with it," the Haireen snapped. "I'm ready. I want to go!"

"What? Why?" Cindy blurted out.

"I'm freezing and I hate this place!" he hissed.

"Wait, so...you're willing to go?" Max asked with disbelief, holding the staff out in front of him. *Is this a trick?*

"Yes! The cold burns my skin and my muscles ache!"

"Don't trust him," Cindy whispered, keeping her staff ready for an attack.

"Even if I could actually overpower you with your weapons, I'm certain I have no chance against your friend. I saw what he did to the Zbal." The Haireen shuddered. "Besides, your other friends are coming."

Cindy put her hand on Ell's leg. "He's right. Ell said the others are on the way."

"How do you want to do this?" Max asked Cindy.

"I would prefer to go without a fight," the creature responded.

Could it be this easy? Max's thoughts raced, and he couldn't help but be suspicious of this deceitful creature.

"Max! Cindy!" Grandpa called from outside the barn. "Are you okay?"

Max and his mother sat around the Christmas tree sipping hot chocolate. Snow had been falling for three straight days; there was a good two feet of it in the yard. Max let the steaming cup revive the feeling in his hands after shoveling the sidewalk for the fifth time in three days. He loved the snow but clearing walkways every morning and afternoon was getting old.

Max stared at the colorful lights thinking about how easy it had been to move Grd back to Kleen. He hadn't realized Grd was cold blooded or that the winter temperatures affected his ability to survive. The weirdest part of the whole situation had been Grd's declaration about him not hunting humans because of all the junk we eat, which he claimed affected the way we taste. The need for good meat had forced him into the wild, where temperatures were usually lower than in the cities. Grd said his life turned miserable and he desired nothing more than to go home.

A sudden frantic pounding on the door brought Max out of his reverie.

"I wonder who that could be." Max's mother put down a book she had been reading and went to the door.

Max's curiosity changed to worry as the rapping at the door became more frantic.

"All right, all right. I'm coming," Mrs. Rigdon called. She had barely unlocked the door when it flew open, almost knocking her backwards. Into the house rushed Max's Uncle Frank, his Aunt Donna, and his cousin Martin.

Frank's agitated state suggested that something was very wrong.

"Frank, what's going on?" Max's mother regained her footing and composure, as she saw the state her brother-in-law was in.

"We have a real problem!" Donna said. She was definitely Rachel's sister. If it hadn't been for the few more gray hairs on Max's mother's head and her leaner build, they could almost pass for twins.

Martin, Max's cousin, was two years younger than Max. He was short for his age with brown hair and a friendly face, while Uncle Frank was average height and weight with flecks of gray hair mingled in with the brown.

"A real problem!" Frank stressed as he paced around the room in an animated manner. "Is Joe here?"

"Not at the moment. What is it?" Mrs. Rigdon asked.

"Frank just showed up on an episode of America's Most Wanted!" Donna stated, her face pale.

"What?" Max and his mother asked. This news propelled Max off the front room floor and into the entryway with the others.

"Yes, it's true," Frank flailed his hands in the air and he continued circling the room. "Now, what are we going to do?"

"Settle down. Take some deep breaths. I'm sure we can think of a solution." Rachel tried to help ease the situation.

"Yeah, no one knows where you are. Olik provided you with a new name and identity," Max added.

"The enemy knows I'm here," Frank stated, holding out his right hand to reveal the mark on his palm.

"I forgot about that," Rachel mumbled as she opened her hand and stared down at the same mark on her own hand.

"Why can't Olik get rid of this evil thing?" Frank asked, shaking his head.

"Take it easy, dear." Donna placed a hand on Frank's shoulder, trying to calm him down.

"We need to work harder on the spell to remove them," Mrs. Rigdon said.

"There has to be an easier way," Frank said, taking a seat in the open armchair.

"Well, there is an easier way, but it's extremely painful," Max added. "Believe me, as long as you can avoid that method, I would."

"Olik has to know..." Frank started.

"They already explained that," Rachel interrupted. "If they try to cut it, it will spread into your arm. They would pretty much have to chop your arm off in one swipe to keep it isolated in your hand."

"Yes, but I find it hard to believe that part about if they try to numb your hand before burning it out, the thing thinks your hand is dying and will also move into your arm?" Frank grumbled.

"Well, believe it," Max replied. "I saw where Marko laid the blade on my palm. He burned the side next to my wrist first. Olik detailed how that trapped the mark in my hand for him to destroy it completely. The mark can feel pain as well and it didn't want to pass through the initial burn."

"I think you should work on the spell to remove it as Rachel suggested," Donna said, sitting on the arm of the chair next to her husband.

Martin sat Indian style on the floor next to the Christmas tree. He had been secretly imprisoned last year, along with Max's mother and his dad. Since his rescue, he had made remarkable progress with his own magical abilities. He could now perform several spells and had made some friends at the school Grandpa Joe had helped establish.

"How long was the segment on America's Most Wanted, then? Did they show your picture?" Rachel asked.

"Too long! And YES!" Frank stated. "They're calling me 'The Cannibal'." Frank made quotes with his fingers in the air as he stressed the name.

"Well, you did eat your victims," Max piped in with a smile. He just couldn't resist the urge to find some humor in the situation.

"Good one," Martin laughed until sharp looks from the adults caused both his and Max's smirks to disappear.

"They even claimed I'm in New York where they found all those victims several months ago—the ones that looked like they'd been eaten. The authorities think I'm on the move and will resurface any day." Frank's voice was getting harsher and more high-pitched by the second.

Rachel sighed and put up a hand to quiet her brother-in-law. "Well, Joe should be back in a while and we can discuss our options then. For now, please try and relax. Panicking isn't helping anyone."

Alan and Hudich waited in the snow, watching Joe's house. They remained in the shadows in order to remain hidden from unwanted observers.

Alan was tall, but Hudich stood a foot taller and kept his skull-like head covered by a large hood. A puff of steamy air issued from the hood every few seconds as Hudich exhaled, and Alan thought he caught a glint off Hudich's solid red eyes as a car's headlights flashed across them on its way up the street.

Alan ran a hand through his graying hair and pulled his long overcoat closer around him to keep out the chill as he stared at the

Christmas lights in Joe's window. For a few minutes, the shapes of figures could be seen moving around, but now there was nothing.

"Tonight was the broadcast?" Hudich's deep voice asked.

"Yes," Alan responded pleasantly.

"Good." Hudich almost purred. "Give it a few days and then make the report."

"It shall be done."

"They have not been as interested in me since my release from the collar as I anticipated. That indicates to me they are probably up to something they deem very important. I want to know what it is." Hudich kicked at the snow with his bare tiger-like foot.

"My plan should work," Alan said, blowing into his hands for warmth.

"You're sure he'll leave?" Hudich asked.

"I guarantee it!"

"His reaction was exactly what we hoped for," Hudich said. His hand disappeared into his hood to scratch his chin. "We need to be ready for him."

"We will be."

###

Max awoke early Christmas morning to more heavy falling snow. The clock by the side of his bed glowed 5:51 A.M. as he noticed the snow falling outside his window under the streetlight across the road. The snow could not contain his excitement for the colorfully wrapped Christmas presents sitting under the tree.

Pulling on a pair of sweats and socks for protection against the chill in the house, Max raced down the stairs, without caring who heard. His feet thumped loudly on every step and he nearly fell when his stocking covered feet slipped on the hardwood floor as he tried to make the sharp left turn into the front room.

The soft glow of the lights on the Christmas tree reflected off the front window, illuminating the rows of presents around the tree. Max paused and took in the festive scene. His eyes danced off the various decorated presents until his gaze came to rest on a brand new baseball glove sitting next to a stuffed green stocking.

"It's about time you got up," Grandpa's voice snapped from the armchair behind Max, causing him to jump. "I've been up for almost an hour waiting for you."

"What're you doing up so early?" Max asked with a smile.

"It's Christmas, isn't it? I wanted to open my presents," Grandpa chuckled. "You didn't think you were the only one excited about getting presents, did you?"

Max's mother entered the room dressed from neck to toe in a thick, pink robe carrying a tray with three large mugs. "Banana bread and eggnog anyone?" She placed the tray on the coffee table.

"How long have you been up?" Max raised his eyebrows in surprise.

"I got up with Grandpa about an hour ago. We were wondering how long you were going to sleep." Max's mother shot Grandpa a wink as she took a sip of her eggnog.

Max smiled and turned back towards the tree. "Who gave me the baseball glove?"

"Wasn't me. It must have been Santa," Rachel said.

"Right," Max said sarcastically, as he picked up the glove and slid it on his hand.

"After everything you've seen, you're telling me you don't believe in Santa?" Grandpa asked with a questioning look. "I thought I had taught you better than that."

"You're not telling me you think Santa Claus is real?" Max folded the glove the way he liked it, but the new leather was stiff. *I'll have to sleep with it between my mattress and box springs.*

"Did you believe in aliens before you met Olik?"

"Well, no."

"So, how can you be certain there's no Santa?"

"He's got a point." Rachel continued to drink her eggnog with the mug cupped in her hands.

They spent over an hour, making their way through the gifts beneath the tree, each taking turns unwrapping presents and snapping pictures.

Later that day, they had a full house for Christmas dinner. Cindy and her parents showed up just before noon to help set up and finish the preparations. By the time they were ready to eat, Uncle Frank, Aunt Donna, Martin, Yelka, Olik, and Sky had all shown up. Yelka brought a strange casserole-type dish she'd made while Olik and Sky contributed some spicy meats.

Max couldn't remember being this happy at Christmas since his father died. Everyone was enjoying themselves, but after a while Grandpa, Olik, Yelka, and Sky disappeared up to the third floor. Martin was playing cards with the adults, while Max and Cindy battled a game on the computer Grandpa had bought, to search news stories, in an effort to catch Kacha.

"Do you think Sky's found out anything new?" Cindy asked, staring at Max's game character fighting several zombies in a subterranean complex.

"I doubt it," Max said, leaning hard to his left as if he could make his player avoid the outstretched claws of an attacker. "She said something about having tracked Kacha to New York, but then the trail grew cold. Grandpa's been checking the news constantly for any strange deaths. There were a couple of people who had died under weird circumstances, but the bodies didn't match what we're looking for."

"What was so strange about them?"

"Well, there didn't appear to be any explanation why they died. The people just seemed to have dropped dead for no reason. The only mark—" Max tilted the other way while rapidly pounding a key on the keyboard, "...was a small bruise on the front of their necks. Dang!"

Cindy chuckled as a group of zombies dismantle Max's player.

"Do you want to go listen to what they're talking about?" Cindy asked as Max moved out of the way for her.

"Sure."

"As I said, he's in New York," Sky stated as Max and Cindy entered the third floor. She held a marker in her hand and was tapping it on the table.

Grandpa and the others sat around the table with a map of New York City spread out in front of them with several red circles drawn on its surface. Grandpa rubbed his chin as he always did while deep in thought.

"So, you think Joseph's theory is correct?" Olik asked, staring at a particular circle.

"I don't know, but the signs are slowly disappearing. I haven't discovered anything significant in over three months," Sky said.

"Well, our experience with Grd leads us to believe he isn't hunting humans for food," Yelka offered.

"What's Grandpa's theory?" Max asked as he and Cindy sidled up to the table.

"You've heard my theory about the unexplained deaths," Grandpa said. "I just wish we had more to go on. They are extremely spread out across the city and happen so seldom."

"We need to find a pattern if we hope to catch him," Sky said.

"So, you think he's building another gateway?" Cindy asked.

"Yes, in fact I believed that three months ago," Grandpa answered.

Sky shook her head. "Three months ago there were a lot of grisly murders all within this area." She indicated a portion of mid-town Manhattan. "Then...nothing."

"You don't think the cops got him in a shoot-out or something, do you?" Max asked.

"Not likely," Sky said. "There would be reports of a major incident. In any case, he is too powerful for the police now. They would not stand a chance in a showdown with him. Not only have his magical abilities greatly increased, he can change identities, remember?"

"I think we need to go deep into the lives of these people who died under these mysterious conditions," Olik suggested. "There has to be some purpose as to why he chose them."

"I agree. These seem too random to be so. Something is tying them together." Yelka added.

"Is that what you want me to do, Joseph?" Sky asked.

Grandpa looked at each of them in turn, rubbed his chin one last time and nodded at Sky. "Until we have something better to go on, I think it's our only option. Right now, we have no idea what he's planning. These deaths may have nothing to do with him, but they do fall into the realm of unexplained, which usually translates into some sort of dark magic."

"I'll start with the last woman, then." Sky stood up and began to prepare for departure.

"Janice and Mike Ostergren, according to the reports. The husband is missing in that one, so the cops do have a suspect," Grandpa offered.

"Still, the woman has the mark," Olik interjected.

"I'll start there," Sky stated.

"Max and I could do some research on the web," Cindy offered.

"Yeah," Max added.

"Let me do that. You two have plenty of other things to do right now," Grandpa smiled.

"Like what?" Max asked.

"Has either of you mastered the blocking spell yet?" Yelka asked.

"No," Max and Cindy said simultaneously and exchanged guilty looks.

A week later, Max sat in school wishing he was out in the snow instead of trying to concentrate on his homework. History was always his worst subject, but with a magical take added in, he admitted he did find it a bit more interesting. The fact people have been using magic throughout history gave a slight edge to the topic—the Salem witch trials, for example, seemed much more realistic knowing there were actual witches and wizards in the world.

He was rereading a section about how ancient religious priests used their magical powers to prey on the superstitions of some cultures to maintain power, when suddenly Cindy's hand shot into the air in the seat next to him.

"Mrs. Jenson?" Cindy's abrupt shout drew everyone's attention.

"Yes, Cindy?"

"I just read how magical powers are passed along the gene pool just like other physical traits, and I was wondering if that means there are more people with magical abilities out there than we know about?"

"I would have to say that is a correct assessment," Mrs. Jenson replied.

"Wait a minute," another student piped in, hand stretching above his head.

"Yes, Billy?" Mrs. Jenson asked.

"So, you're saying some people out there know magic without realizing it?"

"Well, yes. Think of it this way. Everyone in this room can learn to play the piano. With enough lessons and practice you all might play well enough to be a concert pianist, but there are some people, who are born to be masters. It's as if the magic is passed genetically. They just have a greater talent for it. The same is true with sports or math—just about anything. Therefore, what I'm trying to say is that even though we can all learn magic, some people are naturals at it. No matter how hard we practice, we may never be as gifted magically as they are."

"Bummer," a blond girl in the front row replied.

"That means there will be people who will always be better than us?" Martin asked with a disappointed tone.

"I'm sorry to say, yes," Mrs. Jenson replied. "But, a lot of times people who delve in black magic take the easy road. They're a bit like criminals; they would rather not work for themselves, but instead steal from those who already have it. Evil breeds laziness. Even a master pianist who never practices will lose his ability. If you keep practicing and learning new magic, you will eventually pass them by."

"So, back to the original question." Max put his hand in the air. "There are some people who have magic, without knowing it or strange powers they don't understand?"

"Well, I imagine they sense something is different about themselves, but just can't quite put their finger on it. The fact that society tells them magic isn't real keeps them in the dark, so to speak."

"Do you think there are a lot of these people around?" Cindy asked.

"That's hard to say. There could be."

Sky stepped into the alley where Janice Ostergren—and likely her missing husband were killed. She proceeded with caution in the direction Janice had entered the dark alley between the two buildings, her eyes scanning everything from the overturned trashcans to a pile of old tires. The murder had taken place well over two weeks ago, so any hope she had of finding some clues was minimal. All the Christmas snow had melted, washing away anything that might have been left behind.

As she moved deeper into the alley, Sky closed her eyes and held out her hands. "There's definitely been magic here, recently," she muttered to herself. "And not just dark magic. Interesting."

With her eyes clamped shut, she let the traces of magic guide her until she reached the place where Janice had died. Her eyes snapped open and Sky meticulously surveyed the area. "So, you died here," she said, crouching over the area, picturing the woman's lifeless body in her mind's eye. She extended her hand over the spot where Janice spent her final moments and closed her eyes again. "The attack came from there." Her arm swung in an arc to the spot where Kacha had stood.

Sky went to the location of Kacha's attack. She floated her hands through the air as if she were a mime performing for an audience. "And after Janice was dead, you went that way." Sky continued to follow the traces of magic left by Kacha until she stood over the spot where he had killed Janice's husband.

"No wonder they can't find you." Sky whispered, kneeling over the spot. She could see the slight outline of a body on the pavement.

4

The Start of a Beautiful Friendship

A few days after the New Year, Kacha sat comfortably in his leather recliner polishing a strange wooden rod with a pitchfork-like top to a high sheen. Every few seconds he paused to feel its smooth surface and examine his handy work. An old leather-bound book lay open on the expensive glass end table beside his chair. Sliding his palm across the glossy surface of the strange staff, he let his eyes peruse the open page. "Yes, I have everything ready," he said to himself with a devilish grin. "Now, I need only find a suitable test site."

He stood and strode to the computer where a map was visible on the screen. His forked tongue licked his human lips in anticipation as he tapped a small town in the south-middle area of Wyoming on the center of the screen with a clawed fingernail. "You'll do nicely. If this cold weather would break."

Suddenly, a new browser window popped up on his screen. Usually, he quickly closed the annoying advertisements, but this particular one caught his eye. He read the words aloud, "Find your ancestors at ancestry.com."

CRASH! Max slammed into the wall behind him and dropped to the floor as Yelka's spell caught him square in the chest.

"I thought you were going to practice your new spells so you could learn to block," Yelka's voice sang with its melodic sound as she shook her head disapprovingly.

Cindy turned her head to hide the smirk that spread across her face.

"What are you smiling about?" Max protested as he saw Cindy's expression. "You won't do any better." Max climbed to his feet, rubbing his backside.

"Perhaps we should begin with something easier," Yelka suggested, glancing around the room. "Don't you have some sort of strange oblong foam ball?"

"You mean my Nerf football?" Max asked.

"I believe that's what you call it, yes."

"Yeah, that shouldn't hurt your brick head very much when it hits you," Cindy teased.

"At least my head's a small target," Max snapped.

"Children! Run and get this ball before I change my mind and crush you both against the wall instead. At least we can practice the blocking spell. I have some other ideas to help with the mind reading part," Yelka ordered and Max darted from the room. "How much have you two really been working on this spell?" Yelka interrogated Cindy.

"Actually…" Cindy grimaced.

"Actually, you haven't." Yelka frowned, but it reversed into a smile. "I know how youngsters are when it's Christmas and you already have other things to do. But you really should not be neglecting your advanced magic."

"I know." Cindy sighed.

Max returned carrying a blue Nerf football, which he launched at Cindy the minute he entered the room.

"Nice try," Cindy rolled her eyes as she grabbed the ball out of the air. "I don't need a spell to block that weak arm."

"This weak arm could strike you out any day of the week."

"All right, since I have never used this ball before, I'll let the two of you throw it." Yelka motioned to the football. "When I taught Joseph this spell, he didn't have a soft object to use and he had a bruised bottom for weeks," Yelka chuckled.

"I forgot you taught my grandfather," Max stated.

"Yes, and he was a more diligent student." Yelka pursed her lips and widened her eyes in her best stern look. "He never neglected his lessons."

"Yelka, how did you and Grandpa meet?" Cindy asked.

"Yeah, I've never heard that story either," Max added, eager to learn more.

"That's a long tale, I'm afraid, and we must practice." Yelka took Max by the arm and led him to a spot beside the wall. "Cindy, you stand over there." She pointed to the opposite wall.

"Please," Cindy pleaded, "tell us how it happened."

"Yes, we promise we'll practice the spell so we will be ready for our next lesson. Tell us how you met Grandpa," Max urged.

"Hmph. Only if you guarantee me we won't be using this foam ball the next time I'm here. Even if you're not ready, you'll not get away with using a soft object to block," Yelka said, folding her arms and eyeing them suspiciously.

"We promise," they answered.

"Very well, let's go down to the front room where we can sit down." Yelka walked towards the door with Max and Cindy right on her heels.

En route to the front room, they managed to collect Max's mother, who was also interested in the tale.

Yelka hustled through the tall grass towards the trees a few leagues behind her house. *What's wrong with my spells!* For over an hour, she had been dodging these strange invaders. She glanced back at the line of men tracking her. They were the same ones she had studied over the past fortnight. Something warned her that she couldn't trust them. She had witnessed the men capturing several varieties of animal species from her world, and then they would make the beast disappear into nothingness.

I grew careless. After observing them while under the invisibility spell she still didn't feel safe around them, but had nevertheless gradually moved closer to them each day in order to study them further. This morning they had arrived with some peculiar furry animals that seemed to be able to find her without seeing her. These animals ran on four legs and constantly sniffed the ground. *They must smell me.*

Yelka suddenly realized where she must lead them and it wasn't anything she was looking forward too. The Temni Forest held great evil but the scent of the trava grasses in the forest would mask her scent from anything. There were great risks at entering a place where evil creatures could sense a living being from many miles away. It was even more dangerous for beings that used good magic such as Yelka did.

"This way," a stranger shouted from behind her.

Yelka could see the animal and its keeper making their way along the route she had taken. A whistle and wave from him brought the others in his direction.

Taking a deep breath and trying to swallow against the dryness in her throat, Yelka attempted to steady her nerves. *Keep your head or they're going to catch you.* She scrambled down a large hill, which blocked her view of the pursuers. Once at the bottom, she jogged between the hills leading towards the forest.

Her heart thumped inside her chest but she was uncertain if it was because of the men behind her or the perils that loomed ahead in the dark trees. The feeling of being squeezed in a vise crept over her as she approached the forest and the men in pursuit closed the gap. Her short legs couldn't outdistance the swift four-legged beasts or the tall men that drove them.

Not only was her flight draining her but her use of the invisibility spell was exacting its toll. She hoped she could hold her current pace until she entered the forest. Her only advantage at the moment was the fact they didn't know exactly what they were looking for. Sweat rolled down her forehead and off her nose and her lungs ached terribly as she tried to keep her breathing as quiet as possible.

The invisibility spell failed her as she dove into the trees. A shout from the strangers told her they had seen her. The hairy four-legged beasts' howls filled the air with their excitement. Yelka sprinted into the trees and up the first hill. The grass that would hide her scent grew at a higher altitude. She hoped she could make it before they overtook her. A shadow off to her left changed her focus from the men behind her to the dangers within the forest. Another dark, twisted shape jumped across her vision on the right, trailed by several more.

Yelka pulled her dark green cloak tight around her and dove into a group of shrubs. She tried to slow her breathing and calm her thumping heart. The misshapen, dark figures paid her no attention as if they were drawn to the noise of her pursuers. Holding her breath as best she could, she strained to listen, fearing for the lives of the unsuspecting strangers even now, despite their attempt to capture her.

A scream caused her to gasp and throw her hands over her mouth. Then a boom louder than she had ever heard before filled the air followed by several more. The yelps of the four-legged bests rang out and several high pitched shrieks echoed through the forest. Boom! Boom! Boom! Each new explosion increased her heartbeat as she scrambled through the brush struggling to find a better view.

Suddenly the dark, distorted shapes raced past her, dashing away in the opposite direction. The men and the four-legged animals chased after them. Yelka could only stare in shock. She had expected the men and their charges to be wiped out. Her surprise kept her frozen in place. One part of her warned her to grab this chance and get away but her curiosity in the men had increased even more. *What are these ground shaking weapons? Can they actually escape the forest?*

Abandoning her good sense, Yelka chased after the men. She had found them interesting when she first spotted them weeks ago, but now they had driven off creatures Yelka didn't think even her own magic could conquer.

A few hundred yards up the slope, they entered the grasses that would cover hers and everything else's scent. The tall, skinny shafts of grass reached up to her shoulders, and along with the trees, the trava grass provided her with excellent cover, but it also hid the noisy, hairy animals from her sight. The taller men were much easier to track, as the grasses only reached their waists.

What are you doing, Yelka? You know better than to stray too deep into this forest. Evil will sense your magic! The uneasy sensation of eyes on her and on these men made her sink a little lower into the grass. She glanced in all directions, knowing things that existed only in nightmares came to life in this place.

A soft hiss to her left stopped Yelka in her tracks. She knew that sound, and it told her things were much worse than she had thought. *Night Shades!* She waited, holding her breath, but no other noises were forthcoming and she began to wonder if her mind had been playing tricks on her. The men up ahead were slowly moving out of her sight. She was just about to go when three small flashes of light between her and the men cemented her where she stood. Out of the light, three Night Shades advanced towards the unsuspecting men.

They're not after me? Yelka thought with surprise, watching the Night Shades' track the men. From what she had observed of the men, they possessed no magical capabilities except for their unusual weapons. Usually Night Shades just let the creatures of the forest take care of anyone practicing good magic. Their presence here suggested something important was going on. Something Hudich had an interest in. *Why would Hudich care about these strangers?*

This question propelled her forward, causing her to again abandon her good judgment. She crouched lower into the grass and began jogging after the Night Shades. As she hustled to keep up with the shadowy creatures, she spotted even more of them closing in on both sides of the men. *Yelka, what are you doing out in the open with Night Shades about?* Yelka knew she should be fleeing as far from them as possible and going home, but something deep inside was screaming this was very important.

Suddenly, red flashes and fire erupted everywhere, followed by the same kind of deafening blasts she had heard earlier. The four-legged animals were yelping and running everywhere as men and Night Shades scrambled for cover. The Night Shades cast spells while the men used their curious weapons. Men and Night Shades alike howled in pain as the weapons and spells of their enemy struck them down.

Yelka dodged behind a tree for cover as sparks, fire, and other debris flew all around her. Poking her head around the tree for a better look, she collided with one of the four-legged animals fleeing the scene. The force of the impact knocked her backwards. Both she and the beast rolled for several yards back down the hill before coming to a stop in a large bush.

Yelka thrust her arms forward to cast a spell, but the fear in the animal's eyes stopped her. It gave a soft whimper and its entire body trembled. Yelka slowly extended a hand towards the beast, which appeared to ease its nerves. She placed a reassuring hand on the creature's head and began patting it gently. The strange animal huddled closer to her and seemed to be drawing comfort from her. Taking the animal by its leash, she led it behind some trees, making sure to keep as far as she could from spells and weapons exploding nearby.

The thud of footsteps and cracking of branches warned her that something was approaching them fast. Yelka, though terrified, hugged the animal close to her to keep it quiet. She crouched down beside it and watched two men dash by, pursued by several Night Shades. She eyed them until they dashed down the hill and out of sight. A bright flash of light preceded a ground rocking boom behind her, which drew everyone's attention. Through the trees at the top of the hill, Yelka caught a glimpse of Hudich, who raised his hands and sent a shockwave through the forest, throwing up a whirlwind of leaves, twigs, dust, and other debris in its wake.

The strange furry animal jerked under her arm but didn't flee. Yelka gasped, finally coming to her senses. She must rush back home and tell the village council. These men obviously had something very important for Hudich to pay so much attention to them. She gathered her courage and began to sneak down the hill, when Hudich's voice echoed through the forest, freezing her blood.

"Bring me the prisoners! Alive! I want to know how they got here."

What does that mean? Yelka had assumed they had traveled here through the use of magic the same as everyone else. *That doesn't explain how they took the captured animals!* Suddenly the importance of these men hit Yelka in the gut. The knot that was building twisted tighter and tighter. Deserting her desire for home, she bolted from her place of concealment, animal in tow, after the two men fleeing the Night Shades down the hill.

Boom! Boom! Boom! rumbled through the forest as Yelka reached the edge of the trees.

"Get their weapons!" Hudich's voice was only a distant whisper behind her now.

The Night Shades bounded up and down the rolling hills just out of the forest. They seemed to be bouncing rather than running. Every few seconds the red flash of their magic leapt from their hands towards the two fleeing men, narrowly missing them.

A horrifying scream from out of the forest made the hairs on Yelka's body stand on end, causing her to almost lose her balance. It was only the strange animal's leash that helped her maintain her balance. Yelka could tell that the Night Shades would catch the fleeing men if she didn't intervene. She just didn't know if she should, or even if she could take on those evil creatures with Hudich such a short distance away. Still, something inside her told her this was critical.

Maybe a distraction to help them out! But what? Her eyes danced across the hilltops, searching for anything she could use to help the men without giving herself away.

Suddenly several things happened at once: the animal at her side gave a low deep growl, a bright flash of light sent the Night Shades ahead of her flying in all directions, and a spell launched her down the hill. She lost her hold on the rope attached to the four-legged animal as she landed, rolling over and over. Sharp stabbing pain erupted in every part of her body, both from the spell and the impact of her landing.

Yelka scrambled to find her attacker. Too late! Another spell pinned her to the ground.

"Helpingssss the menss. Attacking my peoplessss" the Night Shade hissed as he hastened down the hill towards her. Its arms extended, holding Yelka with its spell.

"I attacked no one," Yelka replied though gritted teeth, fighting the intense ache of burning flesh.

"LIAR! I seesss," the Night Shade spat with venom as it stood over her. Its red eyes flashed with dark intentions.

Off to the left of the Night Shade, a blur of speed slammed into it as the four-legged animal locked jaws on the Night Shade's arm, yanking the evil being to the ground. The Night Shade roared in agony as it attempted to fend off its attacker. Yelka sprang to her feet, her spell ripped the Night Shade from the animal's grasp and smashed the shadow creature into the side of the hill with such force it lost consciousness.

Yelka spun on her heels to find the Night Shades who had been chasing the men, but the only thing that moved was the animal, which trotted up to her.

"Good boy," Yelka knelt to pat the animal's head. "Where are your friends?" she asked more to herself as she scanned the area. Suddenly at these words, the animal began trotting up the hill with its nose pressed against the earth.

Yelka hurried to keep up with the animal as it continued up the hill with its strange, WHIFF, WHIFF, WHIFF, all the while sniffing the ground intently. When they reached the top of the hill, now in a frightening state of destruction from the strange explosion, Yelka peered all about her to see if she could locate the men or the Night Shades. Scanning behind her, she spotted four more Night Shades exit the forest.

"Find your friends," Yelka encouraged the animal as they started down the slope and out of the Night Shades' line of sight. Yelka picked up the animals leash and again placed a hand on its back, before casting the invisibility spell to hide them both.

The fact that they had covered several hills without a sign of the men or the Night Shades worried Yelka. The Night Shades behind them had gained some ground on her. Somehow, the animal seemed to know where he was going and continued following an unseen path in the green grass of the rolling hills.

The sun had set and darkness grew, and Yelka hoped the animal knew where to go. "Hurry! Hurry! We mustn't let the Night Shades catch up with us," Yelka whispered to the animal.

The raspy breathing of the trailing Night Shades drew closer and closer as they reached the summit of another hill. Yelka's furry guide turned left and trotted along a small creek that wound its way through a group of hills. Glancing behind her, Yelka watched four Night Shades remain on their current path, cresting the next hill and not deviating to pursue her and the animal.

After the Night Shades vanished from sight, Yelka considered releasing the spell which kept her and the beast hidden, but the call of a Night Shade changed her mind. Yelka tugged on the leash to stop the animal so she could listen. Only a short time later a reply answered the first Night Shade's call.

"There are more coming," Yelka mumbled to herself as she surveyed the hills behind her.

"Okay, find your friends," Yelka encouraged the animal once again. WHIFF, WHIFF, the thing continued with its nose stuck to the ground.

After they made an additional turn around the base of another hill, they encountered stands of willow-like trees growing along the sides of the creek. All at once, the animal picked up its pace and dragged Yelka towards a thick group of the trees.

"SPREAD OUT!" Hudich's voice echoed off the hills. "I WANT THEM ALL!"

"We need to hurry," Yelka muttered to the animal, hoping it would sense the desperateness of the situation.

When they discovered a thick stand of trees the animal began pulling her left and right, circling the trees several times as it gave off a soft whimper. Yelka tugged lightly on the leash to stop the animal, realizing the men must be hiding in the trees. Yelka patted the animal lightly on the head.

Yelka swallowed the lump in her parched throat. "Hello," she whispered.

After several moments without a response, Yelka tried again. "Hello. I know you're in there and I want to help."

"Where are you?" came a soft reply.

"I'm just outside the trees. I'm with one of your animals," Yelka stated.

"Where? We can't see you!"

"I'm invisible! I can help you get away but you must trust me!"

"Where's the dog?"

"The dog? Oh, the animal. I'm making him invisible too," Yelka said in a hushed voice while constantly eyeing the hills and slopes behind them.

"How?"

"With magic of course!" Yelka stated simply.

"Magic?"

"Here they come," Yelka whispered as two Night Shades made their way down the hill towards them. "Stay still and don't make a sound. I can help you."

Two Night Shades zigzagged down the slope, glancing in all directions. Every so often, one would send a shockwave of magic over the ground. The magic spread over the grass like a shimmering of green light and then disappeared. After a few moments, another Night Shade rounded the corner walking the riverbed. This one was casting a net of magic in its effort to find the men.

Yelka took the dog and slid into the copse of trees. Her heart raced as the Night Shades drew closer to the trees. *You have to be perfect!* She inhaled the cool evening air to calm her nerves. She knew she would need all her energy if she was going to pull this off. Suddenly the dog gave off a low growl as the three Night Shades met up along the creek. Yelka wrapped an arm around the dog's shoulders to calm it.

After a short huddle, two of the Nights Shades jumped the creek and hustled towards the next hill, while the third zigzagged along the creek towards the trees. Again, every few feet, it would extend its hands and release the green pulse of light.

Get ready! Yelka focused on the Night Shade's hands as they prepared to cast the spell of searching magic. The moment the Night Shade started to stretch forth its hands, Yelka used her spell. The trick worked! The Night Shade stayed on its current heading, up the creek.

Yelka, the dog, and the men sat in silence for the better part of an hour. After not seeing another Night Shade either along the creek or hills, Yelka spoke in a hoarse whisper, "I think we're safe. Stay here and I'll have a look around." Yelka released the dog, making him visible for the men. "Take care of the dog!"

The men gasped in surprise when the animal reappeared to them. She had no time to explain right now, however.

"I'll be back shortly," Yelka muttered and climbed to the top of the nearest hill. Even though she was invisible, the evening breeze caught her long blond locks and whipped them gently about her face. Taking a deep breath of the fresh air, she sat cross-legged in the grass. Closing her eyes, she lowered her palms on the ground, slowly sending her magic to the plant life around her.

Soon Yelka received the information she wanted from the lush green grass of the rolling hills. Hudich and the Night Shades were several miles away, still hunting for the missing men.

Funny how evil doesn't pay attention to all forms of life! They could learn so much if they would only open their minds. Yelka skipped down the hill, her heart in a lighter mood thanks to the grasses' positive energies. She decided she would take the men to the village. There she knew she would be able to find help to protect them. Plus, she hoped to discover the answers Hudich sought. *How did they get here without magic?*

At the bottom of the hill, Yelka took one last glance around to make sure no one was around. Satisfied that she was alone, she made herself visible again. She didn't want to surprise the men this time by just popping out of nowhere. Their reaction to the dog's reappearance told her they didn't have an understanding of magic or how to use it. That also meant they were unaware of the dangers they were in not to mention the peril in which they had now put their world and its people.

"Hello," Yelka said as she reached the trees. "I'm the one who had your animal—your dog. You can come out now. I can take you somewhere where you will be safe."

There was some mumbling among them that she couldn't quite make out, but after some moments, they spoke up. "Okay, we're coming out." Limbs cracking and leaves rustling filled the air and the dog nearly knocked Yelka off her feet as he leapt into her. He licked wildly at her face causing her to laugh. "All right! All right!" she giggled.

Two tall men stepped out of the trees. They wore the same dark blue jumpsuits Yelka had seen them wearing before on previous visits.

"We owe you our thanks," the one with a beard said, extending his hand. "Please accept them. My name is Joseph."

"Yelka." She looked at Joseph's hand, expecting it was some kind of greeting, and held out her own to mirror his. He grasped her hand and Yelka's eyes grew large and she felt her heart skip a bit in shock, but after waggling Yelka's hand up and down once, Joseph released it again.

"I am William," the other said, offering his hand as well.

Now understanding the ritual, Yelka shook his hand with confidence.

"And that is how Joseph and I met," Yelka said to her captive audience.

"You can talk to plants?" Cindy asked with wide eyes.

"How did you understand Grandpa and William? I always thought you learned English later in life?" Mrs. Rigdon asked.

"What did Hudich do to the other men?" Max queried.

Yelka blinked at the flood of questions, and then pointed at each asker in turn. "Yes. Through magic. Sadly, he tortured them before eventually killing them."

"Not only was that the first day we met," Grandpa spoke up from the entrance to the front room, "it was the first day we found out about the war and magic. We learned how dangerous it would be if the gateway fell into Hudich's hands. Luckily, a fire destroyed the original gateway before that could happen." Grandpa winked.

"So you and William started the fire?" Rachel asked with surprise. "I always wondered how the fire started."

"When we got back from Yelka's village, we tried to warn them, but they merely acted as if we were crazy. So, we tampered with some of the gateway's wiring to make the fire look like an accident. To be extra certain Hudich could not create his own gateway, we made sure the only known plans for constructing a new gateway were also consumed in the fire."

"Hey, I want to get back to this whole understanding other languages with magic thing," Cindy interrupted.

"If you master the blocking spell, then using magic to understand another language will be easier," Yelka admonished. "The key to successful spell blocking is reading your opponent's mind. That's also the key to understanding a language you don't know."

"Sounds like the two of you have some more work to do," Grandpa said.

"I want to hear how you found out about the other men," Max demanded. "How do you know they were tortured? What did Hudich learn from them?"

A shadow passed over Grandpa's face. "About their families...about all our families."

5

The Hunter's Prey

Max lay in bed that night unable to sleep. His grandfather's words kept parading through his mind. *He found out about our families!* Had his grandmother met with a fate similar to his father's? Somehow, he knew deep down inside that she had. Did she know magic to defend herself before it happened as his father had, or was she helpless at the hands of their enemies?

Max finally understood how critical and dangerous this war is. In addition, the despair about his father and grandmother spawned even more rage against those who sought to destroy him. He hadn't thought that would be possible after the fury he felt when they had kidnapped his mother last summer. *I'm going to master the blocking spell! Next time I meet the enemy, I'll be ready!*

His thoughts remained on his grandmother and his bubbling anger made him long for summer when school wouldn't stand between him and the fight. *Spring break isn't that far away. I can help that week.* It was early morning when exhaustion overcame his busy mind and he drifted off to sleep.

The next morning, Max's lack of sleep caused his head to pound with painful pressure, so he took two aspirin with his orange juice. Cindy came into the kitchen all cheerful and bright as he shoveled cereal into his mouth.

"Hey, punk," she kidded as she poured herself a glass of milk. "You look tired."

"I am," Max muttered with a mouthful of cereal.

"Why?"

"I couldn't get to sleep."

"Thinking about what Grandpa said?" Cindy picked up a piece of toast and started to nibble on a corner.

Max nodded.

"Me too. I don't know about you, but I got the impression he was talking about your grandmother." Cindy stared at him as she munched on her toast. "So, what are you thinking?"

"I'm going to learn the blocking spell, help catch Kacha, and destroy all of the enemy's plans," Max stated, his head throbbing a little more as his anger pushed his blood pressure higher.

"So, I guess we're going to start working on that blocking spell like we should have already been doing?"

"Yep!"

"What else do you want to do?"

"I don't know what else we can do until Sky gets back. I hope she returns soon," Max swallowed.

"I wish school was out. So we could just focus on this!"

Kacha entered the bank vault carrying his briefcase and holding his newly acquired key. He waited for the bank officer to insert the bank's key into the safety deposit box and unlock it before leaving Kacha alone in the vault. The camera above his head in the corner of the room bothered him, but he knew he had to deal with it. He kept his face concealed as best he could and avoided looking straight at it. Sliding his own key into the box's second slot, he turned it until a soft click reached his ears.

Kacha pulled the flat metal drawer from its slot and set it on a tall table behind him. Frowning at the thought of the camera about to film his most prized possession, he placed his briefcase on the table. He dialed the combination to the numeric controls and flicked them open.

Cautiously, he lifted the lid and took out an old, leather-bound book. While cradling it in one hand, he ran his other over the cover with affection. "I can't risk them finding you," he whispered. After staring at the book a few moments longer, he stowed it inside the metal container and returned it to the vacant slot in the vault's wall. Shooting the camera another sidelong glance, he sealed his box with his key. "Mr. Wentworth," he called, and the bank officer returned to the chamber.

Kacha made sure the clerk locked the other side of his box before retrieving his briefcase and departing.

Sky stood in the shadows of the small grocery store canopy on 26th street between Sixth Avenue and Broadway.   Her two days of holding up in the New York City cold hadn't produced any results. This was the fourth penthouse she had staked out over the past three weeks.

The capture of Grd had led her on this new chase.   Grd had stopped eating humans because of all the toxins in their bodies. Perhaps Kacha had done the same. A new diet might be more advantageous for him in two ways. One, it would be healthier—according to Grd—and two, he would be harder to track. *Plus the fact his magical powers had grown exponentially. Fortunately for me, you can't totally hide your use of it.* She had picked up traces of it all around the areas she had been watching.

This was the last of four locations that had been receiving large shipments of beef. Two had turned out to be restaurants located on the ground floor of some apartment buildings.   The third had been the residence of a family who ran a street cart. This fourth building seemed more promising. She figured the cold weather was keeping him from showing as she breathed out a cloud of warm air.

"Hey baby," called a group of rough-looking men, passing by on the sidewalk.

"Not a chance," Sky smiled grimly at the group.

"Why you gotta be like that?" one responded.

"Because you're just not all that interesting," Sky said, turning her attention back to the building. *Keep walking!*

Finally, the men gave up and went along their way.

Suddenly, Sky's target emerged from the building. A tall blond man, wearing designer winter gear turned left on the sidewalk and started towards Broadway.   His scarf was wrapped so tightly around his face that only his eyes were visible.

That's got to be him! Sky followed along from the opposite side of the street. The chilly morning air hovered among Manhattan's tall buildings, but it was otherwise unseasonably warm. Sky wore only a light coat with thin cotton gloves and a quick glance at those around her on the street confirmed her perception of the temperature. Only light winter apparel covered most of the people on the street. She did have a baseball hat pulled low on her head for a disguise, its purpose was not to protect her from the cold.

Suddenly, two dogs started barking and straining at their leashes in an effort to get at the heavily clothed man.

"Stop it! Stop it!" the owner ordered, tugging the dogs back into submission. "What's come over you?" the owner tried to settle the excited dogs. "I'm terribly sorry," the woman apologized, but Sky noticed the wary look she gave him.

"No problem," the man responded politely and hurried on his way.

The dogs continued to bark until he was nearly to the corner of Fifth Avenue and several pedestrians had come between them.

Sky kept studying the man's movements as she waited for the pedestrian crossing light on Broadway. He made another left at the end of the block, disappearing from Sky's view. When the signal finally changed, Sky darted across the street. Hustling at a brisk pace, she hoped he hadn't reached his destination before she managed to catch up to him. She didn't want to get close enough for him to see her or possibly detect the magic she gave off, but she needed to see where he was going and what he was up to. This was the first time in over three months she had actually seen him.

She rounded the corner to witness him cross 27th Street, still heading north. *That's him! He's definitely getting stronger!* She could sense the magic he left in his wake. Its dark, biting touch caused her to shiver. *How can anyone find comfort in doing evil! It is so much the opposite of peace and happiness.*

After several minutes of rushing, Sky's pursuit led her just past 40th Street to the entrance of the New York Public Library on Fifth Avenue. Leery of Kacha picking up her scent, she decided against following him inside. She found a distant spot in a coffee shop across the street from which to observe the entrance.

What could he possibly want in there?

Over the next couple of weeks, Sky trailed him back to the library, where Kacha would spend several hours inside. On an unusually warm early March day, she had managed to get a good picture of him without the scarf covering his face. By the end of the third week, Sky gave up tailing him so closely, instead waiting for him to leave his apartment building before she headed for the coffee shop. She had mapped out a route up Sixth Avenue and then through Bryant Park that got her there ahead of him. She could get settled with a hot cappuccino and watch him appear and then proceed into the building where he regularly spent several hours. Once, she followed him from the library to a large bank a couple of blocks over on Park Avenue, but his primary interest seemed to be the library.

Finally, one morning, upon leaving his apartment building, Kacha went right instead of left. *Pay attention, stupid!* Sky almost hurried onto her alternate path, nearly running the risk of bumping into him, when she noticed his change of direction as well as the long case he carried under his arm. As he reached the end of the block, he whistled for a taxi. Sky abandoned her desire to remain hidden and chanced flagging down a cab herself.

She managed to secure a ride at about the same time as Kacha. "Follow that cab," she ordered as she closed the door.

The driver accelerated and the vehicle plunged into traffic. The cab weaved in and out of cars as the driver kept Kacha's cab in sight. Sky noticed her skilled driver was gaining on Kacha's cab. "Try not to get too close and there's an extra tip in it for you!"

"Yes, ma'am," the driver replied, smiling into the rearview mirror, and continued his chase after the taxi carrying Kacha.

They tailed Kacha down 34th Street towards the midtown tunnel leading out of the city. *Where is he going? What did he have with him?* She sat on the edge of her seat, practically leaning against the glass divider between the front and back seats.

"What are you? Some kind of cop or private eye?" the driver asked, maintaining a constant gap between his cab and the other taxi.

"You might say that," Sky said as she spotted the sign indicating they were heading towards the airport. "What are you doing?" she mumbled to herself as she bit her lower lip. She took out her communicator to send Joseph a message.

They followed Kacha's cab into the drop-off lane. "When they stop, I'll stop," the driver said.

"Thanks," Sky handed the total fare amount with a large tip through the divider window.

Sure enough, when the cab carrying Kacha stopped at the curb, Sky's driver pulled over as well. She jumped out the door and onto the busy sidewalk. She needed to be cautious and daring at the same time, if she was going to figure out where he was going.

As Kacha got in line at the ticket counter, Sky remained at a safe distance, standing among a small crowd of tourists near the entrance. She took up a position where she could see him clearly but not be easily observed herself. Slowly she pulled out an extremely small set of binoculars. Kacha moved closer and closer to the automatic ticket counters. Sky continually glanced around to see if anyone was paying any attention to her.

When Kacha stepped up to the ticket machine, Sky put the glasses to her face and focused on his screen. "Gotcha!"

She fished around in her jacket pocket and retrieved her cell phone. Her fingers danced over the numbers as she placed a call. "Hello, Joseph. He's just bought a ticket to Denver. I'm heading back to his apartment building to see if I can discover anything." She watched Kacha proceed up a flight of stairs and enter the security check line. "I will let you know what I find."

Max, Cindy, and Martin jabbered back and forth as they wandered home from school for the day. The sun shone down on the scene, giving the impression spring was not too far in the future.

"I should have worn a jacket today instead of this coat," Martin said, unzipping his heavy parka.

"I can't wait to wear shorts again," Max added as he followed Martin's example.

"Not me, I love winter. I'm sad the snow is melting. All that's left is mud." Cindy looked off towards the snowline on the hills surrounding the small town.

"So, are you coming over to practice blocking tonight?" Max asked Cindy.

"If I can get all my homework done. I can't believe how much Mr. Randall gave us!" Cindy complained.

"I've heard he assigns a ton," Martin said. "I'm glad I don't have him."

"Don't worry. You'll get your turn and it suc..." Max stopped as the wheels spinning on the pavement behind them caused him to turn. Larry, a large stocky boy, and his gang zoomed through Max, Cindy, and Martin startling the three of them.

Max wasn't sure but he thought he heard a few derogatory comments directed at them in the group's wake. Larry was Max's rival and the son of the man suspected of killing his father. Usually their encounters resulted in black eyes and then waking up wondering what had happened. After last summer when Larry's father had been trapped in another world and Larry and his mother had asked for help in bringing him home, their relationship had reached an impasse. They were not friends by any means, but the rude taunts and magical, as well as physical, battles had subsided.

"Hey, watch it!" Cindy protested.

"Where are they—" Martin stopped short, distracted by something in the distance.

Max too, had caught sight of the police lights flashing in the neighborhood just over the heads of Larry and his gang.

"What's going on?" Cindy asked with a worried look.

"If Larry and his gang know about it, it's not good," Max said, breaking into a run with Cindy and Martin right behind him.

With each footfall, an uneasy feeling spread through Max's body. It was as if he was hauling a heavy backpack that constantly gained weight. The world seemed to grind into slow motion as he rounded the corner and realized it was his uncle's house that was surrounded by police and vehicles with men clad in FBI vests exiting them.

Martin gasped as they all froze, mouths agape.

Everyone in their little town appeared to be there to witness the strange scene. The police kept the onlookers well back as the FBI agents rushed in and out of the house.

Max grabbed Martin by the arm and dragged him between two houses and out of sight. Cindy trailed right behind them.

"Max…" Martin started to protest.

"Shhhh! I can guess what they want," Max whispered. "And since you live there, you can't be seen."

"He's right," Cindy added, peering around the corner of the house.

"What do we do?" Martin's voice cracked with fear.

"We need to get you to Grandpa's!" Max said, still holding onto Martin's parka. He pulled Martin to the back of the house where a short wooden fence blocked their way. Max paused to make sure no one would see them. "Cindy, we're going!"

Cindy hurried to join them. "I couldn't see much."

"Follow me." Max climbed over the fence and dashed through the back yard. There he scaled another fence to get to the dirt road behind the houses. He halted just a moment for Cindy and Martin to catch up.

"Did you see my mom or dad?" Martin asked Cindy.

"No! Which is kind of reassuring," Cindy tried to sound positive.

"I'll bet they're at Grandpa's if they're anywhere," Max said, checking to see if anyone was watching them. Feeling they hadn't been spotted, he led the others along the fence line of several houses in a hunched position. He had to stop twice before darting through an open gap where the houses had a chain link fence or didn't have one altogether.

They paused at the last house that would provide cover before reaching Grandpa's, and sneaked a peek at the activity swarming Martin's house. Max watched as a crowd huddled in the street trying to gather any bit of news they could. Police and FBI agents had the place completely blocked in and the front door looked as if they had smashed it open.

"Maaax," Cindy hissed quietly, tapping both him and Martin on the shoulder.

"What?' Max whirled around to see a cop car stop in front of Grandpa's house. Two officers and a man wearing a tailored business suit carrying a sheaf of papers stepped out.

"That guy looks like a lawyer or something," whispered Cindy, and Max nodded his agreement.

"What are we going to do?" Martin seemed anxious as he fidgeted with his hands while his eyes flicked from Max to Cindy.

"I think we need to go now, if we want to get inside before Grandpa's is surrounded too," Max said in a low voice.

"Let's do it!" Cindy bolted from their hiding spot out into the street.

Max pulled Martin with him as he raced after her. They had just about reached the dirt road behind Grandpa's when a shout came from the street behind them. "Hey, there's their son!"

"Keep going," Max urged, and they dashed through the back gate and up the steps to the back door.

Max's mother had the door open before they gained the top step and waved them inside. "Hurry!"

"What's going on?" they all asked on top of each other as Max's mother bolted the door shut.

"There are cops at the front door," Max informed his mother, motioning towards the front of the house.

"Hustle upstairs, now!" Max's mother rushed them to the stairs just as the doorbell rang. "GO," she whispered and turned to answer the door.

On the third floor, Max, Cindy, and Martin found Grandpa, Yelka, and Martin's parents huddled over the control panel in a deep discussion.

"What's happening?" Martin asked, worry shaking his words. Everyone turned, and Martin's mother rushed to give him a hug.

"Are you okay?" she asked.

"We need to hide for awhile," Uncle Frank said over his shoulder.

"And we're trying to decide on the best place," Grandpa added, flipping through his notebook.

"Why? What do the police want?" Martin's voice quivered.

"We think they want me for the murders Grd committed while posing as me last summer!" Frank stated.

"But how did they find us?"

"That's pretty obvious, isn't it?" Max said, the image of the grumbling Larry and his gang from only a little while ago flashed through his head. "Alan!"

Cindy nodded in agreement. "What about Mir; can't they go there?"

"Frank is marked. Hudich will know where he is immediately and Helania doesn't want Hudich anywhere near her world," Grandpa said, still thumbing through the pages.

Max exchanged quick looks with everyone and noticed the concern and fear on their faces. "Why not Yelka's?"

"Yelka's world is important since we do a lot of staging and teaching there. My hope is to find somewhere else safe, but not too obvious."

"Plus we don't want them to know where Ell is." Yelka managed a weak smile.

"Well, you'd better hurry. The police are at the front door!" Cindy said a bit louder than she'd intended, judging by the blush coming to her cheeks. "I'm sorry, but it's true. I don't want anything bad to happen to any of us."

"She's right," Max added. "Mom is talking to them as we speak."

Grandpa started scanning pages in a frantic effort to find a suitable world.

"I just don't know how we can protect you," Grandpa said. "I don't want to bring a lot of magical firepower down on you."

"Well, we've got to go now. If they have a warrant to search your house too…" Frank stated, eyeing the door.

"How about Pekel?" Max blurted out, realizing his knowledge of other worlds was limited, but desperate to help hurry them along as best he could. "Give us some weapons and we should have the advantage."

"Joseph," Yelka nodded, "that could work."

"You're right," Grandpa agreed. "It's not really considered a 'good' magic world, so your presence there may not even be noticed.

There are still Trogs there, however, so, we'll put you on the other side of their world."

"Where are we going?" Aunt Donna visibly trembled.

"Pekel is the world where we had imprisoned Hudich. It is very difficult to use magic there. That should keep you safe." Grandpa started adjusting dials on the control panel. "Yelka, go get some weapons for their protection. We must hurry. We need to move Finster before we lose Kacha."

"What's this about Finster?" Max asked.

"Never mind that now. Go help Yelka!" Grandpa ordered.

Max darted after Yelka with Cindy right on his heels. They bolted down the spiral staircase and into the first bedroom on the right. Yelka went to the closet and flung the doors wide, incanting, "*Odpri!*"

At Yelka's command, the entire back of the closet opened up to reveal a secret room Max had never seen before. "So *that's* where the weapons are kept," Max said, gazing at the array of strange weapons from swords to futuristic-looking guns.

Before he could move, Yelka shoved guns and supplies into his and Cindy's hands. "Hurry!" Yelka shouted. "I'll close up here."

Max and Cindy bolted back up to the tower and deposited their loads. As soon as Yelka joined them, Grandpa fired up the gateway. The force field spread from the five metallic stands and formed a dome, sealing them off from the rest of the world. The old-fashioned mirror started to revolve until it picked up speed and disappeared into a ball of light.

"I'm dropping you in a forest so there should be plenty of cover," Grandpa said while handing Frank, Donna, and Martin a variety of supplies including bedding, food, clothing, and weapons. "Follow Yelka's commands."

"Cindy and I aren't going?" Max asked. bouncing on his toes.

"No! I need you here," Grandpa said and hurried Frank, Donna, Martin, and Yelka through the gateway.

As soon as they were gone, Grandpa switched everything off. The mirror had just stopped and the force field vanished as several police officers with guns drawn, burst into the room.

"Everybody down on the ground. Now!"

6

Hiding from the FBI

After exiting the gateway into Pekel, Yelka took the lead. They stood in the middle of a forest full of thick and leafy, but relatively short trees. The underside of the canopy was barely above Frank's head. Tall forest grass grew everywhere, giving everyone a claustrophobic sensation. To the adults, Yelka and Martin appeared to be almost swimming in a sea of green.

"We should find a place to hole up. One where we can keep a good eye out, but without being too far from the gateway," Yelka said, holding out her compass to get her bearings.

"Are you sure we're safe here?" Donna asked, glancing in all directions while clinging to Frank.

"Ouch!" Frank gasped suddenly, eyeing the mark on his right hand.

Yelka rushed to him and grabbed his hand for a better look. "They know where we are! That changes our plans."

"What are we going to do?" Frank rubbed his palm on his jeans.

"Locate a good place to defend ourselves and hope Joseph can open the gateway before the Trogs arrive," Yelka replied. "Follow me." She conducted the little group north hoping to find a secure spot.

###

Alan, clad in black robes instead of his usual stylish business suit, strode across the polished marble floor towards Hudich, who sat regally on a throne-like chair on a dais in the main chamber of the stone fortress.

Hudich's head remained hidden beneath his black hood but his muscular forearms rested on the arms of his chair. He appeared to be in deep thought with his head tilted towards the floor.

"My lord," Alan said carefully, bowing low before the imposing figure. "I have good news and," he paused for effect, "bad news."

"What is it?" Hudich's deep voice responded with annoyance at being interrupted, and he lifted his head slightly.

"Our plan to push the brother-in-law and his family into another world has worked." Alan reported, his tall frame still maintaining his low posture.

"And the bad news?" Hudich raised his head enough so that his red eyes reflected the torchlight of the chamber, making them glow.

"They traveled to Pekel." Alan swallowed, his voice barely a whisper.

"The old man is clever, but it won't stop me." Hudich slammed his fists down on the arms of the chair.

"What are we going to do?" Alan elevated his own head slightly, unable to keep a nervous hand from running his fingers through his short brown and gray hair.

"It seems I will have to take care of this personally." Hudich's eyes flared with malice as he sprang from his throne. "Ensure the police keep that old fool busy so he can't bring Frank and the others back right away!"

Alan dropped to his knees putting his hands over his head, "Yes, my lord." He winced as a flash of light filled the chamber, and when he opened his eyes again, Hudich had disappeared.

Yelka led them to a pile of dumpster-sized boulders. From the top of the stones they could see above the forest trees in all directions, and at the base they found a secluded alcove that would provide cover. After taking a thorough look from their newly found vantage point, they sat with their backs against the stones to wait while Yelka sent off a quick message to Grandpa.

"How is your hand, now?" Yelka asked.

"Actually, after that initial burn, it feels pretty much the same." Frank studied his palm, his brow furrowed.

"Well, all they know is we have traveled through the gateway to Pekel. We are in a hard world for them to reach." Yelka glanced through an opening in the trees at the blue sky above, remembering the sky of her own world the day she'd met Joseph. "The only place safer than Earth is Pekel with its natural resistance to magic. I imagine the only person who could actually travel here using magic is Hudich himself."

"Why is it some worlds are better for magic than others?" Donna asked Yelka.

"Every living thing has a spirit. This includes planets and worlds. If a planet can support life, it has a spirit. Some spirits are stronger than others and they have control over every living thing and how each one interacts with other life. Pekel's spirit is weak and must use all its energy just to sustain life here. I have a feeling Pekel is very old and nearing the end of its life cycle," Yelka said, running her fingers lightly through the soil as if in touch with the elements.

Frank huffed at all the talk of planets and spirits and climbed to his feet. "I'm going to take a look from the rocks again." He began to climb the large boulders.

"He still has a hard time believing, even after all he has seen," Yelka murmured as she watched him go. "That is why he struggles with his magic lessons."

"I've tried to tell him that too," Donna agreed, wrapping a protective arm around Martin.

Suddenly, Frank landed on his feet with a thud in the middle of their little shelter, eyes huge with fear. "Something's coming!"

"What is it?" asked Martin.

Yelka scurried up the rocks while typing a message into her communicator. "Come on, Joseph," she muttered under her breath. She reached the top a few moments before the others, in time to see treetops swaying in a long thick line, as if a mole was moving under the dirt, heading in their direction. "How does your hand feel now, Frank?"

"It does have a slight tingle," he responded, indicating he had an idea what she was implying.

Yelka checked her communicator for a response. Nothing! "Those are probably Trogs. We need to leave this place and quickly."

"What about the gateway?" Donna asked frantically.

"Joseph can open it anywhere he wants, but right now, something is preventing him." Yelka scrambled down the rocks in the opposite direction of the approaching threat, with Frank and the others right behind her. *Please hurry, Joseph!*

"This is my house. What are you doing? What are the guns for?" Grandpa asked, raising his hands over his head and climbing to his knees. Max and Cindy followed suit.

"We have a warrant to search the premises." The man in the suit Max and Cindy had seen arrive with the police officers entered the room holding out a sheaf of papers. "And you can get up." The man shot the police a weary look as he handed Grandpa the warrant.

Grandpa took the paper as he got to his feet and began scanning the document. Max and Cindy rushed to peer around his arms from the side.

"What does it say?" Max asked.

"It just gives them the authority to search the premises for your Uncle Frank and anything that might lead to his whereabouts," Grandpa said, handing the warrant back to the man. "Well as you can see, he's not up here." Grandpa waved his arm towards the third floor with only the gateway in it.

"I don't suppose you'd care to explain that loud noise from a moment ago that was making the whole house vibrate?" the man asked suspiciously.

"Why, of course," Grandpa smirked. "It's a machine that just sent Frank to another world." Grandpa winked at Max and Cindy.

"Right, then," the man rolled his eyes. "I am going to have to ask you to wait downstairs while we conduct our business."

"Certainly," Grandpa said, wrapping his arms around Max and Cindy, leading them to the spiral staircase. "Let's leave these officers to their work."

As they reached the second floor and made their way towards the main stairs, they passed several officers exploring the various rooms. Comments like, "What the heck is this stuff?" to, "This is the weirdest house I've ever seen!" floated through the hall.

"Do... Ouch!" Max started but a sharp pinch from Grandpa silenced him.

Downstairs they found Max's mother waiting beside the front room window. "Is everything all right?" she asked with a worried expression as they entered the room.

"Fine," Grandpa answered, observing two more policemen come into the house and rush up the stairs. His gaze lingered on the top of the stairs when suddenly he gave a little start and pulled his communicator out of his pocket.

Yelka, Max mouthed so he could see.

Grandpa gave a short nod but before he could respond the man in the suit reappeared from upstairs.

"I'm going to have to ask you a few questions," he stated. pen and notepad in hand.

"Of course," Grandpa responded, slipping his communicator back into his pocket.

"Do you know the whereabouts of Frank Tracey?"

"I would suspect he is at his house or his place of work," Grandpa replied innocently.

"Can we ask what this is all about?" Max's mother interrupted.

"Well, Frank Tracy is actually Frank Bell. He is the main suspect in the gruesome murders of six people," the suited man explained.

"Really! I would never have guessed." Grandpa rubbed his chin.

"Yes. In fact, we've linked him to a few murders reported here last summer as well. We're pretty sure it's him."

A soft buzzing sound resonated from Grandpa's pocket drawing the man's attention.

"Just a text message. I'll check it later," Grandpa said with an innocuous smile. "Please continue."

"Where are we going?" Frank huffed, jogging alongside Yelka and the others.

"As far away as possible from whatever is chasing us," Yelka replied, checking her communicator again. "Hopefully, we can keep ahead of them until Joseph can open the gateway. I don't want to have to stand and fight."

"What about our weapons? I thought they would defeat anything here," Martin puffed, struggling to keep up.

"Normally, yes, but last year they imported a lot of weapons through their gateway. We could be caught in a deadly situation."

"Keep moving," Donna urged.

They raced through the tall grass under the thick forest canopy, dodging trees and the occasional boulder. Low hills dominated the forest, making their flight easy. The tight space between grass top and the low ceiling from the trees gave them a sensation of no way out.

Abruptly, an explosion some ways behind them echoed through the forest, shaking trees and scattering all kinds of chattering birds into the air. Everyone stopped, glanced back, looked at each other and then broke into a sprint. Another boom followed, and another. The ground-quaking explosions steadily landed closer to their position.

They ran as fast as they could but still it seemed like they were losing ground. The blasts were only a few dozen yards behind them. Yelka's mind whirled, trying to find a way out of this. She knew her magic couldn't save them here, or even aid them much. In her few short visits to Pekel, she had only managed one or two weak spells and her mastery of them wasn't nearly at the level she would want.

Suddenly, the trees gave way to a massive gorge that spanned several hundred yards across. Yelka grabbed Frank by the arm to keep him from losing his balance and falling into the depths below.

Frank blanched and fell to his knees, thanking Yelka profusely. Martin and Donna joined Yelka in pulling Frank back from the edge a bit. The roar of a raging river rose from the deep canyon, but a layer of thick mist covered the bottom of the gorge below, hiding the height of the steep rocky walls.

"Look!" Martin pointed to an old rope-and-plank bridge spanning the drop-off about a quarter of a mile to their left.

"Let's go!" Yelka urged them along the edge of the cliff in an effort to reach the bridge before their pursuers overtook them.

"We'll never make it in time. We're giving them an angle," Frank said as he swung himself over a fallen log and then helped the others.

The deafening explosions began following them along the new route both behind and to their left. A few even went over the edge of the bank to disturb the swirling mists below.

It definitely seems as if they are herding us, but why? Yelka snuck a peek at the unresponsive communicator, hoping a message would appear. The noise of the explosions started to ring in her ears and the smell of dust and chemicals hung in the air, making it harder to breathe.

"They're going to catch us!" Donna screeched as a violent blast sent her and Martin to the ground.

Frank held his right hand up to his face and then swung it out for the others to see, "It's me," he shouted. "They're tracking me."

"Frank, WAIT!" Yelka tried to seize him but he spun around and bolted away from them.

"Frank! Frank! Dad! Frank!" Everyone called after him.

Yelka assisted Martin and Donna up before they trailed after him. "You two continue to the bridge. I'll get Frank and meet you there." Yelka had never been so grim in giving a command before. She hoped fervently that Martin and his mother would listen and obey.

Donna, realizing the severity of the situation nodded her assent. She snagged her son's hand and guided him in the direction of the bridge.

Yelka typed in another frantic message to Joseph as she dashed in the direction Frank had gone.

"This is taking too long," Grandpa sighed as he snuck the communicator out of his pocket for a quick glimpse.

Max, Cindy and Rachel exchanged scared looks with Grandpa and each other.

"They're in trouble!" Grandpa whispered and then grabbed the arm of a police officer who just stepped into the house. "Excuse me, but do you have any idea how long this is going to take?"

"I'm not sure. You'll have to ask someone in charge," the officer replied.

"And who would that be?" Grandpa continued in a calm voice.

"Agent Simpson of the FBI. The one who delivered the warrant, sir."

"I think he's gone upstairs again, Grandpa," Max added and watched wide eyed as his grandfather suddenly bolted up the stairs.

"Things must be serious. I can't remember seeing Grandpa move that quickly without something chasing him," Cindy said with a taut expression.

"I can't either," Max's mother agreed.

Frank's pace created a sizeable gap from Yelka and the others while the blasts veered after him. The Trogs were tracking him by the mark on his hand. She knew he had run off in order to protect his family, but if Joseph opened the gateway, he wouldn't be close enough to escape. Her only hope was to gather the group together again. Yelka checked her communicator again but its blank screen only revealed disappointment.

She hurried as fast as she could but the distancing of the eruptions indicated she was losing ground. Suddenly, Yelka darted behind a group of trees as guttural voices reached her ears.

A squad of heavily armed Trogs rushed by ahead of her and off to her left. Toward the bridge! Only glimpses of their large green bodies and armor flashed between the trees. They acted excited by their work, joking and laughing.

Yelka couldn't stop trembling. She felt helpless. Her magic was useless here. A gnawing in her stomach began to grow, certain this situation was going to get worse.

As soon as the Trogs were far enough ahead of her, Yelka raced after them. She emerged into an area where she had a clear view of the rope bridge spanning the gorge. There was no sign of Martin and Donna, who would be slowed down by having to navigate the edge of the ravine. She spotted Frank already part way across the bridge.

Frank hurried toward the other side of the bridge when he noticed movement on the other side. Several muscular green creatures with large ears and dressed in heavy body armor stepped onto the bridge, causing Frank to put on the brakes.

He whirled around as a group of the same creatures were already moving out onto the bridge behind him.

"Thank you for your patience, Mr. Rigdon," Agent Simpson said as the last of the police officers exited the house. "I must say, you've got a lot of unusual stuff in this house."

"Did you find anything to help with your investigation?" Grandpa asked pleasantly.

"No, but we may be back. In the meantime, if you happen to learn any information about Frank, please call this number." Agent Simpson handed Grandpa a card.

"Of course," Grandpa said, accepting the card.

As soon as Agent Simpson left, everyone dashed upstairs as fast as they could.

"Max, call Yelka and get her location, tell her I'm opening the gateway," Grandpa ordered as he scrambled onto the third floor landing and headed for the control panel.

Max took out his communicator and typed in the message.

Frank's heart pounded in his chest and his mouth was full of cotton. He noticed the Trogs hadn't advanced very far onto the bridge and the explosions had stopped. *I'm trapped!*

"Frank," A deep voice behind him drew his attention.

Frank whirled around to see a dark-robed figure standing on the bridge only ten yards away. The wind threw back Hudich's hood revealing his hideous skull-like head with its red rat eyes. His cape flapped in the breeze that drifted up from the canyon and his huge, claw-like fingers gripped the side ropes.

"Hudich," Frank stammered, fetching the gun Grandpa had given him from his jacket. His hand shook as he pointed it at the leader of the enemy. He had found a way to reach Pekel without a gateway.

"There's nowhere left to run," Hudich smiled, advancing.

7

The Wrath of Hudich

Yelka waited just under the cover of the tree line and grabbed Donna and Martin when they caught up to her. They looked surprised she had arrived ahead of them. The three of them stood petrified as they watched the terrifying scene playing out less than a hundred yards away.

"Oh, no," Yelka gasped as Hudich began slowly approaching Frank.

Frank pointed his gun at Hudich. With the cessation of the explosions, they could just make out the conversation taking place on the bridge. The mist kept the roar of the hidden river at bay, causing their voices to travel.

"There's nowhere left to run," Hudich said in his deep voice. "You're ours now."

"I'm not going with you," Frank's voice cracked.

"That's where you're wrong. My friends have a nice cell set aside just for you," Hudich's voice had a wicked ring to it.

"No, I'm not wrong," Frank said more forcefully, leveling the gun at Hudich's chest. "I'm not going anywhere with you or your hideous friends. You'll have to kill me before I have a repeat of last summer."

Suddenly, Hudich's arms shot out in front of him and a shockwave launching Frank off his feet. He barely managed to hang on to the gun as he landed on his back on the old wooden plank walkway. With the wind knocked out of him, he struggled to get up as Hudich came forward another couple of feet. It took him a couple of seconds to gain his balance, and hold the gun steady. He aimed at Hudich while hanging onto the rope railing of the wobbly bridge.

"You don't have it in you. I can feel your fear. Taste it in the air," Hudich growled.

"Take another step forward and we'll see if I have it in me or not," Frank threatened, the gun bouncing in his trembling hand.

Hudich leapt several yards forward, closing the distance between him and Frank by half, just as Frank squeezed the trigger. A flash of white light tore through Hudich's shoulder almost throwing him off the bridge as it swung him over the rail. He hung on with his good arm and hoisted himself back up.

Frank fired again nicking Hudich's left ear. Hudich whirled on Frank, teeth bared in a glare of ultimate rage. A sound wave escaped Hudich's open mouth that caught Frank in the center of his chest, throwing him completely off the bridge into the mists deep below.

"NOOO!" Donna's scream echoed through the forest.

Hudich and the Trogs turned to see the small group only a short distance away. Martin and Donna were hysterical as Yelka fought to pull them into the trees. Hudich glared at her before he vanished in a flash of light.

Suddenly the explosions were back, erupting all around them. Yelka managed to get Donna and Martin under control as Grandpa appeared.

"Hurry!" Grandpa helped them through the gateway to safety.

Max felt sick. Anger and sadness waged a war in his gut at the news of Frank's death at the hands of Hudich. He couldn't stop shaking and tears rolled down his cheeks. There was no comfort for Donna or Martin. If Yelka hadn't been a witness to what happened, they would probably still be wondering.

Grandpa tried to open the gateway in the bottom of the gorge but each time they poked their heads out, it hovered above a tumultuous river.

"Did Frank have a communicator?" Cindy asked before blowing her nose into a tissue.

"Yes," Grandpa said so solemnly everyone knew there had been no response from it.

Eventually everyone wandered down to the front room. Yelka made everyone some hot cocoa and tried to offer comfort. It was as if a shadow hung over the room where the light couldn't penetrate. It seemed like a bad dream. Frank, dead. Max wanted to scream. Hudich had to pay. First his father, possibly his grandmother, and now his uncle. Hudich *would* pay; Max would see to that.

Suddenly, Grandpa gave a jerk as his communicator buzzed in his pants pocket, drawing everyone's attention. He almost dropped it in his effort to get it out quickly.

"It's Sky," he said disappointedly and turned his back.

"I take it we lost Kacha because of the police?" Yelka whispered at Grandpa's side.

"Yes." Grandpa read the message. "She wants an update." Grandpa's fingers flew over the dials as Yelka peered over his shoulder at the communicator.

"We need to get Finster to New York," Grandpa's voice was still low among the soft crying. "Max, Cindy, come with me."

Max exchanged a confused look with Cindy and his mother. He patted the sobbing Martin on the back and then followed Grandpa and Yelka up to the third floor.

"Wha—?" Max started to speak but Grandpa shot out a finger in a forceful manner to stop him.

Grandpa continued to hold up a finger as he strolled around the room. He acted as if he was seeking something. Max noticed that Cindy was watching him with a shocked expression. Yelka started doing the same inspection-type movements as Grandpa, only in the opposite direction.

"Joseph," Yelka said, standing beside a boarded-up window before moving over to the control panel.

Suddenly, Grandpa flew out of the room and down the spiral staircase. The thumping of his footsteps reached them from the hall as Max and Cindy joined Yelka by the control panel.

Are we? Max mouthed to Yelka.

Yelka nodded her head. She appeared old for the first time to Max. He didn't know if it was from the day's horrible events or something else.

"What?" Cindy whispered.

Max leaned into her shoulder. "We're bugged," he spoke quietly into her ear.

"So, do you think our math test is going to be a tough one?" Cindy said in a carefree manner.

Max grinned, realizing what she was up to, and replied nonchalantly, "Oh, I'm not worried. I studied all last week. That test will be a breeze."

Yelka smiled at their clever ruse, but everyone's smile faded the instant Grandpa returned.

Grandpa had a small electronic device in his hand that resembled an old personal digital calendar. He pressed a small round button on its surface and began circling the room. The small tool began to give off a steady clicking sound, like a loud clock. He passed the device over the walls from floor to ceiling. As soon as he got close to the window Yelka had indicated, the ticking sped up like machine gun fire.

Grandpa found the exact spot and yanked the small object from its hiding place. He then crushed it under his foot after dropping it on the floor. In all, he found four similar devices planted in different areas around the room. One was under the control panel and another stuck to one of the metallic stands next to a joint where it wouldn't have been noticed.

"Some of those had a video feed," Grandpa informed them with a grave expression.

"That means they would have seen us come back from Pekel," Yelka gasped putting her hands over her mouth. "Oh, dear!"

"And look for Frank. Well," Grandpa swallowed as if fighting with his emotions, "at least they didn't see Frank come back through. Otherwise, I think they would have been all over us again."

Max wiped his eyes on his shirt. His resolve to win this war continued to deepen with each vile, evil act the enemy committed. The fear and doubt he had just two summers ago was still there in the back of his mind, but his will to destroy the enemy's efforts had outgrown them. "What do you need me and Cindy to do?"

Cindy nodded as a tear drifted down her cheek, her big blue eyes swollen and puffy.

"You're going to help Sky," Grandpa said.

"For how long? We've got school tomorrow," Cindy said.

"I will have Olik help you get caught up. Right now we need to stop Kacha before we can concentrate on Hudich."

"What about Finster or you?" Yelka asked. "I don't think we need Max and Cindy there."

"I have to stay here in case the police come back. You can't go and you can't deal with the police," Grandpa frowned. "Finster is going to watch the apartment for Kacha's return. I thought about sending him to the airport, but what if Kacha flies into another airport? That means going into the apartment is off limits. Sky is going to find out all she can about deliveries and purchases. She needs Max and Cindy to help her with the library."

"What about a library?" Max crinkled his nose. He had thought this was going to be a chance to get back at the enemy. Going to a library right now didn't sound like much of an attack or seem like it would inflict the kind of pain he wanted on the enemy.

"She'll explain when you get there," Grandpa said. "Now, go get a jacket and some clothes in case you're gone for a few days."

"Are you sure it's okay with my mom and dad?" Cindy asked.

"Yelka will go with you and explain what's happened. I'll get Finster out there while you get ready."

Max raced down the spiral staircase with Cindy and Yelka right behind him. He had just entered his room when the gateway started to vibrate the house. After retrieving his backpack from the closet, he threw in a set of clean clothes, his communicator, and a sweatshirt. Just then, Max noticed several strange cars parked behind the house. *They are spying on us!* Then taking his jacket off a hook behind his door, he headed back to the tower.

As he entered the third floor, he saw the back of Finster, a large man with dark black, wavy hair, disappear through the gateway. Grandpa then shut everything off and pulled out his communicator.

"We are being watched," Max said, joining Grandpa inside the ring of stands that created the force field of the gateway.

"I figured as much, and I'm sure after what they've seen, we aren't going to lose our guests for some time." Grandpa said grimly. He put a hand on Max's shoulder. "Are you okay?"

Max fought to keep his lip from quivering as thoughts of his uncle rushed to the forefront of his mind. He gave a short nod.

"I am so sorry. That's another reason for sending you and Cindy to help Sky. Giving you something to do will be better than sitting around thinking about what's happened." Grandpa said.

Footsteps thumped up the spiral staircase before Cindy and Yelka joined them on the third floor. Cindy had a backpack slung over her shoulder and a ball cap on her head.

"What did her mother and father say?" Grandpa asked.

"As usual, I had to assure her Cindy wouldn't be in any danger, which wasn't very easy given what's happened. They came back with us to try and comfort Donna and Martin," Yelka said, her lower lip trembling.

"Now, I'm sure I don't have to tell you but I will. Do exactly what Sky tells you to do!" Grandpa admonished Max and Cindy.

"We will," they answered.

"Don't take any unnecessary risks," Yelka added.

"We won't."

"And if you have spare time, practice your spells," Yelka tried to sound more upbeat.

Grandpa fired up the force field and then the gateway. "Sky will be waiting," he said as the revolving mirror started to dissolve into a ball of light. "Be careful!"

Max gave Grandpa and Yelka a hug as did Cindy before they walked into the light.

Max stepped down into a dark, garbage-filled alley and then helped Cindy down. A strong sent of urine and rotting trash assaulted Max's nose. Sky stood a few feet away with her back to him as she guarded the entrance several yards away.

"You couldn't have found a better spot?" Cindy crinkled her nose.

"No," Sky said with a worried expression. "This was the safest spot at the moment. Are you both all right? I am so sorry about your uncle," Sky said. Sky's pale, beautiful face, with its dark red lips and her black attire gave her a ghostly appearance that seemed to fit the depressing situation.

"What do you want us to do?" Cindy swallowed hard.

Max nodded and hid his face to wipe his eyes on his sleeve. He wanted to get busy doing anything that could destroy the enemy's work, and part of that included capturing Kacha. They didn't think Hudich and the rest of the enemy knew about Kacha and the book. Otherwise they would be pursuing him as well. Up to now, nothing had happened to indicate they were even aware of Kacha's activities.

"If you'd rather go back home…" Sky started.

"NO!" Max and Cindy almost shouted.

"Okay," Sky flashed a quick smile. "Let us get to it then." She led them out of the alley.

After she had shown Max the room where he'd be staying with Finster, she took them to the room she would be sharing with Cindy.

They joined her around the small table in the corner of the hotel room, which had two queen-sized beds, a TV, nightstand, and other conveniences. There in the center of the table was an aerial picture of several city blocks.

"So what are we looking at?" Cindy asked before Sky had a chance to sit down.

"That is the area I've been tracking Kacha's movements over the last month," Sky said. "It will be good for you to see as well."

"Does it show where Kacha lives?" Max leaned in closer.

"Yes," Sky winked.

Max blushed and Cindy cleared her throat while rolling her eyes.

"Kacha lives here." Sky pointed to a building that was in the lower left center of the small map. "On the corner of Sixth Avenue and 26th Street. Finster is positioned here." Sky's finger slid to the building across the street from Kacha's apartment building. "He is keeping an eye out for Kacha's return."

"What do you want Cindy and me to do?" Max asked.

"For several weeks now, Kacha has been spending a great deal of time here." Sky indicated a rather large building farther north on Fifth Avenue. "The New York Public Library. Your job will be to figure out what he has been up to in there. I do not know how you are going to do it, but I have a feeling it is extremely important and could help us catch him."

"Sounds easy enough," Cindy sighed sarcastically.

"Oh, and one more thing. You are not to use any magic while you are in the library. Kacha's powers have grown immensely. He will detect immediately that you have been there if you leave any trace of magic," Sky warned.

"What are you going to be doing?" Cindy asked.

"I am going to see what he has been doing in his apartment. It will be tricky. We had hoped to track him to Denver and wait for him to leave there. That would have given us plenty of time to get out. Now, however, I will not have much of a warning if he shows up unexpectedly."

"Be careful," Max said.

"You will need to be just as cautious. He has spent a great deal of time at that library. There is a chance, although slim, he could go there before heading home," Sky said.

"Do you have a picture of him?" Cindy asked.

"Yeah, good idea, Cindy," Max said.

"Yes, I have several." Sky extracted some photographs from her pocket and dropped them on the table. "Just remember, he is a changeling. He can impersonate anyone. Although, I think he rather likes his current form. It makes him think he is important; better than everyone else. His pride could work to our advantage."

"How?" Max and Cindy asked.

"Pride leads him to believe he is smarter than others and invincible, thus he'll make mistakes in his arrogance. Just remember, there is always someone better or smarter," Sky smiled. "Too much pride sets you up to fall."

Max and Cindy rummaged through the photos finding the best ones. "Can we keep some?" Max asked.

"Of course," Sky said. "All right, let's get cracking. We do not know when Kacha will return so we must hurry. Get your jackets."

Max hustled to his room to retrieve his coat and communicator. When he returned, Sky and Cindy were standing in the hall.

Sky shoved a wad of cash into each of their hands. "I might not come for you until late. If you need to get some food or something, this should take care of it."

They flagged down a taxi in front of the hotel. Sky told the driver to take them to the library and the car jumped into traffic. The buildings zoomed past Max's window. The pain of his uncle's death seemed somehow far away, as if it was only a nightmare. The emptiness in his gut told him it wasn't a dream, though, and he was glad to have something to do to take his mind off his sorrow rather than just hang around the house.

"Are you going to be okay?" Sky asked, running a hand across his shoulder.

"Yeah." Max turned to gaze at Sky's beautiful face and give her a weak smile. "I want to make them pay for what they've done."

"Just do not let your desire to get even cloud your judgment," Sky warned. "If you can do that, we can cause some serious damage to their plans."

"We're here," the cab driver said as he pulled over to the curb.

Sky handed him some money and told him to keep the change as they all jumped out of the backseat.

"This place is huge," Cindy said, staring up at the building.

"Yes, you have your work cut out for you," Sky said. "I will be back later tonight. Stay on the alert. I need to get to it as well. Call me or Finster if you get into trouble." She gave them each a quick hug and then disappeared down the street.

"Where do you think we should start?" Max asked as they climbed the stone steps to the library.

"Well, we need to be careful how we do this. We don't want to alert anyone that will warn him in anyway," Cindy said.

"Just how do we show his picture around without alerting anyone?" Max grumbled as they entered the front doors. The size of the task before them fell on Max like a mountain. The library was enormous. There were multiple floors with walls and walls of books.

"Maybe we should walk around to see if anything catches our eye," Cindy suggested with a sigh.

"Yeah," Max agreed, craning his neck up at the endless floors of books. "Maybe we should see if we can find a map of this place."

"Good idea." Cindy pointed to an information desk a short distance away.

After receiving a map from the lady behind the counter, they huddled close together studying the various floors and the sections they contained.

"I don't think he'd be looking at anything in the fiction department," Max reasoned.

"Or the computer lab," Cindy added. "I mean, he lives in the penthouse of a high-rise. I'm sure he has his own Internet connection."

"Good point. So, where do you think we should start?" Max asked, adjusting his baseball cap.

"I honestly don't have a clue," Cindy stated as she glanced around.

"Well, let's think about this. We know he's probably trying to design another gateway. He would need materials to build it," Max suggested.

"And the hourglass," Cindy offered.

"Hey, that must be it! I bet it has something to do with the hourglass," Max said a little too loud for a library and ducked his head lower into his shoulders as he checked to see if anyone had noticed them.

"Yeah, keep it low, dummy." Cindy slugged him in the arm. "So, what's the most important piece of the hour…"

Max's eyes met Cindy's and he knew she was thinking the same thing he was. Souls! "So what does a library have to do with that?"

"Newspapers? Obituaries? But they are already dead and gone," Cindy started throwing out examples.

"History?" Max raised his eyebrows.

"I suggest we go check out those areas and maybe something else will jump out at us," Cindy offered, leaning over the map again.

They followed the directions on the map to the newspaper section. They found it easier to search old newspapers online and began scanning for any articles with the word "soul" in it. After an hour without finding anything to give them a clue as to what they were looking for, Max began to feel depressed and frustrated. The thoughts of not being able to help his uncle and not making any progress created a knot in his stomach.

"This seems like a dead end," Cindy sighed as she finished reading yet another article. "I'm drawing a blank."

"Me too." Max glanced around at the other people busy going about their research. He took the map out of his pocket and began examining it.

"Trying to hazard another guess?" Cindy asked.

"No, I have to go," Max said, seeking a restroom.

"Thanks for telling me. I didn't need to know that!"

"You asked." Max gave a small smirk. "There's the closest one," He said more to himself. "I'll be back." He got out of the chair and left Cindy to continue searching newspaper articles.

He followed the map to the restroom, noticing the various departments as he passed them. Before leaving the restroom, he splashed water on his face just to help him regain some focus. His reflection in the mirror revealed his puffy red eyes.

Two men in heavy conversation stepped into the lavatory, startling Max a bit.

"I've traced my lineage back six generations on my mother's side," the one said to the other.

"Wow! Anyone famous in your family?" the second jokingly asked.

Max almost dropped the map onto the wet countertop in his efforts to get it out of his back pocket as fast as he could. His heart raced inside his chest at the possibility that he had just found what they were looking for. *That has to be it.* He exited the restroom, his eyes searching from department to department on the map. "Yes!" he muttered to himself with a short fist pump.

Max made his way back to Cindy as fast as he could without actually breaking into a run. He caught several of the library workers' stern glares as if warning him to slow down but they couldn't contain his excitement. He knew he was right.

Max was almost panting when he plopped down in the seat next to Cindy.

"What are you smiling about?" Cindy asked in a frustrated tone.

"I think I know where he goes in the library and I have a theory on why," Max whispered and checked to make sure no one was eavesdropping on their conversation.

"Where?" Cindy asked.

Max held the map out for her to see with his finger pointing to the spot.

"The Genealogical History section?" Cindy crinkled her nose with doubt.

8

The Descendant

The Hazardous Materials crew rushed through the small town dressed in their protective suits while a wide perimeter of armed soldiers kept news crews and onlookers from entering the small Wyoming town. Military helicopters warned everyone to stay clear as they circled the area. News trucks with satellite dishes on top broadcasted their messages to viewers all over the world.

Kacha stood outside the perimeter, studying the layout and watching the men in their yellow suits hurry around the dead town. The wind mussed his wavy blond hair, but today he was not concerned with his appearance. He sneered as HAZMAT-suited members of the Center for Disease Control collected water and air samples while other groups used electronic equipment to gather scientific data. The sight that brought a gleeful smirk to his face, however, was the rows upon rows of black body bags lining the town's high school football field. And more victims were still being hauled towards the makeshift morgue.

The voice of a nearby news reporter reached his ears. "As of now, we know that 1,135 people are dead in this small Wyoming town. The cause of death remains a mystery. Speculations on what happened here range from a terrorist attack to a local citizen bringing back a rare, but lethal, virus from outside the country. We expect to have a complete report from the CDC within the hour, not only as to what killed everyone in this small town but the condition of the family that stumbled first upon the scene. We can only hope this is an isolated incident and that no other towns or people are in danger."

Oh, you are all in danger. The smirk on Kacha's face broadened into a smile. He cast a spell and disappeared from view.

"Mom! Did you see that!" a small child squawked, adding to Kacha's enjoyment of the moment. "That man just vanished!"

"Uh huh," the mother replied her eyes on the scene below.

Kacha navigated the perimeter. A military dog, sensing his presence, started barking and tugging at his handler's leash.

What? You smell something, boy?" the soldier peered right through the invisible Kacha.

The dog pulled the frustrated soldier towards Kacha as he walked deeper into the sealed-off area. Kacha sent a powerful blast of air which tossed sand and dirt into the face of the dog and his trainer, causing them to stop and turn their heads. This maneuver distracted the dog enough to let him get by.

"Dang, the wind sure blows in Wyoming," the solder complained.

Kacha zigzagged through the large sagebrush that covered the prairie around the small town totally relishing the moment. *Silly humans. Next time, I'll have to set up something to completely scare the life out of them. Maybe release some terrible toxin after the fact just to throw them for a real loop.*

He made his way through the streets of the town towards the hill on the far side, listening to the troubled conversations of the crews as they attempted to solve the mystery.

"There is no trace of a virus or chemical agent, either in the air, the soil, or water," one of the men announced to the other scientists and CDC agents near him.

"None of the bodies show any sign of trauma that could indicate how they died. We won't know anything for sure until we can perform the autopsies," the second reported.

"There has to be some common thread, some infection, something," demanded the third, frustration clearly apparent in his words. This one was without a doubt the highest ranking person among them.

"We did notice one minor peculiarity as we were bagging the bodies, but as I said, we won't be able to determine anything for certain until autopsies have been performed," the second mentioned cautiously.

"What is it?" the third asked, obviously desperate for some clue to go on.

"Each body I've looked at so far—just a cursory examination, mind you—bears a tiny bruise in the front of the neck, at the base of the neck."

"That sounds significant. Get those autopsies going immediately," ordered the third.

They won't show you anything. Kacha almost wished they could see the wicked smile plastered on his face, but he had an errand to finish. He continued his march through the center of everything, softly humming to himself. He couldn't remember ever feeling this kind of euphoria in his life. Since the passing of the great wizards, he and the other Haireens' lives had been one of constant struggle. Now he had the upper hand and was in control, he wasn't about to let it go.

He passed through the town unseen and made his way slowly up the slope of the hill on the far side of town. A hiking trail used by the locals made the climb an easy one as it wound through the sagebrush and rocks. Once he gained the summit, he left the trail to a spot of ground that overlooked the small town.

He glanced down on the chaotic scene, desiring to announce to the world he was responsible for what had happened. *Patience*, he cautioned himself. *That will come much later.* He reached down and with a gentle finger, he caressed the silk-covered jar filled with little lights which hung from his ornate staff. The tiny orbs jerked away from his finger, somehow intuitively avoiding Kacha's evil touch.

"You mustn't be afraid of your new master," he mumbled, gazing at the marble-sized lights fleeing from his finger. He bent towards the jar, whispering a strange word. The lights grew in intensity and rushed to the side of the glass where his finger rested, forming a solid ball of light. "That's better."

Straightening, he yanked the staff out of the ground and looked back down at the milling crowd of scientists and military personnel in the valley. *I really should do something to frighten them some more.* The smile on his face spread to an evil grin as he spotted another soldier with his dog patrolling the area behind him and away from the town. *That should do the trick.* He quickened his pace and proceeded straight for the guard.

When he got to within about ten yards of them, the dog began to bark and tug at the leash, trying in vain to get at Kacha. "What is it, girl? What do you smell?" the solder attempted to calm the dog.

Kacha suddenly made himself visible, startling the soldier.

"Where did you come from? Are you from the town?" the soldier asked, quickly putting a hand on his sidearm, while still struggling to control the dog, now emitting a low growl from the back of her throat.

"Not from the town, no," Kacha said smoothly.

"How did you get in here? It's restricted to civilians," the soldier stressed, but Kacha knew he wouldn't unholster it without provocation.

"It was easy." Kacha cast his spell. The soldier lurched forward as his soul escaped his body and flew through the air to join the others in the jar. His body fell lifeless to the ground. The dog sensing she was no match for Kacha, whined once and tucked her tail before sprinting away, yelping as if she had been beaten.

"That should scare them silly," Kacha muttered as he disappeared again and headed back towards the town. By the time he passed the soldiers guarding the perimeter, news of the dead soldier had circulated to everyone and panic began to set in.

Max and Cindy spent the next several days in the small, glass-paneled room learning how to use the genealogical software in the Family History section. There were several desks with computers to aid people in their searches. A friendly elderly woman with silver-white hair was there every day to help them. She reminded Max of what a fairy godmother might look like, short and plump with her hair tied back in a bun.

The two of them had started a family history chart going back several generations for both of their parents so they could familiarize themselves with how the software worked. They found the process fascinating as they discovered the countries their ancestors had migrated from, but were getting frustrated about the lack of progress in figuring out what Kacha was after.

"Let's go over this again," Cindy sighed, raking her fingers through her blond hair in annoyance. "What makes you so sure he's been coming to this genealogical history section?" Cindy asked.

"Do you remember when Mrs. Ryan talked about magic being passed genetically through family lines?"

Cindy nodded.

"What if Kacha is trying to build an army or something, and he's looking for descendants of magical families, hoping they still contain secret abilities? I know that probably sounds kind of dumb," Max's voice sank along with his shoulders.

"Actually, Max, I think you're onto something," Cindy said, her energy renewed. "But listen. I don't think he's trying to *recruit* anybody, unless he needs help to operate the gateway. I think Sky would have noticed if he'd had people showing up at his apartment or was somehow recruiting people to join him."

"Good point," Max admitted. "Wait a minute. Didn't Grandpa say something about Alan and the enemy using chanters to control the souls in order to operate the gateway, since they weren't the ones who collected them?"

"Ah, I see what you're getting at. So, Kacha wouldn't need the chanters?"

"I don't know for sure, but if he's capturing these souls himself, he should be able to operate his hourglass by himself," Max suggested.

"Well, we definitely think he's building the hourglass in order to create a gateway. And if he doesn't require help to operate it…"

"Then maybe he's trying to collect magical souls for it!" Max interrupted raising his eyebrows. "That makes sense doesn't it? If you're using magic to create this gateway, wouldn't the spirits of people who are magical be better for doing that? Their souls might make the gateway more powerful—or maybe using these kinds of people means he won't have to collect as many of them to make the gateway work."

Cindy practically jumped out of her chair. "Which means we're running out of time."

"Yes, but *now* we have a lead. We have to figure out who Kacha is hunting," Max stated.

"How would he even know who to look for or where to start?" Cindy questioned.

"We know from what Grandpa and Yelka have taught us that magic has been going on forever in our world. I'm sure Hudich would know, but Kacha isn't working with him. So what are some historical events in our world that might be associated with magic?"

"Um, the Salem witch trials," Cindy said, perking up a little. "I'd be willing to bet a number of those people really were witches."

"Well, that's as good as any place to start," Max agreed. "Let's go to the history section to see if we can get a list of names to work on."

"I know we don't want to let Kacha know we've been here, but what if the lady who has been assisting us helped Kacha and can point us in the right direction? We don't have much time. What if he comes back soon?"

"It might be worth a shot," Max nodded, frowning. "She may be able to tell us what we want to know. If she aided him, she might be willing to tell us. We've just got to be sly about how we do this."

"Oh, I'm the master of sly," Cindy smiled and batted her eyelashes.

Max rolled his eyes at his friend, but Cindy was already waving to the librarian.

"Can I help you, my dears?" she asked in a soft, pleasant tone. "Are you having trouble with the software?"

"Uh…" Max started.

"Actually," Cindy smiled and her blue eyes sparkled. "Well, you see. Hmm. I don't quite know how to ask this…" Cindy stammered and bit her lip shyly.

"What is it?" The woman's face emanated friendly curiosity.

"Well, Ms Brown, we're doing a school…project," Max struggled noting the name Margret Brown on her name tag.

"And we were wondering if there were any descendents from the Salem witch trials documented in this section?" Cindy interrupted.

"My my! Does your teacher happen to be a well-dressed, attractive blond gentleman?" the old woman winked and giggled.

"You caught us," Cindy feigned embarrassment. "Our assignment is due tomorrow, but we've both been out of school with bad colds. So we're late getting started."

"So you see," Max paused as if in thought, "We're not planning on cheating or anything. We'll still do all the research ourselves, but…."

"But if you could give us some names to start with, we could finish our project in time to turn it in tomorrow," Cindy piped up.

"Yes, we would be so grateful," Max nodded vigorously.

"Hmmm," the lady glanced up to the ceiling as if trying to remember something. "I think he did find a couple of names from the history section of the library. It's on the tip of my tongue. What was it, now?"

"Did he use one of these computers? Maybe his work is saved on it," Max suggested and Cindy kicked his leg gently, warning him to be less obvious.

"That wouldn't help you I'm afraid. We wipe the browsing history every night. In any case, he's researching something else now. Probably for your next assignment." She smiled conspiratorially.

"Really? Anything as fun as Salem witch trial descendants?"

"Now, let me see. I seem to recall it being something about potential descendants of the wizard Merlin—you know, from the tales of King Arthur."

"I thought those were just legends," Cindy's eyes grew wide.

"So did I. I thought he was a fictional character and the whole story was make-believe," Max added. "So how could you find descendants of someone who didn't exist?"

"Well, you see, there has long been speculation among historians that Merlin and all the others were real people—or at least based on real people," the woman said, still beaming. "And there *are* books about them."

"Do you happen to know which ones?" Cindy asked with excitement.

"Would that help you with your report?" the woman asked as a mother would, reminding her kids to concentrate on their homework.

"No, not really." Max stepped lightly on Cindy's foot. "But I do think it's very interesting. If someone found an actual descendent of Merlin, that would really make history."

"I suppose it would," the woman smiled. "Well, if you want to do that kind of research, you'll have to go to the history section. If your teacher comes in again, I promise to keep your secret. Now, children, if you'll excuse me, that gentleman over there has been waiting for me to teach him how to use the system. Good luck."

"Thank you!" Max and Cindy replied in unison.

"So what do you think about this whole Merlin thing?" Cindy whispered.

"As weird as it sounds, I buy it," Max said. "Grandpa's taught me over the last two years to believe the unbelievable."

"Me too. Down to the history books." Cindy stood and they went to search the historical section of the library. "You'd better send that info on to Grandpa."

"Good idea," Max said as they made their way down a large staircase. He took out his communicator and typed in their new discovery. When they reached the bottom of the stairs, he paused to read Grandpa's reaction. "Hey…"

Suddenly, Cindy hit him with the force of a linebacker. She wrapped her arms around him and pushed him into a section of wall. Before Max could protest, she had pressed her lips against his in a kiss. Max's initial shock changed into a warm rush of heart-pounding adrenaline as he started to kiss her back. But, just as fast as Cindy had kissed him she stopped.

"You enjoyed that didn't you?" She whispered into his ear with a teasing edge to her voice.

"Wha...what did you do that..." Before Max could finish his sentence, Kacha bounded up the stairs behind Cindy, drawing his attention.

"Did he turn?" Cindy asked in Max's ear.

"No!"

"Did you get a message from Sky or Finster?"

Max peeked at his communicator to make sure he hadn't missed anything. "No, nothing. Which means either something is wrong or he didn't go to his apartment first." Max's fingers danced over the controls in an effort to contact Sky.

"Is he out of sight?" Cindy muttered.

"Yes," Max answered, after checking the stairs .

"Well, then you can let me go," Cindy leaned back with a huge smile.

Max's cheeks flushed red with embarrassment. "I was concentrating on my com-mun-i-cat-or!"

"What did she say?" Cindy moved closer so she could read Max's communicator with him.

"No answer," Max said.

"What do you think we should do?" Cindy asked.

"We could go back to the hotel," Max suggested.

"Wait," Cindy said, putting her hand on his arm and biting her lip.

"What?"

"What if we could figure out where he's been getting his information?" Cindy said. "I think these descendants, if they exist, are in big trouble. Isn't it our responsibility to protect them?"

"You have a point. If we don't try to find them and warn them, they could be killed," Max agreed.

"Or worse! Their souls might end up in an hourglass."

"I don't think Sky or Grandpa would want us to do anything," Max said, but he could see the determination in Cindy's eyes that said she yearned to go for it.

"We won't get caught." She flashed a dazzling smile.

"Okay, but we've got to be super careful." Max stated and made sure Kacha could not see them.

"If you see him, you can kiss me again to hide our faces." Cindy winked. "You know you liked it."

"Shut it," Max frowned and eased his way out onto the steps, his eyes glued to the landing at the top.

"Relax! With that constipated expression, people are going to think you are up to something. That will draw his attention for sure." Cindy jumped to the front and hustled up the stairs as if she didn't have a care in the world.

Max inhaled a deep breath and chased after her. Adrenaline rushed through his body as Cindy stopped just before they could see the glass room of the genealogy section of the library. His heart raced inside his chest and his mouth was dry. "How do you think we should go about this?"

"So, not only should we stay out of Kacha's sight but also our old librarian friend's," Cindy said as she peered around the corner.

"Good point. I could see her trying to get us together and that would be a disaster." Max peeked into the room. The old lady sat at her desk while Kacha busied himself at a computer in the far right corner of the room. "We're going to need to get in back of him."

"At least the librarian can't see us."

"Yes, but she'll be able to once we get behind Kacha." Max took in their surroundings in an effort to find the best route to their desired location. "If we make our way over to that section," Max nodded in the direction he had in mind. "We should be able to get in behind him and use the bookshelves to hide us from Margret. We'll be out in the open for only a few seconds, but not in Kacha's direct line of sight."

"Okay, let's go for it," Cindy said, leaning back out of view. "Ready?"

"Go!"

Diverting their faces away from Kacha, they scooted across the floor until they made it to the rows of bookshelves that hid them from his view. They hurried down the rows until they reached the one where Kacha's left shoulder appeared. They flattened their backs and started to slide along the bookshelf when Cindy nudged Max.

"What?" Max hissed, turning to look at her.

"People could be watching." She snatched a book off the shelf and started to flip through its pages.

Max's head swiveled around noting the people who could see them. To his relief, no one was paying them any attention, and he exhaled in relief.

"How about you move and I'll keep an eye out. Then I'll go and you guard. If someone starts to watch us, I'll cough."

"Good plan. Okay, I'm going," Max said and continued to slide with his back along the bookshelf. More and more of Kacha entered his view. After he had covered most of the distance, he stopped, extracted a book from a shelf, got into a comfortable position and waited for Cindy.

"Can you see his screen at all?" Cindy asked as she joined him.

"No. I think we're going to have to move more into the open when we get closer," Max said, staring at Kacha. "I'm going to the end of the aisle." Once again, he crept along the shelf behind him. He swallowed the lump that was building with each step he took. His breathing was so loud in his ears he checked to make sure no one could hear him. When he arrived at his destination, he pulled another book off the shelf and turned his back to Kacha, who was now in full view.

"Stay in that position for a minute," Cindy said when she had covered the remaining distance as well. Her head bobbed to areas around Max's arms and shoulders. "Keep your back to him and step to your right."

Max did as Cindy asked and casually made his way to the bookshelf on the other side of the aisle. Cindy stepped with him, keeping him between her and the glass wall of the genealogy room.

"I can see his screen now but it's hard to make out," Cindy said, standing on her tiptoes and peeking over Max's right shoulder. "There's a name."

"What is it?"

"It's a Richard Bur-something. Burdock? No, Burdick—" Cindy jerked her head to the middle of Max's chest.

"What? What happened?" Max whispered.

"The old lady just came over to his desk."

Suddenly a vibration in Max's pocket caused him to jump and drop his book. Without thinking, he bent over to pick up the book exposing Cindy. When he stood back up, he noticed Cindy's ashen face. Max spun to see Kacha and the old woman smiling at them from the other side of the glass.

9

The Old Woman

It felt as if time had stopped. Max and Cindy stared at the smiling Kacha and the elderly woman on the other side of the glass. The woman waved her hand as if beckoning them to come into the room. Suddenly, Kacha flicked his fingers and books started to jump off the shelves towards Max and Cindy. The old woman gasped as Max and Cindy twirled around, ducked, and sprinted down the aisle as fast as they could go. They covered their heads with their arms to avoid the airborne books that pummeled them from everywhere. No matter which way they turned, books slammed into them and chased them around corners. The harder they ran, the more books from different sections attacked them.

The dive-bombing books caused an outbreak of panic through the entire library. People began scrambling for the exits in droves, knocking over desks, computers, bookshelves, and other people. A mix of screams, children crying, and crashing debris echoed throughout the building as if an earthquake was shaking the entire structure.

In the rush of people and flying books, Max and Cindy managed to reach the stairs before Kacha, when a book struck Cindy in the back of the head, knocking her out and propelling her forward into a wall of fleeing people. Max barely managed to grab her arm and keep her from falling down the stairs to be trampled by the crowd. Without both hands to protect his head, Max received several blows as well. The books hammered away at the unconscious Cindy, pounding her out of Max's hand.

Rage at the situation rushed through Max. *I need to block these*

things! At this thought, Max's mind locked onto the spell he had been practicing. *"Ovirajte,"* Max screamed as he shot his hand at some incoming books. The result shocked Max so profoundly he stumbled forward because of the impact that didn't happen. The books smashed into an invisible wall and ricocheted in the opposite direction.

"Ovirajte, Ovirajte." Max continued, fending off waves of books and dragging Cindy with him. Being jammed in the crowd of people trying to exit the library helped Max and Cindy as it carried them out the front doors and onto Fifth Avenue.

As soon as they reached the front steps the crowd spread out, so Max had to fully support Cindy. Max breathed a sigh of relief, thinking the barrage of books had stopped. Crashing glass and a strange paper rattling sound told him a different story as a new onslaught of books zoomed at him and Cindy.

Max flipped Cindy over his shoulder in a fireman's carry and tried to race past the building, hoping to find some refuge in the park. He continued to cast his spell to shield them from the books, but with his attention diverted, he tripped and fell forward. He clenched his teeth against the anticipated impact with the cement, when arms caught hold of him.

Max looked up to see Finster had snagged them. Sky was there too, her arms extended as she cast a spell. The books smashed into Sky's invisible wall.

"Go!" she ordered.

Finster threw Cindy over his shoulder as if she were a small child. The entrance to the library and the street erupted into mass hysteria. Cars collided and people screamed in panic at the attacking books bouncing off Sky's spell and scattering in all directions.

As the last of the books dropped to the ground, Kacha exited the library, his wicked grin revealing his mouthful of vicious hooked teeth. He focused on Max and the others and gave chase.

Max and Finster, with Sky trailing them, navigated the sea of smashed cars in the street, dodging back and forth between people and vehicles. Cindy regained consciousness as she bounced around on Finster's shoulder. They rounded a car crash where one of the cars almost stood straight up on its bumper as it rested on top of a small SUV.

"Watch out!" Sky yanked them out of the way as the car toppled over, just missing them. The blast of Kacha's spell rushed past them at the same time in a microburst of wind.

"What do we do?" Finster shouted to Sky.

"You go on ahead. I will hold him up. Go to the hotel and I will meet you there," Sky barked as she rotated to face Kacha.

"NO!" Max screamed. "We can fight together." Max tried to stop but Finster seized him by the arm, forcing him along.

"Don't worry about me," Sky smiled and raised her eyebrows. "I can take care of myself. Now, go!"

Max couldn't resist Finster's strength and he had to make his feet run or be dragged. Before they rounded the corner of the nearest building, Max glanced back. He watched as Sky's extraordinary quickness enabled her to dodge multiple spells from Kacha and then catch him off guard with a soaring compact car from behind. Crunching metal filled the air as the car carrying Kacha on its bumper collided with a dump truck.

"You can put me down," Cindy's voice vibrated each time Finster's large feet touched the pavement.

About halfway down the next street, Finster slowed to a stroll and gently placed Cindy on the sidewalk. It was a good thing he didn't let go of her arm as she swayed back and forth, trying to regain her balance.

"He's got a lot of nerve casting spells like that in front of everyone," Cindy said holding her head with her free hand.

"I don't know how nervy he really is," Finster stated, still keeping Cindy from tipping over as they maneuvered down the street.

"What do you mean?" Max protested. He agreed with Cindy.

"Well, nobody probably knows what caused all that. People in your world don't believe in magic do they." Finster added.

"I see your point," Cindy said.

"It's a good thing. Did you see that elderly librarian's face right when the books started flying? If she knew he had caused it, he would never get any more help...from..." Max stopped as if he had run into a wall.

Cindy and Finster turned to see what had happened to him.

"What?"

"That woman!" Max shivered. "He'll kill her!" Max spun on his heels and bolted back towards the library.

"Max, come back!" Cindy and Finster shouted.

"I'll meet you at the hotel!" Fear for the woman's life propelled Max forward. He skipped the side street they had just come from and decided to enter the library from the park side. Surely, Kacha would want to know what the old woman had told them. He must find her before Kacha decided to return to the library. *Hopefully, his desire to follow us will keep him occupied.*

Max sprinted down the street dodging people the entire way. Not only were there the normal pedestrians but the commotion had also drawn additional onlookers as well as extra traffic. Soon he was bumping into people left and right and the nasty remarks and rude comments he received matched the scathing looks on their faces.

"Watch it kid!"

"Slow down!"

Max ignored their orders and glares. Deep down he knew if he didn't reach the old woman, she would die or soon be joining the other souls in the hourglass. *And that wouldn't happen until he'd tortured the information out of her.*

Even though Max had been a part of it, the disaster on Fifth Avenue in front of the library shocked him. A multi-car pileup stretched from the library down the entire block. Cars tossed by Kacha and Sky lay in storefronts and on sidewalks. Torn and tattered books, paper, and glass littered everything. The front of the library looked as if a bomb had gone off inside the building. There were ambulances, fire trucks, and police cars with their lights bouncing off everything. The brave, emergency personnel aided wounded people everywhere. News crews from local and national stations broadcast their confused stories to people all over the world.

Police escorted the uninjured and spectators out of the general area as they attempted to cordon off a perimeter. Max didn't hesitate. As he approached the barricade, he cast his spell and disappeared.

He raced around the side of the building, into Bryant Park, and up to the rear entrance of the library. He wanted to remain invisible until he made it inside the building, but his dash from the library and back and the other events had drained his energy. Sweat rolled down his face and back and he gritted his teeth in an effort to hold the spell. Even though he couldn't be seen, his eyes searched everywhere in an effort to spot Kacha. He noticed there was a straight, unobstructed line stretching from the library down the street, which he'd assumed was Kacha and Sky's battlefield.

Keeping his eyes open for Kacha as he entered the library caused him to smack into a man on his way out. The collision startled Max back to visibility almost giving the man a heart attack.

"Holy cow, you scared me. I didn't see you!"

"Ah. Sorry," Max managed before darting away to avoid further conversation.

Max felt like he was in an apocalyptic movie. He waded through ankle-deep books and papers strewn about the place. He navigated the destroyed novels and tried to hustle up the stairs but his legs didn't want to respond. The day's events had sapped his energy and caused his mouth to become as dry as a desert. He needed a drink of water in the worst kind of way. His pace was only a slow, heavy walk by the time he reached the top of the stairs. He forgot his discomforts, however, as he spotted the old woman cleaning up the disaster.

"Okay, how am I going to do this?" Max muttered to himself as he headed towards her.

As she straightened to put some papers in a trash bag she held in her hand, she caught sight of Max. She brushed back her silver disheveled hair and an expression of relief flashed across her tired face. "Max!"

"Hello," Max stammered. His heart raced worse than if he was preparing for battle. He couldn't figure out where to start or how he was going to convince this woman her life was in terrible danger.

"Hello, I was so worried. I'm glad you're okay. Where's your friend? Is she all right? I just don't understand what happened."

"She's okay," Max managed a weak smile.

"I'm still shaking from all this commotion." She held out her trembling hands. "I was scared to death. I can't for the life of me figure out what could have caused this disaster."

"I can." Max glanced around to make sure no one could hear him.

"What? What are you talking about?" The old woman's eyes were wide with fear.

After double-checking to make sure their conversation wouldn't be overheard, "We don't have much time. The only reason I came back was to get you out of here. You are in terrible danger."

"Why, is the building not safe?" the woman followed Max's example and gazed in all directions.

"Not for you it isn't, I'm afraid." Max took a deep breath in an effort to calm his pounding heart. "That sharp-dressed man you were standing next to when this happened isn't who he seems to be. If you don't get out of here, he will come back for you. He is the one who caused all of this."

The woman's expression went from fear to one of admonition. "Max, you can't be serious," she said putting her hand on her hip.

"I'm totally serious. He is very evil and he isn't even a man."
Max could tell by her face she wasn't going to be convinced very easily.
"Okay, see that small book on that table there." Max pointed.

"Yes."

"*Pridi!*" The book zoomed through the air right into Max's hand.
The woman froze with her mouth agape. "H…H…how?"

"Magic," Max whispered. "This disaster, here, today was caused
by him."

"Why?"

"That man is not anyone's teacher. He's hunting down people
with magical abilities. Cindy and I were sent here to discover what he
was up to, which we did. Now that he knows we have been here, he will
want to find out what we know. Which will bring him to you." Max
frowned.

"But I just can't leave. I have no place to go." Her frightened
expression returned with lines of worry on her face.

"We can help…" Max paused as the vibrating in his pocket caught
his attention. He retrieved his communicator to see he had a message
from Sky. The words GET OUT NOW added to his anxiety. "We don't
have much time. We need to leave here, now! He is evil and he used
magic to try and stop Cindy and me from discovering what he's up to.
He caused this destruction." Max waved his arm at the clutter.

"He did seem strangely calm as I tried to get his attention once
things started flying. I do…don't know," she stuttered as she shook from
head to toe. Even the bag in her hand gave off a soft plastic vibration as
it rattled in her hand.

Once again, Max placed a hand under her elbow and started to lead
her towards the hall. "Don't worry. Come with me. My friends and I
will protect you. At the very least you have to get out of here," Max
tried to reassure her.

"What about my daughter? I can't just leave her." the woman said
as they made their way slowly through the cluttered library.

"Where does she live?"

"She lives with me!"

The words dealt Max another blow. "How far do you live from
the library?"

"Three blocks west of here, just south of the Port Authority," the
woman stared into his eyes and Max could see the concern written there.

"Did you ever tell that man about her?"

"I did, yes. He was so suave and handsome. I tried to set him up on a date with her," the woman's voice trembled.

The pressure of the dangerous situation started to squeeze Max under its weight. "What's the exact address?" He had his communicator in his hand and typed in the message as the woman relayed the information. He continued to check the screen as they walked, waiting for a response.

"My friends will meet us at your apartment," Max said. He almost yanked the woman off her feet because he halted so suddenly as he spied Kacha heading towards the stairs from the lower level. Max had to clamped his hand over her mouth to stifle the gasp about to escape her lips. "Shh."

Still holding her elbow, Max escorted her away from the genealogy section and into another area on the opposite side. They found a spot where they could hide in the shadows but still see the genealogy room. Kacha hustled up the stairs. Max couldn't help but smile at the sight of the ragged condition of Kacha's designer clothes and the slight limp in his gait. *Sky gave you more than you counted on.*

"You're right. He's heading right for my area. Do you think he is here for me?" Margret whispered as Kacha made a beeline right to the genealogy section.

Kacha's head swiveled in all directions, forcing Max and the woman to step back deeper into the shadows. When Kacha's eyes moved over their general location, Max thought his beating heart would give them away. But his gaze moved on until he found another librarian. He signaled towards the genealogy section as he conversed with the distraught-looking library consultant.

"Can you show me the quickest way to the stairs leading out to the park?" Max whispered.

"Yes, follow me," the woman said.

Max tailed her down several rows and hallways until they reached a door with a glowing EXIT sign above it. The door opened to an emergency stairwell that was to be used in case of fire. Max wanted to run down the enclosed cement stairway, but the elderly woman's pace kept him from doing so. Before they reached the bottom, she seemed to be drained of energy. Her descent had slowed to almost a crawl and her breathing was shallow and erratic. Max could tell something was wrong.

"Are you okay?"

"I just can't believe it," her voice barely audible as she almost broke out in tears. "I saw what happened today and what you did with that book. I'm just so scared."

"I know you are," Max said putting a reassuring hand on her shoulder. "I was too when I first found out about all this. I still have a hard time believing it myself."

She got out a handkerchief from her pocket and began dabbing at her eyes as she came to a halt. "I left my purse upstairs. How am I going to get my stuff or into my apartment?"

Max noticed she didn't even have a jacket on and took his off to give her. He glanced back up the stairs as if deciding what to do. "Where's your purse? Is there anything you can't live without in it?"

"No," she said but then clamped a hand onto his arm. "Yes, my wedding ring! My purse is in my desk drawer."

"All right. Wait for me at the bottom of the stairs. I'll be back as fast as I can," Max said. He patted her arm gently, smiled to hide his regret at having asked her the question in the first place, and hustled up the stairs.

He made it all the way to the area where they had observed Kacha question the other library workers. Pausing in the same dark section to search for Kacha, Max swallowed hard to regain his nerves. After a few moments of watching without spotting him, Max rushed to the woman's cubicle, located her purse in the bottom drawer and retrieved her jacket from the back of a chair.

After checking to make sure no one, including Kacha, saw him, he scurried through the debris so he could help the librarian get home. He hustled down the steps and around the corner only to find an empty stairwell. Margret was gone.

10

The Demon's Fork

Max felt sick! His head spun and he wanted to throw up as he exploded out of the bottom door that led outside of the library. He looked out across the park but saw no sign of the old woman. *What happened to her? If Kacha found her...*

"Crap!" Max spat, running his hand through his hair while taking a quick scan in both directions. The park was filled with people milling about, curious about the incident on the other side of the library. A policeman approached him, coming from the direction of the front of the building. *Which way could she have gone?*

"Hey, you'll have to go that way. We're clearing this area," the cop pointed towards Sixth Avenue on the other side of the park.

"Ah, sure," Max said and turned to leave, but stopped. "Sir, did you see an elderly woman come out this way?"

"We had her escorted out by a fireman a few minutes ago," the cop responded.

A feeling of relief spread through Max. "And did she go this way too?"

"Yes. We're trying to keep people away from the disaster out front."

"Thanks." Max smiled and jogged across the park, keeping his eyes peeled for the woman. He passed another officer who was wrapping police tape around some trees, creating a large perimeter around the park entrance of the library in order to keep people back. Once he reached the edge of the park, he could see that Sixth Avenue was relatively unaffected by the events on Fifth. This street was the exact opposite of the front of the library except for the police and their vehicles keeping people from turning up the cross streets that would lead them to the library's main entrance. People walked the sidewalks and cars carried passengers the same as any other day, oblivious to the disaster on the street in front of the library.

Max finally spotted the librarian standing in the entryway of a building on the other side of the street. Before rushing to her, Max double-checked the street and the park for Kacha. After a minute of searching, he decided he had no choice but to risk it. He crossed the street at the nearest intersection when the light changed, then he walked over to her. When Max got closer, he could see she was as white as a ghost and was trembling from head to foot.

"Are you okay?" Max rushed to her.

"I saw him," she stammered and pointed up 40th Street. "He was walking towards my building."

"I'm sure my friends will get to your daughter before he has a chance to," Max assured her as he pulled out his communicator and typed in a message. The response was quick. "They're telling me your daughter wasn't home."

"She must be out grocery shopping," the woman said, a little color returning to her face.

"Come on, show me the way. We'll get her," Max promised and helped her put on her jacket that he'd retrieved along with her purse. She gave Max back his coat.

Max escorted the woman the three blocks towards her apartment. When they were in sight of her building, they were spotted by Sky, who joined them and led them into the port authority bus terminal where they could keep an eye on the woman's building in relative anonymity.

"He is inside," Sky told them, which added to the woman's visible distress. "No women have gone in the front door. I cannot say that about the back."

"Please don't let anything happen to her," Margret pleaded as tears welled up along the bottom of her eyes.

"Do you have a cell phone? Does your daughter?" Sky asked.

"Yes, but I left mine in the apartment this morning," the woman's frown grew deeper as she shook her head slowly.

"Would your daughter use the other entrance to your building?" Sky queried as she kept an eye on the front of the complex.

"I don't think so, but she might," Margret said.

"So we need to cover both exits," Sky said. "Do you have a picture of her?"

"Yes." The woman dug around in her purse and retrieved a wallet. She found the picture of her daughter and showed it to Sky. "Her name is Katrina."

"Where are Cindy and Finster?" Max asked.

"I sent them back through the gateway. Cindy has a concussion," Sky said as she studied the photograph.

"Oh, I do hope she'll be all right," Margret said, still trembling and pale.

"Max's grandfather will take good care of her. Let's just concentrate on finding your daughter and getting out of here," Sky said. "You two stay here and watch the front, while I take up a position in the back. Send me a message if you see her."

"Okay," Max agreed.

Sky waited until the road was clear and then darted across it, soon disappearing from view. Max and the old woman kept watch at the windows of the bus terminal.

Moments later, the librarian jumped. "There she is!"

Max followed her gaze and saw her daughter walking down the other side of the street. "Let's go." Max quickly typed in a message to Sky as he held the door open for the older woman.

Margret exited the terminal, she shouted for her daughter while waving her hands through the air. "Katrina! Katrina!"

Max joined in the shout, until Katrina noticed them.

Margret's flailing arms caught Kacha's attention as he stood in the dark next to the window of Margret's apartment, waiting for Margret and her daughter. He stepped closer to the window. A surge of rage rushed through his body as he spotted Max with Margret and her daughter on the other side of the street.

A snarl curled his lip. He knew from their gestures towards the apartment they were talking about him. "They are starting to get in my way," he grumbled. "I want that witch DEAD!" he spat, eyeing Sky when she joined Max and the two women. He had let her get the best of him today and that did not sit well with him at all. With anger churning in his stomach, he growled, "I will have her! I will have them all!"

It made his blood boil that he couldn't act now and kill them. He wanted so badly to crush them like the bugs they were, but he knew their souls would be more useful to him if he let them live for awhile longer. "I think it's time I unleash the demon's fork on your little town." This comment brought a wicked smile to his face and eased some of the anger burning in his gut. "Just think, a whole town of magical souls. That, coupled with my other targets, would help me complete the hourglass quicker."

He let these happy thoughts play in his mind and ease his anger as he watched Max and the three women hurry off down 40th Street. "I think I'll book my flight tonight," he muttered to himself with satisfaction.

The scene on the third floor of Grandpa's house was surreal as yet another group of people sat there trying to comprehend the strange revelations about magic, gateways, and the existence of other worlds. Max figured for them, the hardest idea to swallow was they had just entered a surreal battle between good and evil involving magical powers and strange creatures.

The thought of war brought to the surface all the sorrow Max had been able to suppress about his Uncle Frank over the last week. He felt lost and wanted to go curl up in his bed and cry.

His mother came to him and put a comforting arm around his shoulder. "How are you doing, kiddo?" She looked into his eyes and Max understood they were both feeling the same pain and sadness.

"Okay, I guess. How are Martin and Aunt Donna?" he asked, fighting against the lump pushing its way up his throat.

"Struggling," his mom answered, tears building in her eyes as she gave him a squeeze.

"And Cindy?"

"She'll be all right. Olik came to see her; made sure there would be no permanent damage. She's at home in bed, now, resting." She smiled warmly. "And it looks like you've found some more willing recruits."

Max snorted.

"What's so funny?"

Max leaned into his mother and whispered into her ear. "You should have seen Grandpa when he met Margret. He practically started drooling. He bent over and kissed her hand," he whispered.

"Really?" Rachel smiled.

Max nodded.

"Good for Grandpa," she whispered back.

Max's exhaustion and grief almost overpowered him making his head fuzzy. He wanted to go lie down, but he needed to speak to Grandpa about what he and Cindy had discovered. He waited patiently while Grandpa took care of Margret and Katrina, but after another couple of hours he got his turn.

Max gathered together Grandpa, Olik, Sky, Finster, his mother, and Yelka in the kitchen once everyone else had settled in for the night. He told them about the discovery he and Cindy had made based on what Margret had told them. He filled them in on details of the resulting battle in the streets of New York City brought about by their attempt to learn more. Finally, he explained how he had gone back for Margret, fearing for her life at the hands of Kacha.

"You were right to get her and her daughter out of there," Yelka said solemnly.

"So he's hunting magical souls," Olik mused, his big black eyes growing even larger.

"I think we need to find this Richard Burdick or his relatives before Kacha does," Sky stated and everyone around the kitchen table nodded in agreement.

"There's more," Grandpa said, drawing everyone's attention. "We have two other issues to deal with as well. First, I think I've discovered what Kacha did on his trip."

"The trip to Denver?" Max asked.

"Exactly. We know he flew into Denver International Airport. But I've been scanning news channels to see if I could spot anything out of the ordinary. And there was something. I think he went to a small town in Wyoming within a day's drive from Denver," Grandpa started.

"What happened?" Sky's tone was impatient.

"Everyone in the town is dead. All of them! And they seem to have the same small mark on the front of their necks as did the bodies of the other victims."

"What's the second issue?" Finster asked with his deep voice.

"We have to assume the magical battle on the streets of New York will draw our enemy's attention," Grandpa stated. "We might not be able to hide what Kacha is doing for long."

"Yes, but don't the others know that Kacha is still loose in our world?" Rachel stated.

"They do, but they haven't known, or seemed interested in, what he is up to. That magical display is sure to raise some flags, however," Olik said. "If they find out what he is actually up to, this whole situation could become even more dangerous."

"I am one hundred percent certain he is building a new gateway," Sky said leaning forward so all could see her. "I did not get into his apartment, but from what I have learned from people who had been inside, contractors and such, they all claimed he was building something 'weird' from stone."

"Sky, Finster, we need you to get back to New York and keep an eye on him. We know he'll probably stay in the vicinity so he can find all the magical descendants he's looking for. I'll send Jax and his men to help," Grandpa said.

Sky crinkled her nose at that comment and sat back folding her arms across her chest. A scowl darkened her pale skin.

"I know. I know, but we need as many people on this as possible. As events are now, we not only have to keep an eye on Kacha, but we also have to watch for whomever else may be trying to discover what's going on," Grandpa said.

"Max, Yelka, and Rachel, I need you to get on this Burdick thing immediately. Cindy can help you when she feels up to it," Grandpa said. "I think Olik and I need to check-up on our other friends."

"My lord." Alan found himself once again bowed low in front of Hudich as he sat on his throne. "I believe there is an incident that bears our investigation."

Hudich adjusted his weight slowly to lean on his right armrest. With his head lowered, it was impossible to see his face concealed behind his black hood. His mood hadn't improved since the events on the rope bridge in Pekel. Alan knew Hudich had intended to capture Frank, rather than kill him. Of course, Frank would have been destroyed in the end, but that would have been much later and slower.

"Sir?" Alan persisted, struggling to maintain his submissive posture.

"What is it?" Hudich hissed, raising his head slightly but not enough for his features to be seen.

"Something very strange happened today in New York City, my lord," Alan said, coming to a standing position. "It seems Max and a few others were involved in a small struggle."

"What does that have to do with us?" Hudich growled.

"It was a magical skirmish. One that almost destroyed an entire Manhattan city block," Alan said with a smile.

"With someone we know?"

"Yes, but not who you would have thought."

"What do you mean?" Hudich raised his head a bit more until Alan could see those glowing red eyes.

"No one currently aligned with us, but most definitely someone we know. My sources tell me it is Kacha," Alan's smile of satisfaction continued to spread.

"Kacha! He didn't have enough mastery over his magic to put up much of a fight." Hudich's eyes blazed like fire. "What does this mean?"

"May I venture a guess?" Alan said, stepping closer to Hudich's throne.

Hudich gave off a grunt and a flick of his fingers and Alan interpreted it as a sign that Hudich wished him to proceed.

"Kacha, as you know, was in Joe's house all that time. We know they have been hunting Kacha and Grd, but we had assumed it was to protect people from them. Suppose Kacha has something they want even more," Alan paused and looked around as if he was revealing a secret he didn't want anyone else to overhear.

"Continue." Hudich leaned forward on his throne.

"What if he has the book? We have learned there was a fight in the street in front of Joe's house. They killed the Zbal there and Kacha managed to escape. Since that day, they have been trying to keep what they're doing a secret."

"So, you believe Kacha to be in ownership of the book and that's how he has managed to develop his powers enough to destroy a city block?" Hudich drummed his fingers on the arm of his chair.

"It only makes sense. Joe has some excellent trackers who wield powerful magic. They should have overtaken Kacha by now."

"We need to verify it was Kacha!" Hudich ordered. "This could be good news. If we had captured Frank, we would have had this information already." He clenched his fists and slammed them on the arms of his chair, sending a loud thud, like the rolling of thunder, through the hall.

"I shall put people on it right away." Alan smiled and then gave another low bow.

"See if we can track down Grd as well. He may know something."

"As you wish," Alan said and backed out of the chamber, his head held low in obeisance.

Kacha turned his Harley down the dirt road, throwing a line of dust in the air as he sped forward. It was a warm spring day. The sun shone down from the sky, coaxing plants to emerge from their winter slumber. Only the occasional patch of snow remained in the shadows of rocks or groups of sagebrush. The mountains surrounding the small town wouldn't lose their white tops for another couple of months.

He gave his hog some more gas. He loved the wind in his hair and the loud rumble of the engine. It made him feel free and even more powerful.

The dirt road curved around a large hill covered with sagebrush and remnants of tall yellow prairie grass leftover from last summer. Kacha found a flat section to park his ride, then pulled off the road. Working the kickstand down with his boot, he let the bike come to rest.

He unhooked a long black case about the size of a guitar from the back of his seat. After throwing his leather jacket over the seat, he proceeded to weave around the sagebrush and up the hill.

"What a nice day to capture magical souls." He smiled to himself, extending his arms to absorb more of the sun's heat. He was ecstatic winter was on its way out. He hated the cold. It made his muscles ache.

His smile turned into an evil grin as he climbed higher and higher up the slope. *This will teach them to meddle in my affairs!* He patted the case affectionately. As he reached the top of the hill, a cool spring breeze whipped around him and on the far side of the hill, Grandpa's small town spread out before him. He stood on the same hill where Max and Cindy sat when they watched the sandlot baseball game two summers ago.

He observed the small town for a few minutes. It had been about six months since he had been here. Things had changed very little. There were one or two additional homes in the new subdivisions, but otherwise the small town was the same. Traffic was minimal, as usual, in a town with only one traffic light.

Kacha knelt and placed the case on the ground in front of him. After unlatching the lid, he extracted the smooth black staff. He ran his hand over its polished surface and then hung the jar with its silken lid over one of the forks. "Soon, you'll be full of precious souls and they won't even know what happened." He smiled in wicked delight.

Coming to his feet, he held the staff before him in both hands. "Take them all," he sneered and stabbed the sharp bottom end of the staff into the ground.

11

Panic in the Streets

Max, Cindy, and Yelka huddled around the computer on Grandpa's kitchen table. They had spent the last several days visiting every family history site they could find. Margret was a great resource. She knew every genealogical site and the means to get them up and going. Assisting them with tracking down Kacha's target seemed to make her transition a little easier.

After a few more magical demonstrations, Grandpa accompanied Margret and her daughter on a quick trip to Yelka's world to help them understand what was happening. He really acted as if he enjoyed Margret's company. Max, on the other hand, wasn't too sure having this many women in his grandfather's house was a good thing. Bathroom time was getting increasingly difficult to come by.

They did manage to trace one of the several Richard Burdicks back to the middle ages and, also, a man named Merlin. This brightened their sprits and they felt they were actually getting somewhere.

"Let's just hope Kacha hasn't found this one yet," Cindy said, sipping some lemonade.

"Oh my!" Yelka gasped and sank down in her chair. Her skin turned as white as a sheet.

"What is it?" Max thought she was going to be sick. Her body trembled and she wobbled as if she was about to faint.

"Yelka, what's going on?" Cindy sprang out of her chair and hustled to Yelka's side in an instant.

Yelka swallowed. "Something's wrong. Something's terribly wrong," Yelka's voice quivered with fear.

Max's heart jumped into overdrive. He couldn't remember ever seeing Yelka this scared before. "What's wrong?"

"Something very evil has just been set loose on all of us," Yelka murmured, her voice barely audible. Her eyes stared straight ahead in fright as if some invisible object were hurtling towards them.

"Max, get some water," Cindy ordered, grasping Yelka's hand tightly.

Max rushed to the kitchen and returned with a glass of water, which he gave to Yelka. He and Cindy gathered close, watching Yelka sip the water and waiting for more information.

Yelka placed the glass on the table and took a few deep breaths, still gazing off into nowhere.

Max couldn't contain himself any longer, "What's going on? What is coming for us and how do we stop it?"

"A fate worse than death approaches quickly. A curse I don't know how to combat has been unleashed on this town. I feel it. It will strike soon and it won't discriminate against anyone."

"What do you mean by that?" Cindy asked.

"It will take everyone, our enemy as well as us." Yelka's eyes suddenly focused on Max. "Find your grandfather. We need to start evacuating people immediately."

"From where?" Max shook his head with confusion.

"From this town!" Yelka's voice suddenly found its strength. She got up out of the chair. "Go get Joseph! Now!"

Max didn't wait to be told again and sprinted from the kitchen. He almost knocked his mother to the floor as she came down the hall.

"Max, what's going on?"

"Where's Grandpa?" Max shouted over his shoulder.

"I think he's at the school," his mother answered.

Max flew out the front door, leaping the entire front porch steps to land on the sidewalk below. Yelka's words played in his mind over and over. "A fate worse than death is coming our way." *What could be worse than death?* The obvious answer to that question dawned on Max and propelled his legs forward at a greater speed. But, before he could round the corner, Larry and his gang appeared on the street ahead of him riding their bikes. *Crap!*

Max hadn't seen Larry since that day when the FBI caused Uncle Frank to flee, ultimately leading to Frank's death. Max knew the enemy was behind the tip that led the agents to Frank's house and then to Grandpa's house that fateful day.

Their casual bike ride changed into a race as their eyes locked on Max. Their legs pumped hard and fast, pushing their bikes forward, closing in on Max.

"What's your hurry, Max?" Larry called as they encircled Max, slowing his sprint to a jog.

"Yeah, Max. What're you running from?" they all chanted.

"And where's your girlfriend, Mindy?" Jo, with her pink hair, taunted.

Max groaned inwardly. Dealing with Larry and his friends was the last thing he had time for right now. He had to get to Grandpa right away. "What do you want, Larry?" Max growled, clenching his fists, ready for a fight.

"We just wanted to say hi," Larry smirked as he and the others continued to circle Max.

"Well, hi then. And bye," Max said, giving a sharp wave of his hand and making an attempt to leave the circling chain of bicycles.

Larry slammed on his brakes, stopping so close to Max he almost drove over his toes with his front tire. "I don't like the fact that Gramps hasn't helped my dad yet," Larry barked in Max's face. "I thought he told my mother he would help, or is he a liar?"

"He's working on it." Max tried to step around Larry when Jo blocked his exit.

"We don't think he's working fast enough," Jo spat, looking like a deranged clown with her bushy pink hair.

"Well, since you don't have the gateway, you don't get to decide when." Max's blood pressure started to rise. He didn't want to waste time talking to Larry and his gang. Yelka's pale, terrified face flashed to the front of his mind, screaming at him to find Grandpa.

"I think we've waited long enough. We need to start motivating your people to work faster," Fred added, closing the circle around Max even tighter.

"If you don't get out of my way, you might never see your dad again." Max gritted his teeth as his patience starting to wear thin.

"Are you threatening my dad?" Larry got off his bike, letting it crash to the ground. He squared his shoulders towards Max and balled his hands into large round fists.

Max put his hands up in a disarming manner. "That's not what I meant. What I'm trying to say is everyone in this town is in trouble. Your people as well as mine." Max couldn't believe he'd just said that. He didn't know if he should have imparted that information to them.

"Yeah, right, like you care about what happens to us," Jo practically screamed in his ear.

"I'm serious. Something bad is going to happen." Max needed to get out of there. He had to get to Grandpa. He wished he understood what Larry was thinking. *What is Larry playing at? Like fighting with me would help his dad's cause.* Max began repeating the spell *beri misel* while concentrating on Larry. The strangest thing Max had ever experienced in his life began happening. He watched Larry and the others' lips move but he couldn't hear what they were saying. It was like trying to find a remote radio station in his head. Every few seconds it would catch a thought but it wasn't a clear signal. He couldn't quite make out the sound.

"I think you should kick his head in," Fred jeered, breaking through the static. All the others began adding their agreements.

"Kick his butt!"

"Waste him!"

Max's mind suddenly locked on a wavelength. The sound wasn't like hearing a word as much a feeling, but Max's brain registered it just as easily as if Larry had spoken it aloud. *Punch face.*

"*Oviraj,*" Max said a second before Larry's blow could make contact. A loud crunch, as if someone had smacked a solid wall, preceded the cry from Larry's mouth. His fist stopped dead in the air just inches from Max's face.

Larry dropped to the ground and curled into a ball cradling his hand, whimpering in pain. "You broke my hand," Larry shouted.

The rest of the group slid away from Max with fearful looks. Jo jumped off her bike and began consoling Larry. Larry wailed in agony, protecting his hand.

Max glared at the others who moved away several more yards. "Now that I have your undivided attention, you really do need to get out of town. Something more evil than you is coming and no one will survive it." Max stepped outside the circle. Then, turning to keep them within his line of sight, he backed up the street.

Jo had managed to get Larry on his feet. He continued to block anyone from seeing his hand as he covered it by hunching over it with his body. He was paler than usual and was breathing in large gulps of air. Jo had to put her arm around him to keep him steady.

"Hey, bring our bikes," Jo ordered as she led Larry slowly down the street.

Max kept walking backwards until they were a good distance down the street from him before turning. He had just kicked his run into a sprint when a disturbance from Larry's gang caught his attention.

"Fred, dude!"

"Hey, something's wrong with Fred."

Max stopped. He glanced at the school at the end of the street than back to the huddle comprised of Larry's gang.

"He's not breathing," sounded a frightened voice.

"We need to get help."

Max exploded towards the school. He ran faster than he ever thought possible. He cut across the grass and then hurdled a bike rack. Bursting into the school through the main doors, he spotted Grandpa in the hall talking to Mr. Kendle, the school principle.

"Grandpa, come quick!"

"Max, what's wrong?" Grandpa didn't hesitate and hustled towards Max with Mr. Kendle in hot pursuit.

Max didn't wait for them to reach him, but dashed back out the front doors. He caught sight of the small group the minute he hit the street and accelerated his pace.

The wail of police sirens echoed through the town and Max could see their flashing lights spinning between houses and buildings.

"What did you do?" screamed Jo, pointing her finger at Max as he approached. "You murdered him!"

"No! I didn't do anything," Max jaw dropped, shocked.

From the other direction came an ambulance followed by two police cars. They sped towards Larry's circle of friends, and Max could only stand frozen, staring at the surreal scene. Fred lay limp in the middle of the street. Larry still held his hand close to his chest but he seemed to have forgotten his pain. Everyone was visibly shaken.

Grandpa rushed past Max and into the center of the group. He took Fred's wrist in his hand and searched for a pulse. "What happened?" Grandpa asked as he examined Fred for any other signs of injury.

"Max did this! He broke Larry's hand and then he killed Fred," Jo shouted as the cops and the paramedics arrived on the scene.

"I did no such thing," Max countered.

"What's this?" Grandpa muttered.

"What's what?" a paramedic asked, pushing Grandpa aside and starting CPR in an effort to revive Fred.

"There's a strange mark on his throat," Grandpa pointed to a small dark spot at the base of Fred's throat.

The police started to inquire about what had happened. Jo stuck to her story that Max had killed him, and Larry and the others, though confused, acted as if that was the best explanation. To hide the fact Larry initiated the fight, they said Max had pushed Larry off his bike, causing him to break his hand.

Max's head was fuzzy. He felt lost, like a boat taking on water, and he didn't like where this was going. When Grandpa mentioned the mark on Fred's neck, Max knew Yelka's fears were correct.

"Don't go anywhere!" An officer signaled Max while he continued to take statements from Larry's gang.

Grandpa walked over to Max, his head hung low as if in deep thought. He rubbed his bearded chin as he always did when pondering a situation.

Conversations with the police floated in their general direction.

"He said we were all in danger and then this."

"Told all of us, we needed to get out of town."

"Is this true?" Grandpa whispered to Max.

"You don't think I killed him?" Max gasped, twisting his face into a knot of disbelief and betrayal.

"No, of course not. Calm down. I know you didn't do this, but did you warn them to get out?"

"Yes. I was on my way to see you." Max relaxed somewhat and explained everything that had transpired, from Yelka to his encounter with Larry. He watched Grandpa's face get grimmer.

"What are you thinking?" Max asked.

"I think whatever happened to that town in Wyoming is about to repeat itself here," Grandpa answered. "Yelka is absolutely right. We need to start moving people now. I just don't know what to tell them about *why* without actually explaining to them what Kacha is doing. That could cause us more trouble than we want."

Max and everyone else watched silently as they placed Fred's body in a black bag and carried it into the ambulance. Even though Max disliked Larry and his gang, he felt bad seeing the lifeless body carried away. It was another fifteen minutes until the police, after questioning all of Larry's friends, got to Max.

Usually when the policemen in Grandpa's small town had something against Max, they wore a slight smirk. Not this time. The whole police force of two men had expressions that were a mixture of grief and rage. One rested his hand on his gun and the other held his handcuffs at the ready.

"Now, Joe, step aside. We have to do our job," the one holding the cuffs said.

Grandpa jumped in between Max and the approaching offices. "Wait! At least hear what I have to say."

"If you want to make a statement, you'll have to make it downtown. We have to place Max under arrest," the second said.

"Turn around, Max and put your hands behind your back," the officer with the cuffs said.

"Grandpa!" Max protested. "I didn't kill anyone! They don't have any proof. It's just their word against mine. Even they admitted they saw him fall off his bike, *by himself.*"

"Yes, but what did you do to cause him to fall?" the first officer asked.

"Nothing! I was over fifty yards *away.*"

"We all know distance doesn't matter, don't we?" the second added.

"Max, don't say another word," Grandpa said, stepping out of the way. "We'll be right behind you." Grandpa hurried as fast as his old legs would move towards the house.

"You have the right to remain silent…" the officer read Max his Miranda rights while cuffing him, clamping the cuffs down extra hard.

"Ouch," Max complained as the metal cut into his skin. Not only were the cuffs hurting him, the police were not in the least bit gentle as they shoved him into the back of the car. With the cuffs as tight as they were, Max couldn't find a comfortable position to sit in. Any way he tried to adjust caused his wrists to throb.

"You are in so much trouble," the cop driving said over his shoulder.

"We all are," Max shot back.

"What's that supposed to mean? Are you threatening officers of the law?" the other policeman asked, glaring at him through the steel cage that separated the back and front seats.

"We'll see how cocky you are once we have you in the interrogation room," the driver added.

"None of us have that much time," Max spat and then went into silent treatment mode. He screwed his face up into the most disgruntled expression he could muster. He had been tortured before and that was in another world where there were no laws, so he knew there was nothing these pathetic excuses for cops could do to him.

Max clenched his teeth to brace against the pain in his wrists as the police pulled him out of the car. He didn't want to give them the satisfaction of knowing he was uncomfortable. They had just gotten him to his feet when Grandpa and his mother arrived in his mother's car.

"Max," Rachel called, hurrying up to him.

"I'm all right, Mom," Max smiled despite the cuts in his wrists as the officer twisted his cuffs.

"Ma'am, please step back," the officer put his arm out to keep her away from Max. "You'll have to wait until after we've processed him and had a chance to question him."

"You can't question him without a lawyer present. He's underage," Grandpa stated. "If you don't hear me out, more will die."

They led Max into the small police station on Main Street. There was a small counter with a couple of desks on the other side. A secretary was typing on the computer of the desk to the left. After they escorted Max past the desks, they shoved him into a room by himself that contained a table with two chairs on opposite sides. A large mirror, which Max assumed was a two-way, hung on the wall behind one of the chairs.

He carried on as if his wrists didn't hurt and everything was right in the world. He walked around the room taking in his environment. He pulled a face at the mirror by crossing one of his eyes while keeping the other straight. It didn't feel right making light of the fact Fred had just died, but he didn't want to look guilty either.

He circled the room one more time before stopping in front of the mirror again. "Any day now. Time's a-wasting."

Suddenly the door behind him flew open, startling him. He whirled around as the officer who had driven the car entered.

"Take a seat." He gestured towards the chair.

"Are you going to take these off? Otherwise, I prefer to stand." Max moved to the side of the table facing the mirror.

"Turn around." The officer retrieved the key from his pocket, unlocked the cuffs and then sat in the chair opposite Max.

Max plopped down and made himself comfortable, ignoring the urge to rub his wrists. He crossed his legs and slouched forward in the chair. The anger in the cop's expression caused Max to smirk a little.

"You think this is funny!" the officer shouted, his face changing to a dark red.

"I don't think what happened to Fred is funny, but I find it amusing I can annoy you. We both know I'm innocent, so I suggest you listen to my grandfather before we all end up like Fred." Max's anger got the better of him and he folded his arms across his chest, glaring at the cop.

"Like I give two shakes about what your grandfather has to say. I trust him about as far as I can bowl him," the officer spat. "You don't seem to realize, we can make up whatever we want here. Like you said, I know you're innocent, but I don't care. Did you really think I was going to interrogate you? You really aren't that smart after all, are you? I'll let you think about that one for a little while and then see how *amusing* you find it. Oh, and by the way, this room is soundproof. No one will hear your screams." He snarled and left the room.

The second the door closed, a siren erupted from speakers lining the ceiling. The decibel level stabbed at Max's eardrums. He covered his ears with his hands in an effort to ease the noise, which was causing pain all over his body. The deafening sound sparked nerve endings, causing muscles to cramp and his nose to bleed.

The room started to spin and Max thought he was going to vomit, when the noise stopped abruptly. He fell to the floor, taking large gulps of air. He managed to crawl up on his hands and knees, when the door opened and the officer returned.

"Not so cocky are we now, hmmm?" the officer taunted. "You see, my friend's son is dead and you're behind it somehow, whether you cast the spell or not."

"Actually, you're behind it," Max spat through gritted teeth. "Your people caused this!" Max was furious. He made it to a standing position using the wall to support him.

"How dare you. We would never do anything to hurt our own!" The officer advanced on Max, his nightstick in his hand.

"*Oviraj*," Max hollered as the cop swung downward at him. WHOMP! The outside of the cop's nightstick crashed into the blocking spell. The club ricocheted over the shield, out of the cop's hand and across the room.

"Aagh!" the cop cradled his hand.

"And that's what actually happened to Larry's hand! He was going to punch me."

"You'll wish you'd never done that," the cop seethed and headed for the door. "I think a little visit from Hudich is in order. While you wait, I'll have the music turned back on."

"*Premakni!*" Max shouted the second the door was open. The table lunched across the room slamming into the door and flattening the officer. Max sprang through the door, over the officer and headed for the front office.

"Stop right there!" the other officer blocked Max's exit, his gun drawn and leveled at Max. "Give me a reason. Please."

Max put up his hands as the door behind the officer exploded outward. The cop spun around as his gun flew out of his hands and into Grandpa's.

"Now, listen to me," Grandpa's voice rang through the building as the officer almost instinctively raised his hands above his head.

Max raced past the officer and out to Grandpa and his mother. The secretary was on her feet with her hands in the air as well.

"We don't have much time. *Any of us.* You need to get your people out of town, now. Something very bad is here and it will strike very quickly." Grandpa removed the gun's magazine and tossed the unloaded weapon back to the officer before waving Max and his mother towards the door.

"Why should we believe you? You've always wanted us gone. This is just a trick," the secretary hissed.

"I assure you, this is no trick, and you are wasting time."

As they turned to leave, Alan's wife rushed through the door. There were tears on her face. "Jessica Rupert is dead. She must have had a seizure or something. She convulsed a few times and then…just died!"

"Get out of town, now," Grandpa stressed again and pushed Max and his mother out the door.

"Hey…What…" Alan's wife tried to speak.

"Drive as fast as you can," Grandpa ordered as Rachel remotely unlocked the car door.

They rushed out of the police station and jumped into the car. Rachel slammed the car into reverse and peeled out into the street before speeding towards home. Max dug his fingers into the back leather seat as the car ripped through the small town. His mother's driving always made him nervous and her doing her Danica Patrick impersonation wasn't helping matters.

"NO!" Grandpa almost grabbed the wheel as Rachel started to turn towards home. "Go back to the school first. We need to let everyone know. I don't think we have much time."

The way his mother zoomed towards the school, Max wondered if they would be able to stop in time. A few of the neighbors had gathered in front of the school and appeared to be discussing what had transpired in the street, when Max's mother laid on the horn and screeched to a halt.

"Wait here." Grandpa jumped out of the vehicle. The people hurried to meet him.

Max watched from the backseat as Grandpa's arms flailed about like a strange bird. He pointed repeatedly to where Fred died and then gesticulated wildly, likely trying to convince people to flee the town. The grave expressions on the peoples' faces, as they nodded their heads or commented, indicated the amount of fear that was starting to spread.

Rachel turned in the front seat to look at her son, face pale and drawn. "Max, what's going on? I mean, this must be more serious than I thought. First, you're grandfather shows up and tells me you've been arrested and we are all in danger. Now, we've helped bust you out of jail, there's been another death, and Grandpa tells me to bypass the house to warn people about something."

"Grandpa didn't tell you?" Max met her gaze.

"Tell me what?"

"We think Kacha set loose some kind of a curse on this town, like he did to that town in Wyoming." Max went back to observing Grandpa.

"You mean the one that will steal our souls?" Rachel shrieked.

"Yes!"

The small huddle on the sidewalk broke up and Grandpa rushed back to the car. "Home," he barked as he slammed the door shut.

Rachel whipped the car around and punched the gas. "What did you tell them?"

"To get out of town," Grandpa said, wiping his brow with his handkerchief. "I was so glad when they moved into town. I just hope it doesn't get them all killed."

"It's that serious?" Rachel's voice cracked as she stopped at her usual parking spot at the side of the house.

"Yes!"

They piled out of the car and hurried into the house. Cindy gave Max a hug as he entered the house. Yelka waited with her as did Margret and her daughter.

"Have you called your parents?" Grandpa asked Cindy.

"Yes." Cindy nodded as she released Max, her cheeks flushing slightly.

"Martin and…" Grandpa started but before he could finish, they entered the house. "Did you close the gates?" he directed his question towards Donna and Martin.

"Yes, what's happening?" Donna broke down in tears and Rachel rushed to take care of her.

Another knock at the door and Cindy's parents joined them. Grandpa asked them the same question about the gate.

"Do you think the protective spells will hold?" Cindy's mother asked.

Grandpa looked to Yelka.

"I think so," Yelka said. "The spells are meant to keep evil magic away and this is definitely evil magic."

"I do think for a necessary precaution, we should move some of you to another world," Grandpa suggested and Donna broke down even more. Martin stood next to her, shaking from head to foot.

"Are you sure?" Cindy's father asked.

"Mom can't! They can track her," Max argued.

"What if they find us?" Rachel continued to comfort the sobbing Donna.

"I'll take you to my people," Yelka stepped forward. "We can protect you there. We've done it before."

"If the spell holds, no one should have to go for long," Grandpa said. "We have plenty of supplies here. I just don't think anyone should venture out of the yard until we figure out how to combat this curse."

Max couldn't believe what was happening. Evacuate! The last place he ever thought he would have to run from was Grandpa's house. Even with the vast majority of its population on the wrong side, he always felt safe here. Grandpa's house was a refuge against the evils that waited for him beyond the yard.

"I will stay behind to operate the gateway," Grandpa's voice broke through Max's musings.

"What if the spells don't hold? We'll be stuck in Yelka's world," Max stated.

"What if I leave the gateway open and the spells don't hold, who knows how far this curse will go!" Grandpa countered.

"You can't," everyone began to object. "We don't want to be stuck in another world!"

"Max, Yelka, or Cindy can all come back with magic and open the gateway if need be. As long as Max is alive, the spells will protect the house. The enemy won't be able to capture it," Grandpa stated.

The complaints and the counter arguments continued for several minutes. Points were made about the tracking curse on Rachel's hand. Traveling to another world terrified Martin and Donna, who were visibly upset from the loss of Frank. Margret and her daughter, as newcomers, appeared confused by the whole situation.

"What about Rachel? We can't protect her if Hudich comes for her," Yelka said.

"I'll stay here with Grandpa," Rachel said.

"Then I'm staying too," Max said, immediately followed by similar protests from Cindy.

"Listen! You all may very well be able to remain here, but we need to take precautions. Rachel and I will stay," Grandpa put up a finger to silence Max. "After we figure out if we are safe, we will let you come back."

"Should we get some things to take with us?" Cindy's mother asked.

"I don't think you should leave this house until..."

Loud, rapid pounding on the front door caused everyone to jump.

Cindy opened the door and gasped. Max and the others rushed to the front window and doorway to see the entire population of the town surrounding Grandpa's house.

12

Hudich Joins the Hunt

Max stared, mouth agape. The population of the whole town really was outside Grandpa's house. Cars and people crowded the streets all the way around as if the house were a stage for a major rock concert and they were all vying for a vantage point. Horns honked, people yelled, and small shoving matches broke out in a few areas because of the close proximity of good and evil people.

"Joseph, we've got a huge problem," the principle of the school said as he stood in the doorway. He was pale with beads of sweat forming all over his forehead. "No one can leave town!"

"What? Why not?" everyone in the house asked on top of each other, along with a hundred other questions.

Grandpa put up his hands and everyone fell silent. "What do you mean? Are we trapped?"

"It appears so, and anyone who tries to leave…" He shook his head. "It…a whole car full…" Tears formed in his eyes.

"Who?"

"The Waltons and their two girls. It was like they all convulsed one violent time and then their car just drove into the ditch right by the city limit sign." He wiped his eyes on his hands.

Everyone in the house gasped or cried out.

"We're all doomed," Aunt Donna moaned out loud.

"Yelka, can your people handle more visitors?" Grandpa asked.

"Yes, but they will not stand for any trouble," Yelka responded as she nodded to a small jinxing contest taking place on the other side of the fence.

"That won't be a problem. I'm not sending *them* there. They will be traveling to Mir. Helaina won't let them get away with anything," Grandpa said. "Yelka, set the gateway for Mir."

"What? You're sending them first!" Cindy's father barked.

"Yes, that's the only way we'll have order and get everyone out as quickly as possible," Grandpa answered and then squeezed his way out onto the porch. He climbed up onto the porch railing and gave a loud long whistle, which brought all the commotion to a stop. All heads turned towards him.

"Listen up! I will get everyone, yes, everyone, out of here, but we are going to do it in an orderly fashion. I will be sending those of you who, how do I say this, don't really like me very much *first*. But only on one condition: there will be no trouble and you are to be blindfolded. You will be traveling to Mir," Grandpa spoke with a loud strong voice. Before anyone had a chance to protest, he continued, "If you don't like my terms, you can stay in the street."

It took almost three hours to move everyone to their new destinations. Despite the occasional grumbling and a few shoves here or there, the operation went smoothly. Grandpa did have to go through with the first batch to Mir in order to explain the situation to Helania. He reported back that she was as equally unhappy about the idea as Grandpa was, but she agreed, under the circumstances. As soon as everyone remaining could fit inside the yard, the gates were shut.

Cindy's parents, Martin, Donna, and the others had managed to pack some travel items while they waited for the others to depart through the gateway. Grandpa had Margret and her daughter accompany Yelka and the first group traveling to Svet. Slowing the process immensely was the fact the gateway had to be shut down each time in order to allow another group to get inside the force field.

Max entered his bedroom to see if he could see anything else he wanted to take with him. His stomach twisted into an uncomfortable knot. He hated that his mother and grandfather were remaining in the house, while he had to flee. *What if the protective spells failed? I would rather die with them than live without them.* Max hadn't felt this hopeless since last summer when Hudich and his followers imprisoned his mother.

Max gave his closet a quick glance for anything that might look important enough to grab. He hadn't really packed anything but some clothes. His overwhelming desire to stay, caused everything else to pale in comparison. He began opening the dresser drawers one by one and closing them again.

After not finding anything in the drawers, he sighed and stared out the window. He gazed at the pit where he had built that huge fire his first summer here. Leaning on the top of the dresser, he plopped his head into his hands.

"Max, let's go," his mother called from the third floor.

Cindy knocked on the open door. "You ready?"

"NO!" Max growled.

"Me either, but we'd better go anyway."

Max stood up to leave when a faint shadow outside his window slid by the gate, stopping him. "Did you..." He remained frozen, wondering if his eyes had deceived him.

"What?" Cindy asked coming to join him. "What did you see?"

He paused, straining his eyes and then the shadow moved again. "There!" he pointed, "on the other side of the fence." His heart raced and all the hairs on his body stood on end.

"I don't see anything."

They waited and finally a wisp of black shadow swirled for a second right up next to the fence.

"There," Max jabbed his finger against the window.

"I saw it, but what was it?" Cindy said, squinting her eyes.

They remained in place for several more minutes until it happened again. This time a darker, thicker shadow drifted more to the side of the house, barely in their line of sight. It floated from the ground, at a slight angle up, into the air before vanishing. A second later and in the corner of the backyard, a dark mass appeared to hit an invisible wall and exploded in all directions, sending small visible fingers that slowly evaporated.

"Max! Come on!" his mother shouted.

"Hey, everyone, come quick!" Max hollered over his shoulder, his focus on the new black mist swirling right in front of the back gate. It hovered for several moments before spinning away. Then another materialized like a giant ghost hand gliding along the back fence, its black fingers growing longer and longer until they stretched so thin they disappeared.

"I want to see something," Cindy said and bolted out of the room.

The strange, shadowy mists continued to form and evaporate just outside the fence. Some would glide up into the air before vanishing from sight. To Max's surprise, now he could spot multiple shadows at

the same time. Goose pimples spread all over his body as a faint, eerie moaning filled the house.

"They're at the front of the house too," Cindy's yelled from another room.

"What's going on?" Grandpa asked worriedly as he, Rachel, and Cindy's parents entered his room.

"I'm not sure." Max glanced at them over his shoulder before turning his attention back to the strange shadows. "I think we are under siege and, for now at least, the spell is holding the curse back."

Everyone crowded around Max's bedroom window to watch the strange phenomena. The mists continued their foreign assault on the protective spells surrounding the yard and house. They sprang up in all shapes and sizes, some thicker than others, taking longer to melt away as they roamed over the shield.

"Can you hear that wailing?" Rachel swallowed, her eyes wide.

"Yes," everyone responded.

"It gives me chills," Cindy's mother added.

"Did you hear what I just said?" Cindy popped into the doorway.

"What?" her mother asked.

"They are on all sides of the house and there seem to be more of them than there were at first," Cindy stated.

Soon everyone rushed in and out of each room in the house with a window to verify the mists were growing in greater numbers and with more frequency. Max shivered as the shadows began to block the sunlight, casting a cold gloom over the house. What had been a beautiful spring day now felt like a cool fall one as the shadows continued to grow and spread. They gave the sensation of being in a heavy, dark fog as they slowly began to block out the light. Shadows swirled and twisted in a dome shape around the house. Some flew up higher than the third floor and over the top of the house.

"It looks like the spells are holding them back for now," Grandpa said as everyone eventually filtered into the front room with its large windows. "I still want to get all of you out of here just to be safe." There was a different tone to Grandpa's voice now. It held a tinge of fear and uncertainty.

"I still think we should all go," Cindy's mother stated, and Max nodded his emphatic agreement.

"We've been over this before." Grandpa shook his head. "I don't want to unleash this curse on Yelka's world."

"Come on, Max," Rachel said, putting her hands on his shoulders and pulling him away from the window.

"I want to stay," Max's voice cracked as his mother led him up the stairs. "I…" He couldn't say what was in his heart without breaking down completely.

Everyone waited without speaking inside the circle of the five metallic stands as Grandpa fired up the gateway. The force field sprang from the poles and covered the small group and the gateway like an electrical wave until it formed the transparent dome. The old ornate mirror that had been in the center was now a ball of white light creating the entrance to Yelka's world.

Cindy's dad gave Grandpa and Rachel a handshake before stepping over to the gateway. Cindy and her mother exchanged hugs with them. Max wrapped his arms around each and held them tight.

"I'll send you a message every hour." Rachel kissed Max on the forehead.

"How long until you're satisfied the spells are going to hold?" Max asked. "We can't search for the Burdick descendants from Yelka's world you know."

"At least twenty-four hours," Grandpa replied. "If nothing has happened by then, I'll bring you back. I agree we don't have time to waste. Kacha is obviously moving, and very quickly. Stopping him is our top priority right now."

"Good luck." Cindy's dad entered the gateway, taking Cindy's mother by the hand and pulling her through behind him.

"Bye." Cindy waved and followed.

"I love you," Rachel said to Max.

"I love you too," Max responded, choking down the lump in his throat before walking into the ball of light.

###

Hudich sat on his throne in his new palace surrounded by his followers, who constantly averted their eyes. They all created a jagged semi-circle on the sunken floor in front of the raised platform that supported his throne. Any eye contact at all lasted only a brief second.

Alan noticed all this from his position at the center of the half circle below. For the first time since being trapped here, he sensed a change in the air. Hudich's mood had improved since the discovery of the battle in New York. For months, he had been in a foul temper, dealing out harsh punishments to anyone who had crossed him. Those who failed him begged for death before he finished with them.

"We haven't found either Kacha or Grd, but we are very confident it won't be long. We think Kacha is avoiding the area in an attempt to stay off the radar, but Grd shouldn't be hard to locate," a hooded figure to the left said.

A sudden flash of light and a Night Shade arrived in a vacant spot in the semi-circle. He gave a low bow and hissed, "They sssstill have ssseveral people in the ccccity of New York."

"Then they think he is still there too," Hudich's deep voice rumbled through the hall.

Another flash of light and the sheriff appeared in an unmoving heap on the floor next to Alan. He lay on his side with his hood drawn back, his eyes wide open, staring into nothing. Under the torch light of the stone hall, his skin was a chalky white color in the torch light of the stone hall.

"Ken," Alan whispered out of the side of his mouth, trying to get a response out of the sheriff without breaking formation. Alan watched Ken's chest but it remained still. His whole body hadn't so much as twitched since his arrival.

"Ken!" Hudich growled, but Ken didn't budge. "What's wrong with him?"

After Hudich asked, Alan felt it was safe to ascertain the sheriff's condition. He knelt next to Ken and began examining him. He checked for a pulse on his wrist first, then his neck. His skin was cold. "He's dead," Alan looked up to Hudich, who was leaning forward on his throne.

"Are there any wounds?" Hudich asked, his voice more curious than hostile.

Alan ran his hands over Ken's body, lifting his shirt, feeling along his torso and neck. As he pulled the collar of Ken's shirt wide, he spotted the mark. He tugged the front of Ken's collar away. "No physical wounds, but he has what appears to be some kind of black mark at the base of his throat." Alan searched for a mark on the back of his neck as well, finding nothing.

Hudich sprang out of his chair and down a couple of steps to the lower floor. The others in the semi-circle flinched backwards a little in response. He crossed the floor to reach Alan and the lifeless sheriff in two large steps. Alan ripped the front of Ken's shirt to better expose the mark for Hudich to see.

"Have you ever seen anything like it before, my lord?" Alan asked, looking up into Hudich's face and away quickly.

"I've not seen one with my own eyes, but I've heard tell of it," Hudich mused as he stared down at the lifeless Sheriff. "Things are becoming clear to me now."

"What things, my Lord?"

"The pieces of the puzzle are starting to connect. I'm beginning to see…"

The doors to the great hall opened inward and in rushed Larry and a few others from Grandpa's town escorted by two Night Shades.

Alan shot to his feet, his heart racing with panic. Forgetting court protocol, he sped towards the intruders to head them off. As he closed the distance, his pace slowed. His son and the others' fearful expressions didn't seem to be caused by their proximity to Hudich.

"Larry," Alan spoke loud enough for Larry and the others with him to hear but low enough to be a soft hiss in the rest of the chamber. "You know better than to enter unbidden!"

Larry opened his mouth to speak, but Alan held out a finger forcefully to silence him. Alan spread his arms wide as if to funnel them backwards towards the doors.

"They ssssaid it wassss very importantsss," one of the Night Shades whispered. "Otherwisssse."

"I'm sure it can wait until we—" Alan glanced over his shoulder and swallowed hard as he noticed Hudich approaching fast. "Take them out of here!" Alan ordered.

The Night Shades got the hint and attempted to lead the unexpected visitors out.

"Wait!" Hudich commanded as he drew near. "I also wish to know what's so important to interrupt my court session by ignoring my orders!"

The entire group seemed to grow smaller as they crowded closer together in fear. Alan bowed and the others followed his example. Larry started to whimper and tried to push his way deeper into the group.

"Isn't that your son?" Hudich asked Alan in a taunting tone.

"Ah…Ah, yes, my lord," Alan kept his head down but his eyes met his son's, whose were tearing up.

"Larry!" Hudich barked causing Larry to flinch so hard he almost lost his balance.

"Y—yes," Larry mumbled.

"What's so important you disregarded my wishes?" Hudich marched around the circle until he stood immediately in front of the trembling Larry.

Larry looked petrified his mouth agape.

"WELL!" Hudich ordered.

Alan managed to make eye contact with his son. He raised his eyebrows and gave his son a short nod as if prodding him to answer.

"W-we had to e-evacuate the town," Larry stuttered.

"Why?" Hudich's voice took on an impatient edge.

"Something, some curse, s-started killing people," Larry stammered as if trying to gain some courage. "It killed my friend, Fred."

"That doesn't sound like something that old fool, Joseph, would do," Hudich stated.

Alan's curiosity got the better of him as he joined Hudich in front of Larry to better hear what his son was saying.

"No," Larry continued. "Whatever it was, it killed people from their side too. We couldn't leave the town, so he sent us to Mir through his gateway."

"Joseph helped you escape?" Alan couldn't contain himself.

"Tell me everything," Hudich commanded.

Larry took the next several minutes, with a few comments from the others, telling all that had happened since Fred's collapse. They told them about the woman and then the family as they tried to leave. They ended with Joseph sending them blindfolded to Mir.

"Go back to Mir and await my orders," Hudich dismissed Larry and the small group. He acted as if pondering the news as he stepped back towards the sheriff's body.

Alan patted Larry on the back before the Night Shades removed them from the chamber. After the doors had closed, he went to Hudich beside the sheriff. "What are you thinking, my Lord?"

"I think we need to see what is going on in your town. Something that doesn't have any regard for ideology and kills whomever it wants; I find that very interesting," Hudich said as he nudged the sheriff's body with his foot.

"We...sir?" Alan suffered a twinge of fear as he glanced at the sheriff.

"Yes, we." Hudich's eyes fell on Alan with an intensity that told Alan he dare not cross his master. "But do not enter the town. Just go to the outside edge of the city limits."

"Yes, my lord," Alan bowed low. When he straightened, Hudich disappeared in a flash of light. The others in the semi-circle stared at him and Alan cast his spell.

Alan landed a few yards behind Hudich. They stood on a hill just off the main road that passed through the small town. Alan immediately caught sight of the car and the four dead bodies only thirty yards in front of them. He then noticed Hudich gazing at something in the town and followed his gaze to the strange event taking place at Joseph's house.

A dome of dark gray mists swirled around Joseph's house as if a slowly rotating tornado hovered over it. The patches of gray and black would expand and contract, devouring each other as they floated in circles. Eerie wailing cries floated with the breeze as if tortured creatures lurked inside the foggy haze.

"What is that thing?" Alan asked, stepping forward to get a closer view. Hudich's muscular arm shot out into his chest, blocking his way forward.

"Do *not* cross into the town," Hudich warned, still peering ahead at the strange spectacle.

"I don't understand. What's going on?" Alan struggled for answers.

"Kacha or Grd has the book. That's what that old fool and his people have been hiding from us. We need to discover everything they know," Hudich said, licking his lips with his black tongue. "That thing is the curse that killed Ken." Hudich pointed at the black mass.

"What?"

"Kacha or Grd have the book and we're going to take it from them! Find out where that old fool sent his people. If he shipped ours to Mir, his went somewhere else. Find them!"

13

Jump in the Dark

Max, along with Cindy and her parents, stepped down into Svet to encounter a waiting Yelka and Ell. They exited from the gateway on the top of a rolling green hill. Knee-high grasses flowed in the wind rippling like the sea. A couple of miles to their left, a vast mountain range towered with white-blanketed peaks that stretched to the sky. Tall, dark green trees, resembling pines, skirted the slopes and foothills. In the opposite direction from the forest, lay a small fairytale-like village with quaint cottages and shops nestled between the hills with a stream flowing merrily through the center of it.

Ell bounced around in earth-shaking leaps like an elephant-sized sheep dog excited at his master's return home. Max chuckled as Cindy hurried to calm Ell down before the ground movement caused everyone to lose their balance.

"Calm down. Calm down." Cindy placed a hand on Ell's side.

"Any news?" Yelka asked.

As Yelka escorted them towards the village, Max related the information about the strange dark mists that had engulfed Grandpa's house.

"So, for now, the spells are holding," Cindy's mom sighed with relief.

"Joe said he wants to give it at least a day before he allows anyone back to the house. The others will have to remain here until we can get rid of the curse entirely," Cindy's father added.

Max walked on the other side of Ell, resting his hand on Ell's neck so he and Cindy could both converse with him at the same time. Max detected a hint of thinly disguised boredom in the way Ell continually asked them what they were doing and if Grandpa needed his assistance anywhere. It had been almost five months since he had helped them capture Grd.

They told him about Kacha and his horrific plans, and filled him in on their attempts to find descendants of Richard Burdick. Right before they reached the small village, Ell came to an abrupt halt.

What's wrong? Max asked.

I'm not allowed in the village.

Why not? Cindy questioned.

I think they are afraid of me and I'm a little too large for their streets and bridges.

As if knowing what was coming, Yelka stated with a frown, "Ell will have to wait here. You can come back once you are settled."

"Maybe...we can sleep outside tonight," Max suggested with a smile.

"Yeah!" Cindy quickly agreed.

"I don't know," Cindy's mother looked to her husband.

"Oh, come on," Cindy pleaded. "I don't think there's anything in this world that would want to mess with Ell."

Yelka chuckled softly. "She is probably correct. I think that would be okay, at least for tonight, but I do not want to overstep my bounds."

Max continued to stroke Ell's large head while Cindy put the biggest pout on her face Max had ever seen. She placed her hands together in a prayer fashion and her bottom lip almost touched the tall green grass.

"All right," Cindy's mother threw up her hands while shaking her head. "You're pathetic with that look, you know."

"Sweet! We'll need some sleeping bags," Max added. Cindy's deplorable act to get her mother's permission made Max feel as if everything would be okay once again. A night under the stars might keep his mind off his mother and grandfather sitting at home trying to weather the assault of Kacha's evil curse.

He took out his communicator and everyone's eyes fell on him as he sent a message. To his relief the reply was quick. "No change," he informed the group.

###

Well, the spell is still holding, Max told Cindy and Ell as he and Cindy lay with their backs against Ell's side. *Mom did say the mists are so thick they can't see through them anymore.* He tucked his communicator back in his pocket. Ell's powers of communication filled Max with wonder. Not only could he convey his thoughts, he could make it so everyone touching him could hear one another. This was a little disturbing though, as Max had to keep some fearful thoughts out of his mind.

I'm sure the spell will hold, Cindy said, staring up at the stars.

It was a clear night, and without any city lights interfering with their vision, the sky was a black canvas with glowing pixie dust scattered generously across its surface. They set their camp on the top of a hill just outside the village, but close to Yelka's home. They chose this spot because of its height and it had the flattest top around, making it seem a bit more comfortable for sleeping. Ell's enormous back created a natural backstop for Cindy and Max to lean against as they wrapped themselves in their sleeping bags and watched for shooting stars.

It wasn't long until the soft snores of Cindy and the deep ups and downs of Ell's breaths told Max he was the only one awake. He didn't expect to get too much sleep tonight as his concentration remained on his mother and grandfather. It took every ounce of will power he possessed to not send them a message every ten seconds.

A cool breeze caused the grass to sway as if it was the ruffling fur of a monstrous creature. A wide range of squawks, growls, and cries that Max had never heard before floated through the air. His thoughts danced from his mother and grandfather to Richard Burdick. *How many descendants could he have now? It could easily be in the thousands.*

A deep menacing growl a few hills away brought Max back to the present, sleeping outside with Cindy and a hideous, elephant-sized Ell. He inhaled deeply before letting the air out in a slow, calming manner. Pulling his bag up around his shoulders, Max let the weight of his eyelids push them shut.

His exhaustion had just about carried him off to dreamland when a small blink of light stirred him. Max tried to tell himself he had only dreamed the white intrusion and to force it out of his mind when another flash snapped his eyes open. *I didn't imagine that!* He cautiously lifted his head in time to see another spark of light on the top of the next hill. When his night vision returned, a Night Shade stood with his back to them where the light had been.

The restless wind currents of the night whipped his black cloak around him, creating distant slapping sounds. Two more Night Shades approached this one from the side of the same hill while another blink of white brought yet another into Svet.

A surge of adrenaline rushed through Max's body, kick starting his heart into a higher rate and replacing his exhaustion with fear. With his eyes glued on the four Night Shades, he placed a hand over Cindy's mouth and shook her shoulder with the other. It required several attempts until a groggy Cindy woke up.

"Shh," Max whispered as their eyes met. "Night Shades." He rotated his gaze for Cindy to follow to the next hill before releasing her mouth.

ELL! They both thought as they laid against the creature's back. *WAKE UP!*

What is it?

Night Shades!

Max thought the Night Shades had spotted them for sure as Ell raised his monstrous head and lifted his body slightly to see what was happening. The constant swaying of the grass with the soft rustling sound and the fact the Night Shades had their backs to them, kept them unaware of Max, Cindy, and Ell's presence.

What do you think they want? Cindy asked.

I imagine they know what's happening in town from Larry and the others. I bet they are trying to find out what's causing it, Max theorized.

What should we do? Ell and Cindy thought at the same time.

Ell, can you pick up what they are saying? Max asked straining his ears to hear above the rustling of the grass and the other night calls.

With their hissing and the other noises, it's just jumble.

The Night Shades took off at a leisurely pace down the slope towards the small village. With their black garb blowing in the wind, it appear as if they floated above the waves of lush grass.

Cindy locked eyes with Max as if to say, *What now?*

Follow, Ell responded, rolling onto his stomach. *Get on.*

Max and Cindy climbed aboard and Ell started to track the Night Shades as they headed for Yelka's small hamlet.

###

Rachel entered Grandpa's kitchen dressed in her night robe and slippers. She had every light in the kitchen on in an attempt to chase away the uneasy feeling enveloping her. The mists swirling around Grandpa's house had completely encased the property in total darkness. The lack of light wasn't the cause of her discomfort. But the nails-on-the-chalkboard-type screeching and wailing that accompanied the mists had continued to grow from a faint vibration to an ear-splitting, spine-tingling cry. It was as if the very jaws of hell had been opened outside.

She pressed the on button to the laptop computer sitting on the table and then made her way to the counter to turn on a small CD player resting there. The soft sound of classical music was no match for the wailing of the damned raging outside in the street, so she changed it to a hard rock CD and cranked up the volume. As much as she considered that type of music noise, it did help to filter out the nerve-racking screams.

Sitting at the table, she typed the password into the laptop and noticed her hands were trembling. She held them out to watch them vibrate for a few moments.

"That bad, huh?" Grandpa shouted above the conflicting wails and music.

Rachel jumped at the sudden interruption. "I can't sleep with this." She motioned towards the windows and the blackness beyond.

Grandpa walked over and put a hand on her shoulder. "It will be all right. I'm fairly certain the spells are going to hold."

"Fairly?" Rachel chuckled. "The spells might hold, but what if the noise drives me so nuts I throw myself off the house?"

Grandpa smiled. He reached into his pocket, pulled out a set of earplugs and handed them to her. "This might help."

"Thanks." She tore off the plastic wrapping and placed the soft foam plugs into her ears. The effect was pure bliss. The wailing and shrieking was at a certain tone the earplugs blocked. Instead of a nerve shattering pitch, the noise was now a dull hum.

"How can these possibly work this well?" she wondered aloud.

Grandpa just winked and replied, "Magic."

"Of course," Rachel grinned. "I should have known."

"Want some cocoa?" Grandpa asked.

"Sure. I thought since I couldn't sleep, I'd see if I could get a little further with this Richard Burdick. I'm just not quite sure where I should start."

"Why don't you see if any Burdicks came through Ellis Island," Grandpa suggested as he stirred a pot of cocoa on the stove. "If any came through there, we might be able to track them from that point forward or backward."

"That's a great idea."

For Ell's enormous size, he glided through the tall prairie grass without making a sound. He kept his body low and steps light so as not to cause the ground to vibrate, the padded soles of his feet softening each footfall. He maintained an adequate distance between them and the Night Shades and he stayed in the shadows as they crept closer to Yelka's small village.

"Crap!" Max whispered as he plunged his hand into his pocket.

What? Cindy and Ell asked as the surprise exclamation caused Ell to freeze.

Max retrieved his communicator from his pocket. *I should at least try to warn them. I hope somehow Yelka wakes up and sees this.* Max entered a message into the device. *Come on. Answer.*

Anything? Cindy asked.

Not yet.

What do you want... Cindy started but a sudden jerk of Ell's furry head interrupted her.

There are more of them. Ell's head swung back and forth and the whiff whiff of his sniffing the air, with his big black nose, broke the swooshing of the waving grasses. *On both sides.*

Max and Cindy joined in the search to find the unseen.

There. Ell's head pointed to their left and locked onto an area off to the side of a low hill.

Max followed the direction of Ell's head but the limited light made it difficult to see anything among the swaying grass as it rolled along. Ell hadn't budged, so Max continued to focus on the same spot. Then it was there. Two shapes darker than the landscape glided through the grass towards the town. Max could only make out about a third of their bodies as the hill and grasses blocked most of his view.

On our right. Cindy thought, causing both Max and Ell to take notice of three more Night Shades descending a tall slope.

Max checked his communicator again. No response.

Signal your grandpa, Ell suggested.

Good idea, Max agreed. He tried to retrieve his communicator when pain exploded in his head and back as if he'd been doused with boiling water. A blur that was a screaming Cindy flashed past his vision and an incredible force dislodged him from Ell's back, causing him to collide with the ground. The impact of his landing jarred his whole body, completely knocking the wind out of him.

Max lay on his back and struggled desperately to suck air into his lungs. He'd lost all sense of direction and had no idea what had happened to the others. Then Ell's roar broke the silence. Judging by the volume of his howl, Ell was several yards away and the distance was growing. Suddenly, something headed right towards Max. He rolled hard down the slope as a blistering ball of fire impacted the place where he had been lying, exploding the area with a shower of sparks and burning grass. Several more fireballs zoomed over the area, charring the grass where they smashed into the earth. Max scrambled on hands and knees in the direction he remembered Cindy crossing his vision. "Cindy! Cindy!" Max attempted to holler without giving away his location. He hoped he could gain a little search time if he stayed lower than the grass.

"Max," Cindy called from a short distance away, and then Ell roared another vicious growl that echoed off the hills.

The ground vibrated under his hands and the shaking became more pronounced. It grew so intense Max's hands and knees actually left the ground a few times. Suddenly Ell stopped almost on top of him.

"Get on!" Cindy screamed, extending her hand down towards him.

Max sprang off the ground and with Cindy's help landed on Ell's back. Jets of red and green fire zipped all around them as the enemy sought to bring them down. Ell raced forward towards a line of Night Shades closing from the top of the nearest hill.

Max and Cindy cast their own counter spells in all directions but it was like trying to shoot a gun while on a bucking bronco. Most of their blasts soared aimlessly through the air.

An intense, increasing white light zooming towards them caught Max's attention. "*Oviraj*," Max screamed in time to block a hot ray of fire that collided with his spell in a display that matched the finale of most Fourth of July firework shows. The speed and force of the impact almost launched him from Ell's back. If it weren't for Cindy's quick reflexes as she clamped down on Max's arm, he would have fallen.

Time froze for a brief second. There was no sound as the light of the blast faded and Max locked eyes with Hudich. Another spell raced from Hudich's hands and threw dirt, rocks, and grass over the three of them as they scrambled behind the cover of a hill.

"Max," Cindy screamed as they hurtled towards a line of Night Shades.

"*Premakni!*" Max's hands pushed towards the center of the line.

"*Premakni!* Cindy shouted.

The results of their spells and the speed of Ell tossed the Nights Shades aside, creating a route of escape.

Ell constantly changed his pattern of flight, leaping, sprinting, zigzagging, and vaulting, never giving the Night Shades a steady target. The resulting strategy carried them away, unscathed, from the pursuing Night Shades and the foul, deadly spells of Hudich.

Max glanced back to see the last of the Night Shades disappear beyond a distant hill.

They're behind the hills now. Slow down. Relief flooded through Max as he patted his front pocket to discover he hadn't lost his communicator. *Is everyone okay?* As soon as Max had asked the question, the burns on his back screamed at him like thousands of hot needles. He wondered if his shirt was still covering his back, but he didn't dare reach back to feel.

Ell slowed to a trot, his breathing hard and fast, causing Max and Cindy's legs to stretch over his back. *I'm all right.*

Just a few bruises. Cindy added.

Max snuck a peek over his shoulder to see Ell was missing several patches of fur on his backside and the exposed skin was blistered everywhere. He expected his back must look the same.

Suddenly Max's communicator started vibrating and he yanked it from his pocket to read Yelka's message.

"WHAT'S HAPPENING? WHERE ARE YOU?"

It's Yelka. As quickly as his fingers could manage, Max tapped in their situation and that Hudich was here. He told her about all the Night Shades surrounding the village. *I've let her know she needs to prepare for a fight. With any luck, the three of us can lead them away from her village,* he relayed to Cindy and Ell.

Ell began weaving around the hills to keep them hidden from Hudich and his minions. The tree line marking the edge of the forest drew closer with each of Ell's strides. Suddenly, Ell's pace quickened and his angles of direction changed. The steady night breeze grew more intense.

They are coming! Ell warned.

Head for the trees, Cindy suggested.

Suddenly, the entire area lit up from all sides with hundreds or even thousands of blinks of lights like cameras busy taking pictures. The scene changed from innocent flashes to a massive fireworks display as the arrival of the enemy brought a barrage of wicked curses. Every color imaginable rained down on Max, Cindy, and Ell as Ell broke into a ground-shaking sprint towards the forest ahead.

In a quick maneuver to avoid a collision with a pile of trees brought down by several spells attempting to block their path, Ell almost threw Max and Cindy. With the aid of his huge tufts of fur, they both managed to remain aboard as Ell dove into the forest. The claw-like fingers of the forest's tree limbs scratched their exposed skin as caution gave way to the need for speed. Max and Cindy leaned as low as possible over Ell's back. Tree branches, sparks, fire, spells and dirt cascaded down on them like a pursuing avalanche trying to devour them in its roaring descent.

Ell proceeded as if he had a sixth sense, jumping to the left or right in time to avoid an inferno of fireballs or falling trees. Max and Cindy tried to help as much as they could. Cindy used the *premakni* spell to clear as much of the path as she could, while Max cast the *oviraj* spell to shield them from incoming attacks.

The endless onslaught by the enemy began to take its toll on all of them. Ell's pace slowed as Cindy struggled to keep their path clear. Max sweated profusely and his breathing came in great labored gulps as he attempted to cast his spell every few seconds. The only bright side was the fact the Ell had created some distance between them and the enemy. Even though their dash through the forest had drained their energy, the constant rain of spells started to dwindle.

I think we are going to make it, Cindy thought.

If we can find a place to rest, Max agreed.

The attack seemed to be losing some of its fervor, which gave credence to Cindy's comment. Ell had slowed to a trot and the spells, which had been flying all around them only moments ago were now landing several dozen yards behind them.

I think they're aiming blindly now, Ell commented.

Max took out his communicator and sent Yelka a message. The response was almost instantaneous. *Everyone in town is safe*, Max informed them.

So, the Night Shades are all chasing us? Cindy asked.

Not sure, Yelka only said everyone is okay.

Ell, do you know where we are? Cindy asked.

We are heading into uncharted territory for me, Ell answered. *I think we need to find a place to hide.*

And rest! Max added as he checked behind them to see the separation between them and their attackers' spells had increased. As Max rotated, the burns on his back sent sharp messages to his brain that they were still there. Without anything to distract him, the pain returned to the front of his mind.

What? Ell asked.

I imagine, my back looks like your backside, Max said.

What? Cindy questioned with confusion.

It can wait, Max assured her.

"MMMAAAXXX," Hudich's deep voice echoed through the forest and the raging storm of spells caught up to them once again. This time the assault's intensity had no limits. It seemed the ground was about to open and gobble them up.

Ell leapt forward as fast as he could but his exhaustion carried them head first into the trunk of a large tree. The impact rocked all of them to the core. Cindy had pulled out handfuls of fur in her effort to keep her and Max, whose weight was against her back, on top of Ell. The blow staggered Ell like a drunken man. He wobbled to and fro, blindly avoiding several spells before they reached a steep downward slope. Ell fell sideways and the three of them started to slide down an ever-increasing decline.

Max and Cindy couldn't free themselves from the unconscious Ell. With Ell's weight behind them, they were at gravity's mercy, zooming down the hill at an incredible speed. Max worried they would fly off a cliff or slam into a boulder or tree. But Ell's fall had seemingly confused the enemy as well, and the attackers had stopped following them.

"I think we are slowing down," Cindy half-shouted as the slope began to level off.

Shortly afterward, they came to a halt as the slope flattened out and the ground leveled off. A soft roar from a short distance ahead of them indicated a river raged somewhere close by. There was no way to tell where they were in the dark. The thick forest trees seemed to increase the blackness.

Judging by the faint fires and spells still erupting on the hill above them, they had slid almost a half-mile on their backsides, and thankfully, the Night Shades had not noticed. "We need to get undercover," Max suggested, staring up the slope.

To both his and Cindy's great relief, Ell was moving.

Are you all right? Cindy asked.

My head hurts and I'm dizzy. What happened? Ell rolled on to his stomach.

You smacked head first into a tree trunk, Cindy said.

Catch your breath. I'm going to see if I can find a place for us to hide, Max indicated. Except for the lights on the hill above and the stars in the sky, it was extremely dark. As Max took several cautious steps forward away from the slope, the soft roar grew in volume. "I think the river is farther down this hill," he whispered back to Cindy. He inched forward and his foot hit nothing. "Wow," escaped his lips as he dropped backwards on his rear end to avoid falling forward.

"Shh," Cindy hissed at him.

"Sorry, but we are on the edge of a cliff. I just about went over!" Max spat back.

"Be careful," Cindy muttered in an apologetic tone. "Ell's okay. I think he just got his bell rung."

Cindy tried to help the gigantic Ell to his feet as Max crept along the edge of a dark chasm, feeling his way carefully as he went. The ledge made a wide half circle as Max traced its entire drop off. He had just finished his second pass around Cindy and Ell when voices above caught his attention. He realized the spells had stopped. Instead of the battlefield firelights, torches now moved along the top of the hill, winking at him as they rushed in and out of the trees.

An uneasy feeling in Max's gut began to turn with the force of a hurricane. "We're trapped," Max whispered.

"What?" Cindy responded.

Max rushed back to Cindy and Ell and placed his hand on Ell's side. *We are on a ledge next to a drop-off. We have no cover. Without any light, I can't be sure if we can make it along the slope.*

How far is the drop off? Cindy asked.

Ell pushed his way through them and advanced to the edge of the cliff. He lowered his head over the drop off. *I can see water about a hundred feet below.* He said when they had both touched him again.

Can you tell how deep it is? Cindy leaned over for a look. *And are you sure there's water down there?*

I'm sure there is water, and it's flowing very slowly, so I think it's a river. I'm not certain of its depth. The roar is coming from farther downstream; perhaps it is a waterfall.

"Find them," Hudich's order rang out from above, drawing their attention.

I don't think we have long, Ell thought.

Me either, Max agreed.

You two aren't thinking what I think you're thinking. Cindy's thoughts indicated nervousness. *What if it's only a foot deep? What if there are ledges sticking out? It could kill us!*

And you think what's going to be raining down on us from above is going to be a lot more friendly when they spot us? At least we stand a chance in the river! Max argued.

Be very quiet! Ell ordered and with his large foot, he kicked a fair sized boulder over the edge. He turned his head sideways and paused.

They only had to wait about three seconds before PLOP reached their ears. Ell remained motionless a moment longer, while the noise above them continued to gain strength.

It is at least several feet deep where the rock went in.

I say we go for it. Max's mouth was dry in nervous anticipation of what he figured was their only option.

Where it went in! What if that was the deepest spot and there are jagged rocks under the surface? Cindy countered.

Cindy's fear surprised Max. He didn't think she was scared of anything. This sudden hesitation told him there was something she was worried about.

"They couldn't have gone far!" Hudich's voice was closer now and his anger apparent. "Search everywhere!"

Before Cindy had a chance to object any further, Ell leapt over the edge and disappeared. A large splash reached them a few seconds later.

"Ell," Cindy whispered as if in shock.

Max extended his hand. Cindy acted stunned, and it appeared to take all the effort she had to reach out and put her hand in Max's. He gave her hand a reassuring squeeze. They stepped to the edge.

"It's going to be all right," Max said before they jumped.

14

Into the Pit

Sky sat in her usual vantage point occupying an empty apartment in the building across the street from Kacha's place. After their struggle to rescue the librarian and her daughter, Kacha had disappeared. The thought Kacha would abandon his apartment upon its discovery had danced at the forefront of her mind for two days now. Only her knowledge about the elaborate stone structure inside his living room kept her from searching elsewhere. *He's building his gateway here!* she told herself over and over.

This Saturday morning the knowledge of what was inside his apartment paid off. Kacha rode up the street on his Harley Davidson motorcycle, the ornate chrome reflecting sunlight onto the surrounding buildings and sidewalks. He wore a big sparkling smile, which matched the bright bike.

He seems very self-assured. He has done something that pleases him. Sky followed him with her eyes until he disappeared into the underground parking lot beneath his building. She breathed a small sigh of relief at knowing where he was once more. She took out her communicator and typed in a message to Joseph, Jax, and Finster.

A quick response from Jax caught her eye, Sky detested any message from Jax: **Two enemy spies heading your way,** flashed across her communicator's small screen. "Joseph was right. That little battle drew some attention," she muttered to herself and sent another message to Joseph. She spotted the two rather easily by their dark apparel as they meandered up the street towards her.

"I could eliminate them easily," she mouthed, duplicating that information via communicator to Joseph and the others.

No! That would definitely let them know something important is going on here. Keep them in the dark as much as possible, Joseph answered back.

"Do you think they know Kacha is here?" Finster joined her and nodded in the direction of Kacha's building.

"No. I suspect they are just widening the circle around the library, hoping to get lucky. Hopefully, Kacha will not go back there or use any magic. These two are just scouting around, searching for traces of magic," Sky answered.

"LOOK!" Finster barked, shooting a finger towards the other side of the street.

Sky's heart stopped as Kacha exited the front doors of his apartment complex at the same moment the two enemy scouts, walking along the sidewalk, reached the front of his building. She held her breath as Kacha paused to let them pass in front of him before he stepped out onto the sidewalk behind them. "Tell Jax and his men what's happening and to get into position," Sky ordered as she dug her fingernails into the palms of her hands, expecting Kacha and the enemy to discern and recognize one another as creatures of magic.

The enemy spies continued at a steady pace, their heads swiveling back and forth, scanning the city streets, while Kacha strolled along as if he didn't have a care in the world. He held his head high, letting the warm sunshine touch his face.

Sky bounced on her heels, waiting for them to get far enough ahead of her so she could start trailing them. She bit her lip as they crossed the street at the light, heading in the same direction. "Stay on your communicator," she told Finster as she bolted out of the apartment building. She kept them in sight from the opposite side of the street.

Her heart rate slowed as the distance between Kacha and the enemy increased because of Kacha's lackadaisical manner. The concern of an unwanted encounter with the enemy revealing their location to Hudich began to ease.

The chase continued for a couple of more blocks. Sky's fears that Kacha would notice the others or vice versa had almost subsided, when Kacha stopped abruptly. His head turned towards the men in front of him. His pace increased as he started to close the gap between them.

He knows! Sky hurried to the crosswalk, her focus on Kacha.

Joe leaned over Rachel's shoulder as he peered at the screen. They had found a Burdick that had registered at Ellis Island upon entering America. With the help of the earplugs and their newfound information, the wailing and crying outside the house had died down to a small annoyance. They had connected the Ellis Island Burdick to several generations further back and felt they were very close to tying him to Merlin, when Joseph's communicator vibrated in his pocket.

"Wonder what's going on?" he said, glancing at the clock. "3:00 a.m., this can't be good." He fished out his communicator.

"Who is it?" Rachel asked over her shoulder as she studied the screen.

"Yelka. We've got a big problem." He dashed out of the room.

"What's happening?" Rachel chased after him.

He rounded the railing and flew up the spiral staircase.

"Max and Cindy are in trouble." He started flipping switches and the force field sprang to life. Retrieving his communicator from his pocket once again, he sent another message.

"What? What happened?" Rachel's voice trembled, climbing several octaves.

"Night Shades showed up searching for our people. Max and Cindy discovered them. They alerted the town, so everyone there is safe and in hiding. However, Max, Cindy, and Ell are on the run, and they're not responding."

"What does that mean?"

"I don't know. They might not be able to answer at this exact moment. I'm sure they are fine," he added, noticing the apprehensive expression on her face.

"I'll go get some weapons," Rachel stated firmly.

"You need to stay here. I'm going to Yelka's village. If Max and Cindy send a message, you have to be ready to open the gateway for them. I'll be back as fast as I can. I'm just going to check on everyone else." He paused momentarily, taking Rachel by the shoulders to face her as the mirror began its slow initial revolutions. "Hey, they'll be all right. Be ready to get them out. I'll be back in about an hour."

Rachel nodded and they hugged. She stood with her arms wrapped tightly around herself as he entered the gateway.

###

Max and Cindy plunged into icy water that nipped and burned their skin. Cindy's fears about the depth of the water proved groundless as there seemed to be no bottom to the river. Max wasn't as worried about the sound of their splash as he was about the loud gasps that escaped them, due to the freezing water's bite, when they broke the surface. Their breathing came in sharp, short pants as they swam in a direction they desperately hoped would lead them to land. The air did not bring relief. Unfortunately, a foul, decaying stench filled their nostrils and their lungs, nauseating them. The thickness of the odor hung in the air like heavy, bitter smog that made Max want to retch each time he drew it into his mouth.

Ell swam suddenly in front of them and they snagged hold of his back, the large friendly creature pulling them through the water. Ell's long legs propelled them forward far faster than Max or Cindy could swim. After a few moments, Ell's haunches started to rise out of the surface of the water as his feet reached the bottom. Max and Cindy retained their hold on his thick fur until Ell made it onto the shore.

What's that smell? Cindy gagged as she conveyed her thoughts to Ell and Max.

It's getting worse. Max put his face into Ell's back to block the overpowering smell of rotting refuse. Even wet-smelling Ell-fur was better than that.

Death, Ell responded.

Max's teeth began to dance against each other in the cool night's temperature. The icy water had soothed the searing burns on his back, and for that he was thankful, but now he couldn't stop his skin from prickling with cold. From the way Cindy wrapped her arms around herself and her teeth produced a chattering noise, the water had chilled her to the bone. Ell in his thick, wintery fur seemed fine.

I'm going to be sick. Cindy struggled to breathe pulling the collar of her wet shirt up over her nose and mouth.

The lights on the top of the hill seemed like distant stars now, disappearing into the background of the night sky. The darkness that had been prevalent before had grown so deep Max could only make out the outlines of Cindy and Ell just a few feet away from him. He placed a hand on Ell's flank. *We need to get out of this disgusting place. Can you see anything?*

Not so much as I can feel it. We're not alone.

What's out there? Cindy asked.

I'm not sure, but I can sense its hunger. There are many. Something very powerful is also out there, controlling the others.

Joe stepped down out of the gateway into a small valley surrounded by rolling hills. He inhaled a deep breath of fresh air into his lungs. It felt good to be outside in the clean air. He hadn't realized how claustrophobic the curse had made it seem inside his house, but now that he was away from the wailing haze, freedom reigned.

He took out his communicator. *Nothing!*

A few hills over, the soft glow from the street lamps of Yelka's village brightened the night. He surveyed the area for any hint of the enemy, but all appeared calm. Switching on his flashlight and turning his back to the village, he marched at a good clip in the opposite direction. When he reached the bottom of the hill, he followed the small stream, which wound its way through the landscape, bubbling and gurgling.

Twisting and weaving around several large hills, the stream picked up speed as the slope grew steeper. It led Joe into a forest of leafy trees, at first sparse, but gradually increasing in density the farther in he ventured. The soft running water changed into the muted roar of a waterfall. At the point where the water threw itself over a high rock shelf, Joe headed left along a trail zigzagging downward. If he hadn't used this path several times in the past, he would never have located it in the dark, even with his light.

He shuffled his feet as fast as he could and checked his watch. *Twenty minutes without a response, they must be in trouble.* The path leveled out and dove into a thick patch of trees. Suddenly, the trees gave way to a small valley nestled against a cliff on the left and impenetrable stands of trees on its other sides. Five almost invisible buildings hugged the cliffs, but the valley looked empty.

With his communicator still in hand, Joe typed a message to Yelka. The response was immediate. After receiving the okay, he waited a minute and then stepped into the valley and found himself surrounded by an escort of armed guards.

"Joseph, glad you let us know it was you," came a voice off to his right. It belonged to a male elf just a few inches taller than Yelka.

"Micho," Joe extended his hand and the other accepted it. "I didn't want to get an arrow in my back."

Yelka hustled through the valley with Cindy's parents right behind her. They pushed through the soldiers to reach Joe. "Get back to your posts," Yelka ordered, nodding to the guards.

"Yes, ma'am," Micho saluted and the guards disappeared into the trees.

Yelka related all they knew and that everyone in the town had gotten out undetected. The knot in Joe's stomach continued to tighten as he continued to glance at his communicator for a message, but without results.

"We've got to do something," Cindy's mom demanded. She appeared on the verge of a breakdown, her skin paled as her body trembled. "We shouldn't have let them sleep out there."

"They actually saved everyone," Yelka said. "If they hadn't been out there, who knows what would have happened?"

"Does Ell know about this place?" Joe asked.

Yelka shook her head, "No."

"Then someone should go back to the village and wait for them. I think only the four of us should go," Joe added, not wanting to waste time arguing about whether Cindy's mother should remain behind. The desperateness of the situation pressed down on him like a car had parked on his chest and he needed to hurry. He'd had to leave her behind last summer and didn't wish to face that scrutiny again. "We can check out the situation and keep an eye out for them."

"Good idea," Cindy's father agreed.

"How long do you think the others should wait here, at the hideout?" Yelka asked.

"Until we find Max and Cindy and only if they don't have an army of Night Shades on their tail. I don't want to involve everyone in a battle."

"Come on, the caves are this way." Yelka waved for them to follow.

###

Maybe Grandpa can open the gateway and get us out of here, Cindy suggested, her teeth still clicking against the cold. She continued to breathe through her shirt.

The cold that had raised goose bumps all over Max's body had increased so much so, that along with the horrible stench, Max's urge to vomit was reaching overpowering levels. He nodded at Cindy's suggestion of notifying Grandpa and reached into his pocket to find *nothing*. He frantically patted each pocket to no avail. "Oh no!" A terrible sinking sensation settled in his stomach.

"What?"

"I don't have my communicator." Max continued to check his pockets as if the communicator might magically appear where it hadn't been a second ago. "I must have lost it during our slide or in the water."

"Not good." Cindy sounded worried.

Max put a hand back on Ell. *Can you get us back to the village?*

Yes, but it might take some time. I'm not sure where we are at the moment. I've never been here before. But that must wait. Right now, I can feel the desire of whatever lurks out there and they know we are here. Get on my back!

Ell lowered to his stomach and Max and Cindy climbed aboard. The cooling relief of the water on Max's back was short-lived as the tightness of his wet skin brought a roaring fiery sensation with each movement.

What are they? Cindy asked.

I do not know. I am uncertain if there is a word for what they are or aren't.

What? Both Max and Cindy responded.

They are neither living nor dead and they are closing in on us. This gut-turning stink, it comes from them. Ell began inching forward at a slow pace. The dark was like a thick veil that covered everything. Max wondered if Ell could see anything at all.

Ghosts, Cindy commented.

No. While ghosts are spirits and a type of matter, these things have bodies. Ell paused. Max could just make out his large head as it swung from side to side. *They are everywhere. They want us, but not as much as the other one does. They are her victims, her slaves.*

What other? They both asked again, as they began to see shadows where there weren't any.

The one who made them. She is very powerful. Ell started forward again through the blackness surrounding them. The trickle of flowing water continued to grow in volume and Max could just make out the dark river only yards to his right.

How do you know all this? Who is this "she" you're talking about? Cindy asked.

The plants and the land know. Did you think I could only communicate with you?

Well, not just us, but not plants and stuff, Cindy responded.

How do you think I tracked you so well before?

I assumed it was your great sense of smell, Cindy thought.

Hey, back to these not-living-not-dead things, Max interrupted as he tried to make out anything in the dark. *What are they? Zombies? That could explain the smell.* Max's mind flashed back to the various horror movies of the walking grotesque, decaying corpses.

What is a zombie? Ell asked.

Cindy and Max explained the concept of a zombie to Ell as he crept along in the dark. They told him how they feed on human brains and could only be killed by shooting them in the head.

I'm not sure how to kill these things or what they eat, but I would say they resemble zombies in the fact they are not living or dead. She that controls them has more of a life source than the others, but still not totally living, Ell went on as he waded a little into the water. *But now you must be extra wary.*

Why's that? Max asked.

They are closing in!

Joe, Yelka, and Cindy's parents shuffled through the underground tunnel back to Yelka's village. Even though the smooth stone tunnel was wide enough for them to all walk abreast, the height of the arched roof had been built for Yelka's people. Joseph and Cindy's parents shuffled along the steady incline, like the hunchback of Notre Dame, to keep their heads from banging against the low ceiling.

Joe attempted to reassure Cindy's parents everything was under control while they traveled from the valley to the large room under the center of the city. From this room, smaller tunnels led to various buildings throughout the city. Yelka paused and glanced at a couple of different branching passageways. "Wait here. I will go make sure everything is okay," she said before disappearing into an opening at a left angle from where they had entered the cavern.

Joe walked around the area casually while he fished his communicator out of his pocket. His attempt to hide the fact he was checking it didn't work.

"Anything?" Cindy's mother asked, her eyes on the device in Joe's hand.

"No," he responded and tucked it away. The feeling something was terribly wrong had been spreading through his mind like an oncoming storm. Surely, Max would have sent word or asked them to open the gateway to get them out. *What could have happened? Are they hurt? Captured?* His forehead creased as he grasped for answers.

"What are you thinking?" Cindy's father asked.

"I'm confused. Why haven't they signaled for help? If they were captured or something, wouldn't the enemy have had them call with their demands?" Joe tossed out these ideas, but it didn't help his concern.

"I don't see how silence is good news then," Cindy's father stated as Yelka re-entered the chamber.

"Me neither," Joe added.

"The town is completely empty," Yelka said as she met their gaze. "And I can't pick up any trace of magic having been used." She turned and the others followed her to the exit. They only had to travel about twenty yards before a door opened into the basement of a small clothing shop owned by a friend of Yelka's.

The village was as Yelka had said. With all the villagers and the people from Joe's town down in the valley, the place looked like a ghost town. The slight tint in the eastern sky hinted at morning's dawning.

"Do you know where they slept?" Joe asked.

"Yes. I can show you." Yelka headed in the direction of Max and Cindy's campsite.

"I'd better tell Rachel what's going on," Joe said, communicator in hand once again as they hurried along.

How much time do we have? Cindy's thoughts echoed her panic.

From which direction are they coming? Max's heart raced. Although the black veil above had changed to a lighter shade of gray in the eastern sky, the forest and the river remained pitch black.

No time at all! And from every direction. Ell took a few steps backwards into the river keeping the shore in front of him.

Suddenly, the silence that had dominated the darkness into which they'd fallen was broken. Loud movements in front of them filled the air. It wasn't the usual thumping of running feet that normally preceded an attack. Hissings and moans mingled with dragging and snapping noises. An occasional thump or crack wafted on the air as if legs and feet were not working properly and the creatures struggled to remain upright.

Ell growled deep in his throat in warning, but it didn't seem to affect the advancing creatures.

Soon, tiny sets of glowing lights floated all along the shore in groups of twos, accompanied with spin tingling cries and shrieks. At first there were only a few but as the scraping and thumping grew closer, more and more lights appeared.

What are those? Cindy thoughts screamed.

I think they are eyes, Max offered, the hairs all over his body standing on end.

Ell's fur bristled as he lowered his head and rumbled a menacing deep warning through his razor-sharp teeth. He backed farther into the water as the hundreds of tiny shining eyes continued to advance, bobbing and staggering at a slow but steady pace towards them.

Don't use fire! We don't want to attract Hudich and the Night Shades' attention, Max thought as he prepared to fight.

What do you suggest we do then? Cindy asked, fear-induced frustration building in her tone.

Suddenly, the water exploded all around them as twisted forms broke the surface of the dark liquid. With clawed, broken limbs with rotting skin and bone they surged towards Max, Cindy, and Ell with their ghostly glowing eyes, trying to grasp them with their decrepit arms and hands. The stench grew to a suffocating level as the swarms of decaying forms attacked them.

"*Premakni!*" Max screamed, throwing back a wave of attackers.

"*Premakni!*" Cindy scattered another group.

Ell bucked like a bull as he bit and tore at anything within reach, throwing the skeletal creatures through the air as he shook his head violently. Max and Cindy continued to knock back more and more of the misshapen forms, but there seemed to be no end to them as the water was now a boiling pool of rotting stench.

Disappear! Max thought, holding onto Ell. He cast the invisibility spell as did Cindy and Ell, but the magic didn't fool the undead creatures.

The fact Max, Cindy, and Ell could no longer be seen didn't faze their attackers, who started to drag them down and back towards the shore. Bony fingers and hands with decaying flesh clamped on to every part of Max and wrenched him from Ell's back. A large splash and a wave of water swept over Max and into his mouth; Ell had been brought down in the water. They pinned Max to the muddy bottom of the water's edge, grinding his blistered back against the ground. Max yelled as he kicked, punched, and cast his spells. Cindy's high-pitched scream broke the moaning and wailing, followed by a roar from Ell.

No matter how many times Max tired to push them off, a new surge replaced the previous one. The putrid air surrounding his attackers stole his energy, as if it prevented him from getting adequate oxygen into his lungs. New and intense pain erupted all over Max's body. Where there had only been the weight and stench of these misshapen creatures, their teeth now penetrated Max's skin. The pain changed to a numbing sensation that flowed over him, stealing away his fears. He felt light as sleep called to him. He closed his eyes to the numbing bliss and lost consciousness.

15

Spider's Web

With the morning crowd on the street and Sky's ability to avoid detection, she managed to get within thirty yards of Kacha. With his focus on the two enemy scouts in front of him, Sky marveled at how he never thought to look over his shoulder. Sky's constant need to be on guard caused her to check for more enemy spies every few buildings. She placed one hand on her communicator for double protection, knowing Finster, Jax, and Jax's men were also keeping an eye out for trouble.

What is he going to do? He cannot seriously be thinking about attacking. That would put an army of the enemy on his trail, if they aren't already. She jumped into the entrance of a building as Kacha and the two men stopped at an intersection to wait for the light. **This isn't good. They could be leading him into a trap,** she typed into her communicator.

Sky let them get halfway across the intersection before bolting after them. She managed to reach the other side of the street before the light changed and continued on as before. As she wove in and out of the crowd, a sudden sensation of magic's touch surprised her. She glanced in all directions, but couldn't spot who had cast a spell.

Anyone know where that magic came from? She tapped in the message.

No, but I'm looking, Finster replied.

Where what came from? responded Jax and his men.

"Idiots," Sky muttered in reference to Jax and his men and then turned her attention back to Kacha. Another hair-teasing caress of magic vibrated through the city streets. Its dark touch suggested something sinister like a black mamba, beautiful but deadly at the same time. This time she tracked its direction to somewhere out in front of her.

The enemy scouts seemed to have sensed it as well. Their head swiveling movements suggested something had sparked their interest as they pointed and conversed back and forth. In that time, Kacha had closed the distance between them. His eyes remained locked on the two in front of him as if they were all that existed in the world.

When they reached the end of the block, a third hint of magic wafted toward them from the left along the side street. The two out in front made a sharp turn with Kacha close behind them.

Where is that coming from? She entered again.

Again, Jax and his men didn't know what she was talking about, and Finster was as much in the dark as she was.

The spies continued to track the wisps of magic that periodically surged in front of them as they went. The trail directed them south, into the Wall Street district, away from the tourist part of the city, forcing Sky to leave a greater safety gap between her and Kacha as the pedestrians started to thin.

An incoming message from Finster caught her attention. **Watch Kacha's hands. I think he's the one doing it. We're heading towards Wall Street. He's leading them into a trap!**

With this new information, sure enough, every time Sky detected the release of magic, Kacha flicked his hand subtly. This knowledge enabled her to really concentrate on what he was doing. He bounced spells off objects out in front of the spies, leading them to believe they were following the source.

Clever! Sky smiled at Kacha's shrewdness, in spite of herself, as she risked closing the gap between them a little. They headed into some darker streets with towering buildings and hardly any people in the area. Weekends always left the streets empty of pedestrians and taxis in this neighborhood.

Kacha continued his spells and lured the two enemy spies down a deserted street, forcing Sky to give up most of the space between them. Not only did she not dare to get too close, she needed to sneak from one hiding place to the other. Fortunately, neither Kacha nor the spies checked to see if they were being followed. Both seemed too occupied with what was happening in front of them, even though Kacha had gradually let the others get farther ahead of him.

Sky wondered how long this would continue and what Kacha had in mind, when suddenly he stopped casting his tempting spells. Sky dove behind a parked sedan in the street and crouched, peeking through its windows. Kacha's next move caused her jaw to drop.

"Gentlemen. Gentlemen," Kacha called to the others with a raised hand while hustling towards them. "I was wondering if you could help me."

The two scouts didn't seem pleased at Kacha's approach, but weren't alarmed either. They acted more concerned about the loss of the trail they had been pursuing.

"I'm not from this neighborhood and you look a little more civil than the other residents here. Could you help me find an address? I seem to be lost," Kacha's voice carried to Sky's hiding place.

The enemy eyed Kacha with contempt more than curiosity. "We're not from this neighborhood either!"

"Oh," Kacha sounded calm. "So…you're lost too?" Kacka's hand flicked at his side down a darkened alley to his left. His spell bounced back towards them causing the two scouts' heads to snap in the alley's direction.

"We're on business," the second snapped. "So, buzz off!"

They left Kacha standing on the sidewalk and proceeded into the alley. Kacha waited a few moments before pursuing after them.

Sky leapt from her place of cover and crossed the street at an angle. She sprinted for a parked car in direct line with the alleyway on the opposite side of the street. With her light feet, she bounded with the stealth of a cat. She reached the car in time to see two marble-size balls of light float from the fallen spies and into a glass container in Kacha's hand.

A greedy smile played over Kacha's face as he exited the alley, gazing at the two small lights in his jar that vanished as he walked into the sunlight. He tucked the jar inside his jacket and patted it gently before departing back the way he had come.

Did you see that? Sky messaged the others.

A few positive and a few negative replies returned.

Stay on him! Sky ordered.

Sky hustled into the alley to inspect the bodies when suddenly one disappeared in a flash of light. The other remained, lying on the littered ground. *He must be from here.* She inspected the front of his throat to find the same dark mark Kacha had left on all his other victims.

###

Yelka led Joe and Cindy's parents to where Max, Cindy, and Ell had planned to spend the night. Their sleeping bags and a few other items still remained at their campsite. Joe's worry grew to the point where he thought his stomach was going to join his throat. He couldn't find Max's communicator among the items. The immediate area didn't give them any clues as to where they had gone.

"I am not a tracker," Yelka said as she searched the hill. "And with the constant sway of the grasses, I can't figure anything out."

"What are we going to do?" Cindy's mother, Stacey, asked. Her eyes were puffy and her face pale.

"I think we need Sky," Joe said. "She's the best tracker we've got. I don't really want to pull her off of Kacha but I think we have to."

"Yes! We do," Cindy's mother stressed.

"We have enough to worry about right now, this is a problem we can't afford to neglect," Joe said, scanning the surrounding hills. "I'll get Sky, but I require your help elsewhere." Joe looked at Cindy's parents.

"What? We're going to help find our daughter," Cindy's dad bristled.

"Okay, just hear me out." Joe retrieved his communicator and his fingers danced over the controls.

"What?" Stacey asked shaking her head.

"I need you to help Rachel. We were making some real progress on the Burdick search. Will you work with her and operate the gateway in case we have to make a quick exit." Grandpa located the gateway with the aid of his crystal and the four of them entered into it.

###

The sun shone down from the eastern sky as Sky moved around the campsite, kneeling in the grass and studying the layout, while Joe, Cindy's father Jim, and Yelka watched her work. It always fascinated Joe to observe a tracker and how they let the land tell them a story.

"They went this way," Sky pointed. "They rode Ell."

They followed Sky down the slope. Every so often she would pause and take in the surroundings, squatting here, and touching there. She led them to the spot of the attack and was able to tell the happenings to the others. She showed them pieces of burnt fur and a section of

Max's shirt, explaining Ell and Max received wounds but they're okay. This process of trailing Max, Cindy, and Ell's flight continued into the forest. The signs of burnt trees and underbrush stood out like arrows signaling the way.

The charred earth and exploded trees put them all on guard. They knew whoever attacked Max, Cindy, and Ell could still be out there. Sky pointed out their trail and a mark in the tree that had knocked Ell senseless, which brought her to the hill. She glanced quickly over the edge and then started a thorough sweep of the area.

Joe, Jim, and Yelka watched for unwanted visitors that might notice them snooping around the forest.

Sky gave a sharp whistle, which startled Joe as he pondered on the events that could have led Cindy and Max here. Sky waved them over to the side of the hill where Max and the others had slid down.

"What's going on?" Jim poured cool water onto his head from a canteen before taking a drink.

"From what I can tell, they fell over the hill right here and the enemy seems to have lost them at this spot," Sky said. "The enemy has since moved on searching elsewhere. I imagine in the dark and without a good scout to spot the signs, they didn't realize where the children and Ell had gone. In fact, it took me a while to figure it out in the daylight. At night it would have been twice as hard. Ell collided with that tree," Sky motioned to the massive trunk. "Max and Cindy were still on his back. He staggered to this point and then fell. He landed pretty far down the slope and that is probably what baffled the enemy."

"Oh no," Yelka gasped. Her tan face drained of color as she put her hands over her mouth. "I hope they didn't go in there." Her eyes locked on the island in the pit below.

"What's down there?" Jim asked as everyone peered down at the giant hole where a heavily vegetated island sat, surrounded by a black slow-moving river.

"I am not sure. I'm going down to that ledge to figure out where they went from here," Sky added.

"A horrible creature dwells down there. Anything that enters that place, never comes out," Yelka said, her face white and taut as she glanced at the others.

"Surely, that's just a myth. You hear that all the time about dark places, even in our world," Jim said.

"Let's just hope they didn't have to go that far." Joe forced a smile to try and ease Jim's concerns but could see Yelka's frown behind him.

"Wait here. I will go take a look. I do not want to have to try and stop any of you from sliding off into the hole," Sky said. She started down the steep slope. She hopped down the side of the hill with the grace of a gazelle, sure-footed and effortless. She paused about ten yards down. "Here is where they landed after Ell fell." She studied the area for a second and then descended along the path left by Max, Cindy, and Ell as they slid.

"I have a strange feeling they went into that place," Jim admitted, his eyes glued on Sky. "I hope it is just a myth about the creature that lives there."

Joe's eyes met Yelka's again and she gave him a frightened expression with a slow shake of the head.

About three-quarters of the way down towards the small ledge, Sky stopped and seemed to be drawn towards something. Suddenly, she stood holding Max's communicator high in the air for them to see.

Grandpa gave a short sigh of relief. "Well, at least we know he just lost it."

"How's that comforting?" Jim asked.

"Better he lost it instead of someone taking it from him, or worse," Joe said as Sky reached the small ledge.

Sky explored the area for a few moments, stepping out to the drop-off point a few times before making her way back up the hill. Her climb back to them seemed to take forever, as they were eager for news. Even Sky's perfect features and dark red lips couldn't hide the lines of worry across her forehead.

She handed Joe Max's communicator. "They went in," she said glancing back down into the pit. "I think they were in a hurry to hide from the enemy and didn't notice the smell before they jumped into the water. That alone should have told them they didn't want to go in there."

"What does a smell have to do with it?" Jim exhaled.

"It stinks of death. It is faint from where I was, but it is there. If I could detect it from that high up, I am sure it is overpowering inside that bowl. Yelka, what kind of creature lives there?"

"Rumors are all I have heard. Anything that goes in is never seen again. That includes humans, elves, animals and monsters," Yelka melodic voice played a worried tune.

"How do we get down there?" Jim asked, fearfully rubbing his eyes with a hand while twisting his head in obvious worry. "I don't care about rumors. If they jumped, they could be injured."

"There is a trail on the other side," Yelka pointed. "It's a steep staircase carved into the rock, but we should get some serious weapons."

"Let's go take a closer look. If we need firepower, we can get them," Joe said.

Max awoke to discover he couldn't move. Not that he really felt like getting up. The urge to sleep was overpowering, but something had awakened him. A scream. Someone had been screaming. He discovered he couldn't even rotate his head but his vision revealed a dome-like chamber that appeared to be made of tree branches, rocks, and other debris glued together in some fashion. Rays of sunshine filtered down through cracks and holes in the ceiling, providing enough light to see by.

"Everything will be all right, my sweet pretty thing," a soft, kind female voice spoke and Max relaxed as if the woman's words rang true.

"Get away from me," Cindy shrieked at a pitch Max had never heard before. Terror filled her voice. "Aagghh! Leave me alone!" echoed in the strange chamber and then a wave of moaning followed. It was a hungry, wanting moan like a starving, beaten dog begging for scraps from its master's table.

Cindy's distress brought Max to his senses, the memory of what had happened on the shore flooding back to him. He tried to get up but found himself completely unable to budge, as if he were stuck in cement. His eyes flicked around to see he was in a silicon-like, transparent cocoon. The only parts of his body that weren't encased in the clear wraps were his face and his right hand and forearm. He searched for any glimpse of Cindy or Ell but with his head cemented in place, he could only guess at Cindy's location from her constant screams.

Max's mind raced for ideas on how to free himself. The fire spell danced through his mind but there was no guarantee it would work and it might ignite the whole place, killing them all. If he launched something, it might land on Ell or Cindy. His thoughts of escape stopped and fear replaced them as he caught sight of the most hideous thing he had ever seen. A giant zombie-like spider crept towards him. It was twice the size of Ell and moved on legs of rotting black flesh with pus and brownish liquids flowing from open sores all over its large bulbous body. Patches of brown and black spiky fur grew in some areas and clung like a loose garment in others. Its glossed-over eyes appeared as if they had cataracts, while giving off a strange light. The stench of foul decaying flesh like rotten eggs caused Max to gag.

"Awake, I see," it spoke softly, soothingly to him.

"*Prizgaj*," Max screamed in terror and a small ball of fire landed on the top of the beast's back. The fire burned and blistered the skin of the monster but it acted unfazed.

"Let's ease your troubles a bit, shall we," she comforted and her large fangs sank into Max's forearm. A cold numbing sensation spread from his arm to his mind, as she held tight for several seconds. "Ah, fresh young blood. Delicious. Soon you will be one of my own," she whispered kindly after letting go.

Somehow, she soothed Max and repulsed him at the same time.

Max awoke again to hear Cindy crying. The tone and pitch of her wailing had a creepy, spine-tingling moan to it as if she suffered a pain deeper than physical wounds could cause. Something was wrong, and not just with Cindy. Max was cold. Not in a way he needed a fire or additional clothing to improve his condition. He could sense his body was transforming somehow, as if a foreign cold liquid flowed through his veins instead of warm blood.

"Cindy," Max's own voice rang differently in his ears, as if his voice was mutating. The moment he called her name, her cries stopped. Max expected an immediate answer but only silence returned.

"Cindy!" he forced out louder than before. Even his breathing felt odd, as if he didn't require as much air.

"We're dying, Max," Cindy's sobbing started again.

Max struggled to free himself but his bindings held him trapped in place.

"We're…we're—she's changing us," Cindy's wept.

Fear pumped through Max's body with a slight warming effect. His eyes jumped to his arm. There were two decaying holes where the strange spider's fangs had bitten him. The black, blue, and green flesh around the wound showed signs of decay. Panic pumped through Max's veins like fire burning his desire to live as Cindy's words cranked his mind into action. *What do spiders do? They inject venom and drink the fluids of their victims!* His thoughts brought all of his spells to the forefront of his mind. There had to be one to help them.

"*Presilims se, Earthu!*" he screamed. The force of his determination and spell jerked him forward a few feet with a loud cracking and crunching as if tree branches were breaking under the weight of heavy snow, but his cocoon held. His energy spent, he fell back a few feet and settled.

"Mmm, yummy magical creatures," the comforting female voice rose from somewhere below him. "I haven't had such a treat in ages."

A clacking and creaking of joints passed close by and then Max's cocoon started to vibrate. "I see you need a little more tending to."

In his peripheral vision, Max witnessed a clear goo seep out of the decaying spider's backside as she repaired her web. "That should hold you, my delicious treat."

"*Premakni,*" Max screamed in despair, but it was only a word, there was no energy behind it.

Yelka guided the others around the strange hole to a set of steep sandstone stairs that descended between a deep crack in the mountainside. When they reached the bottom, they stood on a flat stone slab surrounded on all sides by the dark, sludge-like water. An old wooden rowboat floated at the front of the slab, tethered in place by a rope attached to a wooden pole topped with a sign.

The sign had been made from a flat piece of bark and fixed to the pole with a length of rough string. On its surface, a faded white message had been scribbled. They noticed the nauseating odor Sky had mentioned before their descent down the stone steps, but when they set foot on the landing, an overpowering stench clogged their noses and watered their eyes.

"You weren't kidding about the smell." Jim buried his nose in his elbow, bending his arm around his face.

"Yelka, can you read this?" Sky asked, staring at the writing.

"It is an old tongue in Svet, but it says, 'Keep Out, Payek's Lair,'" Yelka answered, worry creasing her brow.

"Who is Payek?" Joe asked, pressing a hanky over his mouth and nose. Sky and Yelka's ability to put up with the odor that had brought the contents of his stomach into his throat, amazed him.

"I am not sure if that is a name. Payek is an old word for spider," Yelka said, meeting everyone's stares, her eyes wide, and her skin pale and blotchy.

"What are the stories?" Joe asked, his words muffled by breathing through his handkerchief.

"She is more than a spider. She is very magical and controls an army of the walking dead. An army she created from her victims."

"And you believe these stories?" Jim asked, cocking one of his eyebrows.

"You cannot deny the overpowering stench of decaying flesh," Sky said, countering Jim's doubts. She turned her head back to the small rowboat. "I am the only one who should go in. If I chop off the head, the army dies."

"What?" Jim barked from under his elbow, stepping towards the boat.

"I think we should stick together," Joe suggested. "I can go back and get us some heavy firepower."

"I agree," Yelka nodded.

Suddenly, Max's *premakni* reached their ears, drawing their attention.

"Max," Yelka said.

"We do not have time to wait for weapons." Sky leapt from the rock and into the rowboat. In one fluid motion, she cut the rope and pushed out into the water.

The others raced to the edge of the platform.

"Wait," Joe shouted.

Yelka's hands jerked out to grab him. "Do not touch the water," Yelka stressed, her eyes wide.

"What are you doing?" Jim yelled.

"You would be overpowered," Sky called back. "You are not quick enough."

They watched her row in smooth strokes towards the opposite shore. The small boat glided across the slow-moving water, creating an ever-widening v-shaped wake. As the boat hit bottom on the far shore, Sky removed her jacket and adjusted an array of daggers across her back. She quickly assembled two swords that had been hidden inside her jacket. She whipped them through the air with the grace of a baton twirler and rose to her feet.

"I will be back," Sky promised soberly and stepped into the shallow water at the shore's edge.

Suddenly a twisted black mass erupted from the water, spraying foul liquid everywhere. Joe, Yelka, and Jim retreated towards the stairs reflexively as a hulking, moss-draped beast faced Sky. The moan that escaped its mouth launched a twinge up Joe's spine and caused all the hair on his body to stand on end and his skin to crawl.

Sky faced the thing with a determined smile and a gleam in her eyes.

16

Hudich in the Big Apple

Sky didn't flinch as she waited ankle-deep in the water facing the large beast. It stood half-submerged, its exposed upper torso giving the impression of rotting death, itself, rising up out of the water. With its head already higher than Sky's, requiring her to stare upward at the dead glowing eyes protruding out of its dead-flesh face.

With one long step, the green-skinned creature moved its cracked and rotting body closer to Sky by half the distance and rose farther up out of the water, moaning as if to curse the sun in the sky above. An excited smile spread across Sky's face as she watched the hulk lift its other leg out of the water to close the distance. Already in position for battle, Sky extended her arms, spun in the air like a top, and severed one of the beast's legs from its body. Without the limb for support, it fell face forward. Sky was a blur, whipping her weight around instantly in the opposite direction. With her blades still extended, the motion sliced off the monster's head. A foul, oily liquid issued from the beast's corpse as it splashed down into the shallow water.

The others had made it to the front of the slab, giving a brief, relieved cheer in support of Sky.

"Be careful," Joe yelled across the water.

"Hurry—" Cindy's father stopped short when he glimpsed the forest behind Sky coming alive with terrifying moans and activity.

Sky rotated the hilt of one sword around the back of her hand, flipping the blade in a large circle before catching it by the hilt. She inhaled and exhaled a quick, deep breath and sprang into the trees and thick undergrowth. Once she entered the shadow of the dense forest, flashes of creatures danced toward her from all directions.

An array of grotesque living-dead advanced on her, teeth, claws, and hands attempting to grasp and bite. Sky flew at them like a deadly tornado, her blades whirling and slicing. The slow, plodding beings, though they greatly outnumbered Sky, simply didn't stand a chance against her agile speed. Every swipe of her hands and arms cut down anything in her path, sometimes two or three at a time. Limbs and heads of Payek's servants flew through the air and their black oil-like blood oozed across the forest floor. With each blow, Sky's blade brought release from their horrible fate.

Few things ever surprised Sky, but the sheer numbers of those trying to overpower her, amazed her. After her initial siege, any normal life form would have realized they shouldn't mess with her, but these attackers showed no concern for their personal well-being and surged forward without regard for their life, such as it was. Sky couldn't stop for a second or she would be overrun. Her skill kept her enemy at bay, but how long could she last before growing weary?

A hundred yards into the trees, she spotted her goal about a half-mile deeper into the center of the pit. The strange timber, branch, and mud dome was clearly her ultimate destination, as it was the only structure in sight. Max and Cindy must have been taken there. With her new target located, Sky hacked and slashed with all her might, leaving a trail of dismembered bodies and decapitated creatures in her wake. Headless bodies oozing black goo.

Sky's speed and ability delivered death at every turn, and she broke past the lines. She hustled through the trees with the moans and wailing of her pursuers spurring her on. Swords at the ready, she sprinted at top speed, fully expecting to encounter more of Payek's monsters. Several times her race to the dome brought her on top of a straggling zombie that barely registered her presence before she cut it down.

After reaching the debris constructed dome, Sky noticed its architecture was one of logs, branches, bushes, and mud. She circled the structure, searching for the entrance, which she found located on the opposite side from the platform where Joseph and the others waited.

Before Sky could enter the basketball court-sized shelter, she encountered another line of defense. These new soldiers surprised Sky as spells erupted all around her, causing her to twirl and dance in and out of the trees, using the trunks to shield her from this change of tactics.

Sparks and fire ignited bark and weeds as Sky avoided the assault of the living-dead.

These magical things must be leftovers from Yelka's race!

Sky cast a spell that created an illusion of herself some distance away, and the trick worked, confusing the sluggish magical attackers. Before they had a chance to realize what she had done, Sky released them from their prison.

As she entered the dome, a gasp escaped her lips. She tried to catch her breath at the shock of the horrifying scene. A monstrous, sore-covered, pus-oozing spider, twice the size of an elephant, rested on a web that filled the entire dome. She lay above Ell with her fangs dug into his leg. It rose up, thrashing its front legs and hissing as it caught sight of Sky.

The web had several vertical levels like a parking garage. Max hung in the top level with Cindy on the level below him. The clear, thick strands held Ell in its lowest section. Its sticky surface contained an array of other life forms for its creator to feed upon.

Sky dropped and rolled to avoid another spell from a human-like figure to her right. As she sprang to her feet, she slashed through one of the strands suspending the web. The strand snapped back, knocking the creature off his feet. The impact distorted the crumpling body even more as it struggled to stand. Sky separated it from its head with another swift cut.

"What do you want here?" Payek asked in her calm soothing voice.

"I have come for my friends," Sky said, severing another support strand, causing Ell's body to drop closer to the ground.

"Your friends no longer exist. Only my children are here," Payek said as she climbed to the next level. "Surely you must see that."

"For your sake, you better pray it is not so." Sky shuffled to her left, slashing two more support strands from the wall.

Payek scurried backwards across the web away from Sky at a surprising pace. When Payek reached the spot directly beneath Cindy, she started to climb up towards her.

"Oh no you don't!" Sky raced into the midst of the web's strands and leapt onto a particularly thick one which obviously provided some support to the whole structure. She slashed at the support strand and the tension released, catapulting Sky through the air. Sky rotated her body in mid flight to avoid a collision with another weaving of sticky strands before landing higher up, on the same level as Cindy.

The surface of the web was like tacky glue, but not as adhesive as she'd feared. Able to free herself fairly easily, she dashed across one of the web's thick lines, cutting cross-sections above and beside her as she went. After every other section was released, the line on which Sky ran sagged more and more.

Sky reached Cindy before Payek could close the distance. The great, ugly beast hissed and scampered up to the top level. Sky's blades diced several additional lines above her head and the top layer shifted towards Payek. The sudden swing caused Payek to fall back down to the same level as Sky.

"Wh-what?" Max's shaky voice awoke to the sudden jerking of his cocoon.

"Max!" Sky shouted as she jumped to another main line on her right, opposite of Max. Slashing more of the web above her, she altered the balance of it again.

"Sky," Max voiced as if in a dream.

"Sky. Sky," Cindy joined in the chorus, her voice echoed with both panic and relief at the same time.

"I am here," Sky tried to offer assurance. "And I am taking you out of this place."

Suddenly, the moaning and wailing of Payek's army of zombies rose in pitch as they poured in through the entrance charging Sky.

Payek laughed a soft sound. "You will be one of my greatest children."

Sky smiled back at the beast. "It will be very hard to control anyone without your head," she countered.

Payek let go of the main strand she was holding and her weight caused the surrounding supports to give as well. Dropping to the next level, she snagged an angled strand of web that would carry her into the midst of her children. She used her mass and gravity to her advantage and zipped down the line at an incredible speed.

Sky sprang forward off her line, slipping down through two levels to catch hold of another angled support. Her blade swung up, releasing the web above her head. The recoil of the support shot her through the air like a whip at a downward angle towards the escaping Payek.

Sky released her hold on the falling support right before she overtook her target. Rotating her weight, her blades swung outward. The first took off the front two legs of the unsuspecting Payek, who tumbled face forward just as the other blade sliced off her head. The

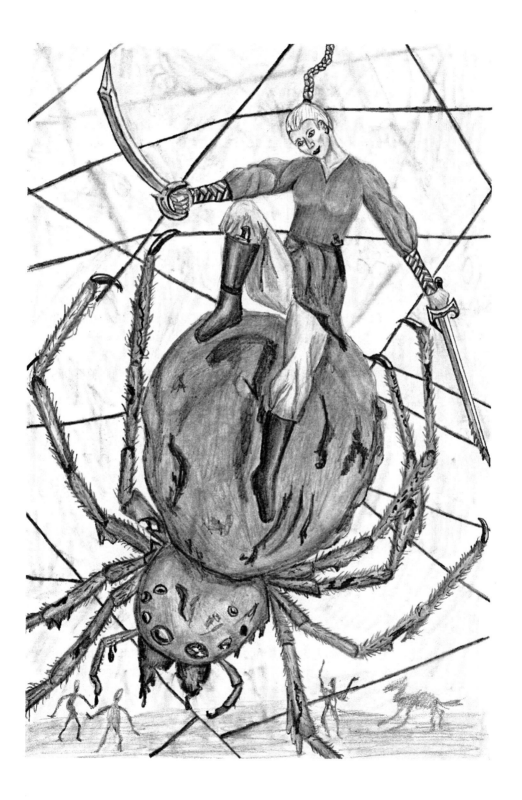

zombie spider's body smashed into the falling bodies of her "children," scattering them as if a bomb had gone off.

Sky hit the ground hard, shattering the blade of one of her swords on a stone protruding out of the dirt floor. She rolled to her feet holding the hilt of the broken sword in one hand and a whole sword in the other as she prepared to face the living-dead. But with the zombie spider dead, her controlling spell evaporated with her, freeing them to succumb to their deaths. In the wake of their fall, silence followed. The moaning, wailing, and cracking of the living-dead finally ceased.

"Sky," Max and Cindy broke the stillness.

"Sky, what happened?" Cindy asked.

"She is dead. Along with her army," Sky informed them. She withdrew her communicator and sent Joseph the news.

Sky climbed to the top level and cut Max free with her knife as Joseph, Yelka, and both Cindy's parents exited the gateway into the dome. "Help Ell," Sky called down to the others as Max fell into her arms. He wrapped his arms around her and hugged her harder than she had ever been held before. She could feel him shake as he wept. "I have you," she soothed and rubbed his back as a mother comforting a sick child. *I can't lose you. I will always be there for you!*

"Thanks for coming for us," Max said, wiping his eyes as he pulled away.

Sky refused to go back to New York until everyone was back at Joseph's.

It took them almost an hour to get the weakened Max, Cindy, and Ell back to Joseph's house. Ell was the most difficult. In his poisoned state, he could only remain on his feet for a few moments at a time. They finally got him into a makeshift bed made of blankets in the corner of the third floor.

"Everyone's safe. Now I can go," Sky sighed with contentment.

"What's the verdict?" Joe asked Olik as he and the others waited anxiously around the kitchen table. Soothing classical music played throughout the house to drown out the wailing and crying from the wall of night that had fully encapsulated Joe's house. Every light in the house burned to combat the ever-increasing darkness.

"I'm not completely sure. I don't think they will ever fully recover from the effects of the spider's poison. The fact she hadn't finished feeding on them seems to be what saved them," Olik said. His large, black, circular eyes looked at everyone in the room.

"What does that mean?" Rachel asked, voice tremulous with fear. Cindy's parents' pale, terrified expressions indicated their concern.

"Will they be—different?" Jim asked with a dark expression, clearly remembering the things he had seen on the island.

"Yes, they will, but I'm not able as yet to determine how. They are getting stronger as their bodies produce more blood. The fact they had been drained of so much is what weakened them in the first place. The magic of the spider's venom will have some lingering effects but with her death, she has no hold on them," Olik continued. "I believe the more time that goes by, the more they will return to their old selves."

"Are they at all like—like zombies?" Cindy's father finally put to words the horror of what he saw on the island.

"In a small way, yes, but not like the minions of Payek. Their wounds around the spider's bite are healing extremely slowly. I'm giving them the most advanced medicine in the universe to try to cure them and it is only yielding minimal results. I've also discovered a strange phenomenon in their blood. It's as if each cell has a life separate from the life they support. In a way, it's as if their blood cells would fight to keep themselves alive. Where if you or I receive a cut, the blood would just run out of us, theirs might actually fight to seal the wound. While we have platelets that help to clot blood, this is a passive physiological reaction. Theirs is active, almost intelligent."

"Do you think this will go away as well?" Joe asked.

"I do not know," Olik responded.

Kacha stood on the hill next to the demon's fork, sneering at Grandpa's town. He had been in great spirits until he climbed the hill to see the strange spectacle in the town. It wasn't the wall of black spinning mists that had engulfed Grandpa's house that had soured his mood, but the fact he had only managed to extract seven measly souls.

Dark storm clouds and a cool breeze, pushing over the mountains, added to his disappointment. He wasn't sure what to do next. He didn't know how the magic would react if he removed the staff from the ground. Would the magic stop its assault on the small town? He knew it usually ended when it had collected all the souls within its radius.

On the other hand, it could keep them busy while I go after the descendants. After the business at the library, he knew they too must be seeking these people and he was running out of time if he wanted to capture them. *My gateway is almost complete. I must hurry.*

A stiff gust blasted him in the face, ruffling his hair and causing him to tighten his jacket against the cold. *I wish I could wait till summer, but the sooner the better. I think I'll leave you in place, my sweets. Keep them occupied.* He reached down and stroked the crooked devil like fork with his hand.

A small flicker of light broke the night and Hudich appeared next to the body of his fallen servant. He kept his hood and cloak pulled tightly over his body as he kicked at a rat nosing around the body. Another blip of light and Alan stood next to him.

"What do you think, my lord?" Alan asked staring at the body.

"This is the work of Grd or Kacha."

"But the bodies are uneaten," Alan pointed out. "And I thought they didn't know any other magic but how to change shapes."

"No, he didn't eat either victim. Clearly, he's getting smarter and evolving." Hudich glanced down both directions of the alleyway and noticed a group of suited traders out for a smoke eyeing them suspiciously from the street. "I'd wager he lives nowhere near this neighborhood."

"You think he's covering his tracks? Why would he do that? Why would he need to? He can change his appearance to someone new every day if he wants. Why would either Grd or Kacha care about what people find? No one here is a match for them, except that old fool and few others."

"I think this one doesn't want anyone to know what he's up to. One of our old friends has the book we want," Hudich growled, crouching down, he reached with his clawed, black hand and twisted the dead man's head to reveal the mark on his neck. "He needs secrecy to build the gateway. I don't simply think it anymore, I know it. That old fool and his people did a good job of keeping it from us for the past eight months, but no longer. Put everyone on this!"

"Here in New York City!" Alan sounded surprised.

"Yes. I care not about witnesses. I want that book! With the book, we will have our gateway and the power to rule all."

Just then, another group of young suits appeared in the alley. "Hey yo! What you two freaks doing back here?" one cocky suit called out, his tone and harsh Bronx accent unable to hide his attitude as much as his expensive pinstripe suit did.

"We need to examine the location of the battle," Hudich said, rising to his feet.

"Hey, losers, I'm talking to you. Where's your ID? You're not supposed to be back here!" The suits behind him sniggered, but did nothing to retreat from the alley.

"Better call building security," another spouted.

"Yeah, that'll teach you for trying to sneak into our bank. Go try somewhere else with your little schemes, freaks!" the brave one stated, pulling out his cell phone and tapping in a number.

Hudich waved his hand and the phone flew from the young man's fingers and disappeared in the night. As he stretched forth his hand, the suit flew neck first into his grasp. Hudich clamped down on his throat and his eyes bulged with fear.

"Whoa," several of the others gasped.

"What the—" the others stated, stepping back towards the street.

"Listen to me, worm. I suggest you do your posturing to some lesser life form. I could snuff the breath out of you with the snap of my finger," Hudich hissed, leaning his face close enough for the man to see under Hudich's hood.

The blood drained from his face, "What kind of freak are you, man?"

"Run worm. Run now." Hudich launched the guy back into his friends, knocking them all to the street.

The men whimpered and whined as they scrambled over each other to get away. Hudich watched them flee for a moment, and then disappeared. Alan followed.

They both landed atop the building opposite the New York Public Library. They stood silently on the ledge observing the cars and people move below and taking in the general area. All the signs of the strange events that had occurred here over a month ago had long been cleaned up. All the windows in the library had been replaced and the smashed cars hauled away.

"His place of residence is close," Hudich's deep voice grumbled.

"What makes you so certain?" Alan asked.

"What would we do to anyone who got in the way of our plans?" Hudich asked.

"Destroy them."

"Exactly. They discovered something he was up to at this build..."

"Library," Alan added.

"At this library. It was obviously something he didn't want them interfering with and he tried to eliminate the threat," Hudich mused. "What is a library?"

"A library houses books, newspapers, and magazines on all different types of subjects. They also do other things as well," Alan informed him.

"Are there many libraries on earth?"

"Yes! Probably several hundred right here in New York City."

"I'd be willing to bet his interest here has something to do with building the gateway. Get people on it. NOW!" Hudich growled. "We need as many people as possible into this area. If there are as many libraries as you claim, then he must live in close proximity to this one. Have our people keep an eye out for Joseph's people as well. If they had a battle with him here, they are likely still in the vicinity."

As they stared down on the street below for several more minutes, something attracted Hudich's gaze. It was a familiar face from his past. Excitement flooded through him as he hopped back off the ledge pulling Alan with him. "I was right!"

"About what?" Alan asked, ducking low following Hudich's example.

"I see an old friend, standing in the shadows of that building below." Hudich's long crooked finger extended in the direction he had indicated. "An old friend who betrayed me."

"I'm afraid I don't have your vision, sir," Alan said, squinting to see who it was.

"Jax, that disgrace to my race and to his brother." The edge in Hudich's voice filled with malice. "Bring him to me."

17

Death in the Forest

Max awoke in a cold sweat. He jerked and slashed around as if fighting an invisible force attempting to hold him still, before he realized he was in his own bed. Even with the earplugs and the thumping of his heart in his eardrums, the wailing and cries outside reminded him of being trapped in Payek's web and seeped into his nightmares. The slight tingle in his arm and a growling stomach were the only sensations, other than the strange numbness, that told him he was alive. He held up his arm to inspect the bandage.

He breathed a sigh of relief and wondered how long he had been asleep. A day? A week? He cocked his head in his pillow to read 6:45 a.m. on the alarm clock. He swung his feet out of bed and put on some clothes. The fact his body obeyed his commands shocked him. He felt so weird, as if his head controlled a robot shell. Fear he might still be dying caused him to tremble and stole what comfort he had of being home.

Out the bedroom window, the dark eerie mists swirled and twisted over the house, giving him the feeling it was 7 p.m. instead of 7 a.m. He had lost track of time. Sky's rescue seemed like a distant dream.

He went downstairs to find Grandpa leaning over his and Cindy's mothers, as they huddled around the computer at the kitchen table. He couldn't explain it, but he knew Ell rested upstairs in the far corner of the third floor, while Cindy's dad sat next to a sleeping Cindy in the room just below Ell.

"Max," Grandpa said, straightening as he caught sight of him, causing the others to look up as well.

"Sweetheart." Max's mother raced to him, putting a hand on his forehead as if to take his temperature. "How do you feel?"

"A little hungry," Max said, seeing the worry on their faces. "How long have I been asleep?"

"Almost three days," Grandpa said. "Have a seat, and I'll fix you a nice big breakfast." Grandpa pulled out a chair for Max and then headed for the fridge.

Max's mother gave him a big hug and a kiss on the forehead before helping him into the chair. "We do have some great news. We've tracked down some descendants of Richard Burdick."

"Really? Where?" Max asked as Grandpa set a tall glass of orange juice in front of him.

"In Alaska," Cindy's mother added, keeping her eyes on the monitor.

Max swallowed a mouthful of juice and it took all his restraint to keep from spitting it out on the kitchen table. It tasted worse than a mouthful of puke. "Blah!" Max wrinkled his face and stared at the glass. "Are you sure this juice is okay?"

"I think so." Grandpa poured himself a small glass and tipped some in his mouth. "It's fine," he said with a wrinkled forehead.

Max's mother snagged the glass from him and sipped at it. "It tastes like regular orange juice." She pressed her hand against his forehead again.

"It must be the effects of the spider's poison," Grandpa said and brought Max a glass of water instead.

"Look who's finally awake," Cindy's dad said as he escorted Cindy into the kitchen and onto the chair next to Max.

Max fought back a smile as Cindy's mother performed the same ministrations as his own mother had done. "How're you feeling?"

"Weird."

"Me too."

Soon Grandpa had set out a huge breakfast for everyone. Max and Cindy found the only thing they could stomach to eat was the eggs and sausage. Everything else caused them to gag or heave. Max wondered if the spider's venom affected his appetite. While everyone ate, Grandpa told Max and Cindy about what had happened and how their fight with the Night Shades on the hills above Yelka's village probably saved everyone.

Grandpa voiced concern about the fact Hudich had been there in person. He explained to them how Sky had tracked them down and single-handedly taken down Payek and her army of living-dead. Max and Cindy received a lot of "I don't knows" about their condition and recovery. They were nevertheless happy to hear how Ell seemed to be getting better faster than they were. Grandpa informed them about Olik's theory on how it was Ell's sheer size and volume of blood that contributed to his faster recovery rate.

"What are we going to do about these Burdick descendants?" Max finally asked.

"Sky is on it. We know the family moved to Alaska in the 1970s, but we are not sure where," Grandpa informed them.

After breakfast, a fully-armed group escorted Max, Cindy, and Ell through the gateway for some fresh air on the hills where their adventure had started. Martin, Aunt Donna, and others were there waiting for them and gave them a hero's welcome. What Max really wanted was some time alone with Cindy to discuss the bizarre things he was noticing about his mind and body. But she beat him to the punch.

"We need to talk," Cindy whispered to him amidst the celebrating. Max nodded his emphatic agreement.

Brian sat in class, head resting on his thin arm, gazing drearily out the window at the steady drizzle. He was ten now, and had known he was different for almost two years. It had started with what he called his "wish gift" and an incident on his bicycle when he'd decided to ride full speed ahead of everyone through the forest. If he wished for something hard enough it usually happened, but it did have its limitations. It couldn't bring him money or things like that. It only affected the people, animals, and environment directly around him.

Thoughts of the first time still made him quiver a little, the fear he had when he rounded that bend of trees right into the mother brown bear and her cubs. He thought he was dead for sure.

What happened next still excited him today. *I actually communicated with the bear, and she understood me!* A smile twinkled in his eyes beneath his messy brown hair as he remembered pleading with the mother bear which towered over him ready to devour him in order to protect her young. He had begged the bear to spare him and even apologized to her. Suddenly, her manner changed. She stopped growling at him and cocked her head to the side like a curious dog.

He didn't know how he'd done it, but he spoke to the bear and she understood and obeyed him. By the time his mother and father had caught up to him, the bear and her cubs had wandered off the trail and into the trees. The fact he sat in the mud with tears running down his face alarmed his adoptive parents, but after he told them about the bear they wouldn't let him ride ahead of everyone again. He didn't tell them he'd talked with the bear, just that he had encountered one that left him alone. Because of their understanding expressions, he suspected they knew what had happened, but they didn't say anything.

Later that night, with a great deal of effort that ultimately resulted in a headache, he found he could get the family dog to do almost anything he wanted. He tested his efforts in the privacy of his own bedroom. Twice, his dad had walked in to see the dog doing some strange tricks but again he said nothing. He thought people might fear him if they discovered his abilities and so he lived with his secrets. Although his mother and father encouraged him to develop his talents and to not let anyone or anything get in his way, he kept them hidden.

Brian wondered if his real parents had the same powers and felt a twinge of sorrow. Even though he was only two at the time of the accident, he could still remember his mother and father. His adoptive parents were good people, who let him hang onto photos and keepsakes from his past. These items didn't tell him anything about any unusual talents or skills his real parents may have had. So in his mind, he viewed the abilities as special powers, which he surely would have inherited from one or both of them.

He returned from his reverie to the teacher's boring lecture. She had been going on and on about subject-verb agreement for thirty minutes and Brian decided that was long enough. He liked Mrs. Kelley Harvey but he hated when lessons dragged on, so it was time to do something about it. He had performed it several times throughout the school year and today seemed like a good time to befuddle her again. With summer vacation only weeks away, he'd no longer have Mrs. Harvey as a teacher. Next year, he would be spoiling a different teacher's lessons.

While Mrs. Harvey wrote examples on the chalkboard, Brian concentrated on the steaming cup of coffee sitting on the edge of her desk. In his mind's eye he pictured it sliding off the desk and creating a mess as it hit the floor. *Move!*

The mug jerked a little towards the edge, giving off a slight vibration that caught Mrs. Harvey's attention. She glanced over her shoulder at the desk. Her eyes floated over the objects on its surface before returning her attention back to the board.

Move! The cup of coffee wobbled to the edge and dropped over. The ceramic cup shattered to pieces and black coffee flew everywhere.

Mrs. Harvey jumped at the crash as did many of the other students. "Not again," she sighed as she turned to see the mess.

That should take the rest of the hour to clean up. Brian smiled to himself.

Hudich stood under the center of the stone archway built in the middle of Kacha's large penthouse apartment. The construction of it was perfect. It had all the same pieces as its predecessor on Kleen.

"I can't believe he's building it right here," Alan said, handing Hudich a jar full of tiny white orbs. "The hourglass is in the other room, it appears he hasn't entered the souls yet."

"And the book?" Hudich eyed the souls as they sank to the other end of the jar after he had tipped it upside down. When all the souls had collected at the bottom, he slipped the jar inside his cloak.

"I don't see it, but we will tear this place apart if we have to," Alan said.

"See that you do." Hudich ran a clawed, black hand over the smooth stone surface of the archway. "I want several people watching this building at all times. The minute he appears, inform me immediately. I will deal with him myself."

"Yes, my Lord." Alan bowed. "And Jax?"

"Keep him alive a little longer. He has given us a lot of good information. The tip on this apartment proved correct." Hudich strolled to the window and admired the view of the city. "It's nice what you can do to someone who has no record of existence in this world. It's like they were never born and you can just make them disappear."

Alan walked over to a laptop sitting on the bar in the kitchen and pressed the "on" button. "What about these people they are searching for? Do you think he's trying to trick us?"

"No, we broke him. They are real. It seems he doesn't know everything that old fool, Joe, is up to," Hudich replied.

Alan uttered a strange word and the password appeared in the correct spot on Kacha's computer.

"What are you doing?" Hudich asked joining Alan at the bar.

"Maybe his computer will tell us something of what he's up to. The keys are worn, he's been using it," Alan stated, pointing out the letters on the keyboard that were faded or almost gone.

Alan brought up a web browser and opened Kacha's viewing history, "Hmm, seems like he is showing a great deal of interest in Alaska. Even bought a plane ticket to..."

"Let me guess, Juneau," Hudich said.

"Yes."

"That's very interesting. What else does it show you?" Hudich asked.

"A family name..." Alan started to read the screen aloud.

"Lackey?"

"Yes," Alan's tone changed to one of surprise.

"That is very interesting indeed. He has been very busy poking his nose around. I sense his magic and it has greatly increased, but his thinking is limited."

"Yes, he's using the travel techniques of the general population, which is slow and clumsy." Alan continued to scan the files on Kacha's computer. "He's looking for the son of a deceased man and woman, who were killed in a car wreck, but I have a feeling you already know that."

"He's also taking pictures of himself," Hudich said with an evil smile as he stepped over to an end table and snatched a photograph of Kacha from its surface. "Not very smart of him, is it?"

"No," Alan agreed observing the photograph. "Perhaps his vanity will get the better of him."

"Pass out copies of these to everyone," Hudich ordered.

"Yes, my Lord. If he's traveling by plane, we could intercept him when he changes planes in Anchorage," Alan suggested.

"No, I'm curious why he would be hunting this human. Let's track him a while longer. Tell our people to be on the alert. He was able to detect those two buffoons before and dispose of them."

Even after a week, Max still felt . . . wrong. He had all his strength back, but an ever-present icy sensation dominated his flesh, especially his extremities. The sharpening of his senses seemed to stick out to him most of all. Somehow, he could detect things before they happened. He found Yelka suspicious when his and Cindy's blocking skills improved dramatically, but she only smiled, probably deciding it was just their normal progression.

Several days after transferring Ell back to Svet, Max finally got the chance to speak with Cindy alone. "How do you really feel?" he asked in a low voice as they sat on his bed playing a card game.

Cindy glanced over her shoulder at the open doorway before answering, "Different. I don't know how to explain it. I think I'm stronger and I know what's going on around better than before."

"Me too. I also have an all-consuming cold or numb feeling through my whole body. And this constant wailing and moaning from that mist won't let me forget about that horrible zombie army." Max waved a hand towards the window.

Cindy nodded. "And my arm, where that thing bit me—it looks like the flesh of her victims, dead, like something out of a horror movie. It's gotten better, but not by much."

Max glanced down at the bandage around his arm. "I know what you mean. Olik doesn't seem to really understand what is happening to us either. Or if he does, he's not telling us."

"Do you think we are dying?" Cindy whispered, leaning closer towards Max, her eyes wide.

"No, but I'm not a hundred percent sure we aren't partially dead either," Max whispered back. "Remember the burns on my back? They look just as bad as my arm but they don't hurt one little bit."

"Did Olik give you anything for the pain?" Cindy asked.

Max shook his head. "And the only food that tastes good to me now is meat."

"Same here. And only water to drink."

Max nodded and laid down a pair of sevens and mouthed, "Grandpa's coming."

"We've got trouble," Grandpa said as he poked his head in the door. "Come on."

Max and Cindy dropped their cards and followed Grandpa up to the third floor where Sky, Yelka, and Max's mother Rachel waited. Their drawn faces and pursed lips indicated something was very wrong.

"What's going on?" Max and Cindy asked as they reached the others around the control panel.

"Jax is missing," Sky said. "The enemy may know everything he knows."

"Jax and his men, or just Jax?" Max asked. An ever tightening knot spread from his gut through his body. Jax, the brother of Marko the traitor, had *disappeared*. Max believed, as did Sky, that Jax could not be trusted. Marko had almost gotten all of them killed two years ago, why should his brother be any more loyal?

"Just Jax. Two of his men are dead and the third just managed to escape," Sky said. "I have never trusted Jax, but the lone survivor claims he only got away because of Jax and that he put up a huge fight."

"Do you believe him?" Cindy asked.

"Yes, I do. I used magic to read the mind of the survivor while he was in a state of panic. He spoke the truth," Sky said reluctantly.

"Another note for you to remember when blocking or keeping the enemy from anticipating your moves," Yelka smiled. "A distressed mind is easier to read than one that is under control. It's because they allow their emotions to get in the way."

"Anyway, they have been to Kacha's apartment and the enemy is crawling all over the area. I pulled Jax's men back and only Finster remains close enough to keep an eye on things," Sky continued, interrupting Yelka's quick lesson.

"The fact they know where Kacha's apartment is tells us they probably got the information directly from Jax," Grandpa stated.

"Then he is working for them," Max erupted. "He's just like Marko."

"No, I believe he didn't give them the information willingly," Grandpa frowned.

"How do you know that?" Max argued.

"Olik has been in touch with our inside source. We know Jax suffered greatly before giving in to their demands. I know you don't trust Jax, Sky, but he was the one who helped us imprison Hudich in Pekel."

"Really?" Cindy cocked an eyebrow.

"Yes, really. Now we have to assume the enemy knows everything that is going on," Grandpa said. "We've managed to find a family of Burdicks in Alaska. Apparently the parents were killed in a car wreck in Anchorage and a baby boy of two was put up for adoption."

"Who adopted him?" Cindy asked.

"If you'll let me finish," Grandpa smiled. "A family in Juneau, Alaska."

"We do know Kacha is heading that way," Sky said. "We need to find this boy before he does and set some sort of trap for him."

"Which is going to be difficult enough without Hudich and the enemy getting involved," Rachel added.

"So what's the plan?" Max and Cindy asked together.

"We don't have one yet, but the first thing is to get up there and locate the boy. We have to move quickly before Kacha seals him away in an hourglass. Do you two think you're ready to go?" Grandpa asked.

"Yes. I am so ready to get out of this house," Max said.

"Go get your things," Grandpa ordered. "We'll be leaving as soon as possible. Sky's already got a place to stay."

Max could hear Cindy's mother starting to object about staying behind to help Max's mother manage the gateway, but he let his mind wander on to other things as he raced down the spiral staircase to fetch anything he might need on a trip to Alaska.

It was past midnight when Hudich and Alan arrived on Mount Roberts. They stood knee-deep in the snow, staring down at the city lights of downtown Juneau and Douglas Island. The last of the cruise ships drifted away from the city and out into the channel. High clouds hid the moon and stars as a gust of wind whipped their cloaks and shards of frozen snow blasted them in the face.

"I like this place," Hudich mused.

Alan put a hand up to block the blowing snow. "Why's that?"

"It's nice and isolated; we can do all sorts of damage and no one will find out about it until we're long departed."

"Very true," Alan agreed. "Our people are all in position, my lord."

"Good…" Hudich stiffened and cocked his head to the side as the unmistakable scent of magic filled his nostrils.

"What is it, my lord?" Alan asked.

"There is magic here, in this town. I can smell and taste it." Another wind gust yanked Hudich's hood off his head to reveal the smile on his black, skeletal face. His red rat eyes blazed with fire.

"What kind of magic? A talisman? A person? A place?"

"A person I have been looking forward to meeting for a long time. I can sense a small residue of his magic and it is extremely powerful. And knowing Kacha is looking for the same person in this place has really piqued my curiosity."

"A human?" Alan whispered.

"Yes!"

A foul mood dominated Kacha as he exited the plane in Juneau. He had been in airports for three days and the necessity to eat human food left him unsatisfied. He craved raw meat. With only a small carry-on bag, he headed down the stairs towards the exit. The day was gloomy and a slight drizzle permeated the air, causing Kacha to zip his coat all the way up and pull a hat down grumpily over his ears.

He hailed a cab the second he hit the curb and climbed inside. "Take me out the road."

"How far?" asked the cab driver, confused by the unusual request.

"Until I say stop or you reach the end of the road," Kacha snapped. He had studied several maps of Juneau and the surrounding areas and since food dominated his thoughts, he knew where he needed to go.

Kacha watched the landmarks, he had noted in his studies of Juneau, flit by the window as the cab passed the ferry terminal, the shrine of Saint Therese and the Herbert River. He knew this was where he would find what he desired and told the driver to drop him off at the start of the Herbert Glacier trail.

He slapped a large wad of cash in the driver's hand. "Can you pick me up in about four hours?"

The driver's jaw dropped to the floor of his cab as he peered happily at the sum of money. "You bet!"

"Good," he said as he closed the door.

Four other vehicles occupied the small parking lot as the cab drove away. After checking that none of their owners were around, Kacha found a thick patch of trees to shed his clothes. The cool spring temperatures bit his skin viciously as his body changed to that of a silver-scaled reptile. His forked tongue tasted the air through his hooked teeth and on all fours he stretched, digging his long claws into the muddy earth.

A wave of freedom washed over him and he took off at a sprint to generate some body warmth. His keen sense of smell told him where to go. He had so missed the hunt. The hunger for meat propelled him forward faster than any animal on the planet. He hurtled down the main trail letting his instincts lead him. Trees became a blur as the distance between his front and back legs touching the ground increased to several yards.

Even at top speed he could detect his prey. He rounded a corner flipping mud, dirt, and other debris as he spotted his dinner a short

distance off the trail. The massive brown bear had barely raised its head when Kacha slammed into him.

A ferocious roar echoed through the forest only a short distance from where the hikers had paused to drink some water and eat some snacks. The howl both terrified them and sparked their curiosity at the same time.

"What was that?" Nancy asked, eyes wide.

"Sounds like a bear fight," John responded as he reached back and took hold of the shotgun strapped across his back.

Mitch, camera in hand, took a couple steps towards the battle. "I say we go sneak a peek."

"Are you crazy?" Karen responded.

"We're heading that way anyway. We can't stay out here all day," Mitch pointed out. "Besides we've got a gun."

John checked to make sure both barrels were loaded and then nodded to Mitch.

"We'll wait here," Nancy said and moved to sit next to Karen, who had been resting on a fallen tree.

Suddenly, a high-pitched yelp rang out and then silence. John and Mitch looked at each other and then headed carefully up the trail.

"Idiots," Karen said as they watched them go. "What do you think that noise was?"

"I think one bear just lost the fight," Nancy said. "I don't want to be messing around with an angry bear even with a gun."

"Me neither. Besides—"

"RUUNN," Mitch's terrified voice triggered the hairs on Karen and Nancy's neck to stand on end. They froze, petrified to the spot until another deep menacing roar launched them down the trail.

They raced along the trail, splashing through mud puddles and around trees. They had only covered a short distance when two shotgun blasts preceded a scream from John.

"W—what's happening?" Karen whimpered as they dashed ahead, driven by fear.

"I..."

Mitch shrieked and then silence.

Mitch's cry sent them scrambling through the trees. The branches scratched and clawed their faces, slowing their escape. They screamed as fast, thumping footfalls drew nearer and nearer. Suddenly they broke through the trees and tumbled down the bank of the Herbert River and into the icy glacial waters. The current of the spring runoff carried them downstream.

Gasping in the life-stealing cold, they paddled quickly back towards the shore when they caught sight of the silver nightmare pacing along the bank, waiting for them to get out. It touched the water with its clawed foot and howled with pain. The beast continued to follow them downstream, jogging along the bank.

"Swim for the far shore," Nancy screamed.

"I can't make it." Karen's teeth chattered as she struggled to keep her head above the freezing water.

Nancy grabbed hold of the back of Karen's jacket and dragged her to the other shore, kicking hard under the water, using the current to help her. They staggered out of the water shivering and exhausted when they glimpsed the silver monster before it disappeared back into the trees.

"We can't go back to the car," Nancy said, coughing against the cold.

"Why not? I'm freezing," Karen stuttered.

"That thing is fast and it was moving in that direction. We need to head for Wind Fall Lake and the Montana Creek Road. We can warm up in the cabin at Wind Fall Lake."

18

Juneau

"We need to act now," Sky said as she entered the hotel room and threw a newspaper on the bed in front of Grandpa.

Max, Cindy, and Yelka rushed to look over his shoulder as he started to read the main article entitled "Two men killed on Herbert Glacier Trail."

> Two men were killed in an apparent bear attack on the Herbert Glacier Trail. Two women hiking with the men managed to escape by swimming across the frigid waters of the Herbert River. Police and the National Forest Service are still investigating the deaths, on the claims by the two women, that a strange, silver beast was responsible for the deaths and not a bear. Although the county coroner claims the signs are atypical of a bear attack, the police are not willing to acknowledge the presence of a mysterious beast.

"We've been watching the airport. How did he arrive without us knowing?" Max asked, pointing to the spotting scope set up by the window.

"He must have slipped through," Grandpa said. "With the size of the airport, we weren't able to get any closer."

"And this rain doesn't help much either," Yelka added grimly.

"We've got bigger problems. The enemy presence around here has increased considerably," Sky said. "We need to get these people out of here quick."

"How do you propose we do this?" Grandpa asked, skepticism and worry tingeing his voice.

"I think we should go after the boy and his parents directly. The enemy isn't completely aware of our movements yet. Let's use that to our advantage," Sky suggested.

"I agree. We don't want to give them anything they can use as leverage. What day is it today?" Grandpa asked.

"Thursday. That means he's likely to be in school," Cindy said, still reading the article in the paper.

"Do both parents work? Does he have brothers and sisters?" Max asked.

"He's an only child and his parents both work. I'll pick them up; you four fetch the boy," Sky said. "Meet me at the Mendenhall Glacier visitor's center." Sky pointed at the local map they'd studied earlier to ensure they all knew the exact layout of the area. Satisfied they all knew what to do, she went on her way and the rest of them gathered up their things in preparation for their own side of the mission.

They caught a taxi out toward Mendenhall River Elementary School. Reaching the general area, they got out and walked through the neighborhoods to the south side of the school discussing how they were going to try and convince the boy, Brian, to come with them. A steady drizzle dulled the colors of the moss covered houses and dense vegetation. The dampness penetrated Max's mind like dark thoughts speaking of dangers unseen.

Suddenly Max and Cindy froze, both of them getting a sensation simultaneously. "Grandpa. Yelka." Max whispered as loudly as he dared to stop Grandpa and Yelka from proceeding any further towards the school.

Grandpa halted and glanced in all directions. "What?"

"Did you see something?" Yelka asked, stepping back to them.

"Kacha is near," Cindy said in a hushed voice.

Max lifted his head and could feel it in his body. It was as if the air was telling him, or the rain was whispering it in his ear. "There are Night Shades too."

Grandpa waved them protectively into the pine trees. "How do you know?"

"Are you reading their magic?" Yelka asked with a curious expression. "Because I can detect some magic, but it's coming from inside the school."

"I don't know if that's it, but ever since Payek poisoned us, we both can . . ." Max met Cindy's eyes for a second, "sense things around us. It's been very accurate."

"To say the least," Cindy added. "For example, Kacha is east of the school. The Night Shades seem to be everywhere."

"I'd better warn Sky." Grandpa took out his communicator and sent a message. "Which of them is closer to the school, the Night Shades or Kacha?"

"Kacha is," Cindy answered with utter certainty.

"The Night Shades are holding farther back. They seem to know Kacha is here, but they don't know about us," Max added.

"At least not yet," Grandpa winked. "Can we move closer without being spotted?"

Cindy shrugged her shoulders but Max listened—to the rain? He wasn't positive—for a moment and then nodded tentatively. "I think so," he added.

The thick forest blocked their progress and it forced them to hustle from one section of trees to another. When they arrived at the front of the school, they paused to check things out. Cars occupied the front parking lot, but other than that, no one came or went.

Grandpa motioned towards the playground. "He must be going to make a grab for him during recess and we can't let that happen. We need to get closer to that playground without being seen. Can you pinpoint Kacha's location?"

Cindy and Max stared into the trees just beyond the fence that surrounded the playground.

"I make him out to be in the northeast corner, close to the road," Cindy said.

"Yes, I agree—"

Before Max could finish his sentence, a bell sounded and a huge mass of children poured out onto the playground.

"Come on!" Grandpa said. "I hope Kacha doesn't know what Brian looks like. I'm guessing he's going to track his magic. Yelka, we're going to need you to do the same."

"I'm on it," Yelka said and moved with determination to the front of the group, her eyes on the students running around and climbing on the playground equipment.

Max's heart jumped back and forth in anticipation. He expected a fight to break out any minute. He wondered what Kacha had in mind.

"You'd think he'd just spot Brian and follow him home," Max mumbled under his breath.

"What did you say?" Grandpa's mouth fell open.

"I was just thinking, why would he attack here in front of all these people when he could just tail him home and take him in secret?" Max stated.

Yelka and Grandpa exchanged a look. "I bet he's right," Yelka said.

"Still, everyone be ready to act. We'll wait for a moment and see what happens," Grandpa said.

"I'm amazed you thought of that all by yourself." Cindy smiled and punched Max in the arm.

"Shut it," Max smirked.

"He is still inside," Yelka said after a few moments of studying the kids and their activities. "The source of the magic is very strong and it is not outside."

Shortly after the current group of students entered the building, a second group rushed out to the playground. Yelka inched forward a few paces, her eyes locked on a particular group of children.

"Look," Cindy pointed to the fence on the northeast corner of the playground.

Kacha had stepped out of the trees. He appeared to be eyeing the same group of kids as Yelka. He clutched the fence with his hands as a steady rain replaced the soft morning drizzle.

Max's heart beat accelerated and his mouth grew dry. All the muscles in his body tensed in anticipation of a fight, but Kacha held his position on the fence, still watching the particular group of students.

Suddenly, Cindy, who had been in a crouched position, cranked her head around. Her eyes were wide and her face pale. "Max," she seemed to be seeking his verification.

"Ah, Grandpa," Max answered Cindy's unasked question. "Something really bad is coming!"

"The Night Shades?" Grandpa asked.

"It is the skinny, brown-haired boy with the blue jacket," Yelka interrupted, singling out a student in the group.

"Worse," Cindy added.

A flash of light illuminated the dull rainy playground, causing kids to shriek and scream as if a bolt of lightning had touched down in the center of them. When the flash faded, Hudich stood in the middle of the terrified children, his cape flapping in the wind. His black skull-like head with its red rat eyes sat on his broad shoulders, fully exposed for all to see.

He cocked his head toward the small boy Yelka had singled out. "Brian, it's so nice to finally meet you," his deep voice rumbled.

Brian fell to the earth in shock, his eyes wide and his mouth agape, the color completely draining from his face.

Hudich whirled around in time to block an incoming fireball causing it to explode into thousands of harmless sparks that sizzled and fizzed in the rain. A wall of steam appeared and slowly drifted away revealing an unharmed Hudich facing Kacha in his reptile form. For a brief moment everything stopped and then screams rang out and panicked children fled towards the school to get out of their way. Several teachers bravely rushed to the aid of the few straggling children, leading them back into the building.

"You must be Hudich," Kacha hissed his tongue flicking out through his hooked teeth.

"Kacha," Hudich launched a blast of power across the playground that knocked Kacha back into the trees.

"Come on," Grandpa said as the four of them hustled forward to reach the playground. Grandpa extracted one of Olik's guns from inside his jacket and melted a hole through the fence. They ducked through the opening, racing as discreetly as they could towards Brian who was scrambling on hands and knees through wet sand away from Hudich.

Kacha cast several more spells and launched himself out of the trees towards Hudich. With every spell Hudich had to block, Kacha got closer and closer to him. Hudich ducked and dodged and landed another blast, sending Kacha crashing into a jungle gym. Hudich then located the escaping Brian, who had managed to crawl several yards away.

"Going somewhere?" Hudich asked and sent an immobilizing spell at the boy. Brian fell over sideways into a puddle of water.

Kacha sprang forward, advancing in a tactical manner. Forward a few more sprints then left, leaping right, barely avoiding Hudich's spells, which threw dirt, gravel, and playground equipment everywhere.

In the commotion, Max, Cindy, Grandpa, and Yelka managed to reach the fallen and paralyzed Brian. Grandpa and Max carried him back towards the hole in the fence while Yelka and Cindy guarded their backs.

"The Night Shades are coming," Cindy called, drawing Hudich's attention.

"No," Hudich roared as his eyes locked on them. As Hudich raised his hands to attack Max and the others, Kacha reached him.

The collision between Kacha and Hudich carried the two twisting and clawing into the side of the school, the power from their collective spells collapsing a wall of the brick building. The roars and growls from the combatants filled the air, terrifying all.

With the rain growing heavier, the shrieks of the panicked students, and the battle raging behind them, Max and the others were able to slip through the line of Night Shades hurrying to help Hudich.

"Yelka, can you free Brian so he can run on his own?" Grandpa and Max struggled to keep him from dragging along the ground.

###

Sky hopped out of the cab and onto the sidewalk in downtown Juneau. She tightened her cloak around her shoulders to warm herself against the steady rain. Thousands of tourists busied themselves along the street and in and out of the various shops, eager to find the best deals on souvenirs.

Sky crossed the street by the Red Dog Saloon and headed for the shop she knew belonged to Brian's adoptive parents.

Suddenly a massive explosion blew out the front of a small souvenir shop. Glass, splinters of wood, bricks, and dust shot across the street. The force of the blast toppled tourists and set off car alarms all along the street. Frightened screams and alarms rang out like swarms of seabirds. *I'm too late!* Sky dashed towards the scene, dodging and weaving through the hysterical visitors that scrambled to get away.

She wound her way quickly through the crowd as six cloaked figures, faces buried behind their cowls, emerged from the damaged building, dragging Brian's parents bound and blindfolded. The abductors' heads turned towards Sky when they spotted her breaking through the line of fleeing tourists.

Spells exploded all around Sky, but she somersaulted, flipped, and dodged everything they sent. Four of the abductors carried Brian's struggling parents back in the direction of the Red Dog, while two attempted to deal with Sky.

Sky waited for Brian's parents to be dragged out of range before attacking the two abductors who remained, knowing she would not accidentally injure Brian's family. Regretting the damage, but understanding what she had to do, Sky launched one of them through the window into another shop. She dodged a spell from the second and was about to counter when two armed policemen hustled towards the lone cloaked figure.

"Freeze!" they yelled, guns leveled at the enemy's servants.

As he spun towards the officers, Sky bolted after the others who had taken Brian's parents. Fortunately, Sky's speed proved to be a big advantage. She overtook her prey as they bolted up the dock behind the town library. Deciding to risk shooting at them despite the presence of Brian's parents, Sky threw a spell into the group. The two bringing up the rear were propelled into the ones in the front and everyone's balance was upset; down they all tumbled.

Spells whizzed inches from Sky but she was too quick and evaded them with ease. The abductors scrambled to their feet and burst their way, with Brian's parents, onto a cruise ship as they blasted the panicked guards out of their way. Frantic tourists and cruise workers dashed everywhere to find cover from the volley of spells sent by the small group. Fire alarms blared as flames broke out everywhere in the wake of the fight.

Sky pursued them up several flights of stairs and down hallways. She forced her way into a cabin by breaking down the door in an effort to avoid a blast that flattened several fleeing tourists. For the sake of not injuring any innocent bystanders, Sky decided to remain on the defensive as far as spells went. She threw up several blocking spells and extinguishing spells, but refrained from launching a counter attack.

The battle moved out onto the upper deck of the cruise ship. Police and fire engine sirens rang out from the dock and street below. The group rushed around the side of the boat with Brian's bound and blindfolded parents in tow. Sky hurried to keep up and the empty deck gave her an opportunity to slow her targets. She threw several spells causing the group to stop and deal with her. They blocked her assault and then retaliated with several deadly curses that almost blew a hole in the top of the ship. Sky dove out of the way just in time to avoid being hit squarely with a deadly lightning bolt.

The group suddenly leapt over the rail and glided down to the top of the library a couple of stories below. Police shouted for them to stop while aiming their guns at the group as it hurtled across the parking lot on top of the building. When Sky reached the rail of the boat a dark smoke swirled around the group shielding them from everyone's view. The smoke slowly dissipated and the group was gone.

Suddenly all the attention went from the vanishing act to Sky as people began to indicate her involvement in the morning's spectacular destruction. Sky backed away from the edge and cast the disappearing spell.

"Who are you people? And what were those things back there?" Brian asked as they hustled him through a neighborhood heading east towards Loop Road.

"Believe it or not, we are here to help and those things back there are your worst nightmares come to life," Yelka said, jogging beside him with an arm looped through his.

Grandpa led the way, with Max and Cindy bringing up the rear.

"The fight's over," Cindy said, glancing back over her shoulder.

"Who won?" Grandpa asked as he ushered them across Loop Road and into a neighborhood on the eastside.

"Ah, neither," Max said as he ran. Another strange thought occurred to Max. They had been sprinting for several blocks now and he wasn't even tired. His legs still felt fresh and his breathing was smooth and relaxed. He wanted to ask Cindy if she had noticed the changes, but the way she loped next to him in a calm, easy manner, he knew she must.

"They're chasing," Cindy said.

"Who?" Grandpa asked.

"Not sure," Max stopped, and everyone else halted as well. Max noted Cindy's fresh state compared to the other three who held their sides gasping for air, confirming his suspicions about more affects of Payek's venom. Cindy stepped back towards the school, her head tilted sideways as if she was listening. Max detected a connection to the world around him as if it was an extension of his nerve endings. He reached out to trees and plants alike.

"I'm not sensing Hudich or any Night Shades at all. It's like they disappeared," Cindy said.

"Hudich? Is that the name of that skull-headed thing?" Brian asked.

Max could interpret the same information in the vibes passed along by the living plants. He could read the signs of the panicked teachers and children and then he could see Kacha in his mind. "Kacha's searching for Brian's magic. He's putting out feelers."

"My magic?" Brian said with surprise. "How do you know I have magic?"

"I can feel it," Yelka said. "Unfortunately, so can those monsters back there and they want you for that very reason."

"How can anyone sense magic?" Brian asked between gulps of air.

"I suggest we continue to the rendezvous point. Hopefully Sky is there and we can get out through the gateway," Grandpa suggested as he rested with his hands on his knees.

"We have to hurry," Max said, peering back in the direction they had just come as two cop cars and an ambulance sped around the corner towards the school, their sirens wailing.

"I think we need to keep out of sight. I'm sure most of the children heard who Hudich was after. That means the police will be searching for Brian as well." Grandpa straightened and escorted the small group north towards the Mendenhall Glacier.

They went as far as they could go through neighborhoods and up a small trail before they finally had to travel out onto the main sidewalk. Pulling their jackets and hoods up, they sprinted towards the Visitor's Center. Grandpa continued to lead with Max and Cindy in the rear.

"Are you sensing anything?" Max asked Cindy.

"No, I think the arrival of the police caused Kacha to lay low," Cindy answered.

Before they reached the Visitor's Center, they scurried back across the street and down a bear viewing trail. Grandpa guided them around the path to a spot where one could observe bears during the salmon runs. He took a seat on the bench and pulled out his communicator. "I'm getting too old for all this running around."

"Will you please tell me what's going on?" Brian pleaded with tears forming along the bottom of his eyes.

"We will, I promise. But first we need to get you to a safe place." Yelka put a reassuring arm around his shoulder.

"No. Now!" Brian's words carried a whole new form. It was not a request but a command. A demand with a wave of forceful magic behind it that was extremely powerful.

Max's desire to tell his deepest secrets and everything he knew built inside him like a volcano about to blow.

"Stop!" Yelka said, staring into Brian's eyes and the overpowering urge that had crept over Max seconds ago disappeared. "You must not do that. You will give away our location."

Max exchanged a worried look with Cindy. He wanted to ask the question but Grandpa's eyes were on Brian. Suddenly a vibration rushed through the forest. "Too late."

"What's too late?" Grandpa asked.

"Kacha located his magic. He's coming," Cindy added.

"I can see we need to teach you control," Yelka patted Brian's hand. The flushed look of mastery on Brian's face, when he'd demanded answers, had faded to one of ashen fear.

Suddenly, Sky materialized out of the forest behind them, "We have problems!"

"Where are Brian's parents?" Grandpa asked, rising off the bench.

"That is the problem. The enemy grabbed them before I even got there. We had a battle right in front of thousands of tourists. Then they vanished," Sky said.

"What happened to my mom and dad?" Brian started to cry.

"Ah, we need to go," both Max and Cindy said.

Grandpa tapped another message into his communicator and a few minutes later the entire group exited out of the gateway and into the third floor of Grandpa's house. Brian appeared to be in a state of shock, but Yelka did her best to comfort him. She tried to explain the situation to him as simply as she could.

Sky related to the rest of them what had happened when she went to find Brian's parents and about her battle with the enemy on the cruise ship. Now she looked more determined than ever. "What's our next move?"

"I expect we are going to get some demands from Hudich pretty soon. Some kind of a trade," Grandpa said with a frown. "And probably for things we don't have."

"Do you think Hudich knows Kacha's interest in the boy?" Sky asked, nodding in Brian's direction.

"Yes, he knew him by name and they knew where he was. He didn't seem all that surprised to see Kacha there either. This thing Kacha unleashed on us might be his undoing. It brought Hudich into the fray. It went from a dangerous game to a fight to the death," Grandpa said.

"What about the kid?" Max whispered. "What the heck did he do back there in Juneau? I was ready to spill my guts to him."

Cindy nodded. "And it was instantly powerful enough to let Kacha know right where we were."

"He is very magical and he doesn't know how to use it fully. You've been trained to focus your spells on certain things. He doesn't have that focus and his magic goes everywhere," Grandpa explained patiently.

"What do you think Hudich wants with him?" Sky asked, pacing the room.

"Leverage," Grandpa stated and walked over to where Brian sat with Yelka. The others followed.

"Are you going to help my parents?" Brian wiped a tear from his eye. "I didn't have a clue what I had or that others were out there like me."

"We're going to do everything possible for your parents." Grandpa squatted in front of Brian so he could be at eye level. "Do they know anything about your powers?"

"No," Brian said shaking his head.

###

Hudich stood on the balcony of Kacha's luxury apartment letting the cool evening air blow over him. He was in a good mood. He could feel his grip beginning to tighten around worlds everywhere. He had come so far in the last three years, and now victory was in sight. He had gained his freedom from Pekel and the collar. Now, he just needed a gateway to give him and his armies lasting access to worlds everywhere. He had always assumed it would be the old man's gateway until he had found those records back on Pekel. Now, if he could get the book that would show him how to harness the power of creating his own gateway, all would be under his reign.

"The child's parents have just arrived, my lord," Alan informed him as he joined him on the balcony. "What do you want us to do with them?"

"Put them in the largest bedroom and see that they are comfortable for now," Hudich ordered.

"Can you tell me what we need these people for? Who is this boy?" Alan asked.

"He is the descendant of a very powerful wizard from your world. I've kept track of people like him for centuries." He extracted the jar of souls out of his cloak. "I think Kacha discovered that magical souls are better for operating the gateway."

"So, you want to lure Kacha out with the child?"

"No, I don't really care about Kacha. I would have already killed him back in Juneau if I'd known where the book was. We can use the boy Brian in two ways. He can be leverage against Kacha to find the book, or we can barter his parents to get that old fool Joseph to find the book."

"So what is our next move?"

"Contact Joseph. Tell him we'll trade the boy's parents for the book. You can even throw Jax's name in for good measure," Hudich hissed.

"How am I going to get them the message with that thing in my town?"

"Go to Svet. Just you. Deliver the demands. I'll meet you back at the castle."

"And what are we going to do about Kacha and the boy when we are done?" Alan asked.

Hudich held the jar out in front of his face and watched the small round lights for a moment. "It seems we have a nice spot for them all. Not for just the boy and Kacha, but for all our enemies."

Hudich handed the jar to Alan. "Since we can't keep that with us on Kleen, put it someplace very safe."

19

Valuable Object

Rage consumed Kacha. The time for being the suave businessman was over. He swore in his wrath he would have his revenge on those who stuck their noses in his business. He would take as many of their souls as he could. Others, he would be just as satisfied with destroying them. This anger boiled in his gut all the way home. He knew they had discovered his secrets. Joseph and his allies wished to stop him from building the gateway. Hudich and his followers wanted to steal it. It was time to stop them all and his apartment was the starting place.

Kacha could sense something was out of place when he stepped out of the cab in front of his apartment building. Even with only the street lamps and cars lighting the night, he could feel eyes on him. They wouldn't attack him in the street. They waited in the shadows for their chance to strike. He glanced up at the building before him. *And in my apartment.* He seethed. *We shall see who is the hunter and who is the hunted.*

He had chosen a new identity for his return so if he kept his magic hidden, they would not know he was there until it was too late. His appearance now was that of an elderly man with a scraggly white beard and tattered clothing. He strolled down the street as if he was heading to another destination, leaning upon a cane to complement his disguise. He reached the end of the block when a spell revealed him.

Suddenly groups of black-cloaked figures hurried his way from all directions. They occupied the sidewalk on all sides of the intersection and several came from behind him. A smile twitched at the corners of Kacha's mouth. *They mean business, but so do I!*

Kacha cast a spell and a car approaching the intersection from his left spun out of control and plowed into the group of Hudich's unsuspecting minions as well as innocent bystanders. Kacha bolted to his right, dashed up onto the crashed car and vaulted from its roof over the surprised soldiers and spectators. Hidden beneath his loose pants, he allowed his legs to transform into his normal muscular reptilian legs. They propelled him forward at a rate unattainable by anything that might be following.

An assortment of spells rained down all around him, knocking over people, lampposts, and signs and disrupting traffic. Confused people rushed everywhere at the bizarre spectacle of colorful lights, sparks, and explosions. As glass flew everywhere, screams, crunching metal, and cracking mortar rocked the street. Kacha dove into a crowd and in mid-run took off his outer layer of clothing and changed into a brunette woman wearing sweats. He ducked between two parked delivery trucks and when he emerged on the other side, he walked back towards his apartment building, remaining as calm as possible, and hiding his magic. As he made his way down the street, he watched the spells trail the disappearing crowd around the block. He continued up the sidewalk until all of the obvious soldiers of Hudich had passed and then he turned and followed.

Kacha's forked tongue flicked across his hooked teeth as he pursued the straggler, a short, plump man who was having trouble keeping up with the others. *Vzame Duh!* The man jerked as if an electric shock had been sent up his spine before he dropped to the ground and the small marble-sized light that was his soul floated into a jar in Kacha's hand.

"What did you just do?" a terrified onlooker exclaimed.

Kacha spun towards the man and the brunette woman's face he was wearing transformed into his reptile features. A growl rumbled in his throat, which sent the man fleeing in his wet britches. After the witness left, Kacha lifted his victim into the bed of a crashed pickup truck as a line of police cars arrived on the scene, their lights flashing and sirens blazing.

Kacha hustled on, reverting to his woman form, steering back towards his apartment building. He jogged up the street to complete his disguise, running past the entrance and down into the parking garage where he ducked behind a cement barricade that separated a parking spot from the main exit.

He waited for a few moments before running feet told him what he already knew. The building was still being watched. These poor, unsuspecting fools had come to check on the strange woman. Kacha changed within the sweat suit into his muscular clawed-reptile self as two men in black attire hustled into the parking structure.

The attack was quick and deadly. The men had only a second to realize their mistake before Kacha ripped into them from behind. He hid the bodies in a dark corner of the parking structure. *There will be more.* He smiled. *I only need one thing before I go.*

From a bedroom of a vacant apartment building opposite Kacha's, Sky and Finster watched the two men hurry across the street. "I told you he'd be back."

"I told you I didn't want to bet against it," Finster chuckled. "The wager should have been how many of them it would take to stop Kacha or how long until Hudich shows up."

"Yes, those would have been interesting odds."

"Should we call it in?" Finster asked.

"Yes. Joseph wanted to know the minute we spotted Kacha. Power has become very important to him. We don't have much time before all the damage here turns this place into a crime scene circus."

"What are you thinking?" Finster asked.

"I'm wondering what could be so important to bring him back here."

"I agree. I don't think he is here to take back his apartment. You think he's after the jar of souls? He could always get more of those. Especially with that thing he can unleash on a whole town," Finster put his thought into words.

"There is definitely something he wants and it is important enough to take on Hudich's army to get it. I'm thinking it's time to take a peek in Kacha's apartment."

"You can't be serious. Hudich will have the place crawling with his followers."

"Yes, but at the moment, neither Kacha nor Hudich are worried about me. Call it in. I am going to take a closer look." Sky hurried to the door. "I will be back." She smiled and raised her eyebrows before leaving.

"We've got a message," Grandpa said, bursting into the kitchen where Max, Cindy, Brian, and others ate dinner. He turned down the music used to stifle the constant moaning so he could talk to them without shouting.

"From whom?" Max's mother asked.

"Alan. He contacted Yelka in her world," Grandpa said.

Everyone rushed up the stairs to the third floor where Yelka waited. She studied a piece of parchment in her hand. "They want a trade, of course," Yelka said as the group surrounded her.

"What for what?" Rachel asked.

"They want Brian to deliver the book and then they will release him, his parents, and Jax," Yelka said. "The good news is it appears Jax is still alive and they don't have the book."

"Is there a time frame and a location?" Cindy's mother asked.

"Three days," Yelka frowned. "They will contact us then and give us the location."

"What's the bad news? Besides the fact we don't have the book or a place to plan things around," Max asked.

"Do they know we don't have it?" Cindy asked.

"My guess is yes. If they got enough info out of Jax to track us down in Juneau and know Brian and his parents were the target, I'm thinking they've been in Kacha's apartment. Which leads me to believe they didn't find the book there either," Grandpa said.

"What is this book?" Brian asked. His eyes were red and puffy. Max assumed it was from a night of crying and lack of sleep.

"Something very evil, which will make things really bad for all of us, if Hudich gets his hands on it," Grandpa said.

"But I thought..." Brian started and a sniffle stopped him.

"Yes?" Grandpa asked.

Brian just shook his head. "I want my mom and dad back."

"So basically, we are at square one again," Rachel stated. "We have to get Kacha before we can deal with Hudich."

Grandpa took out his communicator, which had suddenly started to buzz. "It's Finster. Kacha is back in New York."

"Well, at least we know where he is," Max said.

"Yes, and I think we need to be in New York as well. We can't plan anything here. We need to be where things are going to happen and study the layout and get—" Grandpa looked down at his buzzing communicator again. "Hudich and the enemy have taken control of Kacha's apartment."

"When do we leave?" Max asked.

"As soon as we can. Go get ready!"

Sky reached the elevator in the parking garage to see that it had stopped one floor below the penthouse. Thudding feet forced her into the shadows as a young couple eager for a night of fun on the town bustled to their car. After the couple sped away, Sky pushed the button to call the elevator. To Sky's relief, it reached her before anyone else arrived in the parking garage and she tapped the button to floor 37—two below the penthouse.

The ride up was quick and uneventful but the higher the steel cage went, the stronger she could detect the presence of dark magic. When the doors opened, she glanced both ways before entering the hall. *How many are there?* The whole top floor of the building pulsed with dark magic, as if a strange cold seeped through the building, like fog. *They've thrown up a net for you, Kacha.*

At first she thought she would be able to track Kacha's movements by feeling his magic, but the power on the top level was so dominating, she was having trouble making anything out. She tiptoed down the hall, listening as she worked her way back and forth along the front doors of the various apartments. After making a couple passes up and down the hall, she paused in front of a door that emanated no sound. She took another quick survey of the hall before rapping on the door in a light tap.

After waiting several moments without a response, she took a deep breath. She focused all her energy on the door's lock, knowing she must not let her magic get away from this tiny area. Very slowly, she reached out with her magic, holding it under strict control. Even after hearing the bolts click, she maintained her concentration until she had reined in her spell.

The process lasted several minutes. Glancing in both directions before opening the door, she stepped into the dark apartment and pushed the door shut. She stood still for a moment while her eyes adjusted to the lack of light before checking the apartment for its occupants.

It was in the back bedroom of the luxury apartment that she found what she'd hoped for, a balcony. She slid open the window and peered up and down. A dark spot on the ground below her caught her attention. As it came into focus she could see a Night Shade observing the street.

As nimble as a cat, she slipped up onto the balcony's railing and climbed to the top of the building. She kept one eye on where she was going and the other on the Night Shade standing guard. When she reached the top, she sat just below the window ledge and pulled out her communicator to type in a message to Finster. The response was fast. **No one visible on the top floor. Be careful!**

The sensation of oppressive evil hovered over the top floor of the building like a crown. Sky pushed her magic deep down inside her, hiding it away from the world as she raised her eyes up over the ledge. She almost rattled the windowpane as she dropped out of the line of sight of a patrolling Night Shade.

She gave the patrol a few minutes to move along before peeking over the top again. The top floor of the building had a walkway with a large atrium in the center. In the dark it was impossible to see what lurked on the other side of the plant-filled glass building. *I need a diversion. Where the heck is Kacha? I thought he would have been up here by now.* Her eyes fell on an open window at the back of the atrium.

Before she could talk herself out of it, she hopped the ledge and slipped into the glass building. Without any light, the shadows cast by the plants and bushes took on monstrous forms. Several calls outside the glass structure forced her to wedge herself in a large, thorny bush. There seemed to be some excitement but not the full-scale battle she had expected when they discovered Kacha. *They must have found the bodies in the parking garage.*

A flash of light and a Night Shade appeared before Hudich as he sat upon his throne, head down in thought. Alan stood to the left and a few paces back.

"He issss backsss in New Yorkss, my lordssss." The Night Shade bowed.

"Do we have him?" Hudich grumbled.

"No, but he issss in the buildingsssss. Killed sssssseveral."

"I suggest you find him," Hudich lifted his head.

"Yesss." The Night Shade bent low and disappeared.

"Shall we go, my lord?" Alan asked.

"Yes!"

###

Two lifeless bodies with strange black marks at the base of their necks slumped in the love seat in front of the television as Kacha paced around the apartment. He could feel the wave of magic above him and it worried him. Finding a spot in the apartment kitchen, he determined he was just below his master bedroom, he transformed into his reptile self, stretching the sweats to their limits.

Kacha paced out the dimensions of the room above in his mind as well as he could. To represent the objects in his room, he placed kitchen items in specific spots. The table he arranged to represent his bed, a chair for his nightstand, another for his large ficus plant, a third for the main chest of drawers and the last for the armoire.

After he double-checked his measurements, he centered his efforts on the dresser. He mapped out its dimensions more precisely using other items around the kitchen. The rage that burned inside him drove him to focus wholly on his task. With the various kitchen utensils representing the dresser above, he stood on a chair, and with a marker he had found in a kitchen drawer, he drew a square marking out the area of the dresser on the ceiling.

With his target now depicted on the ceiling, he kicked everything on the floor out of the way. Then crouching, he sprang to the ceiling, sinking the claws on his hands and feet into the plaster and sheet rock above. His weight and strength ripped out a fair chunk of the ceiling before he toppled to the floor. This time he launched himself up and dug his claws into the floor beams exposed from his first attempt.

In four attempts, he had torn out a section of beams, sheetrock, particleboard, and wiring, leaving only the hardwood above. Voices and footsteps descended from the room above and the hallway beyond the apartment. The breaking wood and drywall caused by his destruction had alerted them that something was happening. He smiled at the thought of their confusion and leapt to the ceiling one last time.

The impact of his upward motion cracked the wood floor above and his claws and weight tore a hole all the way through right under his dresser. His claws sunk into the furniture, smashing it in pieces as he pulled it down through the hole into the kitchen below. A woman's scream rang out as he snagged the small gold item he had been looking for under a drawer.

The scream disappeared in a roar of spells and explosions that erupted all around him through the hole above. Kacha dashed through the apartment and crashed through the front door, knocking over two Night Shades waiting on the other side. People exited their apartments, startled by the disturbance as Night Shades shoved them aside to capture the fleeing Kacha. What was first curiosity changed into a full-scale panic as the people beheld, not only Kacha in his reptilian form, but also Night Shades.

People scurried back inside their apartments at the sight of Kacha barreling down the hall with spells chasing after him. He didn't slow as he sprinted towards a window at the end of the hallway. He leapt at the same instance a spell propelled him forward through the window. With wildly scrambling hands and feet, he managed to grab hold of a balcony railing on that side of the building. The force of the spell combined with his sheer strength ripped a section of railing away from the wall, sending debris to the sidewalk several stories below. He held tight as the torn-away section swung him out over the pavement between this building and the next, before swinging back again and smashing into the building.

A spell aimed at Kacha from above, destroyed the balcony completely and the whole thing crumpled downward and began to fall with high-pitched bending metal screeching and breaking bricks. Kacha just managed to catch his claws onto a window ledge further down, the building's base widening out on the lower floors.

The wailing of approaching sirens told Kacha it was time to change. He swung his feet onto the ledge and transformed back into the brunette woman.

###

Sky made no sound as she crept to the front of the atrium, always staying close to the next possible hiding spot. The door to the front of the glass structure was within reach when the first thud vibrated under her feet. She peered through the glass to see Night Shades running everywhere when another thud rippled through the air.

Small flashes of light appeared in front of the atrium that carried more Night Shades into this world. The door to the atrium flew open, and Sky dove behind a leafy palm tree just as a third thump rolled through the floor. The head of a Night Shade popped into the room and hovered as if waiting for something. After the fourth thud, the Night

Shade acted convinced it wasn't coming from the atrium and closed the door.

Sky stepped out from behind the plant when a loud crash followed by a woman's scream stopped her cold. A few more blinks of light and Night Shades rushed everywhere and then the sounds of battle followed. Sky waited for a few minutes more, listening intently, as the floor seemed to be clearing of all its occupants.

After not seeing any movement through the glass walls, Sky knew it was time to act. She opened the door to the atrium, verified no one was around and sprang into the apartment. She didn't know what she was looking for as she raced through the abandoned rooms. When she entered the master bedroom, the hole in the floor made it clear what the strange thumps had been about. *What was in the dresser?*

Sky hopped through the hole and began examining the splintered furniture. Cries and blasts floated through the demolished front door. A drawer off to the side caught her attention. She picked it up and rotated it all around in her hands when she spotted the small groove under and up against the center of the back piece.

"What's going on?" Hudich's rough, deep voice floated through the hole above.

Sky leapt to a position out of sight from the opening and tried to listen.

"What did he take?" Hudich's voice grew stronger as he moved towards the hole above.

"We are notss ccccertain," a Night Shade responded.

"Whatever it w-was, it must have been c-concealed in the dresser," Alan stated a slight stutter to his voice. "I assure y-you, we checked it and f-found nothing, my lord."

As the voices increased in volume, Sky started to back towards the entrance of the apartment.

"Did you see anything?" Hudich grumbled.

"No, my—" a woman's voice started.

"He isss on the balcony."

Sky eavesdropped a moment longer then slid towards the door and exited the apartment.

Hudich raced with the others to the side of the building. He sprang on top of the ledge and gazed down as Kacha flew out the window and snagged hold of the balcony railing. From the top of the building the streets were a swarm of activity. Red and blue lights flashed everywhere and encircled the building. Hudich raised his hands above his head and sent a white-hot blast of energy at Kacha.

The broken metal railing swung with the force of Kacha's weight, twisting him out of direct line of Hudich's spell. The balcony crumbled away and fell more than 30 floors to the pavement below.

"Will you go after him?" Alan asked, leaning over the side of the ledge to glimpse Kacha transforming into a woman and escaping down to the street.

"No," Hudich bellowed as swarms of people and police gathered around the building. "We need to figure out what was so important that it brought him back here."

"Yes, my lord," Alan said as they lost Kacha among the crowds of curious people.

"Do it quickly and get everyone who is not needed out of here. I want pictures and a hologram of his gateway taken," Hudich ordered. "Grab everything we can."

Max hauled his pack up to the third floor where the others were waiting. Yelka seemed to be explaining more about the gateway and what was happening to Brian. Grandpa busied himself by giving Max and Cindy's mothers instructions for the gateway.

"You will need to open the gateway for Olik. He'll help you get everything ready. Just wait for his message," Grandpa instructed.

"What's up?" Cindy asked as she arrived with her pack in hand.

"Not sure. Olik is coming to help our moms with something," Max explained.

After Grandpa finished his instructions to Rachel and Cindy's mother, he turned to Max and Cindy. "He went back to his apartment for something."

"What?" Max and Cindy asked.

"Sky has an idea and we need to move fast. So you two had better be ready to work," Grandpa said.

"We are!"

"So, you, Cindy, Yelka, Brian, and I are going?" Max asked.

"No, just Cindy, you, and I will be going to New York. Yelka and Jim will be taking Brian someplace safe until we have dealt with Kacha.

When we have the book, we'll get his parents back. We are just waiting for Sky." Grandpa threw a small bag onto the floor.

Before Sky showed up, Max's mother, Cindy's mother, and Yelka admonished Max and Cindy to do everything they were told. Max knew they were keeping something to themselves.

"Okay, what's really going on? Why are you all acting so strangely? What's the plan?" Max couldn't take it any longer and the questions just poured out.

"We are going to rob a bank!" Grandpa said with a wink.

20

Dealing with Kacha

Shortly after Sky had stepped out of the gateway, Grandpa sent Yelka and Brian through it.

"It is 11 p.m. I think we only have, if we are lucky, a few hours to do this. I am positive he will not wait very long," Sky said, looking at everyone in turn, checking their resolve.

"I agree," Grandpa stated. "I'm sure he wants to go into hiding fairly quickly. The sooner we can act on this, the better."

"So, how are we going to do this?" Olik asked. "We don't have the book. We are only guessing it is in the vault of Kacha's bank, and we definitely don't have the key. Since we've no hope of getting the key from Kacha, it feels like we only have half a plan."

"Would Hudich be willing to trade for Kacha?" Cindy asked hopefully.

Max rolled his eyes impatiently. "Hudich isn't even willing to swap Brian's parents. You can never bargain with the devil. He always has other intentions and he never wants to give up anything."

"I guess you're right," Cindy sighed.

"You have taught your grandson well," Sky smiled.

"Well, he is a little slow, but eventually he picks up on things," Grandpa chuckled.

"So, did you get the items I asked for?" Sky questioned.

"Yes." Grandpa unloaded a pile of gloves and ski-masks onto the floor from his pack. "Everybody grab a mask and a set of gloves."

Cindy picked out a set. "We're going in like real bank robbers?"

"Yes," Sky smiled and raised her eyebrows mischievously. "But we aren't going to be stealing anything."

"As for our plan," Grandpa explained, "we have a way to get Kacha out of our world, but we will still need his key to get the book. I admit we haven't figured that part out yet."

Rachel turned to face Sky. "I hope you are right about this. We could all get into serious trouble here."

"I followed him to the bank one day and he was very secretive. Also, based on the key-shaped slot beneath the drawer, I am certain that's why he returned to his apartment." Sky's tone was fiercely determined.

"Why the masks and gloves, though? Can't we just use the invisibility spells?" Max asked.

"Kacha is more powerful than you know. I don't think he will be expecting us. So, we have surprise on our side, but we need all of our energy in case we have to fight," Sky said.

"Where's Finster?" Grandpa asked.

"He and a few of Jax's men are watching the bank and will be able to alert us once we are inside," Sky replied.

"Once we are in, we must be careful. There are probably a million ways to set off an alarm. The masks are so none of our faces show up on cameras and the gloves are so we don't leave any fingerprints, so don't take them off," Grandpa said.

"How are we going to break into a bank?" Max asked.

"I think you are right, Grandpa. He is a little slow. The gateway of course," Cindy said with a smirk.

"Good girl," Grandpa winked.

"Remember you two…" Rachel started.

"We know. Follow orders," Max and Cindy sighed in unison.

"Let's get to it," Sky urged. "I want to be inside before Kacha gets in. That way we can finalize the plan before we have to execute it."

"Oh, you'll all need these." Grandpa handed them a set of Olik's unique night vision goggles.

Before Rachel switched on the gateway, Max and Cindy had to endure another round of warnings and cautions from their mothers about obeying orders. Max caught Grandpa and Sky chuckling as he rolled his eyes and exhaled in exasperation. Finally, when the gateway was open, Max kissed his mother on the cheek and tailed Grandpa and Sky through.

Max stepped down onto the marble floor in the darkened main hall of the bank. With the emergency lighting and the streetlights shining through the huge glass entryway Max could make everything out, but still he slipped the night vision goggles over his eyes. The bank went from semi-darkness to almost full light with the aid of the goggles.

Sky waved them over into a small nook near a window, and motioned them to get lower to the floor. She pointed to the various cameras mounted on the walls around the large room with its three-story pillars.

"You two will need to use that new sixth sense of yours. I imagine Kacha will use magic to get in," Sky whispered as she checked every direction. "Do you detect anything now?"

"Security guards, but they aren't in the main chambers of the bank," Max said.

"They are behind the cameras," Cindy added.

"Wait here, I will find the bank vault and the quickest way to it." Sky hurried off into the darkness.

Max and the others watched her dart about the main hall of the bank. She moved quickly but with caution, trying to stay out of the cameras' views. After she inspected the main hall, she disappeared from sight.

"What if he doesn't come tonight?" Cindy asked in a hushed voice.

"I've thought about that," Grandpa answered. "The way I see it, if he waits until morning when the bank is open, he would have to enter the bank as the man he's been posing as. If they check IDs and stuff, his information would have to match. I'm fairly certain Hudich knows what that man looks like as do his people. Kacha would risk losing the book then. No, tonight makes better sense. Get it and get out of town."

"Are we going to execute the plan before he has the book or after?" Max asked.

"I'm thinking before. At least then we don't have to fight him for the book. It can sit in this bank while we figure out how to get it later," Grandpa said.

Suddenly Sky appeared again right in front of them, startling Max and setting his heart jumping. Grandpa flinched and Cindy gasped.

"Sorry," Sky whispered. "I've found the vault. It is downstairs and it is laid out fairly well for what we want to do. Follow me. Step where I do and pay close attention for my signals."

Sky led them in a precise pattern through the bank, pausing here and sprinting there, always aware of camera angles and other hidden alarms. They followed Sky down a marble staircase with brass railings into a large hall with offices running along both sides. In front of the offices sitting on carpet were desks and chairs for customers to open accounts. A long strip of marble ran through the center of the room right up to the caged vault at the far end. Sofas and standing tables lined the walkway for those who had to wait or to finish last minute details for an appointment.

Before they could reach the vault for a closer look, Sky stopped suddenly and took out her communicator.

"Kacha's here," Max and Cindy whispered before Sky could read the message.

"You were right. Let's get ready," Grandpa said.

They hustled down to the vault to take a peek at the spacious room behind the steel bars. Each wall resembled a post office with square, polished, shiny doors of various shapes and sizes running from floor to ceiling. Each door had two keyholes that guarded the treasures held within.

"How long do you think we have?" Grandpa asked, glancing back at the room.

"He's not in the building yet," Max noted, head cocked to one side, listening.

"I hope you two do not mind playing the bait?" Sky asked.

"No," they both answered.

Even as Max said it, he couldn't believe the answer he had given. His mouth grew dry and his palms started to sweat. Although he had been in battles many times before now, it still didn't make it any easier and he had never purposely put himself in the line of fire. Cindy didn't seem to be too comfortable with the idea either as she fidgeted next to him.

"What do you think? This is your plan," Grandpa asked Sky.

"Max and Cindy, you hide under a desk close to the stairs. You might have to cast a few spells to provoke him," Sky eyed them through the night vision goggles.

"We can do that," Cindy answered and elbowed Max in the side.

"Joseph and I will conceal ourselves on opposite sides of the vault. With any luck, he won't be expecting us, so he might not be paying attention."

"If he comes after you, get up the stairs as fast as you can. We will have to time this just right in order to let a few spells make it down the hall," Grandpa said rubbing his chin.

"He's in the building now," Max said.

"And he's killed several security guards, if not all of them," Cindy added, fear causing her voice to tremor slightly.

"Get into position," Grandpa ordered.

"Don't use any magic until it is time. We don't want to give ourselves away before we have him," Sky stated.

Max and Cindy raced down the room towards the stairs. They found a section close to the stairs where two desks had been put together in an L-shape and decided to hide there. Max had to force himself to relax and he took a deep breath. Kacha was coming. He could feel it. If only they could get the key. To his relief, he couldn't see Grandpa or Sky at the end of the room, even with the night vision.

"What are you thinking?" Cindy asked staring at him.

"How bad I want to get the key. I mean, the plan is great and all, but if Hudich ever gets his hands on Kacha, the book could still end up on the wrong side."

"Do you have an idea?"

Max quickly explained his scheme to Cindy but the constant shaking of her head told him she wasn't a fan.

"What if it doesn't work? You could be dead or worse," Cindy whispered worriedly.

"I know it will work, I'm sure of it," Max insisted. "I don't think I can stand it for long, so you'll need to set off the alarm to the building."

"Are you positive?"

"Yes. So do you think you can sneak back down there without Grandpa and Sky knowing?"

"Yes!"

"Then you need to go now. I'm sure you can tell Kacha is making his way through the main hall. And Cindy, be quick," Max pleaded.

"I will, but I might be tempted to set off the alarm sooner if it looks bad." Cindy hugged him in encouragement and then scurried back towards the vault.

Max watched her go. She kept low to the ground and behind the row of desks so as not to let Grandpa and Sky see her. He swallowed the lump that had built in his throat. This wasn't the first time he had faced death, but now he was going to look it directly in the eye and give it a free shot at him. His mouth and hands were a complete contrast; his palms were damp with nerves, but his mouth felt as dry as a desert.

The hair on the back of his neck stood on end and he could sense Kacha approach the top of the stairs. The thumping of feet hurrying down the stairs echoed off the marble floor. He plodded along as if he didn't have a care in the world. He didn't even check the room, instead strolling straight towards the vault. Kacha hummed a happy tune to himself as he proceeded through the room.

He is cocky! Sky might be right. Pride could be his undoing.

Kacha walked right up to the bars of the vault. Max crawled on his belly to a better position from which to observe. He wondered if Kacha could detect his heart pounding through the floor as he lay on his stomach. Kacha spread his arms and opened his hands towards the bars. He stood without moving in the same position for several minutes when the bars started glowing red hot.

Kacha's body started to vibrate as the heat spread and intensified. Soon the bars were white with steam rising off their surface. Kacha's arms began to descend slowly to his sides. When they reached just below his chest, his arms shot forward and the bars to the door broke apart in the center leaving a large hole for Kacha to step through.

Kacha swung the key on a chain around his finger as he went straight to his box and slid the key into one of the locks.

This is it! Max climbed to his feet and crossed to the center of the marble walkway. He advanced several feet towards Kacha, who remained in front of a safety deposit box to the back right of the vault. Taking a deep breath Max pushed his arms forward, "*Premakni!*"

The spell slammed Kacha into the back of the vault and dropped him to the floor. He managed to hold onto the chain, which pulled the key from the lock. Kacha shook his head as if dazed and then spun to his feet jamming the key back into his pocket. Max ducked, letting Kacha's curse fly over his head and crack the marble stairs behind him. Max rose to his feet facing Kacha. The fact Max did not flee seemed to worry Kacha as he approached the front of the vault.

"Why don't you run?" Kacha said, ducking his head delicately through the whole in the bars.

"*Premakni!*" Max's spell caught Kacha right in the center of the bars with nowhere to move. Once again, his body collided with the unyielding metal lock boxes.

This time Kacha scrambled to his feet and jumped through the opening in the bars. He faced Max, his chest heaving with rage. "You're dead! *Vzame duh!*"

Pain ripped through Max's body and drove inward as if a swarm of insects were boring into his body. He struggled against an icy hand that had plunged into his chest and wrapped his soul in a death grip before

slowly beginning to extract it. Max's frame heaved and jerked forward, though he had the sensation of observing the whole scene from outside his body. Suddenly, the poison living in Max's veins came awake and every one of his cells acted as if they had a life of their own. Blood and tissue clamped down solid, trapping the cold hand of death inside him, refusing to let go. Everything went blurry.

Fear gripped Joe like he hadn't dealt with in years as he watched the scene unfold before him. What had happened to Cindy? Why was Max the only one who was acting as a decoy for Kacha? Worse, Max didn't run, he attacked. Joe froze as Kacha unleashed a vicious spell and Max lurched violently. Joe couldn't tell if he was dead.

Suddenly a flame erupted against the ceiling, setting off the fire alarms. Water poured down on everything as the siren rang out. In shock, Kacha released Max, who collapsed on the floor. Grandpa used the suffocating terror to unleash his spell.

"*Premakni*," he and Sky yelled at the exact same moment, lifting Kacha off the ground and forward through the air towards the staircase. He flew about a dozen yards and disappeared.

Suddenly, a sopping wet Cindy appeared beside them and they all sprinted towards the unmoving Max.

Deep inside somewhere, Max was aware of his body feeling encased in ice. His limbs wouldn't respond. He could hear his name being called from a great distance away. The voices carried a sad tone, as if pleading for something. It took a great deal of effort just to pry his eyelids open.

The faces of Grandpa, Cindy, and Sky came into focus. He could tell he was being held but something was not quite right about it. It was as if he floated a short distance above the floor.

"He's coming around," Sky said pointing to his eyes.

Max realized it was dark and his goggles had been removed as well as his mask. No one else wore theirs either. "W—what happened?" his voice sounded weak and hoarse in his ears.

"We thought you were dead, that's what," Grandpa tried to scold him. "What do you think you were doing? And Cindy, what were you up to? Where did you go?"

Max's eyes met Cindy's and he saw her face transform from drawn and concerned to a sly smirk. "Did you get it?"

"Get what?" Grandpa and Sky asked.

The smirk on Cindy's face grew to a happy smile as she wiped the water from her face and, Max suspected, a few tears. She held the key out for everyone to see. "Yes."

Kacha flew towards Olik, Rachel, and Stacey before crashing face first into an invisible wall on the third floor of Grandpa's house. The three flinched at the loud thud caused by Kacha colliding with the inside of the force field.

They stood outside it, around the recently moved control panel, and stared at Kacha. With the help of Olik, they had transformed the layout of the control panel and turned the gateway into a small prison behind the force field. Kacha and the gateway were the only objects inside the force field.

"Quick! Punch in the new setting," Olik ordered as Kacha climbed to his feet and shook his head to clear the cobwebs.

"Why is he all wet?" Cindy's mother asked out of the side of her mouth.

"I'm not sure, but we need to hurry. If they are in trouble, they may need an escape route," Rachel whispered back.

The gateway flashed brighter and changed its opening to a new location. Kacha paced around the gateway, jabbing the force field with his finger as if checking its strength. Each punch threw his arm away. He knelt and knocked on the floor.

"The force field runs under the floor," Olik said, approaching the transparent surface. "We made sure that protection was in place long ago."

"Where are you planning on sending me?" Kacha sneered and revealed his hooked teeth beneath his human exterior. Water dripped from his soggy clothes, leaving small puddles all around the gateway.

"That depends on you," Olik stated, shuffling back and forth in front of the force field.

Kacha's eyes followed him like a cat stalking its prey. "How do you mean?"

"Tell us how to stop the curse you put on this town. If you do that, we will return you to your own world," Olik stated. "Unfortunately, that's not where the gateway is open to at this moment."

"If I refuse?" Kacha snarled.

"Then I will have to demonstrate some of the unique features of this gateway. Did you know we can make it grow and shrink in size? We can make it expand to the entire size of the area behind the force field. You've got no choice."

"There's nowhere you can send me that will make me give up the curse," Kacha laughed an evil throaty sound. His face morphed to his reptilian self and he licked the air as if tasting their souls.

"Well, you see I happen to know a thing or two about curses. Namely, a curse only lives until it has fulfilled its purpose, or as long as the one who cast it is alive. So, in theory, if you are dead, the curse ends." Olik smiled back his thin-line smile.

"That's not how you people operate. You don't have it in you," Kacha challenged.

"Oh, you're right about that, we aren't going to be the ones to kill you. You are!" Olik answered.

"How do you figure?" Kacha's smirk changed to an expression of curiosity as his cat-eye pupils narrowed to slits.

"The gateway is now open to halfway down the street outside the front gate of this house. I believe that's your curse raging out there. Shall we make a small wager? Will it or will it not recognize its master?" Olik asked innocently.

Kacha glanced around at the blazing gateway a few yards behind him.

"I personally believe it will take the soul of anyone trapped inside the town and that includes its master. In fact, I'm guessing this is the type of curse that doesn't even know it has a master. It just fulfills its purpose. Actually, I'm surprised it hasn't found its way into the gateway already. We," Olik motioned to Rachel and Cindy's mother, "already have a bet going on how long it will be until it finds you."

Kacha fidgeted with his hands and the strange reptilian smile faded. It seemed as if he couldn't keep his eyes off the gateway.

"Rachel, increase the size of the gateway a little," Olik directed.

Rachel twisted a dial on the control panel and the gateway expanded slightly.

Kacha's head twisted back and forth from the gateway to Olik.
"Oh, a smidge more, don't you think?" Olik instructed pleasantly.
Soon Kacha's eyes were as large as saucers. "All right, I'll tell."
    "And I warn you. We have someone on the outside waiting to make sure you tell us the truth," Olik cautioned.
    "Fine!" Kacha breathed out in a long, drawn-out hiss. "There's a staff."

    Jim hurried as fast as he could towards the spot Kacha had designated. He had to jog almost a mile and a half to get to the hill where the demon's fork stood. He wiped the sweat off his brow as he gained the top of the hill, holding his side against the stitch aching there. The evil tool for collecting souls waited at the front of the hill as if watching the town. A glass jar, with a cloth covering it, hung from one of its branches with a handful of small lights resting on the bottom.
    Cindy's dad gazed down on the strange black dome of mist covering Grandpa's house. Even this far away, the chilling call of death's wail sent shivers up his spine. He reached down, grasped the fork with both hands and yanked it free. A shockwave spread from the fork across the town like a great blast of wind. Once the wind had covered the town it snapped back as if imploding into the fork. The mists drew back with a returning force that knocked Cindy's father to the ground as it impacted on the staff and vanished in a shower of sparks.
    With eyes wide in surprise, Cindy's father lay on his back clutching the stick. He carefully removed the jar from the fork and lifted the lid. "You're free," he said as a ray of light caught the freed souls and they disappeared.
    As he climbed to his feet, he broke the demon's fork over his knee and peered down on the town to see everything was as before.

"Can you move?" Grandpa asked.
Max tried to make his limbs respond without success. "No."
"What a wimp!" Cindy rolled her eyes.
"Hey, I just about died here," Max complained with a weak smile.
    "You are lucky I do not kill you myself," Sky smiled. "After scaring us like that!"

"Good luck. Kacha couldn't do it," Max laughed.

"Yes, but I know how to do it," Sky said, raising her eyebrows and sliding her hand across her throat as if severing her head.

"How long have I been out? And why are we not wearing our masks?" Max asked as he attempted to sit up but couldn't.

"Almost five minutes," Grandpa said.

"We believe Kacha disabled all the cameras and security alarms when he came in. You're just lucky Cindy went for a fire alarm instead of a security alarm," Sky added.

"Hopefully, they can open the gateway to get us out of here soon or we are going to have to avoid getting caught. With Kacha not around, I'm sure they will think we murdered the security guards," Grandpa stated, water running off his face and dripping onto Max.

"Ah, we might need to hurry," Cindy said glancing at the stairs.

Max couldn't sense anything there. He only felt as if he had been run over by a steamroller. He hurt everywhere. Even breathing took a great deal of effort and his chest muscles ached.

"Let's move out of the center of the room," Sky suggested and the three of them hauled Max behind a row of desks close to the wall next to the stairs.

Max grunted as they set him down and pain lanced through his body. "At least my nerves are working!" he stated as the water and the fire alarm stopped.

Grandpa checked his communicator. "No message!"

"It has only been fifteen minutes. I am going to take a look," Sky responded and dashed from sight.

She had only been gone a few moments when the lights came on.

"What are we going to do?" Cindy asked, eyeing the stairs and then the lights.

"Hopefully, we can get out through the gateway before we have to do something else," Grandpa took a peek towards the steps. "I don't know how long Sky and I will be able to keep Max hidden with our magic."

Sky flew down the steps and over to them, "They found the bodies and are calling for more backup. That should give us a little time, but when they arrive, they are coming in full force."

"You'd better keep an eye out, but be careful," Grandpa advised. Sky nodded before heading back up the stairs.

"Come on. Get up, wimp," Cindy tried to make light of the situation, but her drawn face showed the concern mirrored in her eyes.

"Don't worry, I'll be able to kick your butt any minute now," Max chided through gritted teeth.

"Should I go get what's in the box?" Cindy asked.

"You need two keys, so we are going to have to get it later. Let's just hope Hudich doesn't find out about it before we get the chance," Grandpa said. He checked the communicator again as if he could make it respond.

"They are coming." Sky joined them again and soon voices and feet running across the marble floors echoed around them. "Move back deeper into the corner," she whispered and they dragged Max right up to the edge of an office.

Cindy reached out and turned the handle to discover the door was open. "Quick." she motioned to the others as they hauled Max inside. Cindy managed to close the door as a wave of armed police officers rushed down the stairs.

They huddled down behind the desk and watched through the frosted glass wall as the police hurried about outside. The hole burned through the vault cage luckily drew the attention of the police, who gathered at the end of the room.

Their disbelieving voices carried through the door as the cops saw the melted bars. This was immediately followed by office doors crashing opening and then thudding closed, as the officers searched each office. The thumps grew closer and closer.

"If they open this door, use the invisibility spell," Sky whispered.

"Get ready, "Grandpa added when the communicator in his hand started buzzing. Everyone looked at him as he read the message. He quickly typed a reply.

"It will have to wait," Sky mumbled and they cast their spells and disappeared.

The door to the office burst open and three armed men stormed in, guns at the ready. As they made their way around the room, one collided with Max who was unable to move. The cop fell to the ground and then a loud crack followed.

"What the…"

Crack! Crack! All three men lay unconscious on the floor as a result of Sky's surprise attack.

"Where's the gateway?" Sky asked, appearing over the officers.

"Right behind you." Grandpa said. "Help me get Max through."

"What's going on in there?" A voice called outside the office. The officer rushed in to witness the backs of Cindy and Grandpa carrying Max's legs through the gateway.

21

Trades and the Uninvited Party

Everyone crowded into Max's room to watch Olik perform a thorough examination, anxiously awaiting the results on his condition.

"I'm afraid you might be bruised for quite some time because of the way your body heals now. Fortunately, the bruising only covers your main torso so it will be hidden beneath your clothes. It did creep up your neck and down your arms a little though." Olik said, holding Max's shirt up over his head as Max lay on his bed. Everyone gasped as Olik examined Max's purple, green and black chest and abdomen.

Olik had given Max a powerful pain killer that normally would have knocked out anything that ailed him, but it barely eased the sharpest edge of Max's suffering. It had just been a few hours since they had arrived home and he could now move all of his limbs, but the pain and joint stiffness inclined him to remain as still as possible.

"Well, you're not in too bad of shape for someone who's died twice in the last month," Olik smiled.

"Thanks," Max responded with a grin. "At least that wailing has stopped. When do we go back to get the book?"

Grandpa's brow furrowed. "I think we will have to bluff our way through this. If Hudich didn't know about the bank before, he certainly must now. Even if the news of a heist weren't enough to alert Hudich, Kacha missed a security guard, and reports of a horrific beast and what appeared to be a magical battle are already circulating. Hudich may be evil, but he's far from stupid, and if he's heard news of all the strange happenings at the bank, he will no doubt have put two and two together. That means more than just the police will be keeping an eye on that building. Our only advantage is none of them know that the book wasn't taken from the vault."

"What's our next move, then?" Cindy's mother asked. "And shouldn't we bring everyone back?"

"That's what we need to decide," Sky stated, leaning against the wall.

"I'm for leaving Larry and those losers in Mir," Cindy piped in.

Grandpa chuckled. "It would make things easier, I suppose, but I did promise Helaina I wouldn't do that to her."

"So, do you have any ideas?" Max asked, sitting up with a muffled groan after Olik had finished poking and prodding him.

"I'm hoping they will be willing to trade for Kacha instead of the book," Grandpa said. "I will make the point that we can't try and pull a fast one if we don't have the book in hand."

"How are you going to get Kacha to cooperate with that plan?" Cindy's mother asked.

"There are ways," Sky smiled slyly.

"Olik, do you have another collar ready?" Grandpa asked, rubbing his chin as he always did when he had an idea.

"Of course."

"What are you thinking?" Max questioned. "You can't hide the fact you have a plan with that kind of a poker face."

Everyone in the room smiled.

"I'm thinking *you* need some rest. We can talk more about our plans tomorrow," Rachel said. She started ushering everyone out of the room.

Max felt drained and sleep overtook him in a hurry.

###

Max awoke sore, but better. Even though it hurt to move, he didn't moan and groan to do it. He realized if he wanted to participate in any rescue mission or trade, he couldn't let on he wasn't a hundred percent. He got dressed and hurried downstairs, as best he could, to find out the latest news.

The kitchen was full. Cindy and her parents were there, as well as Max's mother, Brian, and Yelka. Yelka, who hadn't seen him the night before, rushed to give him another check up.

"I'm fine. I'm fine," Max forced a smile as Yelka began questioning and inspecting him.

"I'll be the judge of that," Yelka informed him with her sing-song voice.

Max struggled to maintain a straight face as Yelka squeezed and jabbed him. "See. I just need something to eat. Where's Grandpa?" Max sat down at the table next to Cindy.

"He's upstairs with Olik. They sent Sky on a little scouting trip," Max's mother said, placing a plate full of ham and eggs in front of him.

Max once again found himself wishing for some time alone with Cindy so he could discuss what was really going on and how he felt, but as usual, it would have to wait. He inhaled his breakfast and then he and Cindy went upstairs to find out what was happening. Sky stepped out of the gateway as they entered the third floor. The gateway control panel had been moved back inside the force field, which faded a few moments after Sky appeared.

Grandpa read a document that Sky had handed him. "It can't be. I refuse to believe it!" Grandpa's face was white and taut.

"What's going on?" Max and Cindy asked as they joined Grandpa, Olik, and Sky.

"Oh, Sky has been on a little scouting trip," Grandpa said, shaking his head as he sat down in a chair next to the gateway. "My old friend. I thought you were dead," he whispered under his breath.

"What's that all about?" Cindy asked as she pointed to the piece of paper.

"Oh, just a little confirmation on a suspicion we had," Grandpa smiled unconvincingly. "So, how are you feeling today?"

"Much better," Max stated firmly, hoping his resolute tone would be convincing enough. "Ready to help Brian."

"Good, because we need all the help we can get. Do you think the two of you can use the travel spell?" Sky asked.

"Yes," they both replied.

"You may need it before this is through," Sky said.

"I think we should deliver the message," Olik interrupted. "We are running out of time. We need to figure out if they will accept Kacha instead of the book."

"Joseph, do you think Max and Cindy can accompany me to give the message?" Sky asked.

"Huh, ah, what for?" he asked, seeming dazed.

Max wondered what had come over Grandpa. His usual jolly self disappeared. "I want to go," he spoke up. Max thought this could be a good opportunity to get some time alone with Sky and Cindy.

"Me too," Cindy added.

Grandpa, who acted preoccupied with his thoughts, sighed. "Very well. Go get your stuff."

Max, Cindy, and Sky exited the gateway on the borders of Reeka. Max and Cindy hadn't been back here since their trip to retrieve the medicine to help Grandpa recover from the poisoned knife blade after the Night Shade had stabbed him.

"So, who are we delivering the message to?" Cindy asked.

"The people from your town," Sky said. "You won't be going all the way in with me, but I wanted to talk to you."

"I kind of figured," Max responded. "What's up with Grandpa?"

"He just learned that an old friend he thought was dead is in fact alive. That friend is going to play a major role in the trade tomorrow," Sky said, motioning them off the trail and into the forest.

Sky led Max and Cindy quite some distance before finally finding a secluded spot with several large boulders and a fallen tree. Sky sat on one of the rocks and beckoned them to take a seat on the tree truck. "I'm worried this will affect your Grandfather's judgment. We need to come up with some options in case things go wrong."

"What do you think could go wrong?" Cindy asked.

"Yeah, it's just a simple exchange. No real power will be involved," Max added.

"You're wrong there. Brian is much more powerful than he realizes. Hudich wants him for other purposes. If I'm right, I can see the enemy inside Joseph's house with the gateway. That's what I want to plan against. If I'm wrong, no harm in being extra prepared, right?" Sky asked.

"True." Max agreed.

"We will need Ell. Do you think you can make a quick trip to Svet to explain things to him?"

"Sure. What's the plan?" Max asked.

###

It was late afternoon when they returned to Grandpa's house. Hudich, surprisingly, had agreed to swap Kacha for Brian's parents and Jax. The arrangement would take them to an old dirt road a couple miles south of town. Max, Cindy, Sky, Grandpa, Jim, and Yelka traveled to the spot immediately to get a feel for the layout of the area.

"We are being watched," Max whispered to the others as they all walked up and down the dirt road, examining everything.

"Of course," Sky smiled. "I didn't expect otherwise."

Grandpa appeared troubled and not totally focused as they meandered along. His response time to conversation took much longer than usual.

"Keep your comments and ideas until later," Cindy's father suggested. "We don't want to give the enemy any more to work with."

"Very wise," Yelka agreed.

Even though they mainly surveyed the selected dirt road, Max noticed that Sky scouted the whole area taking in every detail of their surroundings. Her head swiveled around like the eyes of a chameleon lizard. Max suspected there wasn't a thing she missed on the two passes they made. He tried to remember every possible thing he could, but every step still caused him some pain and pulled his mind away from the task.

Later that evening, they sat around the dinner table discussing their strategy. They knew whatever Hudich had told them wasn't what he intended, which caused them to look at things from every possible angle.

"I'm sure they will have people hidden everywhere, which means we should do the same," Olik suggested.

"That also means we need those people in place before it gets light," Sky added. "I would like to place Max and Cindy in the culvert beneath the road."

"What? That's right in the middle of the exchange zone," Rachel protested.

"Yes, but they are the only two small enough and young enough to fit," Sky countered. "And they would be protected by several feet of dirt."

"There was a culvert?" Max tried to remember the layout and pictured the dry wash bed running from both sides of the road.

"What do you think, Joseph?" Yelka asked, pulling Grandpa out of his thoughts.

"Ah." Grandpa twisted a map of the area around for a better look. "We could open the gateway here." He pointed to a spot on the road.

"I think that would work," Cindy's father agreed.

"So first thing in the morning Olik will bring Kacha through the gateway with the collar," Grandpa added.

"I suggest we move our people into position sometime tonight," Sky emphasized again and everyone nodded in agreement.

"Armed, of course," Cindy's father said.

After a lot of discussion, everyone finally decided on the best locations for Max, Cindy, and the others. Max and Cindy would be hiding in the culvert under the road as Sky advised. Everyone would be in their respective positions by 4 a.m.

Max lay on his back, finding sleep difficult to come by. His body still ached from the effect of Kacha's spell. He worried whether he would be quick enough after sitting in a drainpipe for several hours.

When the knock came at the door signaling it was time to go, Max doubted he had slept. He slipped into some dark clothing, retrieved the backpack he had loaded the night before, and rushed downstairs to eat a quiet breakfast with the others. No one acted as if they had anything to say about the upcoming trade.

As Max and Cindy were getting ready to leave, Max leaned close to his mother's ear as he hugged her goodbye. "Make sure Ell is ready," he whispered.

"Don't worry. I will take care of it. Be careful!" She embraced him tightly.

"I will." Max and Cindy went out the front door, down the walkway and through the front gate into the night.

Cindy checked her watch. "We've got about half an hour to get there. How are you feeling?"

"Sore," Max responded, but thought he felt ten times better than the previous day. "Let's keep out of the streetlights as much as possible."

"So, what did it feel like?" Cindy asked as they turned onto Main Street heading towards the opposite side of town. Normally, they would have avoided this side of town. Max still had vivid memories of the Zbal that had been sent to hunt and destroy him. Even now, with its occupants in Mir, the street gave off an unsettling vibration. The whole area gave off the air of a ghost town with active poltergeists.

"Like being run over by a semi-truck. Really, it was as if every blood cell and all the tissue in my body had trapped an invisible hand inside my body and that hand was trying to rip my soul from my chest," he said thinking back on the experience. "It wasn't anything I would want to try again."

"Doesn't sound like any fun at all." Cindy shuddered in sympathy.

"Definitely not fun."

They reached the edge of town and quickly located the dry riverbed with the aid of the street lamps. Risking a quick jaunt from the shadows, they reached the ditch and moved out of the light. They had only traveled a short distance up it when they both stopped and glanced at each other.

"You feel that?" Cindy whispered.

"Yep! They are out there but not aware of us, as of yet. Let's hope they don't spot the others," Max responded in a hushed tone.

They hurried up the small dirt canyon in hunched over positions, trying to keep their backs below the top of the ditch. With only a dozen yards left to the large galvanized tunnel, Night Shades moving up the road caused Max and Cindy to take cover. Max forced himself to slowly exhale the air in his lungs as his racing heart screamed for more oxygen to aid its beating.

Once the way was clear, they hustled forward and ducked into the opening under the road. The height of the culvert was tall enough for Max to sit on the silt-covered bottom without having to slouch. They decided to crawl to the opposite end, away from town, which was on the north side of the road. This would keep the nearest opening in the shadows of the early morning light.

"I say we stay close to the exit," Cindy suggested in a whisper that echoed and was way too loud for Max's comfort in the small enclosed area. "I don't want to be trapped in the middle if we are discovered."

Max nodded, hoping Cindy could see him in the darkness of the tube. As he sat, waiting for morning, he tried to be at one with his surroundings. He knew his and Cindy's new-found senses were the result of the spider venom, but were they spider-type senses or were he and Cindy in fact partially dead, and that put their spirits more in touch with nature? He wondered if they would ever know the answer.

Olik stepped out of the gateway with Kacha in tow. He wore his normal silver jumpsuit and had a futuristic gun aimed at Kacha's chest. Kacha appeared in his human form and wore a simple t-shirt and jeans, a far cry from the expensive business suits he was used to wearing. Encircling his neck was a round tube-like collar.

"Everything ready?" Olik asked as Joe shut down the gateway and the force field.

"I hope so." Joe blew out a nervous breath.

As the force field disappeared, they joined Yelka, Brian, Sky, and Rachel who had been waiting on the other side. Sky entered the room dressed for battle, covered in black with two swords strapped across her back, her beautiful pale skin contrasting with the dark clothing. She could have been mistaken for a ghost. Yelka wore her usual work dress and a cloak, while Brian and Rachel wore normal attire for the springtime.

"Are Jax's men ready?" Joe asked.

"Yes," Sky responded. "Everything is the best we can hope for."

"Only nothing ever goes as planned," Rachel pointed out.

"Let's get this over with," Joe said, taking a ball cap out of his back pocket and pulling it down low over his forehead. He then drew a silver laser gun out of the back of his pants and pointed it at Kacha. "After you." He waved his hand towards the door.

The small group proceeded through the house and out the front door.

"Be ready for any changes to the gateway," Grandpa advised Rachel.

"I will. Keep an eye on Max and Cindy. Those two seem to take risks I'd rather they didn't. I'm sure Cindy's parents would agree but at least they are there to help," Rachel said.

"Shall we?" Olik nodded towards the door.

Before they departed, Sky gave Rachel a hug. Rachel nodded her head as they released each other.

"What was that all about?" Joe asked, not having seen Rachel and Sky be that friendly in the past. Not that they were at odds with one another, but Sky usually remained emotionally detached.

"Um, nothing really. I just wanted to reassure her we would look out for Max," Sky said as she passed them to open the front gate.

They marched out in the open on the small town's streets, not trying to hide their presence. Sky, Olik, and Joe escorted Kacha out in front of Yelka, who walked with a comforting arm around Brian.

They reached the edge of town right as the sun peeked its head over the horizon, giving light and warmth to the small city. They followed the main road out of town and turned down the dirt road leading to the spot where they would make the exchange. The area in the low rolling hills surrounding the dirt road was fairly open, with large clusters of sagebrush growing everywhere.

"Ten more minutes," Sky said as they arrived at their designated location on the road.

Joe squinted against the early morning light from under the visor of his cap. He noticed Sky taking in the surroundings and possible hiding places for the enemy. The tension in the air hovered so thick it made it difficult to breathe.

"Everything is going to be okay," Yelka spoke to Brian. He had grown paler and began trembling as they waited.

It seemed like they had been waiting forever when the first Night Shade appeared on the road at the enemy's marked position. Suddenly more and more of them popped into view on and off the road, surrounding the enemy's position. A few minutes later, Hudich within his hooded cloak, Alan, and two Night Shades, escorting Brian's blindfolded parents, walked around the curve of the dirt road that had been hidden by a hill. They were followed by another Night Shade pulling an unsteady Jax by his bound hands. Jax had a bloody wrap around his head, which covered one of his eyes, and every visible part of his skin looked bruised and raw. Once, twice Jax fell to the ground and the Night Shade showed no mercy in yanking him up by his hands and dragging him forward.

"Here we go," Joe whispered to the others, inhaling deeply.

"Give Brian the key to the collar and send him and Kacha this way," Hudich called, his deep voice breaking the morning silence and rumbling over the hills. "We'll send Brian's parents and Alan will escort Jax. Once we have the key and Kacha, you're free to go."

"Like we believe that," Olik whispered.

Joe took a key out of his pocket and kneeled before Brian so they were at the same eye level. "Take this." Joe put the key in his hand. "Walk a few paces behind Kacha. Stay calm. We have people everywhere looking out for you and your parents."

Brian nodded.

Yelka, who still had an arm around his shoulder, gave him a squeeze. "You'll be fine."

Joe whirled towards Kacha. "Don't do anything stupid or we'll vaporize you without a second thought." He waved the gun for Kacha to start forward.

The two groups of people began walking towards each other. All eyes focused on the two small processions.

Max's sore body started complaining about its cramped condition not long after he and Cindy had taken up their spot in the steel culvert. He found himself constantly shifting positions to ease the aches and pains. He even laid flat on the dirt-covered bottom for a long time. Once the light of the rising sun spread over the area, he told himself he wouldn't be in the little tube much longer.

They sensed Grandpa and the others' presence right before the Night Shades and finally Hudich. They prepared to get into a ready stance to spring from the pipe, when they detected the Night Shades approaching from both directions of the wash way.

Max pointed to himself and the other end of the tunnel then at Cindy and the opening in front of her. Cindy nodded and Max crawled towards the other end. His muscles screamed at him and he wished he had sent Cindy to this end. His heart raced and his breathing echoed in the small tunnel as he shuffled along. *It's a trap!*

He reached the other side just in time to catch sight of a Night Shade ducking back around the bend in the wash. He could feel the people up on the road but couldn't tell how close they were to the center.

"Take off their blindfolds," Grandpa's voice called from above.

Max wiped his sweaty palms on his jeans and kept his eyes locked on the spot where he had seen the Night Shade.

"It is you," Grandpa's shocked voice rang out again.

"Yes."

Suddenly, two Night Shades sprang around the bend of the dried-up creek bed. Max didn't hesitate. *"Premakni,"* he yelled, springing out of the tube. The spell caught the unsuspecting Night Shades, throwing them through the air and into the sagebrush.

Cindy's voice rang out as she cast the same spell on the other side of the road.

Joe watched the two groups head towards each other, every step bringing them closer and closer. About ten yards before they arrived at the spot where they would make the trade, Joe called, "Take off their blindfolds."

Everyone stopped short of the rendezvous spot and Alan glanced over his shoulder back at Hudich. There was a tense moment of waiting when Hudich gave a sharp nod. Alan took out a short dagger and sliced the blindfolds off of Brian's parents.

Joe lifted his cap higher on his forehead to expose his face. A rush of disbelief raced through him as his eyes met those of Brian's father. It was his old friend. A man who had worked on the original gateway with him. A man he believed dead. *How was this possible?*

"It is you!" Joe said aloud as the two groups met in the center of the road.

Brian's father gathered his son in his arms and smiled a wicked grin. "Yes."

Suddenly several things happened all at once. Everyone in the center of the road turned to head back towards Hudich. Several Night Shades flew wildly out of the ditch on both sides of the road while spells began zooming everywhere. Everyone dove for cover behind mounds of dirt or clumps of sagebrush. Sky dashed from her position towards the center of the road, a sword in one hand and a gun in the other.

Alan kicked the weakened Jax to the ground and raised the dagger still in his hand high over his head. As he swung his hand downward to deliver the fatal blow, a spell from Cindy, who was still down in the ditch, knocked him to the road.

Suddenly, on the road between Sky and the small group, there was a flash of light and a second Kacha appeared in his lizard-like form. He wore his hooked toothy grin and there was fire in his eyes. A spell erupted from his fingertips missing Sky as she danced for cover.

"WHAT?" Hudich roared as he and Alan remained the only two from the enemy's side on the road.

"NOW!" Sky screamed.

Suddenly the human Kacha with the collar spread his arms wide and bolted towards Brian and his parents. The impact of his collision threw them off the road over the ditch, where they fell and vanished in the air. The human Kacha then whirled around, scooped up Jax in his arms and leapt from the road right where Brian and his parents had disappeared. They, too, evaporated from sight.

22

Showdown

A surprised Brian and his parents landed on the third floor of Grandpa's house. They didn't even have a chance to gather their bearings when Grd and Jax came through the gateway and knocked them down again. Rachel held her communicator in one hand and controlled the gateway with the other. She shut down everything so everyone could move out of the force field.

"We need to hurry. They will need the gateway soon. Grd, take Jax to a bed. You three will just have to hang around until everyone returns," Rachel directed.

They wore shocked expressions, but Rachel didn't have time to explain anything, as she rushed back to the control panel and turned everything back on. The large old-fashioned mirror began to revolve and in a matter of minutes, it once again became the ball of light that was the gateway.

###

Kacha roared with rage as Brian, his parents, Grd, and Jax disappeared through the gateway. He broke after them and dove to the spot they had vanished, but the gateway had closed. He landed hard in the dirt beneath.

Kacha impacted the bottom of the ditch in a cloud of dust out in front of Max. Spells and gunfire continued to echo through the air all around them as Kacha rolled back to his feet. Max felt it coming before Kacha sent it.

"*Oviraj!*" Max blocked Kacha's first spell.

"*Oviraj!*" The second ricocheted away, but the force of the impact of Kacha's spell with Max's smashed Max into the hill on the side of the road, knocking the wind from him. The third spell caught him full on. His already sore body burned with fire, causing Max to cry out.

A black blur with slashing silver rained down on Kacha and the two of them tumbled to the ground in a tangle of black and gray. Kacha howled with fury as Sky sliced a deep gash in his left thigh. Sky danced away from Kacha's gnashing teeth and slashing claws as the two faced each other. Fire and sparks flew as magic, swords, and claws clashed, each in an effort to overcome the other. Max struggled to his feet. His movements were slow and painful. He wanted to help. He desired to fight, but his body wasn't functioning correctly. The risk that a spell might catch Sky was too great.

Suddenly a blast from Kacha caught Sky square in the chest, driving her back through the air and pinning her to the ground. Kacha raced forward, claws and teeth ready as he fell upon on her.

"*Premakni!*" Max screamed. The spell threw Kacha from the ditch just before he could grasp Sky in his claws and teeth.

Sky jumped up and turned to Max. "My thanks," she said, rushing to him and snagging him right before he toppled over. "Where is Cindy?"

"She's on the other end." Max pointed to the culvert, gasping for breath.

"Do you think you can make it through the pipe on your own?" Sky asked. Her eyes darted everywhere in search of an attack.

"I'll try." Max dragged himself to his feet.

"Go. I won't leave until you make it to the other side," Sky ordered.

Max, against all the complaining of his body, crawled into the culvert again.

After Cindy attacked the unsuspecting Night Shades, she glanced back to see she was below the group up on the road. She watched in horror as everyone seemed to be moving without a fight back towards Hudich. *Sky was right!*

Alan kicked the already injured Jax who crumpled from the blow and then raised his hand, exposing the dagger. He tried to deliver Jax's death sentence, but Cindy sprang into action. *"Premakni!"* she called and blasted the unsuspecting Alan to the road.

Grd managed to get everyone into the gateway when Alan spun on Cindy. Cindy dropped to the side of the hill as a wave of extreme heat flew over her. Letting gravity take her, she rolled down the hill, avoiding a ray of energy that tore a hole in the ground where she had been standing. Before Alan could give chase, spells and gunfire broke out giving him no option but to flee for cover.

Cindy found herself back in the ditch and decided it was the safest place to be. The power of the spells and the blasts from the guns were just too overwhelming for her. Dust and debris flew and crashed everywhere. She took up a position where she could guard against anyone coming down the ditch towards her and still keep herself shielded from their view. From her vantage point, Cindy sent three Night Shades flying as they tried to leap across the ditch at a narrow spot.

"Prizgaj," a familiar voice called from out of the metal pipe and then a roar of anger rang out as Max ignited a Night Shade who had sneaked around behind Cindy.

"Max!" Cindy raced to him. "Are you all right?"

He staggered as if he would fall over from pain and exhaustion any second, but replied, "Yes. I think we need to get out of this ditch. If they want to, they could trap us pretty easily in here."

Cindy agreed. "Do you need help?"

"No, but we're going to have to move slowly."

They worked their way through the ditch, trying to spot a good exit point. Right before they rounded a bend, they both froze and glanced at each other knowingly.

"They're waiting," Cindy mouthed.

Max nodded and pointed to the side of the ditch where a large section of sagebrush grew. They started to climb from the ditch when a high, piercing shriek from above drew their attention. A chill ran over Max's skin as he recognized the call of the winged black gargoyle-like creatures he had first encountered on Tabor. Max and Cindy dropped back into the ditch and started casting spells at the new terror from above.

Joe's stomach continued to do back flips as he, Olik, and Yelka jumped off the road in search of cover. They rushed behind a large pile of dirt with dry weeds growing out of it. His old friend was alive and somehow he had adopted a very powerful wizard. The wall of I-don't-believe-it started to crash before him as the impossible coincidences continued to hammer away at it.

"You guard our backs, I'll protect the front," Joe shouted over the tumult of the full-fledged battle being waged, and crawled on his belly to the top of the mound.

Spells smashed sections of the dirt pile away as Joe peered over the top, squinting to avoid getting dirt in his eyes. Night Shades and Jax's men engaged each other in an all-out war. Night Shades would send a barrage of spells while Jax's men attacked with laser blasts and other weapons.

Joe saw Sky dive off the road after Kacha. Clouds of dust and flying sparks indicated a fight was taking place just below his line of sight. *Run Max! Run Cindy! You can't beat him!*

Alan scrambled for cover but Hudich stood like an immovable force in the middle of the road, launching his deadly assault on any who dared oppose him. One moment he blocked laser blasts from Jax's men, the next he burned a whole section of sagebrush to the ground, exposing them to attack.

Without warning, Joe, Olik, and Yelka came under bombardment from Night Shades' curses and slashing claws from the air as the black-winged beasts swooped down on them. Joe rolled onto his back and started shooting at the descending animals, which viciously tore and clawed at them. His heart raced and the feeling of being in a small boat taking on too much water crept over him. Olik had also dropped to his back to keep from being grabbed from behind. Yelka used her magic to hold them at bay as she put up a wall of fire around her.

The constant dive-bombing from above sapped Max's energy. He gulped air with great difficulty and sweat poured off him. Each new attempt from the black-winged devils brought their sharp claws closer to him and Cindy. At first, his spells landed punishing blows to his enemy, but now they were just delaying the inevitable, and he wanted to cry, to give up, but knew he couldn't. Fear of Hudich winning it all pushed him to fight on.

Max couldn't see Cindy, but could hear her screaming and casting spells nearby. By the tone of her voice, he sensed she was losing ground as well. Desperation seized him and he tried to locate her amidst the constant assault. Out of the corner of his eye, he spotted her fending off attackers.

Suddenly howls of agony from the throats of the winged nightmares to his right caught his attention. Sky was there, tearing into the gargoyle-like beasts with the fury of a mother bear defending her cubs. Her sword was a constant silver blur flashing pieces of sunlight in all directions as it cut down the enemy.

Pain erupted in Max's thigh as a flying menace raked him with its claws an instant before Sky split it in two. Max couldn't stop the horror or the gagging in the back of his throat at the sight of the almost black blood that oozed from the wound.

With no time to stop to check on him, Sky twirled past and on towards Cindy. A few minutes later, Cindy and a protective Sky were at his side. Cindy helped him bind his leg while Sky fought off more attackers.

"We need to fall back to Joseph," Sky said, crippling a winged devil that ventured too close.

"Where are they?" Cindy lifted Max to his feet.

"About a hundred yards down the road behind a large dirt pile." Sky pointed. She sprang from the ditch and leaned over to pull Max and Cindy up.

Max managed to regain some small amount of energy from the short break in the action under Sky's protection. The second they made it out of the ditch, his new sense screamed its warning. Both he and Cindy threw up the blocking spell but Hudich's curse pulsed with enormous power. The impact of the collision, although somewhat shielded by their spells, threw them into Sky and the three of them went down. Sagebrush scratched and cut them as Hudich's curse forced them through the branches.

The air assault began anew the instant they hit the ground, but Sky put an end to the gargoyles' fruitless attempts. The three of them could no longer use the sagebrush to hide from Hudich's spells with the constant ring of flying creatures following their every step. It was as if they sprinted through a minefield. Spell after spell erupted earth, rocks, and plants all around them as they tried to stay a few steps ahead of the bombardment. Max's lungs burned inside his chest, but he kept running towards the dirt pile as fast as he could with Cindy's aid.

Another ring of circling vultures told him that Grandpa, Olik, and Yelka were also there. The sagebrush gave them minimal cover from the Night Shades and Hudich, but Max knew they were going to be easy targets when they tried to cross the road to reach Grandpa and the pile of dirt.

"Keep go—" Sky stopped dead out in the open at the side of the road, and Max and Cindy looked to see what the problem was.

For the briefest of moments, time stood still as they faced Kacha on the other side of the road. A hateful fire blazed in his eyes as he poised to strike. Sky twirled her sword in her hand and then taking the hilt in both hands leveled it at Kacha.

A snarl spread across his reptilian face as he flexed his clawed hands. Kacha sprang towards them at an incredible speed. Sky twisted away at the last second and slashed with her blade, cutting a gash across Kacha's stomach. Max and Cindy barely avoided Kacha's outstretched claws as they dropped to the dirt out of his reach.

Before Max and Cindy could pick themselves up, Kacha's heavy tail and foot pinned them to the ground. His foot was more like a large clawed hand as he pressed down and pinched them in his sharp-powerful grip. A strange word rolled off Kacha's tongue and a spell reached out, freezing Max and Cindy in place.

"Get away from them," Sky threatened through gritted teeth.

"Come and get them, my pretty." Kacha's tongue licked out across his lips.

Sky reached around behind her back, pulled out a laser gun, leveled it at Kacha, and squeezed the trigger. The blast threw Kacha from his captives and into the sagebrush beyond. Sky rushed to Max and Cindy, who remained cemented within Kacha's spell. With Sky's attention on Max and Cindy, Kacha advanced again, driving into her with his full force. The two of them landed on the dirt road and Sky used Kacha's momentum to roll over, pushing with her legs to send him on by, but not before his claws ripped into her, blood spilling everywhere.

Kacha hit the dirt and spun back up. He charged towards her, leaping at her with outstretched arms. Sky dropped to the ground and let Kacha fly over grasping at air. This time she jumped back up with the gun at the ready.

Max watched the fight in horror and wanted to help, but he couldn't move. He couldn't even blink. This invisible cast was stifling and claustrophobia began to eat away at his remaining calm. He knew Sky couldn't match Kacha. She possessed more skills and more magic, but Kacha was a machine. He was muscle and speed; he could endure pain in order to overpower his victim. And with his newly acquired magical skills, he was a perfect predator and he would not stop.

Sky fired multiple times at the blur speeding towards her. Suddenly several laser blasts from the side sent Kacha spinning through the air away from Sky. He landed in the middle of the road, rolling over and over. Max was able to rotate his eyes enough to see Grandpa and Olik standing in the road, guns aimed at Kacha. Yelka stood on top of the dirt pile to help shield them from the air attack.

Grandpa uttered a strange word that released Max and Cindy from Kacha's spell and then returned his focus to the stunned Kacha. "On three," Grandpa called out and started to count.

A shock wave rolled over the road and threw everyone backwards through the air. Max and Cindy bounced and tumbled over the top of each other as Grandpa, Sky, and Olik landed against the hard dirt road.

"Kacha," Hudich roared as he marched towards them. He sent another wave of power that forced Kacha to dig his claws deep into the ground to keep from being blown backwards. When the spell subsided, it was as if all the air had been sucked out of everything and everyone.

Grandpa, Sky, and Olik helped Max and Cindy scramble back behind the mound of dirt. They all found a spot from which to observe the battle about to commence on the road. Even the flying creatures and Night Shades seemed to be captivated by the two combatants as they squared off.

Alan stood rooted to the ground at the other end of the road, his eyes on the two in front of him.

"Come with me," Hudich ordered, continuing towards Kacha. "I can teach you so much more. Together we can conquer the universe."

"What makes you think I need you?" Kacha hissed through his hooked teeth, looking like a coiled snake, muscles tensed and ready to strike.

"Because I have something of yours." Hudich took out the small jar of souls for Kacha to see. "Together, with my resources and your newly acquired knowledge, we can rule all! You can't defeat me, but you can join me. Otherwise I will destroy you."

"I think we should get out of here," Cindy advised, but no one budged.

Max knew she was right, and he was sure the others did as well, but something of momentous importance was playing out in front of them. If Kacha went with Hudich, it would give the enemy a great deal of information Grandpa didn't want them to have. They had to know where they stood in terms of protecting their world as well as others.

"You think me a fool?" Kacha questioned with venom. "I've seen how your kind has used my race in the past. Treated us like slaves. Once you have what you need from me, I would be eliminated."

"NO!" Hudich barked in response. "I would give you great power and command."

"Even now you act superior. You think to control me. I am not your slave and I do not need you. I am more powerful than you think. I would rather die than serve you! "

"So be it," Hudich's deep voice rumbled with anger. "Goodbye, Kacha." Lightning flew from Hudich's fingertips, exploding into the dirt road as Kacha leapt clear of the destruction at the last second.

Hudich sent out curse after curse, trying to catch up with the springing Kacha, who chewed up the distance between them with every jump. Hudich managed to land a spell right before Kacha could reach him. The force of the spell catapulted Kacha high through the air to crash into a barbed wire fence some thirty yards off the road. The force of his impact tore out a section of wire and narrow metal tee posts cut through Kacha's scaly armor in a few spots.

"His thinking is primitive," Olik muttered as they all gazed, entranced.

"Yes, he's still trying to use his brute force instead of magic," Grandpa added.

Once again, Kacha launched himself towards Hudich, dodging spells with speed and agility. Every time it looked as if he would grab Hudich, Hudich would land a spell that would propel him back. Hudich's spells, although powerful and punishing, only seemed to enrage Kacha to the point of deranged frenzy. His howls were not the cries of pain but of madness. Every time he advanced towards Hudich, Kacha got a little closer before being tossed back again.

After propelling Kacha back for the eighth time, Hudich started to laugh a deep menacing gurgle in his throat. "You can't win. You have no chance. This is only a game. Join me before the game becomes more than you can handle."

A smile spread across Kacha's reptilian lips. He threw dirt and rocks as he exploded towards Hudich at a blinding speed. He was a silver blur avoiding fire and explosions all around him as he closed the gap. A second before Hudich could fling back Kacha's advance, two Kachas appeared to be closing. Hudich cast his spell at the fake Kacha, dissolving the illusion a second before Kacha slammed into him. The force of the blow propelled them backwards.

Kacha kicked and clawed with unhindered abandon, trying to rip his enemy to pieces. His teeth snapped as he attempted to lock onto Hudich's throat. Hudich roared with anger as he struggled to release himself from Kacha's grip.

It amazed Max that Hudich wasn't dead. No normal life form could withstand that viciousness. Suddenly, out of the corner of Max's eye, a white light flashed and then another. He wondered if more of Hudich's followers had come to witness his death. Or were they here to help him? Soon the little lights were appearing all over the area.

"What are those?" Cindy commented, noticing the same blinks of light that Max had.

"I think more of the enemy has arrived," Grandpa stated, still mesmerized by the conflict in front of them.

"No," Sky interrupted. "They are leaving! Something is happening."

"What? What could be more important than this battle at the moment?" Yelka asked.

Suddenly Hudich rose to his feet. His red eyes blazed as if they were fire, his clothes shredded and soaked with dark red blood. With a strength that surprised Max, he peeled Kacha from him, tearing off portions of his own flesh in the process. He held Kacha high over his head and slammed him to the ground with a force that rocked the entire area as if a small earthquake had taken place. Cracks spread out in all directions like veins from the crater where Kacha impacted with the ground.

A white light appeared on Kacha's body, but Hudich spoke a strange group of words and locked Kacha in a spell of blue flame that reminded Max of the terrible flare worms. "No! No! No!" Hudich admonished. "I can't have you fleeing this world for shelter before the fight is over." The blue light danced over Kacha's body and Hudich clasped his hands together and began to twirl in a circle. Kacha flew outward as if connected by an invisible cable and spun around Hudich's body as he moved. Hudich periodically lowered and raised his hands, driving Kacha into the ground, through sagebrush and into boulders.

After rotating and smashing Kacha into various objects for several minutes, Hudich released him back into the fence. With a snap of his fingers, the barbed wire coiled around Kacha like a python and tightened, cutting into his scaly body. Kacha howled, but the rage was gone and only pain remained. After he was securely twisted inside the barbed wire and fence posts, Hudich cast a spell that carried Kacha back to the middle of the road.

As Hudich walked towards the immobilized Kacha, he looked more terrible than ever. He had lost most of the usual majesty he carried and now acted like a battle-hardened nightmare.

Suddenly, Alan, who had been standing some distance behind Hudich and out of the fight, vanished.

"Where's he going?" Yelka asked.

"I have a bad feeling," Max said.

"Me too," Cindy added with a worried look.

"Something's wrong!" Grandpa said. "Dang it!"

All eyes fell on Grandpa as he fished his communicator out of his pocket. "THEY'RE IN THE HOUSE!"

"What? Who?"

"The enemy!" Grandpa jumped up, as did everyone else.

Max suddenly noted the number of enemy fighters had diminished by more than half. Yelka disappeared in a wink of light and Sky followed a second later.

Max turned as Hudich stood over the helpless Kacha, the blue flame still dancing over his skin.

"Too bad. You could have had so much power, but not anymore. Now you have nothing. Not even life!" Hudich yanked one of the tee posts from the tangled mess and stabbed it down through Kacha. Kacha jerked and twitched on impact and then became motionless. The blue flame that anchored him to this world dissolved as a bright light consumed Kacha's body and he disappeared.

Hudich kicked at the empty wires and then flicked his eyes on the small group next to the dirt pile.

"Go now!" Grandpa ordered.

"What about you?" Max asked.

"We'll be right behind you."

Max took Cindy by the hand. *"Presiliva se home!"* The trip was instant. They arrived in the front yard at Grandpa's house in the midst of an all-out battle. Max fell to his knees, overcome with fatigue. The front gate stood wide open and Night Shades raced everywhere inside and out.

23

Battle for the Gateway

Grandpa's house and yard had been transformed into a battlefield. Smoke flowed from a second-story window. Glass breaking and fighting rang through the air. Sky battled several Night Shades at once on the side of the house but there wasn't any sign of Yelka, Rachel, Brian, or the others.

The second Max and Cindy touched down in Grandpa's front yard curses blasted them from all directions. A terrifying roar distracted everyone as Ell appeared from around the side of the house and attacked several unsuspecting Night Shades. Anyone within his reach fell victim to his deadly bite.

"Ell," Cindy screamed drawing his attention. While Ell's presence distracted the Night Shades, Cindy helped Max to his feet. "I guess this proves Sky's theory correct!"

"Yes!"

Ell dashed to give Max and Cindy cover by shielding them from the curses of the Night Shades with his enormous bulk and his terrifying presence. Max and Cindy joined in the fight sending counter spells at the evil invaders. The thought that the enemy had invaded Grandpa's home gave Max the second wind he needed. His newly acquired senses let him feel what was happening all around him.

A flash of light on the other side of the fence revealed Hudich, still disheveled and enraged from his fight with Kacha. With long, quick strides he advanced towards the open front gate.

"Close the gate!" Max screamed at Cindy as he sent a Night Shade flying with the *premakni* spell.

Cindy jumped into action and raced towards the gate. She caught the gate with outstretched arms and started to swing it closed when a curse from Hudich threw her away like a rag doll. She crashed into some bushes growing just below the porch.

"Ell," Max shouted, waving towards the gate, hoping Ell would follow him and understand what he wanted.

"*Premakni!*" Max aimed his magic at the gate, but Hudich countered before the gate could close and threw off Max's enchantment, leaving the gate wide open.

As Max advanced towards the gate, he could see that he and Hudich were going to arrive at the rusty metal barrier approximately at the same time. He knew Ell was behind him because of the ground shaking vibrations caused by Ell's enormous body when he ran and his new senses told him it was so.

"Don't worry about me," Max screamed to Ell, hoping Ell would understand.

Max reached the bars a second before Hudich and pushed with all his might to drive it shut, but Hudich stopped it about a foot short.

"No! No! N—" Hudich started right when Ell drove into the back of Max, forcing the gate closed with his weight. Hudich bounced away from the impact of Ell's drive.

Max gasped sharply as Ell's body pinned him to the gate. As Ell released him, Max managed to secure the latch before slumping again to the ground.

"NOOO!" Hudich roared in desperation. He rushed the fence and slammed into the spells, protecting Grandpa's yard and house, sending sparks flying. The protective magic surrounding the house repelled him like a trampoline.

Ell spun with his razor-sharp teeth bared as Night Shades rushed to try and capture the gate. Ell howled as spells pounded him from all directions but the Night Shades kept their distance, wary of Ell's deadly bite.

"Close the front door," Sky yelled at Cindy, who had crawled from the bushes and onto the front porch. Sky then launched an assault from the rear of those Night Shades who fought with Ell. Sky's push from behind drove the Night Shades forward into Ell, who snatched several with his large jaws.

"The back gate," Max gasped and used the bars of the fence to pull himself up. He staggered past the small battle while the enemy's focus remained on Sky and Ell. Out of the corner of his eye, a white flash enveloped Hudich, and in an instant he disappeared. Fear gripped Max. He found himself running faster than he thought he could.

Before Max arrived in the backyard, he paused behind a large oak tree in the back corner. His heart pounded in his chest and ears as he peered into the deserted area. Hudich popped up on the other side of the closed back gate. Max knew he couldn't get in with the gate closed, but Hudich waited there, as if waiting for someone. His hood was once again lowered, his skull-like face with its red eyes and sharp fangs exposed.

But who would possibly... Max didn't have to finish the thought to receive his answer.

Alan slunk from the rear of the house through a small group of bushes towards the back gate, his head jerking in all directions at the sounds of battle from the front of the house. He paused right before stepping out into the open.

"What are y—" Cindy about gave Max a heart attack as she joined him behind the tree. "Oh no! We can't let him open that gate!" she whispered.

"Make haste, fool!" Hudich growled at Alan.

Alan rushed for the back gate.

"Bump him over the fence on three," Max said. "One, two, three!"

"Premakni," Max and Cindy called and their combined spell caught the unsuspecting Alan as he extended his hand to unlatch the back gate and threw him up and over the fence outside of the yard.

Hudich threw his arms wide and threw back his head in a frenzied roar of anger and frustration. The shriek scattered birds from trees for blocks around. His red eyes burned a darker shade of red and he let loose several curses towards Max and Cindy, which bounced harmlessly off the shield protecting the house.

"That was fun," Cindy raised her eyebrows and smiled at Max.

Hudich and Alan, looking nasty-tempered and very disappointed, disappeared in flashes of light.

"Yeah, good work." Max felt the exhaustion creep in again and he turned his back to the tree and slid along it to the ground. "Go check the back door, will you?"

"Hang on," Cindy took off.

Just then, Max heard a scream from inside the house. Fear pumped through him like cold water as he recognized the voice, "Mom!" He struggled to get up when Cindy returned to assist him.

"The back door was locked. We're good." She wrapped his arm around her shoulders and they made their way back towards the front yard where they spotted Olik, Grandpa, and Cindy's parents jogging up the street. Their clothes were singed and torn, but otherwise they appeared to be unharmed.

"We need to teach them the transportation spell," Cindy said, shaking her head.

"Indeed."

Max and Cindy rounded the corner and saw Ell still guarding the front gate. Sky came up behind them, startling Max's heart once again.

"The yard is clear," Sky reported as she escorted them the rest of the way around the house. "I see Joseph, Olik, and your parents decided to join the party."

Sweat ran down Grandpa's face and his chest heaved as he gulped down air. "I'm really getting too old for this. What's left?"

"Is everyone okay?" Cindy's mother asked.

"We don't know for sure. There is someone or something still in the house," Cindy replied, glancing worriedly up at the smoke issuing from the second floor window.

Another loud scream issued from the house and the front door flew open. Out raced Brian's mother. She scrambled down the front steps, caught sight of everyone in the yard, and then dashed to the gate and out into the street.

Yelka came out onto the porch seconds after. Her hair completely disheveled and her skin and clothes smeared and dirty. She brushed her hands together as if finishing a chore.

"Close the gate." Grandpa motioned towards the gate and Sky quickly latched it shut once again.

"We need to check the house!" Yelka shouted.

Everyone stared at the house for a moment and then they dashed towards the door.

Rachel stood next to the control panel. She continued to peek at her watch and back to the gateway. *Come on!*

Suddenly the light of the gateway increased in intensity and then Brian and his adoptive parents came through, landing on the floor. They appeared frightened and confused as their eyes flicked everywhere, taking in the change of scenery.

"Move out of the road," Rachel called, waving them away from the gateway.

Brian and his parents attempted to scramble away from the gateway, eyes wide, staring at the light. Before they could get clear, Grd, transformed to look like the human Kacha, leapt through the gateway carrying a battered Jax. They collided with Brian and his parents knocking everyone to the ground.

Rachel shut down the gateway and the force field then rushed to Grd as he held the wounded Jax in his arms. "Let's get him down to a bed. Brian, there is a first aid kit in the kitchen. Can you run and grab it?"

Rachel led Grd down to a guestroom on the second floor where they placed Jax on a bed. Brian arrived carrying the first aid kit a second later.

"Can you look after him?" Rachel asked Grd and Brian. "I have to get back to the gateway."

"I don't know how to help him," Grd responded.

"I can try," Brian said.

"I can tell them what I need," Jax winced as he grasped Rachel's arm. "Go man the gateway."

Rachel fished out her communicator as she rushed back up to the third floor. No message! She flipped on the force field, tapping her foot on the floor. *Come on!* The waiting and the not knowing were unbearable. She returned to glancing from the communicator to her watch.

After what seemed like an eternity of waiting, Yelka suddenly entered the third floor on the other side of the force field.

"Whatever happens, don't turn off the force field," Yelka's muffled voice pierced the gateway, barely audible through the hum of the protective dome.

"What about Max? Grandpa? The others?" Rachel screamed back.

"They are on—" But before Yelka could finish her sentence, a half dozen Night Shades burst into the room from the direction of the staircase and a battle began.

Rachel's heart jumped into her throat at the sight of the hideous black creatures. It seemed like someone had accidentally set off a box of fireworks. Blue, red, and green sparks mixed with fire filled the whole room as a magical war commenced.

Yelka's magical skills surprised Rachel as Yelka dodged, blocked, and attacked multiple attackers at the same time. One by one, Yelka destroyed them all, their bodies disappearing in blips of light. Rachel fought an inner struggle between helping Yelka and protecting the gateway. She knew with the force field up, they couldn't get to it. *How did they get in the house? What was happening?* The suspense gnawed at her. *What about the others in the house? Brian? His parents? Jax and Grd? Had Grd betrayed them?*

Once Yelka had cleared the room of Night Shades, she rotated back to Rachel. "Definitely do NOT turn off the force field!"

"Where is everyone?"

"They should be here any moment. I'll be back," Yelka's distorted voice came through the force field. She spun and rushed from the room.

Glass shattering and the heavy thudding of feet caught Brian, Grd, and Jax's attention. Thumping feet followed with joyous hissing laughter.

"Night Shades," Jax gasped, struggling to sit up.

Grd leapt to the door and shut it quickly.

"My mom and dad?" Brian asked with wide eyes as the color drained from his face.

"Do we have any weapons?" Jax asked.

Grd flashed a wicked smile. He held up a human hand and then jerked it as if opening a switchblade knife and all his reptilian claws appeared. "Just me."

Brian gulped.

"Whatever happens, stay with him," Grd nodded to Jax. He then took several steps back from the door.

Brian started to blubber under his breath, making a soft whimper. Jax reached out, took Brian's arm and pulled him closer.

The running of feet pounded up the stairs and in the hall. A few moments later, doors began to bang open. They started at the opposite end of the hall and worked their way nearer.

"Sssearch the houssssse. Sssecure the gatewaysss."

Footsteps rushed by on the other side of the door. A second after, a loud bang sent the door flying inward. The surprised Night Shades on the other side didn't have a chance to get out of the way. Grd launched himself into the hall on top of the startled Night Shades.

Yelka raced down the spiral staircase, surprising two Night Shades who waited below. Her spells sent them fleeing from the house. As she rushed down the hall, she spotted Jax and Brian waiting in a bedroom.

"Stay there!" she ordered as she continued by.

As she moved into the opening above the stairway, a curse caught her from the side and slammed her into the wall. Before she even hit the floor, a second attack ignited her clothing. Yelka rolled into the hall beyond, suffocating the fire as she trapped it between her and the floor.

"Is that you, Yelka?" a woman's voice cackled. "I've been waiting so long to destroy you. Soon the gateway will be ours."

Yelka kept out of sight, using the hallway wall to block her from view.

"You won't be able to hide for long. Hudich is on his way and soon you'll all be dead."

Yelka cast a spell that sent a slow, floating mist bobbing down the hall. A counter-curse flew into the mist from below. With the distraction, Yelka jumped around the corner and fired a blast into the chandelier over the entryway. The glass and metal structure rained down on Brian's mother. She ducked and covered her head to protect herself.

Yelka cast a spell that hammered downward onto Brian's mother, flattening her to the floor. A second spell threw her into the wall. Before Yelka could send a third, several curses from the end of the hall sent her tumbling down the stairs. Yelka, although stunned, bounced up ready to fight.

Brian's mother, who had just caught her breath, ducked in time to avoid Yelka's next assult. She dashed for the door and out into the yard.

"Are there more in the house?" Grandpa asked Yelka as everyone proceeded up the porch steps.

"Yes." Yelka nodded breathlessly and brushed several strands of her hair out of her eyes before returning to the house.

"How about you three wait here and make sure the gates remain closed," Grandpa suggested to Cindy and her parents.

Jim gave a quick nod in acquiescence but   Cindy looked sidelong at Max in disappointment. Max could only shrug before stepping into the house with Grandpa and the others.

"Where's my mom?" Max asked.

"She's safe behind the force field," Yelka stated.

"Max, you and Sky check out the main floor. Yelka, Olik, and I will take the second," Grandpa ordered rapidly.

Sky motioned for Max to follow her towards the kitchen as Grandpa led his group up the stairs. Sky and Max did a sweep of the kitchen, the dining room, the front room, the study and Grandpa's bedroom. They were just leaving the study when Max noticed the door leading into the basement wasn't closed completely.

"Sky," Max whispered and pointed to the door.

Sky nodded and waved him behind her. She then opened the door and a loud thud followed by an array of spells from the floor below caused them to jump.   Max took a deep breath as Sky poked her head around the opening and peered into the darkened basement.   Max scrambled around her and peeked in from the other side.

From their current position, they couldn't see much. A section of stairs went down to a cement floor.   Only the bottom rows of some shelves were visible against the far wall.   Max extended his arm around the doorway, but before he could turn on the light switch, Sky grabbed his hand.

Sky shook her head and put a finger to her lips. She released his hand and proceeded down the first couple of steps.   Max waited for her to move farther down the steps before trailing after her.

Max could feel it coming before it happened. He dove into Sky, pushing them clear of the curse that shattered the entire wooden structure of the staircase, though he wasn't convinced their landing was any less severe than being thrown to the floor by the spell. Before Max could get his aching body to respond, Sky dragged him behind a wall as another curse slammed into a shelf, scattering its contents all over the floor.

"They're back behind the generator," Sky whispered.

Max ventured a quick glance, but jerked back out of the way as a spell flew so close to his head the wind of it ruffled his hair before crashing into the cement wall where the shelves had been.   Pieces of broken cement and dust flew everywhere, and Max quickly flung his arm around his mouth and nose to breathe through his sleeve.

"Do you think you can make it to the wall over there?" Sky motioned to another section of the basement that was hidden from their attacker's position.

Max swallowed hard as he nodded. He didn't think he could go anywhere at the moment. He felt like he should be in a full body cast, not dodging spells intended to kill him. He got into a crouched position and focused on his destination.

Sky put a hand on his knee. "Wait until after their counter-curse. I'll send a volley to which they will react. When I respond to those, go!"

"Okay," Max coughed on the dust in the air.

Sky rotated her palm upward and a ball of blue flame materialized, resting on the surface of her hand. She cocked her arm and threw the magic across the room. The flame grew into a white-hot beach-ball-sized projectile that hammered into the back of the basement.

A moment later, another curse pounded the corner of the wall protecting Max and Sky from the direct line of fire. Max covered his face to shield it from flying sparks and broken cement.

Sky shoved him with one hand while sending another spell with the other. Max was only halfway across the room when waves of magic started trailing him all the way across the basement. A wake of exploding shelves and junk followed his passing. He went right into a baseball slide behind the wall in time to avoid a curse that would have caught him directly in the face.

When the dust settled a little, Max tried to see Sky. She was gone. His heart raced and his throat burned. He chanced a peek around the corner but a wave of energy sent him further behind the wall. Reaching out with his senses instead, he found her again, and stayed his hand against sending spells blindly across the room. He didn't want to accidentally hit her or reveal her to the enemy lurking in the back corner.

"Max! Sky!" Grandpa's voice called from the open door where the steps used to be. "Are you down there?"

"Yes, we are. So is someone else," Max called back.

"I'll be back. I'll go get a ladder," Grandpa responded, and his footsteps receded.

With that, another blast exploded next to Max and a chunk of wall broke free, colliding with his head. Max was furious. *That's enough of that stuff!*

Max let his senses run out through the basement as he climbed to his feet and stepped clear of the wall. "*Oviraj*," Max blocked a spell and sent it flying away from him at an angle. *"Oviraj!"* Max screamed, using all his frustration to repel his attacker's magic back at them.

"Arggghh," came a gurgling sound that preceded a loud thud as the enemy hit the back wall.

"Move and you're dead," Sky's voice called. "Max, I've got him."

Max walked into the light streaming down from the open door above and the prisoner Sky escorted over was Brian's father. She had one of the man's hands pushed up behind his back and a knife in her other hand dug into his throat.

"All your friends are gone, and now Joseph knows the truth," Sky said as they waited for Grandpa to return with the ladder.

"What truth?" Max asked, coughing occasionally on the dust still permeating the air.

"That Terry here betrayed him. He betrayed us all," Sky stated, twisting the knife a little, causing the man to squirm against its sharp point.

They eyed each other in silence, waiting for Grandpa to return with a ladder.

"Do you have a gun?" Sky called up before they ascended the ladder.

"Yes," Grandpa responded.

"Good. I'm sending Max up first. Then I want you to put your sights on Terry as he comes up. I'll be last," Sky said. "And if you so much as attempt to wipe your nose, you will be dead before you reach the main floor," Sky threatened Terry through gritted teeth.

Max felt like he had a two hundred pound backpack on as he forced his arms and legs to move up the ladder. Terry and Sky followed right behind him. The look of total disgust on Grandpa's face surprised Max. Even though Max had grunted and groaned under the pain of climbing the ladder, Grandpa seemed unconcerned about his injuries or discomfort. All of Grandpa's focus was on Terry.

"Terry," Grandpa spat. "Now I understand the full story. I had refused to believe it until I saw you out there on the road." Grandpa waved the gun for Terry to head towards the front room.

"What are you going to do, Joseph? You don't have it in you to kill me!" Terry hissed back.

"No, I have a better idea for you. Up the stairs," Grandpa ordered.

"You can't make me do anything, Joseph," Terry refused to go.

Sky's hand shot out like a striking snake and landed a blow right in Terry's sternum, causing him to bend over gasping for breath. Sky's face held the same expression of loathing that Grandpa's had. "No, but I can. So unless you want me to beat you senseless right here and now, you'd better do as you are told."

Terry glared at Sky with an expression of utter rage. His face beet red, he rubbed his chest and panted a few times before relenting. The small procession headed up to the second floor and down the hall towards the spiral staircase.

"Dad," Brian's excited voice popped out of the bedroom where he and Jax had been hiding, but the group marched past and climbed their way up the spiral staircase.

They entered the top floor to a surprised Yelka, Rachel, and Grd.

"You know you can't win, Joseph," Terry continued in a confident manner. "Hudich will be victorious in the end."

"He lost today," Grandpa said.

"What are you doing to my dad?" Brian broke through the group and threw his arms around Terry's waist.

"He's not your real dad," Grandpa said still holding the gun at Terry's chest.

"He adopted me, I know," Brian said as tears streamed down his cheeks. "My real parents died in a car crash."

Terry put a hand on Brian's head. "That's right son."

"Your adopted father is a murderer," Grandpa spat the words out as if they left a foul taste in his mouth.

"Don't listen to them, son. He's a liar. I haven't ever killed anyone." Terry stared into Brian's eyes as if there was no one else in the room. "These people are the enemy."

"Brian, why don't you ask him how your real parents died," Sky piped up. "Ask him what really happened to their car."

"He knows what happened." Terry sneered at Sky. "It was an accident!"

"Their car slid off an icy road," Brian added, peering at Sky.

"Funny how it was in the summer and the police couldn't determine what had caused the car to jump off the road. There were no skid marks or brake marks. It was as if the car leapt into the canyon, all on its own. Somehow it *magically* avoided the guard rail as well," Sky stated with pursed lips.

"That's not what happened." The blood drained from Terry's face and his eyes widened.

"Really?" Sky produced a document from a pocket inside her jacket. "I have the police report right here." She whipped the paper open.

"So, you killed Brian's real parents, just as you helped kill my son," Grandpa stated, the gun trembling in his hand.

Upon hearing this last, Max experienced a blow to the abdomen as if he had been kicked in the stomach by a mule. The pain of his battered and bruised body disappeared and only the ache in his heart remained. Even his vision blurred slightly, around the edges, growing dark from the shock. Was he really going to find out more about his father's death?

Brian began to tremble as he glanced up into Terry's eyes. "Is that true?" His voice didn't ring with accusation, but was rather one of an innocent child who had just been devastated by a loved one.

"No, son. It's a lie."

"How about my son? We never knew how Alan found him that day. You were the only one who could have told him, but since we thought you had been killed as well..." Grandpa's voice cracked. "There were other signs he had been attacked by more than one person. Did you participate?"

Max glanced from Grandpa to Terry to his mother. Her face was pale and it appeared she was using the control panel to keep herself upright. With her mouth hanging open and chalky complexion, Max couldn't remember ever seeing her look so appalled. Max slowly circled around behind everyone to stand next to his mother. He took her by the hand and then activated the force field.

Everyone jumped with the sudden change to the tension in the room. All eyes fell on him and then back.

"Get away from him, Brian," Max ordered through gritted teeth.

"I'm not going anywhere without my son," Terry barked and pulled Brian tighter to him.

Brian appeared small and frightened. His head danced around the room as if he was trying to read the truth from everyone's face. "C-can I see the document?" he stuttered.

"It is a trick, son. A forgery," Terry protested.

Sky stepped forward and gave the document to Brian, who pushed away from Terry. He took the report in both hands and started to read.

Max adjusted the dials on the control panel and switched on the gateway. The mirror began to rotate with a soft swooshing sound that changed to a hum as the glass disappeared into the ball of light.

Brian turned towards Terry with tears in his eyes. He held the paper out with one hand. "Is this true?"

"No. No, of course, it's not true," Terry shook his head. "I would..."

"Does mom know about this?" The paper rattled in Brian's hand, tears tumbling down his cheeks.

"I told..."

"DON'T LIE TO ME! DID YOU KNOW ABOUT THIS?" A wave of magic enveloped the area inside the force field. Terry went rigid, as if fighting against some struggle raging inside him. "TELL ME!"

The muscles in Terry's face started to twitch and his bottom lip quivered. Brian's magic was very powerful. "Yes, we both knew," Terry gasped as Brian's will forced the answer from him.

Brian's magic faded and Terry dropped to the floor breathing heavily.

"That is why they adopted you, Brian. They wanted your magical abilities. You have the potential to be one of their most powerful weapons," Sky said.

Yelka jumped forward and with an arm around his shoulder, she led the sobbing Brian away from Terry.

"Get up," Grandpa ordered.

"What are you going to do?" Terry spat. "There's nowhere you can send me that I can't come back from. You'll have to kill me and I don't believe you can."

"You see that boy by the control panel. That's my grandson and he's one smart boy," Grandpa started.

"He's a fool just like you and your son. He'll end up like his father in the end," Terry hissed.

"I doubt it. Like I was saying, he's a smart boy and I'm sure he is sending you someplace special. See you in Pekel, Terry," Grandpa said with a smirk. "You think you can come back from there?"

Horror flashed across his face as he glanced back at the gateway.

"Do the honors, Max," Grandpa spoke.

"*Premakni,*" Max released his anger and his spell threw Terry into the light.

24

Choices and Surprises

"Dad," Brian sobbed into Yelka's shoulder after Max blasted Terry through the gateway into Pekel.

Everyone stared at the gateway in silence for quite some time. Finally, Max reached over and shut everything off after which he and his mother exchanged a hug. All of Max's muscles screamed in protest, as the climax of the day's events ended, bringing his mind back to his surroundings. His mother had to hold him up to keep him from collapsing on the floor. Sky rushed to help her get him to the chair.

"Max! Max, what's wrong?" His mother sounded frantic.

"I—I'm all right," Max tried to talk as the room started spinning. He felt as if Kacha had tried to extract his soul all over again. None of his extremities would respond.

"Talk about leaving everything on the battlefield," Sky smiled as she knelt down in front of him.

Olik began examining him.

"What's the matter with him?" Rachel asked.

"I think it's an old-fashioned case of complete exhaustion. He hadn't completely recovered from the events at the bank and today's battle drained him even more," Olik responded, and though Rachel was still worried, she did look somewhat relieved.

"Plus, I think someone has been hiding the fact he hadn't healed as much as he pretended," Sky winked at him.

Max couldn't hide the smile. At least his face muscles worked. He then had the sensation of being in a dream and floating unaided from the third floor down to the second floor to his bed. People appeared and disappeared before everything went dark.

Max awoke to what seemed like early morning, but he couldn't be certain. He wondered how long he had been out. All of the events over the last week paraded through his mind. Before succumbing to fatigue, he had learned more about his father's death, than he had known in his entire life. His father had been betrayed by someone he and Grandpa had believed to be a friend, and Alan had an accomplice. *Just like Marko! How do these evil people keep worming their way into our lives?*

"Unggh," Max gritted his teeth at the pain rushing through his body when he attempted to sit up.

"You're awake," Cindy's voice rose from the floor.

"Geez, you almost gave me a heart attack!" Max exclaimed, with his heart pounding in his ears. "I didn't know you were there. How long have I been sleeping?"

"For two days," Cindy dragged the sentence out as if her patience with Max had been wearing out. "You didn't even budge. You didn't even toss or turn once."

Max grimaced and squirmed himself up to a sitting position on the edge of his bed. "And I can see why," he exhaled. "It freaking hurts to move."

"Yeah, Olik said that huge bruise had spread. You can see it farther up your neck. Good thing it didn't reach your face. You'd be uglier than you normally are."

"Thanks." Max chuckled, but even laughing caused his chest to ache. "Did I miss anything while I was sleeping?"

"We found another Night Shade hiding in a closet on the second floor. He wasn't the bravest Night Shade I'd ever seen. He knew his buddies were gone and just wanted out. Otherwise it's been quiet. We did transfer all the townsfolk back."

"Really? Even Larry and those wackos?"

"Yep! We left Ell in the front yard and had Grd, as his monstrous self, watch them through the house. They were blindfolded, of course. Grandpa made it a point to let them know that Ell and Grd were there. It took almost all of yesterday. Martin and your Aunt Donna seem to be dealing with the loss of Frank a little better, now."

"What about Brian?"

"He's a mess. He only talks to Yelka and doesn't even come out of his room for meals. I've heard him crying for his mom when I've walked by his room."

"Is Grd gone?"

"Yes, I was happy to see him go too. He kept his word, but I never really trusted him. I hope we never have to work with him again," Cindy concluded.

"Oh, I'm sure Olik and Grandpa will try to get info from him in the future, but it might not be safe for him. Hudich and his followers must know it was Grd who helped us," Max said as he struggled to put on a pair of socks. "Then again, they may not have realized he had been back in his own world gathering information for us all along. They might have thought he had still just been living here."

"Yeah, maybe." Cindy started laughing.

"What?"

"You act older than Grandpa."

"I feel like rigor mortis has already set in," Max laughed at his inability to pull his sock past his toes.

"I can imagine. Even I'm really stiff in the morning since..."

"Yeah."

Over the next few days Max noticed a gradual improvement in his mobility. The bruise had receded a little and with the aid of Olik's painkillers, he could move about without grimacing at every step. Yelka didn't seem sympathetic to his plight as she put him and Cindy through the toughest spell lesson in a long time. Max wondered if she was taking out a little of her frustration about not being able to pull Brian out of his funk.

Sky showed up to tell them she would be starting them on a weapons and self-defense regimen soon, but cut Max some slack because of his condition. Max could tell that his and Cindy's relationship with Sky had grown stronger, because the usually serious Sky joked around with them.

Jax, under Olik's care, made great strides towards a full recovery. Soon he was up and about eating meals with everyone else. Olik commented on how he should be able to get back to work in about a week.

Max decided with this new information about his father, it was time to approach Grandpa about the subject. He wanted to know what had really happened to his dad and what part Alan and Terry had played in his death. The only problem was he never could catch Grandpa alone. He wouldn't have minded asking Grandpa for more information in front of his mother, but he didn't care to have anyone else listening in on the conversation.

Late one night, a week or so later, when Max couldn't sleep, he discovered Grandpa sitting in the kitchen by himself sipping hot cocoa.

"What are you doing up?" Grandpa asked, eyeing him over his mug of hot cocoa.

"Can't sleep," Max yawned.

"Are you still in pain?"

"It's not too bad, now. But I've got a lot on my mind." Max realized he was nervous. His heart raced like he was getting ready to go into battle.

"Is there something you want to talk about?"

"Uh, yes, actually."

"Let me get you a cup of cocoa, then, and you can tell me all about it." Grandpa went to the stove and poured some milk into a pan.

"It's more like I have something to ask," Max struggled, scrunching his face as if expecting his grandfather to decline his request.

"You want to know more about your father," Grandpa stated without surprise, stirring the warming milk.

"Yes. What happened to him? How did Terry betray him?" Max fidgeted, trying to find a comfortable position in the chair because his body was still sore.

"Terry betrayed us all," Grandpa started as he ladled cocoa into an empty mug.

"Just like Marko," Max said.

"Well, no, not exactly like Marko. I'm not sure Marko was ever a good person. It seems he had been working for Hudich all along. I'm convinced Terry was on our side and a decent man at one point in time, but alas people change. Something had to have subverted him," Grandpa sighed, returning to the table with the mug for Max.

"He came onto the project towards the end. He helped us destroy the original gateway and build this one." Grandpa stared past Max as if watching the events play out in front of him again.

"So what happened? With Dad?" Max's voice was almost a whisper.

"It was after we had banished Hudich to Pekel of course. Actually, a lot of it makes sense now. We had received a tip, which I am sure was part of Terry's betrayal, that Hudich's followers had found a way to bring Hudich back."

"Had they?"

"No. Like I said, it makes sense that this was just a lie. It is my belief they wanted to capture your dad in order to make a trade. Well, your father was a very brave man and he didn't let them take him."

Max noticed tears building along the bottom of his grandfather's eyes.

"So, Terry lied to you about the plot to free Hudich?"

"In a way, yes. There was a plot to free Hudich, but it involved taking your dad as hostage. Terry led us to believe Alan and some of the others had discovered a way to get Hudich out using magic or something. So, Terry and your father went to do a little reconnaissance. That's when the enemy ambushed him. Your dad and Terry were supposed to go spy on an enemy camp in a world called Gozd when we lost communications with them. We were all there, but approaching the camp from different directions. We knew Alan..." Grandpa wiped his eyes.

A tear rolled down Max's cheek.

"We know Alan was involved because Yelka saw him deliver the spell..." Grandpa swallowed hard. "Anyway, by the time we had abandoned our original plans and discovered your father, Terry was missing. We found his pack and signs of a struggle, but no Terry. We just assumed they had taken him or killed him. Even his communicator was destroyed. I think that was what really convinced us he was dead. We thought they would have done anything to get a communicator."

There was a long moment of silence before Max decided to ask another question. "The other day you said something about him joining in the attack?"

"Well, another disturbing thing we noted was, of course, there was no camp at all. Neither Marko nor Jax—not even Sky—could find any tracks except Alan's, Terry's, and your father's, but the area around your father's...body showed spells coming at him from different directions. We just figured somehow the other person had hidden their tracks."

"I suspect Sky didn't think that way," Max muttered, taking a slurp of his chocolate.

"No, Sky suspected something funny had happened all along. And Jax tended to agree with Marko when it came to tracking and reading signs. So, when Marko betrayed us, Sky lost all her trust in Jax as well. I think in her mind, she believes Marko was in on that plot."

"Which made her naturally suspect Jax?"

"Oh, don't worry. I think she's softened a little after seeing the torture Jax received from Hudich. Sky is naturally leery of everyone but is a lot different once you get to know her."

A smile spread across Max's face.

"What?" Grandpa asked.

"Oh, I was just thinking how my and Cindy's friendship with Sky has changed since we first met her last year. You're right; she has warmed up to us a lot since then."

Grandpa chuckled. "Oh, I think she is very fond of the two of you. You both have qualities she admires. I haven't ever seen her give anyone as much trust as she has given the two of you in such a short time."

"She told us you had saved her life. How did you do that? I could use a happier story about now," Max tried to smile, but the thoughts of his father and how he was murdered was fresh in his mind.

A smirk crossed Grandpa's face. "Oh, I don't know if she'd want me to tell you that story. It might cause her a little embarrassment."

"What? I've helped rescue her a couple of times. Why would you telling me how you saved her before embarrass her? Now I'm more curious."

"Sorry, but I think she should be the one to tell you," Grandpa chuckled. "It's a secret that gets people from her race into trouble every now and then. It's something they can't control and it scares them to death."

"Come on," Max rolled his eyes. "You can't tell me things like that and then leave me hanging."

"Sky would pulverize me if I told you." Grandpa winked and polished off his cocoa.

"Please. Tell me!" Max begged, putting his hands together as if in prayer.

"I can't. I'll just say there is a reason they are like genies. With the right item, you can make them your slave." Grandpa grinned mischievously.

"You're killing me here." But no matter how much Max pleaded with Grandpa to give more information, Grandpa refused to divulge anymore. When Max finished his hot chocolate, there was nothing for him but to head back to bed.

The next day, Max told Cindy Grandpa's partial revelation about Sky, and the two of them discussed what could possibly be so embarrassing to a warrior like Sky.

Sky continued their defense lessons and although Max's mobility had improved, his body still felt like it had been run over by a car. Sky and Cindy seemed to be finding it all very amusing, pausing between each activity to laugh hysterically at Max's facial expressions as he landed on the mat.

But Max was anything but angry. In fact, he couldn't stop himself from smiling every time they did this. "I'm glad you are getting so much joy out of my pain."

"We are," Cindy held her stomach and Sky had tears rolling down her face.

Max decided since Sky was in such a good mood, it was time. "So, Sky...how did Grandpa rescue you?" Max asked with the biggest smile of curiosity.

Cindy's laughter stopped and Sky wiped at her eyes and continued to chuckle. "What?"

"How did Grandpa rescue you?" Max's grin spread even wider.

Sky's smile faded and she put her hands on her hips. "What did your grandfather tell you?"

"Nothing. I tried to pry it out of him but he said I'd have to ask you. He did say you might not want me to know and so he wouldn't tell me," Max tried to reassure her.

"Then why are you smiling like that?" Sky raised her eyebrows suspiciously.

"Well, he did hint it might embarrass you. So, my imagination has been running wild with ideas. And as good as you are, I can't come up with anything."

"I think you should tell us," Cindy added.

"Oh you do, do you?" Sky smiled. "All right. I'm not going to give you all the details, but I will tell you some of the story. You have to agree right now that you don't get to ask any questions."

Max and Cindy nodded.

"I want to hear you say you agree," Sky said in a schoolteacher's voice. "No questions."

"Agreed," they both responded.

"Okay," Sky sat cross-legged on the mat and Max and Cindy got comfortable as well. "There are those who think my race is rather fair."

Cindy elbowed Max in the side.

"Hey!"

Sky smiled. "Because of our magical abilities and other talents, there are many who desire to control us. There is a rare, but extremely effective, way to do so and those who know about it sometimes spend a lifetime searching for it. It's partly why Joseph calls me his genie. This item is kind of like our bottle and once someone has it, they can control us."

"So what—" Max started but Sky's finger shot out stopping him.

"No questions." Sky slowly shook her finger, pursing her dark red lips. "Anyway, this item is so powerful to my species we cannot resist it. Because of it, I had fallen under the domination of an evil creature. I knew I was a prisoner but because of this thing, I couldn't free myself. It was a living nightmare. I wanted to escape but I couldn't. My will was gone.

"The creature, which held me prisoner, worked for the enemy and had information your grandfather needed. I was away when they fought or I would have been forced to destroy Joseph. When I returned, my master was dead and Joseph now owned the item."

"Did Grandpa know what he had?" Cindy clapped her hand over her mouth. "Sorry."

"No, he actually thought I was going to attack him and disappeared through the gateway. He failed to comprehend the power the item he brought back with him had on me. I followed him here. Granted, I would have to return home every couple of days because this wasn't my world, but I couldn't stay away very long either. He found me sleeping on the porch swing one morning. I think the fact that I was able to come through the front gate convinced him I wasn't evil. To make a long story short, it took a couple of days until I was able to make him understand he owned me and it was this object that made it so. Then your grandfather did something unheard of by my species. He told me I was free, and he destroyed the object, releasing me from its hold."

"So he rescued you from a type of slavery," Max stated.

"A very real slavery," Sky said. "So, I have worked with him ever since. My race would never help anyone under this object's spell. Every one of us fear that by trying to help someone in that condition, they might also end up trapped, which is a very real possibility. In your grandfather, and the others, I have friends who would do whatever they could to help me if I wound up back in that situation. I would rather be a willing servant to these types of people than in forced slavery to some horrible creature.   And before you open your mouth, remember no questions. I will not tell you what the object is."

"Ohh," Max whined.

"Now, let us get back to the lesson.   We have wasted enough time." Sky sprang to her feet. "Besides, I have never gotten this much pleasure from a lesson before." Sky winked at Cindy.

"I'm glad I can help." Max massaged his sore arms and legs.

"Well, if you weren't such a wimp," Cindy chided.

"Even wounded, I can still kick your—"

"BRIAN.   BRIAN, WHERE ARE YOU?" A woman's voice penetrated the house through the open windows, letting in the warm early summer air.

"Who is that?" Max asked. Cindy jumped to the window.

Cindy's face turned pale.   "It's Brian's mother.   She's in the street."

"BRIAN, I'M HERE FOR YOU," his mother called as she stood on the other side of the gate.

Max and Sky crowded around the window for a look.

"She is not alone either," Sky said, pointing at a crowd of the enemy a little farther down the street.

"Alan," Max hissed as Alan and a police officer separated themselves from the crowd. Alan wore his best suit and tie.

They moved directly towards Brian's mother, stopping a few yards behind her. "Joseph, I have a court order demanding you turn the boy over or we will have to get the authorities involved," Alan shouted up to the house.

Footsteps rushed though the hall of the house, which launched Max, Cindy, and Sky after them. Grandpa disappeared out the front door as they reached the top of the stairs.

"Mom," Brian cried as he, Yelka, and Rachel came up behind Max and the others, causing Brain and the others to pause.

"He can't go out there," Rachel said.

"Joseph," Alan's voiced floated in through the open front door. Max and the others hustled down the steps and out into the front yard.

"We have a court order.   If you don't turn the boy over, we can have you arrested for kidnapping," Alan smirked, holding the paper in front of him and stepping closer to the fence.

Max, Cindy, and Sky joined Grandpa while Yelka and Rachel stayed with Brian on the porch. Grandpa glanced at Brian with sad eyes and waved him forward.

"Brian, son, come to mamma," his mother pleaded, but Brian clung to Yelka while they inched their way forward at a snail's pace.

Brian shook from head to toe. He looked like a mouse with nowhere to run from the cat. "M-mom," he stuttered. It appeared as if he wanted to ask a question but seemed terrified of the answer.

"Don't let these losers have him," Cindy spat.

"You have no choice, Joesph," the policeman added. "You don't want to cause an incident."

Grandpa crouched down to eye level with Brian when he reached him. "We will try to help you all we can. I'm sorry." He put a hand on Brian's shoulder. "Be mindful, they will try to convert you."

"Oh, come on, Joseph! Let the poor kid come to his mother," Alan rolled his eyes.

"I don't see Brian in a hurry to get to her," Max said, annoyed at Alan's display of contempt.

"Shut your mouth, kid," the policeman pointed at Max. "Give me a reason to run you in."

"Hey, Brian," Max shouted as if Brian was on the other side of the house. "Remember how we told you about the spell protecting the house when you first got here?"

Brian wiped a tear from his eye and nodded.

"And how evil cannot enter the gate unless it is open?" Max's voice returned to a normal level.

"I think we've heard enough of you. Give us the boy," Alan spat.

"Come to mama," Brian's mother said extending her arm.

"*Pridi*," Max called and pulled Brian's mother forward into the fence. Her arm went through the bars and ignited into flames, even catching a portion of her face on fire. A look of horror spread across her face as her eyes widened and mouth gaped open. She shrieked a high-pitched wail of pain that startled everyone as she jerked back from the fence.

Brian's mother jumped away from the bars and started to pat herself in an effort to put out the flames, but all that remained was a small amount of smoke rising from her arm and chin.

Max was uncertain now if that had been the best thing to do. Brian appeared more frightened than ever, but Max decided he had made his point about evil being unable to pass into the yard.

Brian's mother narrowed her eyes and pinched her lips together before she composed herself and tried to act like nothing had happened.

She brushed at her clothes as if they had lint on them and took a deep breath. "Come on, Brian. We're going."

"That was completely unnecessary," Alan stated, his face turning a dark shade of red.

"Oh, but it was." Sky advanced closer to the fence, causing Alan to take a couple of steps back.

"We will try to help you," Grandpa said as he rose to his feet. "Just always try to be good."

"Good luck, Brian," Yelka gave him a quick hug.

Grandpa led him to the gate, opened the latch and sent him out to his "mother." Brain watched over his shoulder the whole way down the street.

Everyone stared in silence until long after Brian had gone.

"Do you think he has a chance?" Rachel asked in a doubtful tone.

"No, I'm afraid I don't," Grandpa said, shaking his head slowly. "Not unless we can get him away from them soon."

Grandpa and Grd, disguised once again as the human Kacha, strolled into the bank in New York City. They walked across the main hall towards the vault area. The bank was full of busy customers concerned about their own business. Several security guards preformed a lackluster job over the crowded building. Grandpa led, being familiar with the bank's layout. He quickly found the stairs in the back leading to the room below where the security deposit boxes were.

"This favor better make us even," Grd hissed out the side of his mouth.

"Consider it paid for us letting you go home a free Haireen," Grandpa agreed.

Grd presented Kacha's ID at the desk. After showing the man his key, the three of them proceeded into the vault. The man escorted them to the correct box and after inserting his key and turning the lock, he left them to their business. After the man had given them some privacy, they used their key to open the final lock. They pulled the large metal drawer out of its slot and lifted the lid. Grandpa gasped at the sight of the empty box.

Spell Pronunciations and Definitions

The following words are from the Slovene language

Stress marks: [bold type] indicates the primary stressed syllable, as in news·pa·per [nooz-pey-per] and in·for·ma·tion [in-fer-mey-shuhn]

pridi (pri·di) [prē-dē] – Moves objects towards you.

zaspi (za·spi) [zä-spē] – Causes sleep.

prizgaj (pri·zgaj) [prē- 3g ī] – Use to create fire.

ugasni (u·ga·sni) [oo-gä-snē] – Use to extinguish fire.

premakni (pre·ma·kni) [prā-mä-knē] – Moves objects away from you.

vstani (vs·ta·ni) [oos-tä-nē] – Stops moving objects.

pochasi (po·cha·si) [pō-chä-sē] – Slows moving objects down.

izginem se (iz·gi·nem·se) [ēz-gē-n äm- sä] – Makes one invisible.

prikazi se (pri·ka·zi·se) [prē-kä-zē-sä] – Makes one visible.

izbrisi znamenje (iz·bir·si·zna·men·je) [ēz-brē-shē znä-menyē] – Removes
curses.

preselim se(pre·se·lim·se)[pre-se-lēm-sä] – Transports one to another world.

vrnim se(vr·nim·se)[vr-nēm-sä] – To return from transport.

odkri (od·kri)[ōd-krē] – Reveals something hidden.

razkrij zlo (raz·krij·zlo)[räz-krē-zlō] – Reveals a person who has been using evil magic.

razkrij dobro (raz·krij·do·bro)[räz-krē-dō-brō] – Reveals a person who has been using good magic.

unichi (u·ni·chi)[oo-nē-chē] – To destroy something.

vrtinchim se(vr·tin·chim·se)[vr-tēn-chēm-sä] – To twirl like a tornado.

zadravi (za·dra·vi)[zä-drä-vē] – To heal something.

oviraj (o·vir·aj)[oo-vēr- ī] – To block something.

beri misel (beri·mi·sel)[berē-mē-sel] – To read another's thoughts.

Symbols and their examples:

ē bee
ä father
3 vision
ī pie, by
oo boot
ā pay
ō toe
e bet

James Todd Cochrane

The Max and the Gatekeeper Series

Max and the Gatekeeper

The Hourglass of Souls (Max and the Gatekeeper Book II)

The Descendant and the Demon's Fork (Max and the Gatekeeper Book III)